SUEE AND THE SHADOW

by **GINGER LY**

illustrated by **MOLLY PARK**

AMULET BOOKS
New York

CONTENTS

HOW TO PRONOUNCE THE NAMES

SUEE	SOO-EE	수이
HAEUN	HA-OON	하은
HYUNWOO	HYUHN-WOO	현우
YEJIN	YEH-JIN	예진
SEOYEON	SUH-YOHN	서연
MINSEO	MIN-SUH	민서
BYUNGTAE	BYUHNG-TEH	병태

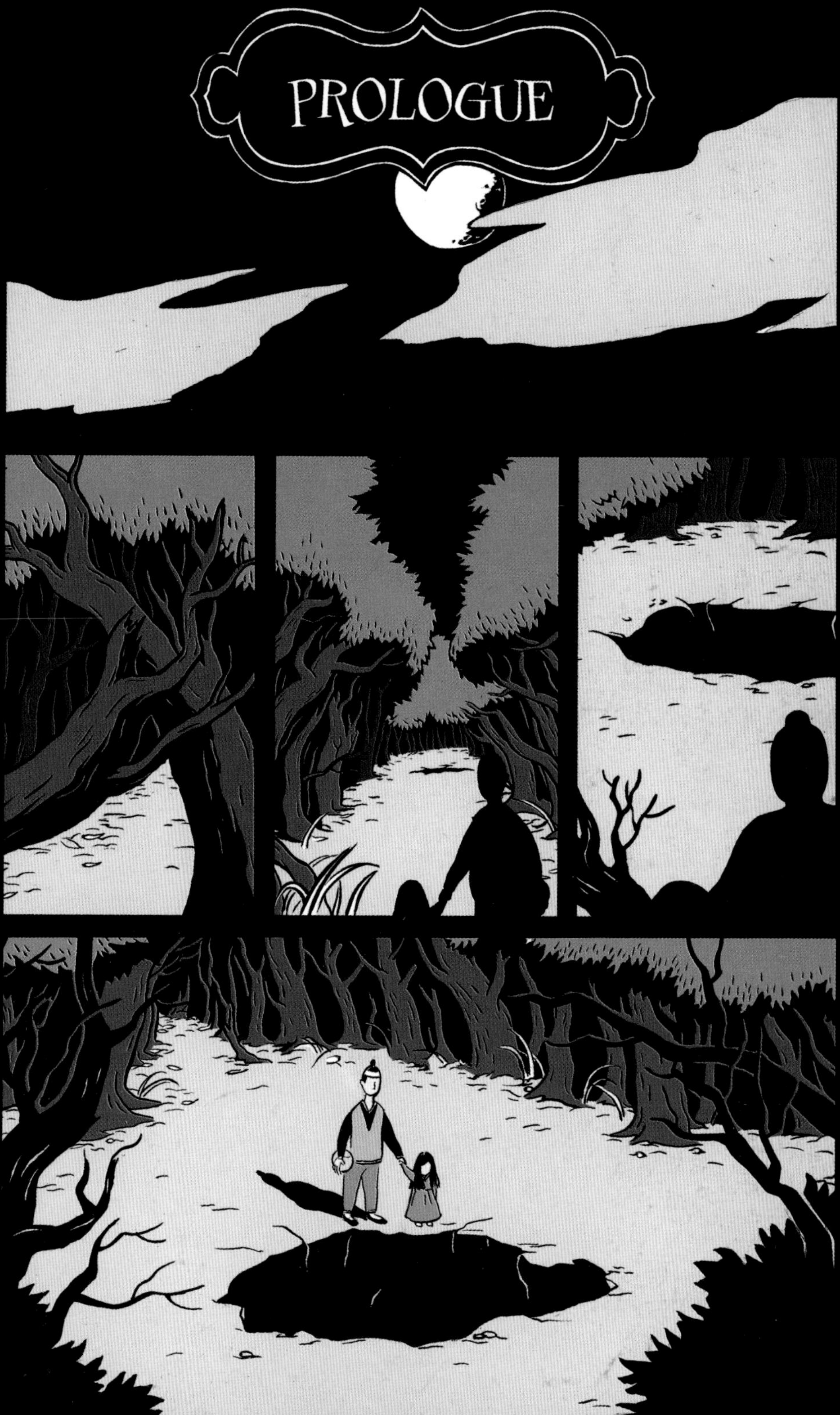
PROLOGUE

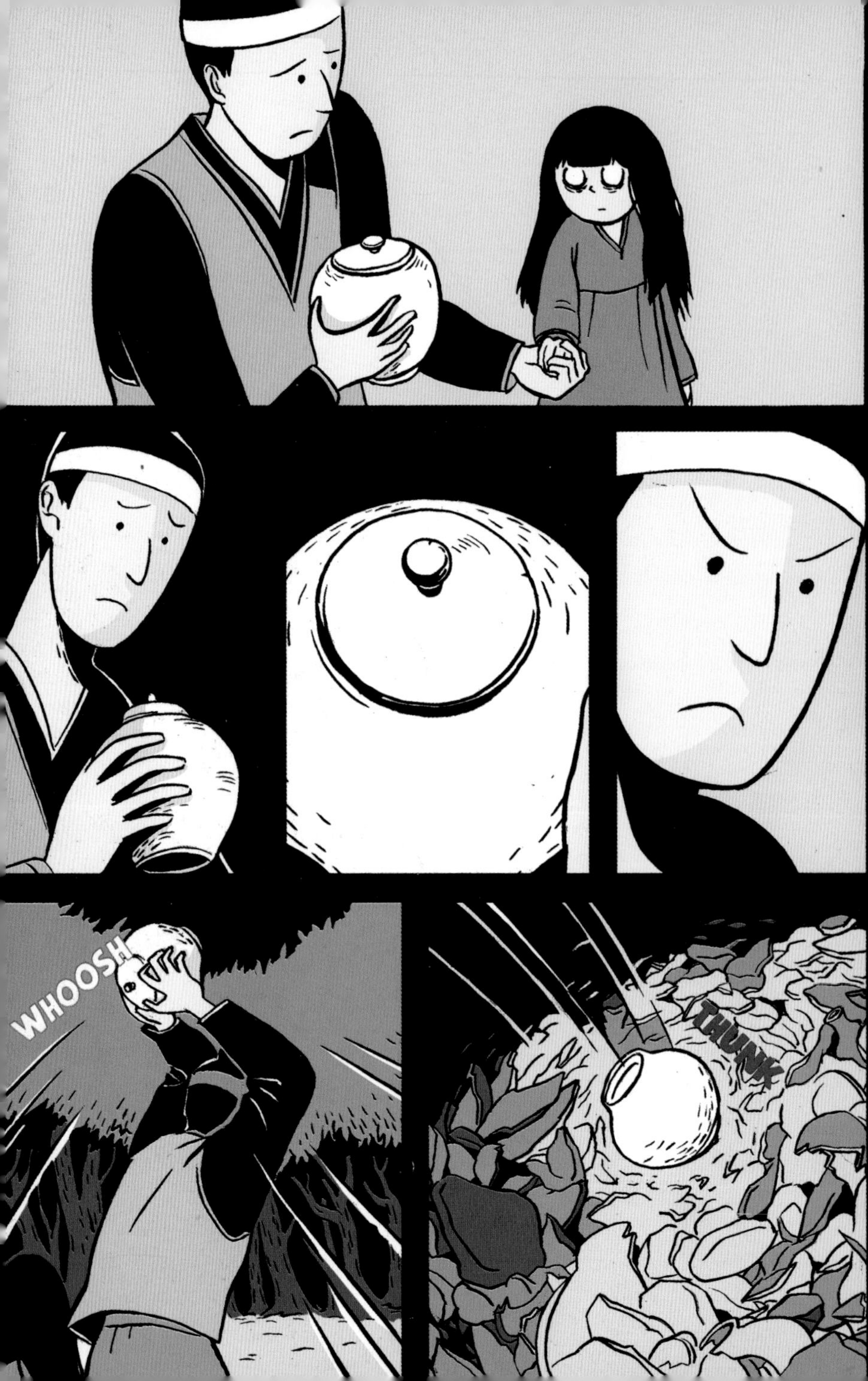
WHOOSH
THUNK

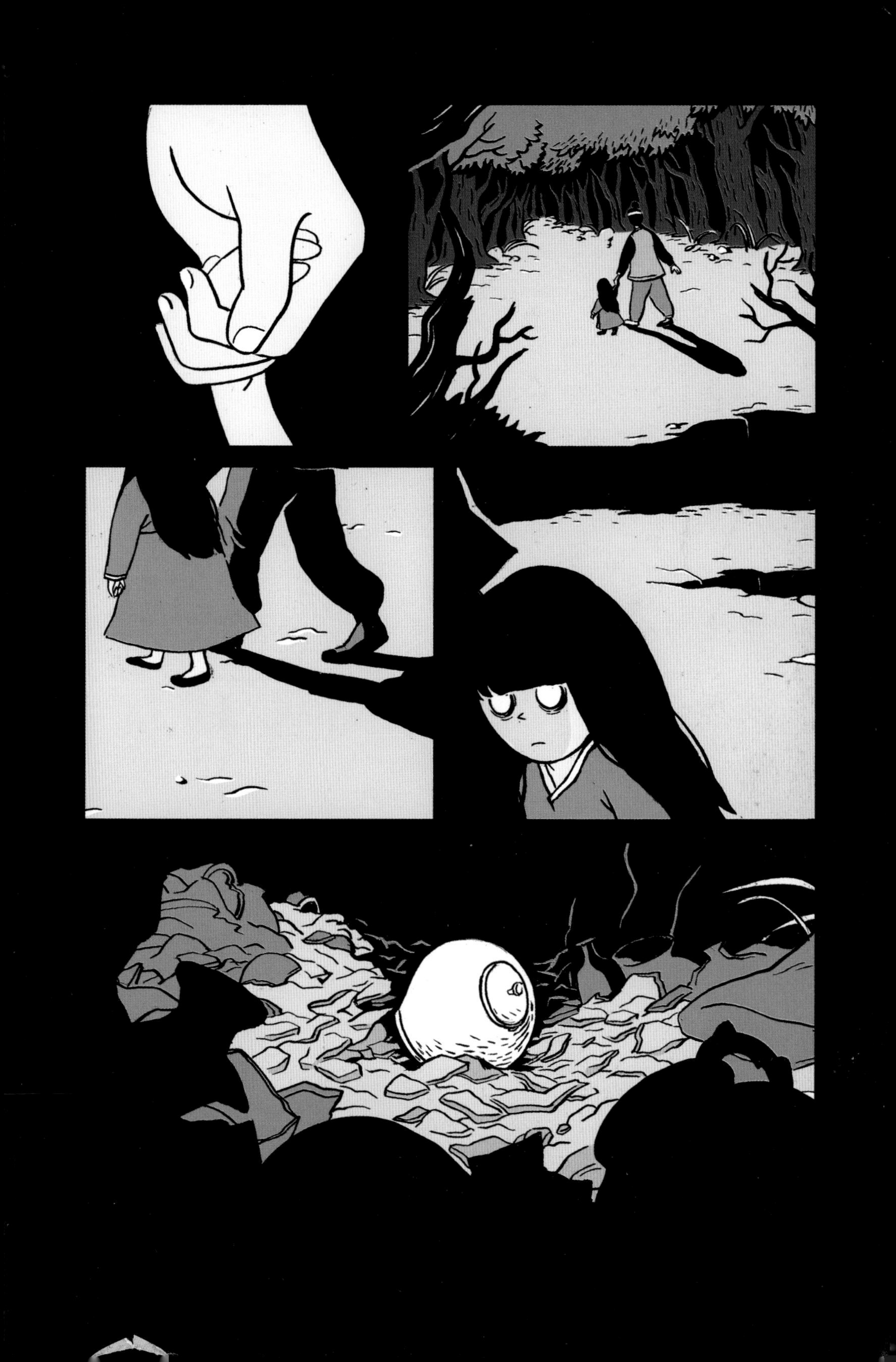

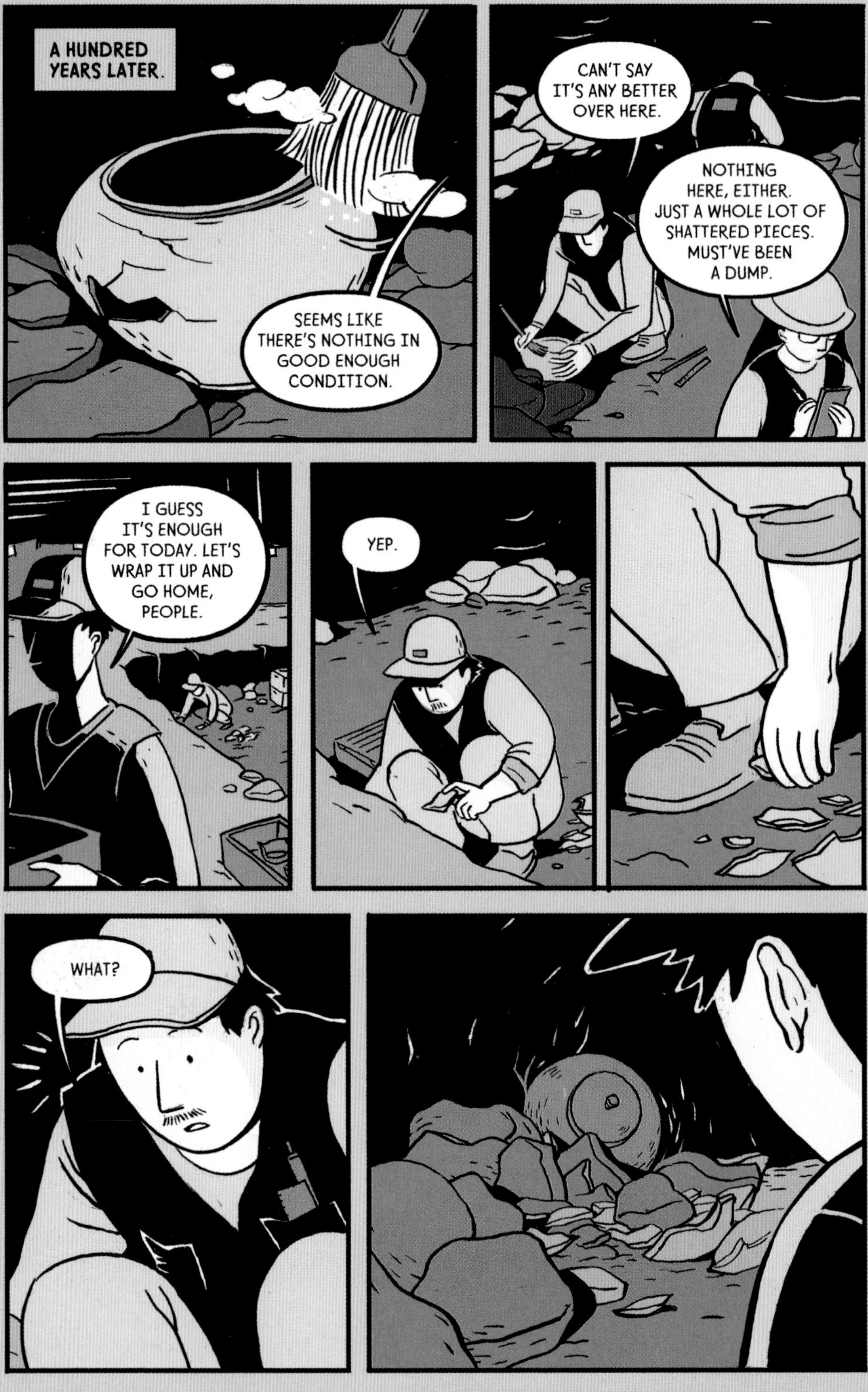
A HUNDRED YEARS LATER.
SEEMS LIKE THERE'S NOTHING IN GOOD ENOUGH CONDITION.
CAN'T SAY IT'S ANY BETTER OVER HERE.
NOTHING HERE, EITHER. JUST A WHOLE LOT OF SHATTERED PIECES. MUST'VE BEEN A DUMP.
I GUESS IT'S ENOUGH FOR TODAY. LET'S WRAP IT UP AND GO HOME, PEOPLE.
YEP.
WHAT?

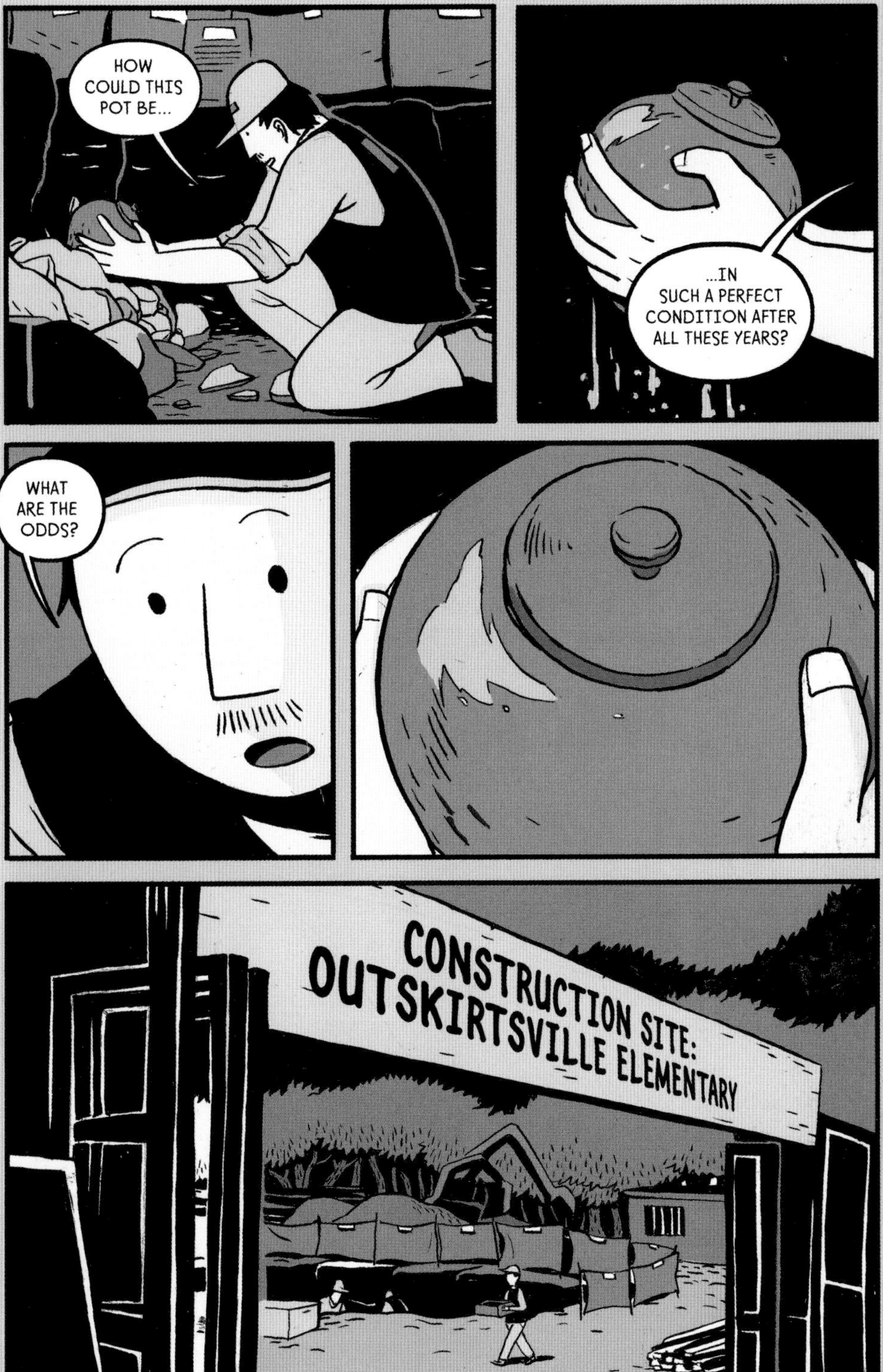
HOW COULD THIS POT BE...
...IN SUCH A PERFECT CONDITION AFTER ALL THESE YEARS?
WHAT ARE THE ODDS?
CONSTRUCTION SITE: OUTSKIRTSVILLE ELEMENTARY

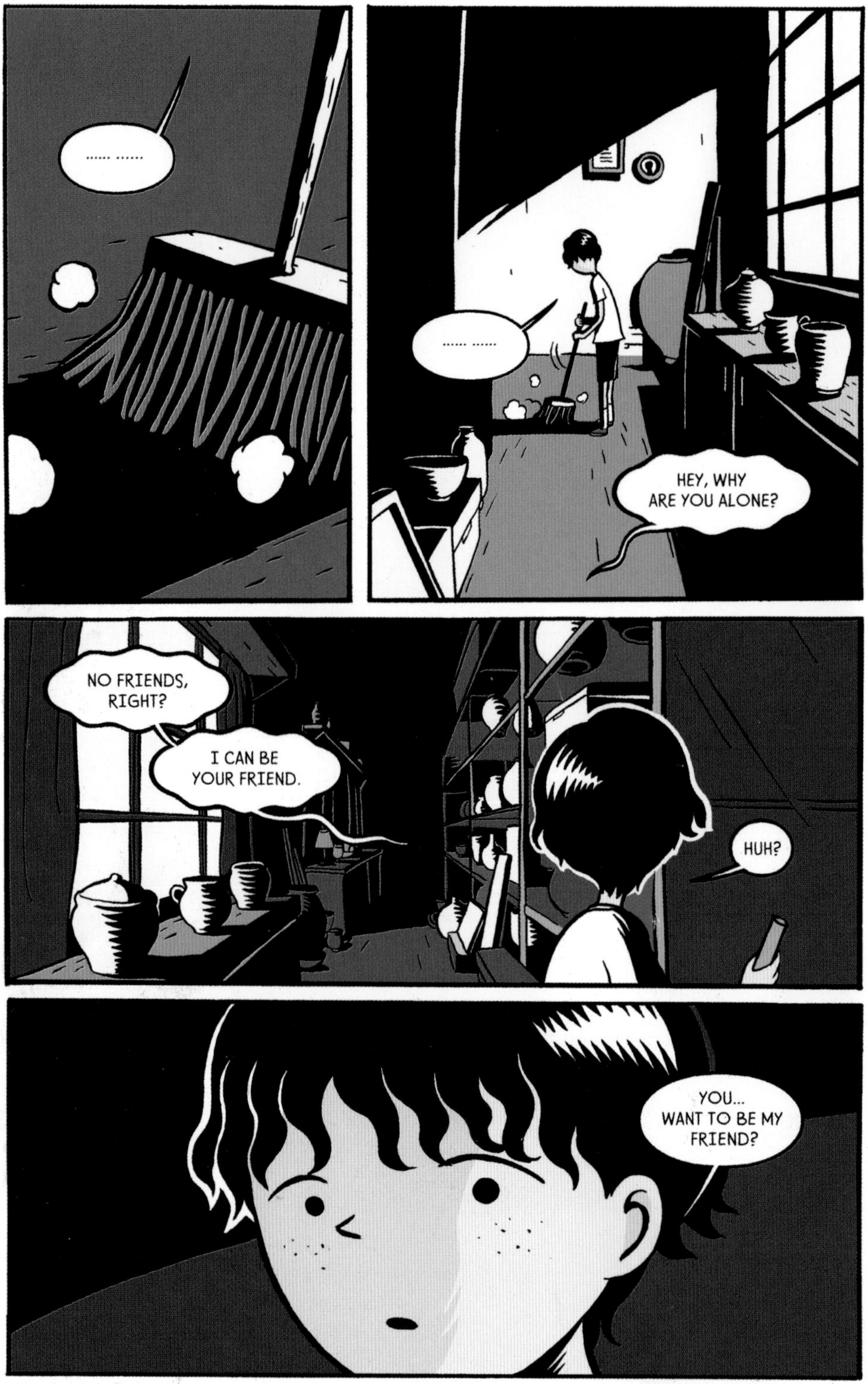
....
....
HEY, WHY ARE YOU ALONE?
NO FRIENDS, RIGHT?
I CAN BE YOUR FRIEND.
HUH?
YOU... WANT TO BE MY FRIEND?

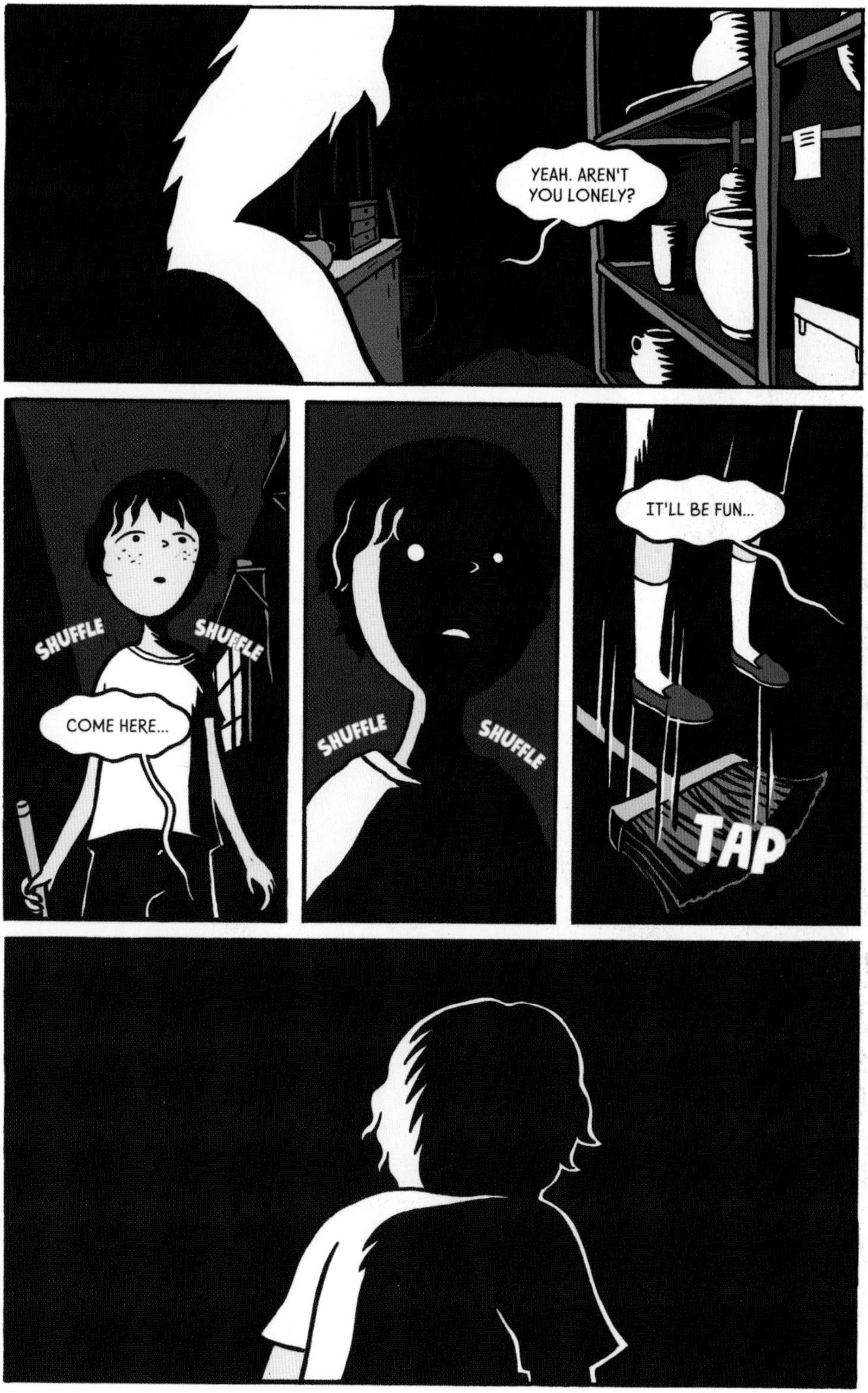
YEAH. AREN'T YOU LONELY?
SHUFFLE
SHUFFLE
COME HERE...
SHUFFLE
SHUFFLE
IT'LL BE FUN...
TAP

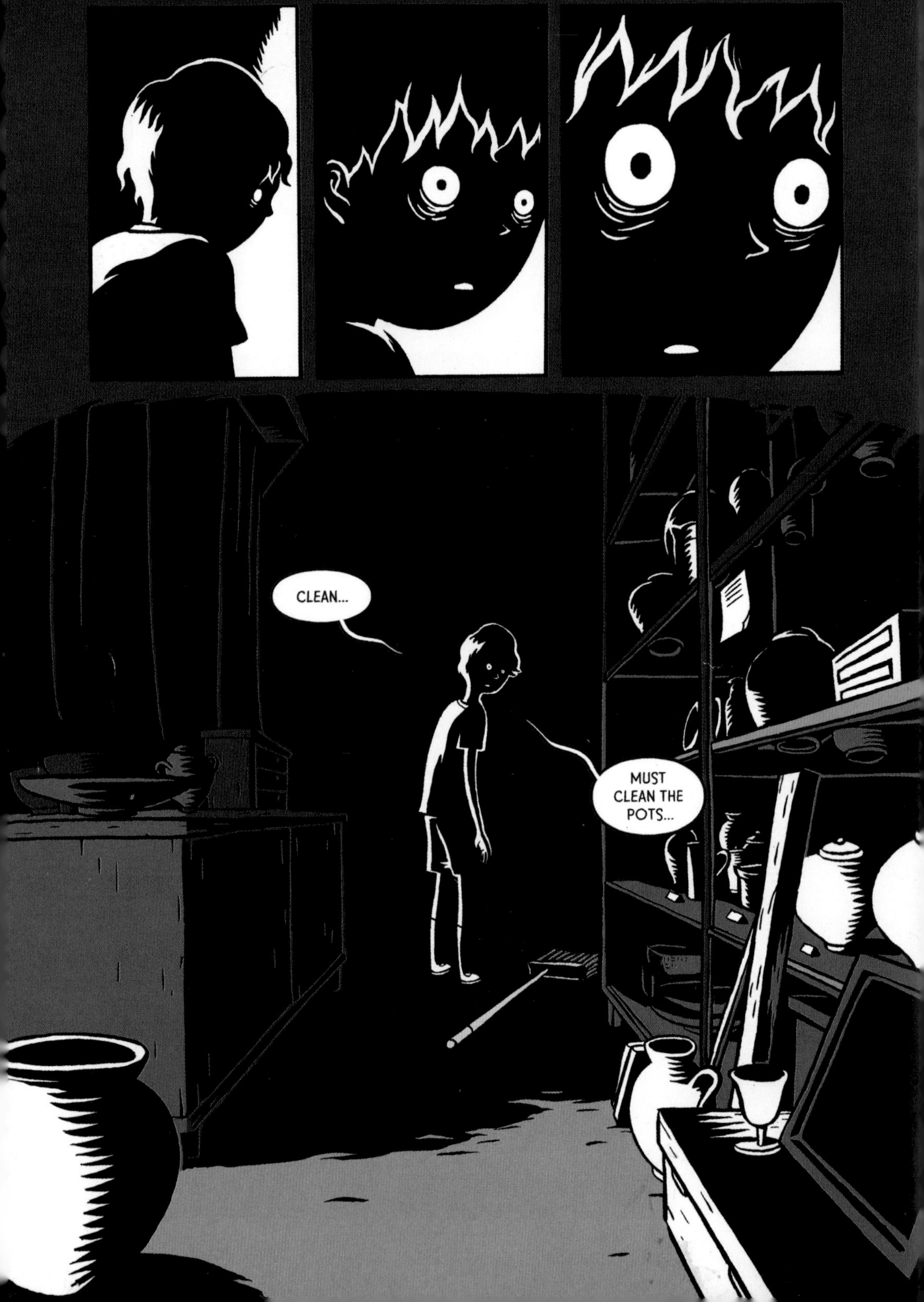
CLEAN...
MUST CLEAN THE POTS...

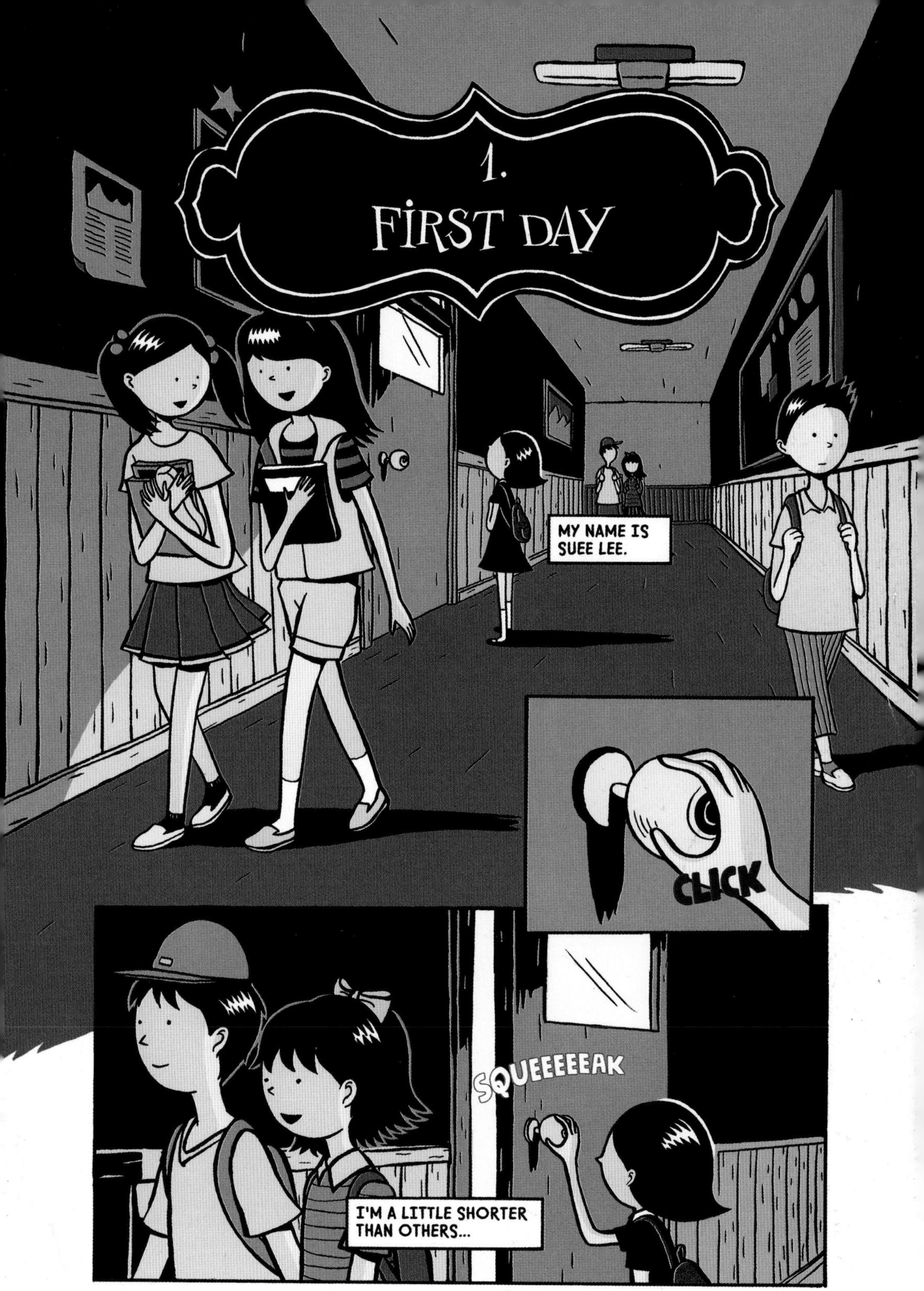
1.
FIRST DAY
MY NAME IS SUEE LEE.
CLICK
SQUEEEEEAK
I'M A LITTLE SHORTER THAN OTHERS...

I DRESS A LITTLE DIFFERENTLY...

GRADE SUBJECT	3	4	5
LANGUAGE ARTS	A	A	A
WRITING	A	A	A
MATH	A	A	A
SCIENCE	A	A	A
HISTORY	C-	C-	C-
SPANISH	C-	C-	C-
MUSIC	A	A	A

AND MY ACADEMIC PHILOSOPHY IS SOMEWHAT UNIQUE.

GLANCE

SHE LOOKS SO STUBBORN...

BUT OTHER THAN THAT I'M A VERY NORMAL TWELVE-YEAR-OLD.

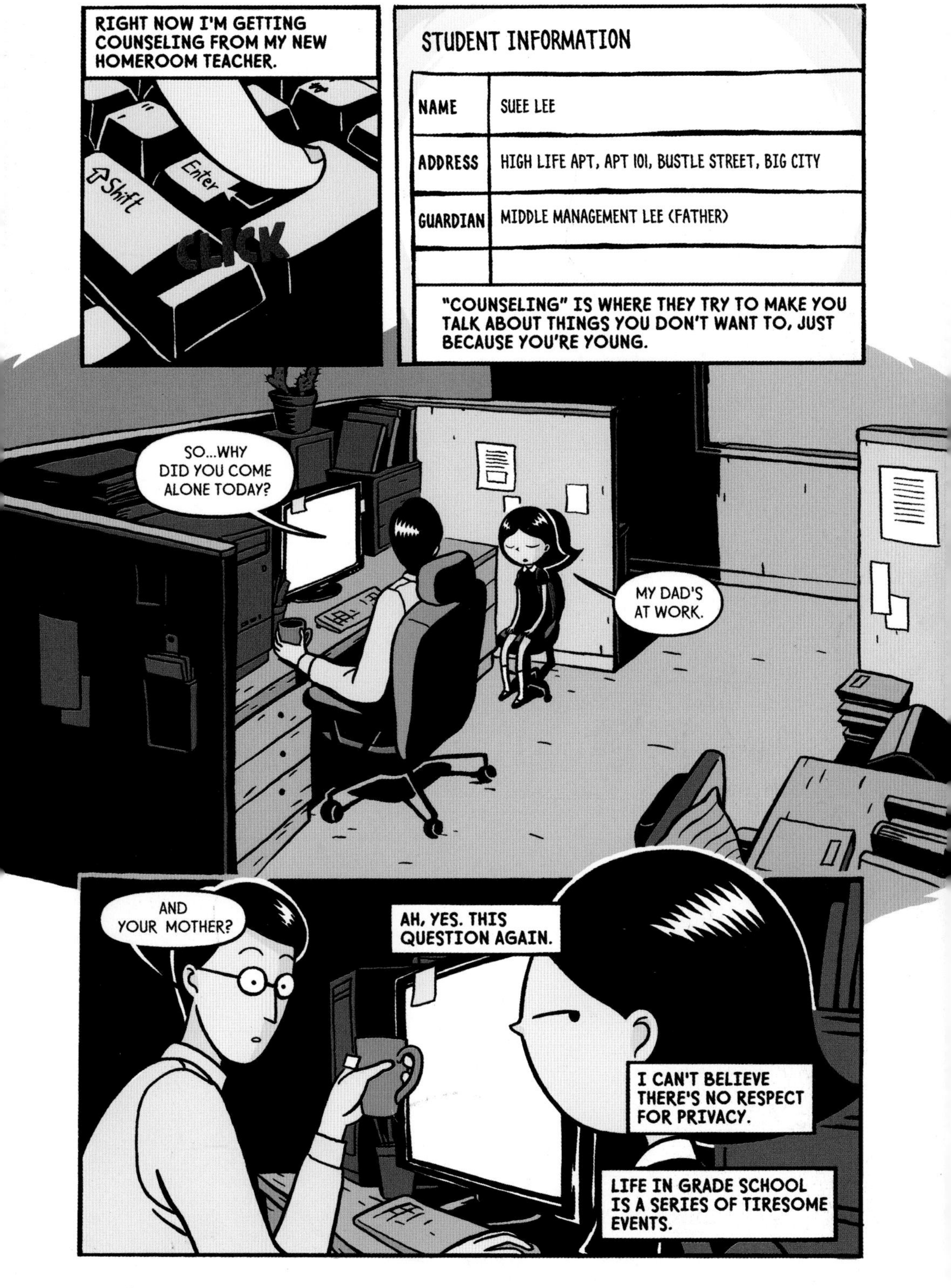
RIGHT NOW I'M GETTING COUNSELING FROM MY NEW HOMEROOM TEACHER.
Enter
Shift
CLICK
STUDENT INFORMATION
NAME
SUEE LEE
ADDRESS
HIGH LIFE APT, APT 101, BUSTLE STREET, BIG CITY
GUARDIAN
MIDDLE MANAGEMENT LEE (FATHER)
"COUNSELING" IS WHERE THEY TRY TO MAKE YOU TALK ABOUT THINGS YOU DON'T WANT TO, JUST BECAUSE YOU'RE YOUNG.
SO...WHY DID YOU COME ALONE TODAY?
MY DAD'S AT WORK.
AND YOUR MOTHER?
AH, YES. THIS QUESTION AGAIN.
I CAN'T BELIEVE THERE'S NO RESPECT FOR PRIVACY.
LIFE IN GRADE SCHOOL IS A SERIES OF TIRESOME EVENTS.

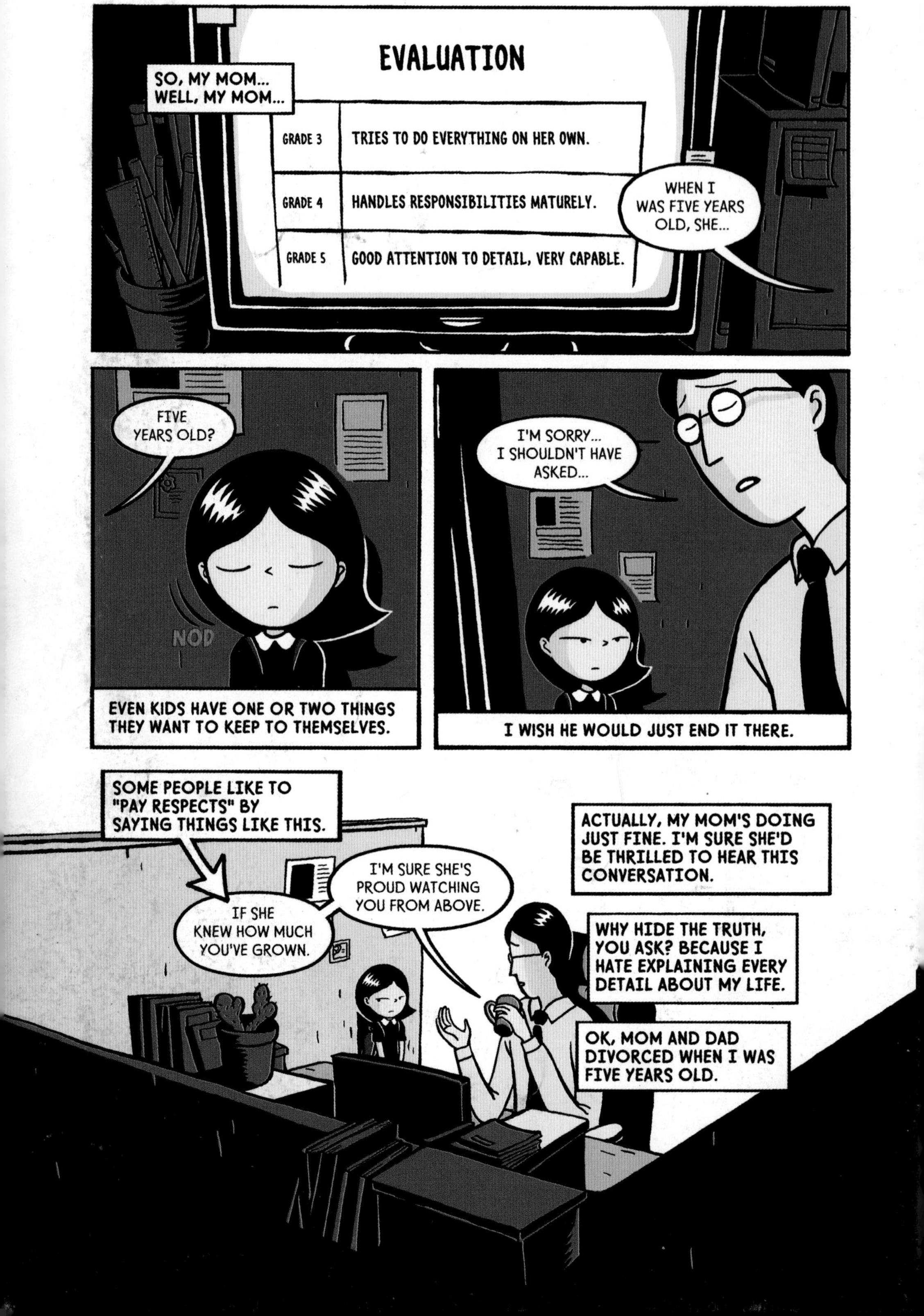
EVALUATION
SO, MY MOM... WELL, MY MOM...
GRADE 3 | TRIES TO DO EVERYTHING ON HER OWN.
GRADE 4 | HANDLES RESPONSIBILITIES MATURELY.
GRADE 5 | GOOD ATTENTION TO DETAIL, VERY CAPABLE.
WHEN I WAS FIVE YEARS OLD, SHE...
FIVE YEARS OLD?
NOD
EVEN KIDS HAVE ONE OR TWO THINGS THEY WANT TO KEEP TO THEMSELVES.
I'M SORRY... I SHOULDN'T HAVE ASKED...
I WISH HE WOULD JUST END IT THERE.
SOME PEOPLE LIKE TO "PAY RESPECTS" BY SAYING THINGS LIKE THIS.
IF SHE KNEW HOW MUCH YOU'VE GROWN.
I'M SURE SHE'S PROUD WATCHING YOU FROM ABOVE.
ACTUALLY, MY MOM'S DOING JUST FINE. I'M SURE SHE'D BE THRILLED TO HEAR THIS CONVERSATION.
WHY HIDE THE TRUTH, YOU ASK? BECAUSE I HATE EXPLAINING EVERY DETAIL ABOUT MY LIFE.
OK, MOM AND DAD DIVORCED WHEN I WAS FIVE YEARS OLD.

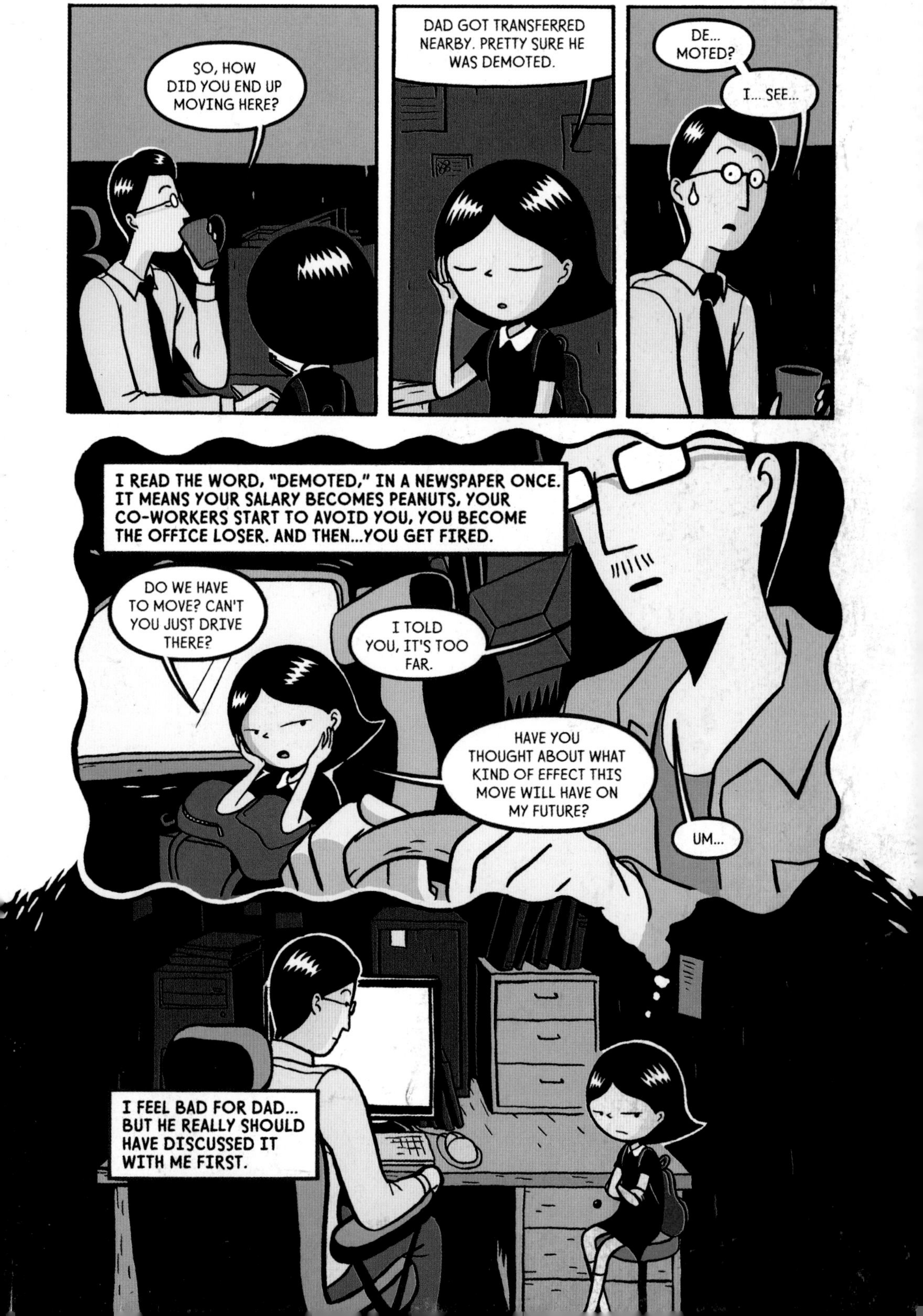
SO, HOW DID YOU END UP MOVING HERE?
DAD GOT TRANSFERRED NEARBY. PRETTY SURE HE WAS DEMOTED.
DE... MOTED?
I... SEE...
I READ THE WORD, "DEMOTED," IN A NEWSPAPER ONCE. IT MEANS YOUR SALARY BECOMES PEANUTS, YOUR CO-WORKERS START TO AVOID YOU, YOU BECOME THE OFFICE LOSER. AND THEN...YOU GET FIRED.
DO WE HAVE TO MOVE? CAN'T YOU JUST DRIVE THERE?
I TOLD YOU, IT'S TOO FAR.
HAVE YOU THOUGHT ABOUT WHAT KIND OF EFFECT THIS MOVE WILL HAVE ON MY FUTURE?
UM...
I FEEL BAD FOR DAD... BUT HE REALLY SHOULD HAVE DISCUSSED IT WITH ME FIRST.

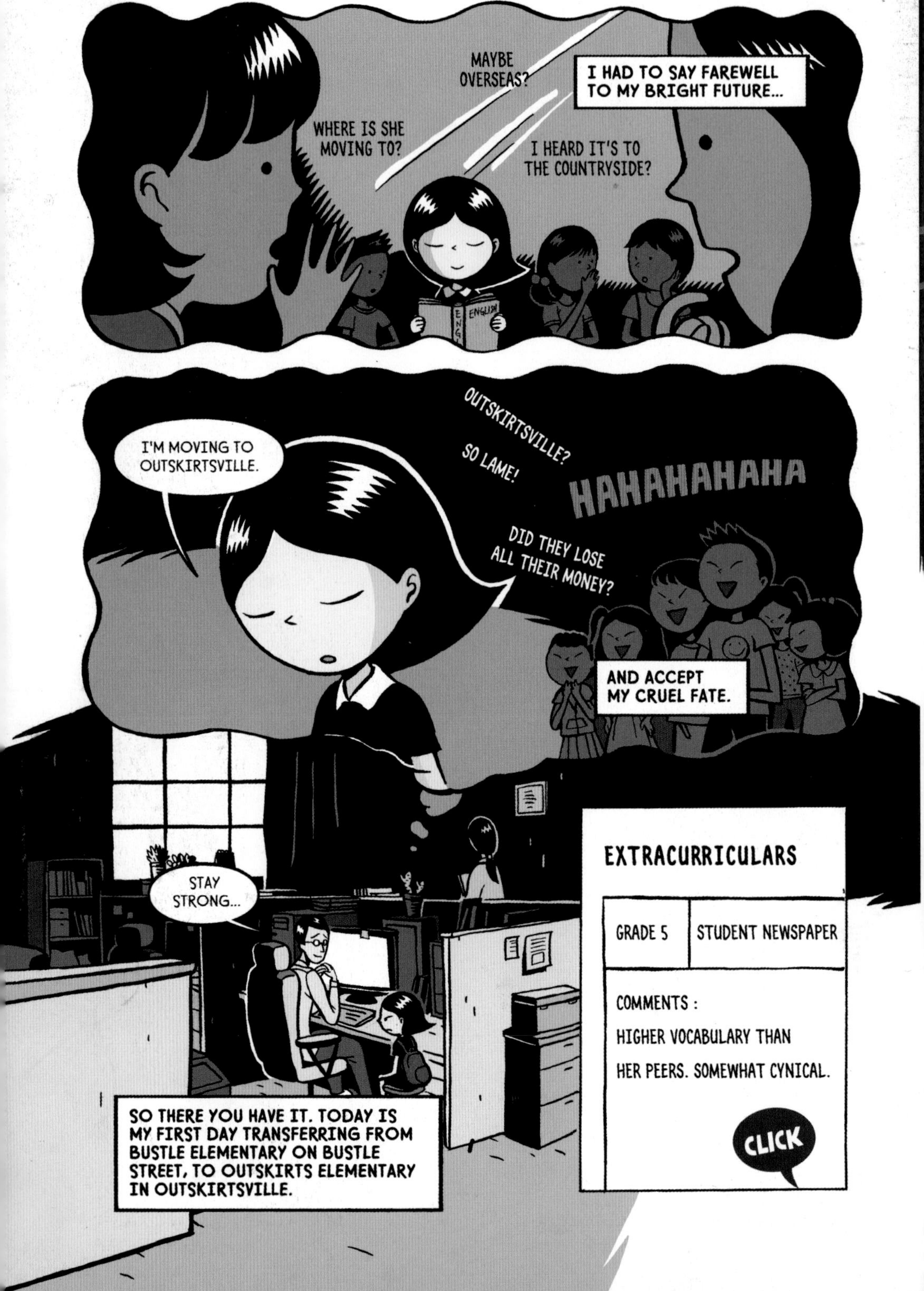
I HAD TO SAY FAREWELL TO MY BRIGHT FUTURE...
WHERE IS SHE MOVING TO?
MAYBE OVERSEAS?
I HEARD IT'S TO THE COUNTRYSIDE?
ENGLISH
I'M MOVING TO OUTSKIRTSVILLE.
OUTSKIRTSVILLE?
SO LAME!
HAHAHAHAHA
DID THEY LOSE ALL THEIR MONEY?
AND ACCEPT MY CRUEL FATE.
STAY STRONG...
EXTRACURRICULARS
GRADE 5
STUDENT NEWSPAPER
COMMENTS :
HIGHER VOCABULARY THAN
HER PEERS. SOMEWHAT CYNICAL.
CLICK
SO THERE YOU HAVE IT. TODAY IS MY FIRST DAY TRANSFERRING FROM BUSTLE ELEMENTARY ON BUSTLE STREET, TO OUTSKIRTS ELEMENTARY IN OUTSKIRTSVILLE.

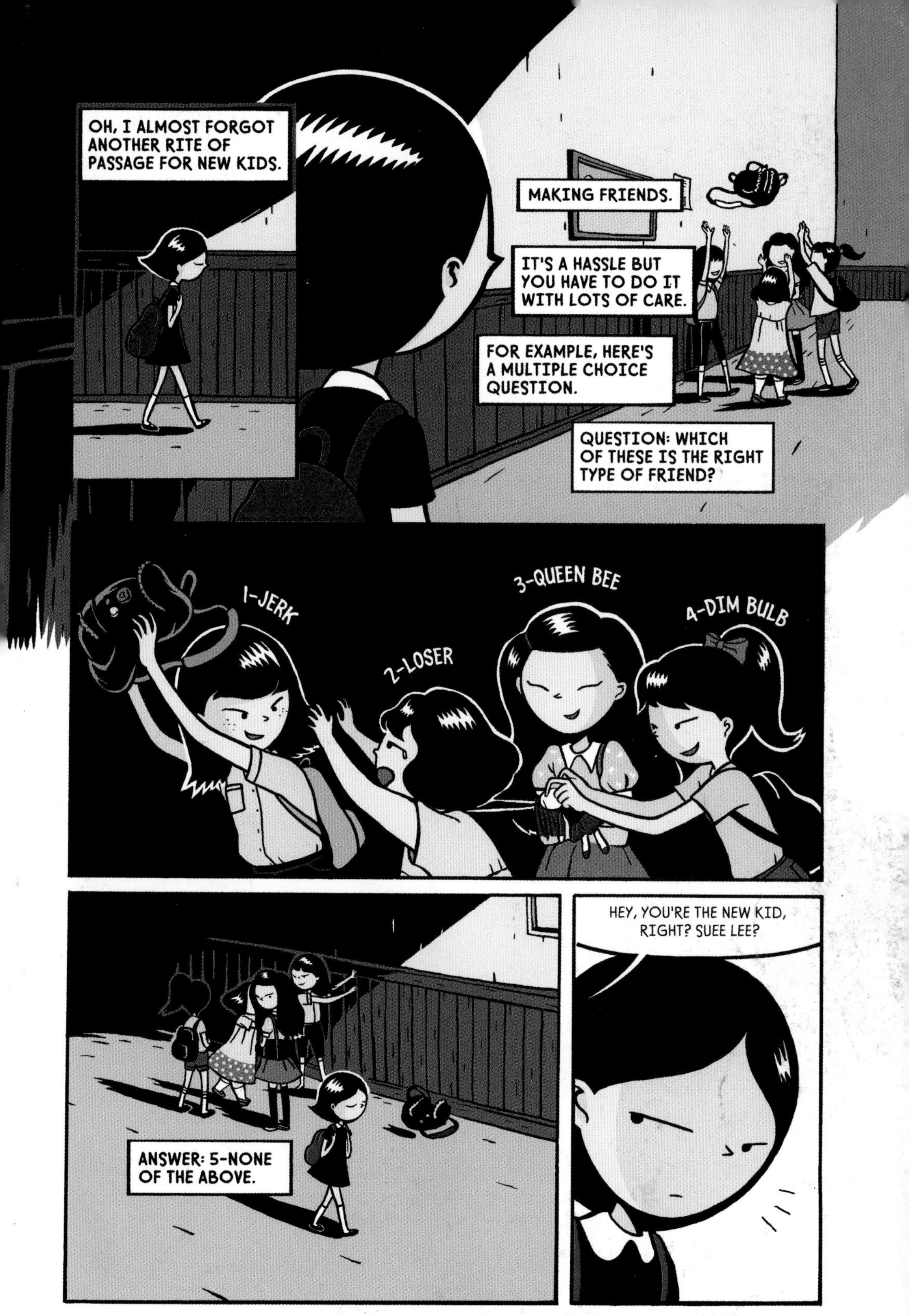
OH, I ALMOST FORGOT ANOTHER RITE OF PASSAGE FOR NEW KIDS.
MAKING FRIENDS.
IT'S A HASSLE BUT YOU HAVE TO DO IT WITH LOTS OF CARE.
FOR EXAMPLE, HERE'S A MULTIPLE CHOICE QUESTION.
QUESTION: WHICH OF THESE IS THE RIGHT TYPE OF FRIEND?
1-JERK
2-LOSER
3-QUEEN BEE
4-DIM BULB
ANSWER: 5-NONE OF THE ABOVE.
HEY, YOU'RE THE NEW KID, RIGHT? SUEE LEE?

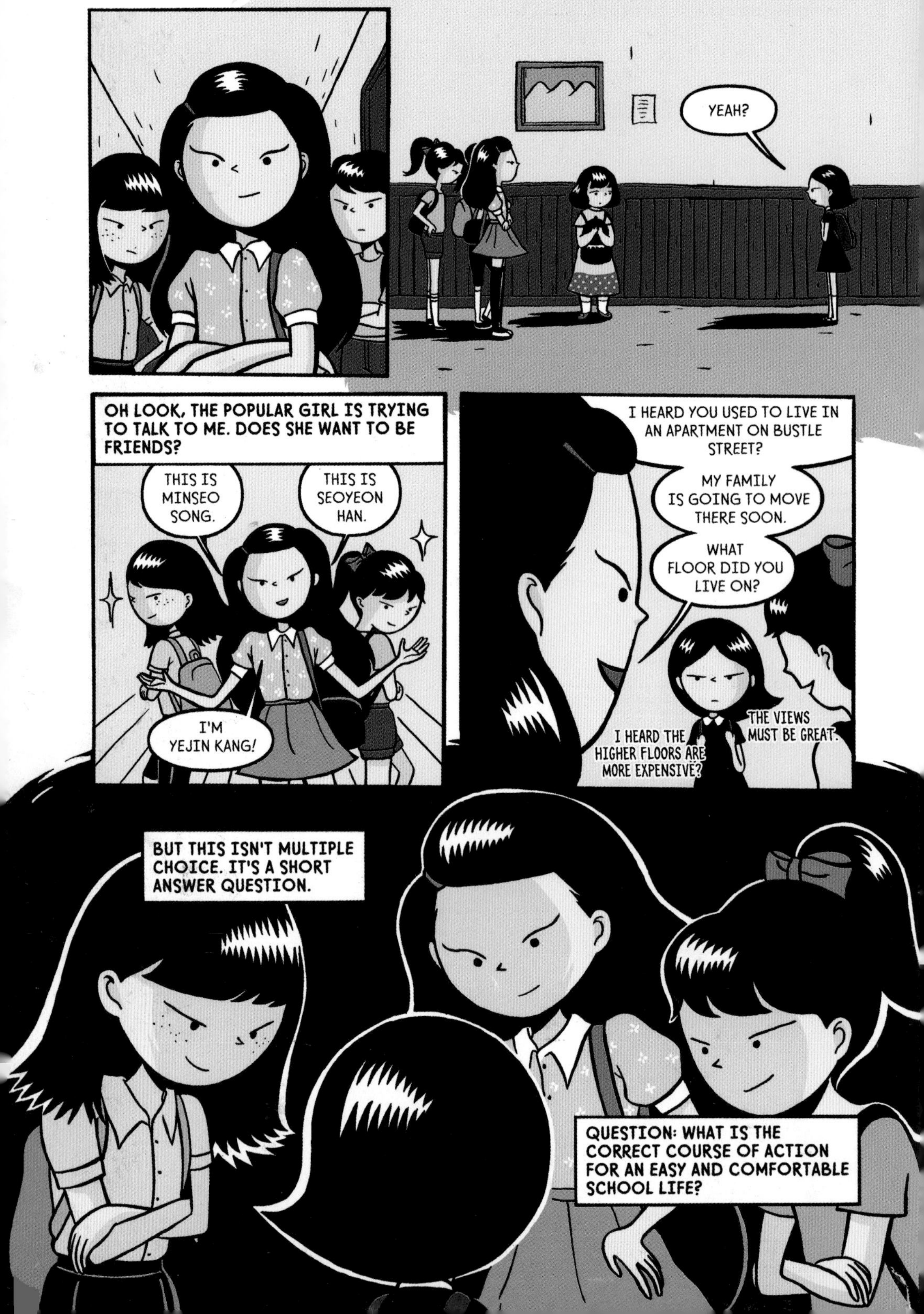
YEAH?
OH LOOK, THE POPULAR GIRL IS TRYING TO TALK TO ME. DOES SHE WANT TO BE FRIENDS?
THIS IS MINSEO SONG.
THIS IS SEOYEON HAN.
I'M YEJIN KANG!
I HEARD YOU USED TO LIVE IN AN APARTMENT ON BUSTLE STREET?
MY FAMILY IS GOING TO MOVE THERE SOON.
WHAT FLOOR DID YOU LIVE ON?
I HEARD THE HIGHER FLOORS ARE MORE EXPENSIVE?
THE VIEWS MUST BE GREAT.
BUT THIS ISN'T MULTIPLE CHOICE. IT'S A SHORT ANSWER QUESTION.
QUESTION: WHAT IS THE CORRECT COURSE OF ACTION FOR AN EASY AND COMFORTABLE SCHOOL LIFE?

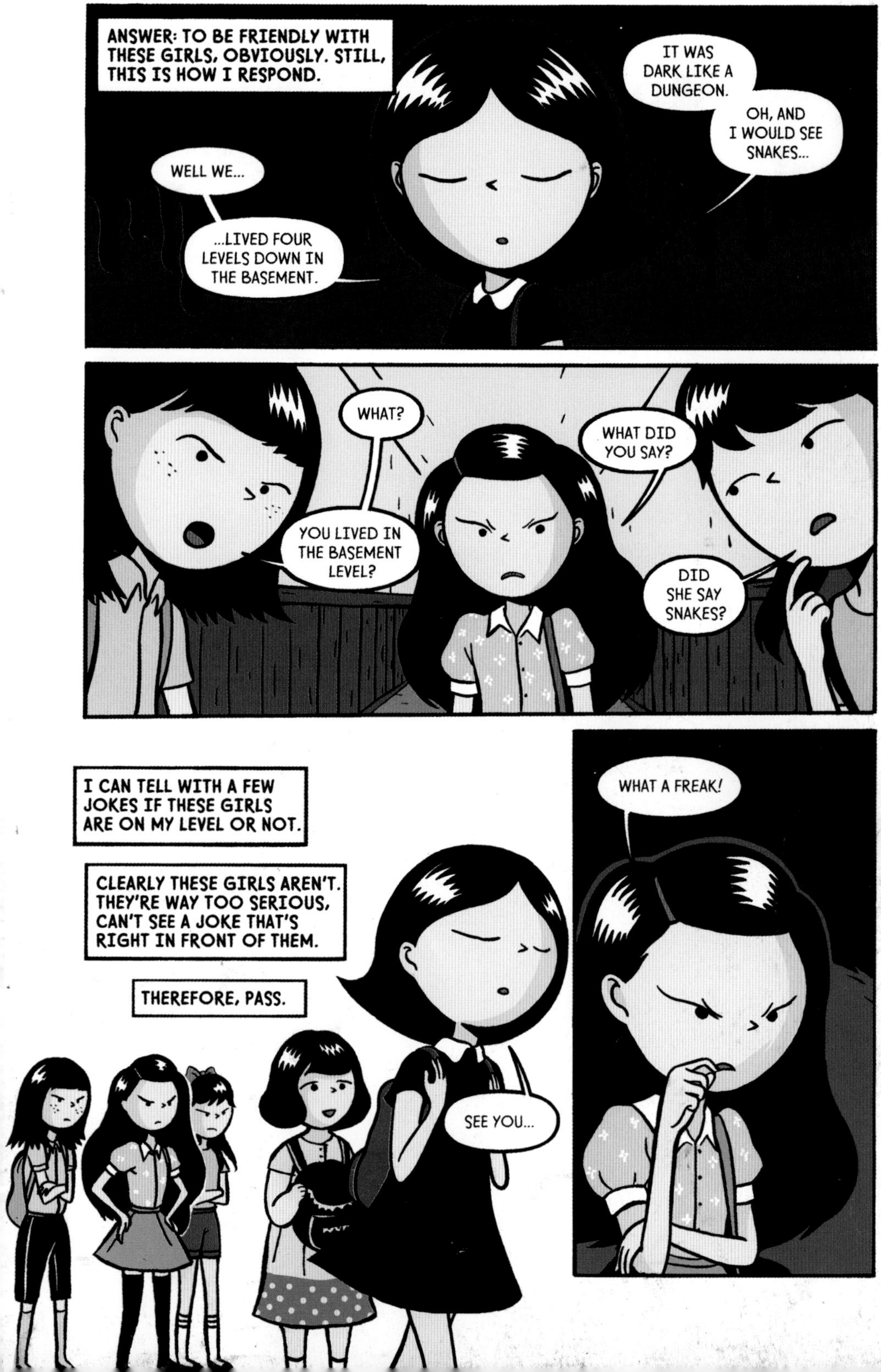
ANSWER: TO BE FRIENDLY WITH THESE GIRLS, OBVIOUSLY. STILL, THIS IS HOW I RESPOND.
WELL WE...
...LIVED FOUR LEVELS DOWN IN THE BASEMENT.
IT WAS DARK LIKE A DUNGEON.
OH, AND I WOULD SEE SNAKES...
WHAT?
YOU LIVED IN THE BASEMENT LEVEL?
WHAT DID YOU SAY?
DID SHE SAY SNAKES?
I CAN TELL WITH A FEW JOKES IF THESE GIRLS ARE ON MY LEVEL OR NOT.
CLEARLY THESE GIRLS AREN'T. THEY'RE WAY TOO SERIOUS, CAN'T SEE A JOKE THAT'S RIGHT IN FRONT OF THEM.
THEREFORE, PASS.
SEE YOU...
WHAT A FREAK!

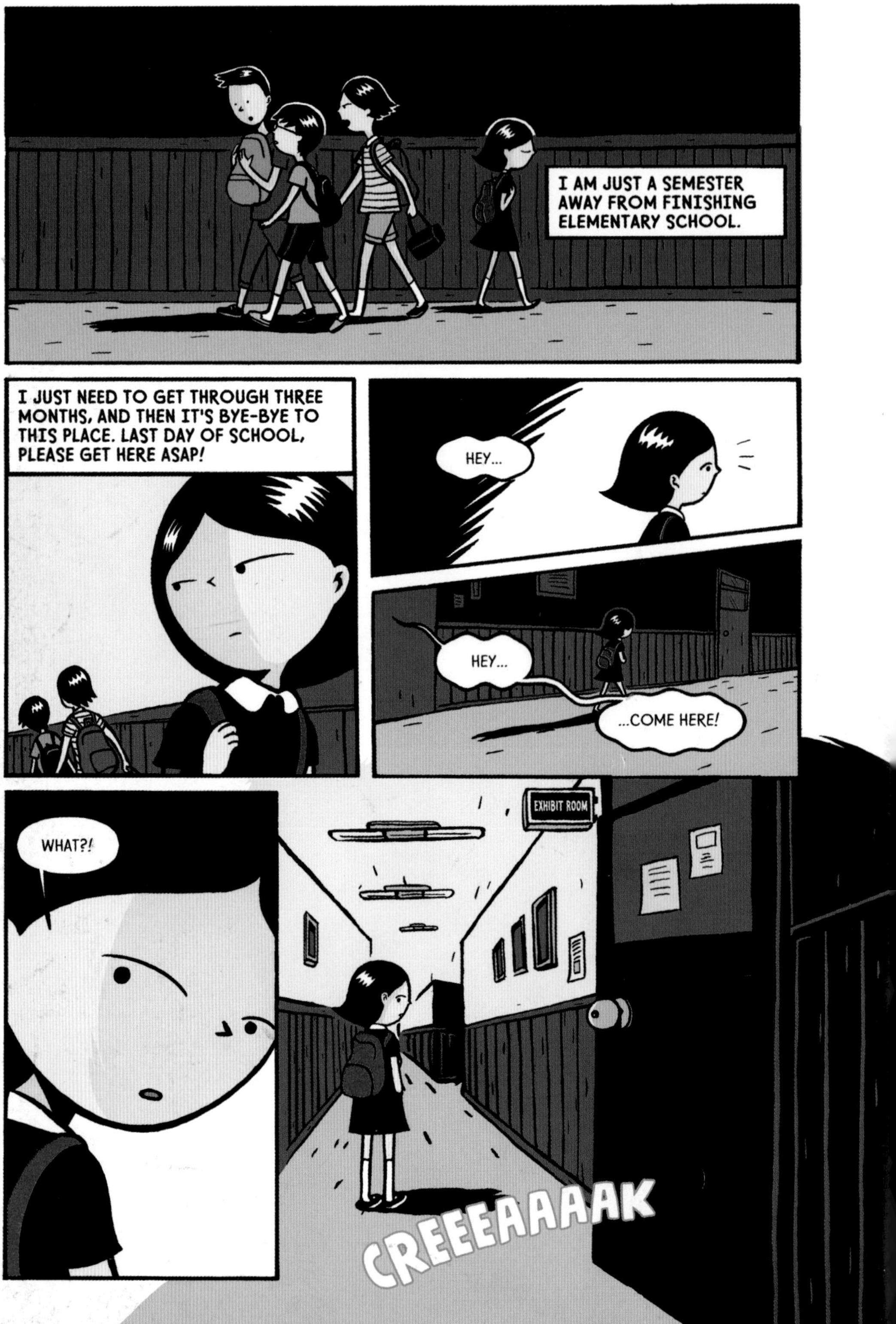
I AM JUST A SEMESTER AWAY FROM FINISHING ELEMENTARY SCHOOL.
I JUST NEED TO GET THROUGH THREE MONTHS, AND THEN IT'S BYE-BYE TO THIS PLACE. LAST DAY OF SCHOOL, PLEASE GET HERE ASAP!
HEY...
HEY...
...COME HERE!
WHAT?!
EXHIBIT ROOM
CREEEAAAAK

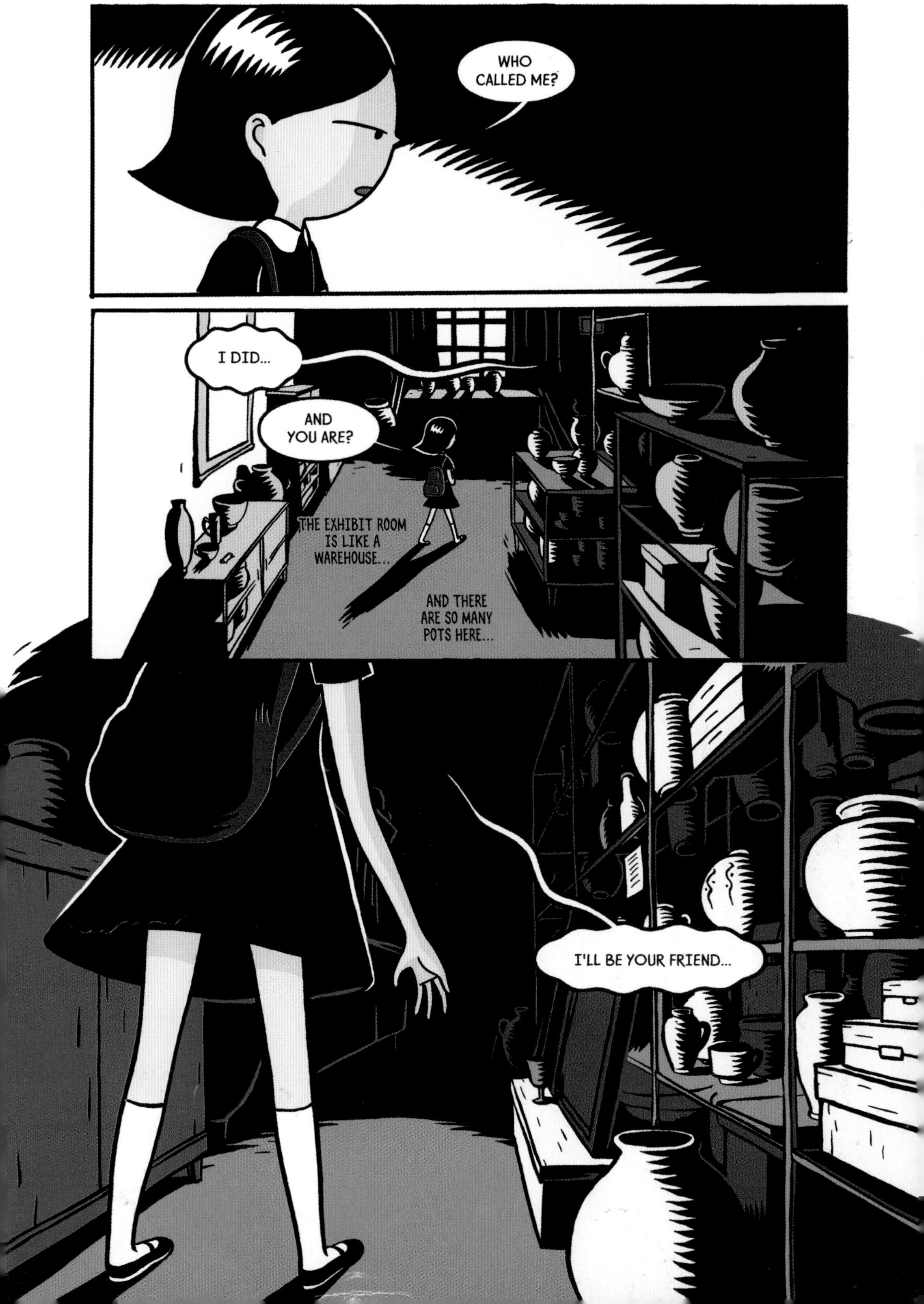
WHO CALLED ME?
I DID...
AND YOU ARE?
THE EXHIBIT ROOM IS LIKE A WAREHOUSE...
AND THERE ARE SO MANY POTS HERE...
I'LL BE YOUR FRIEND...

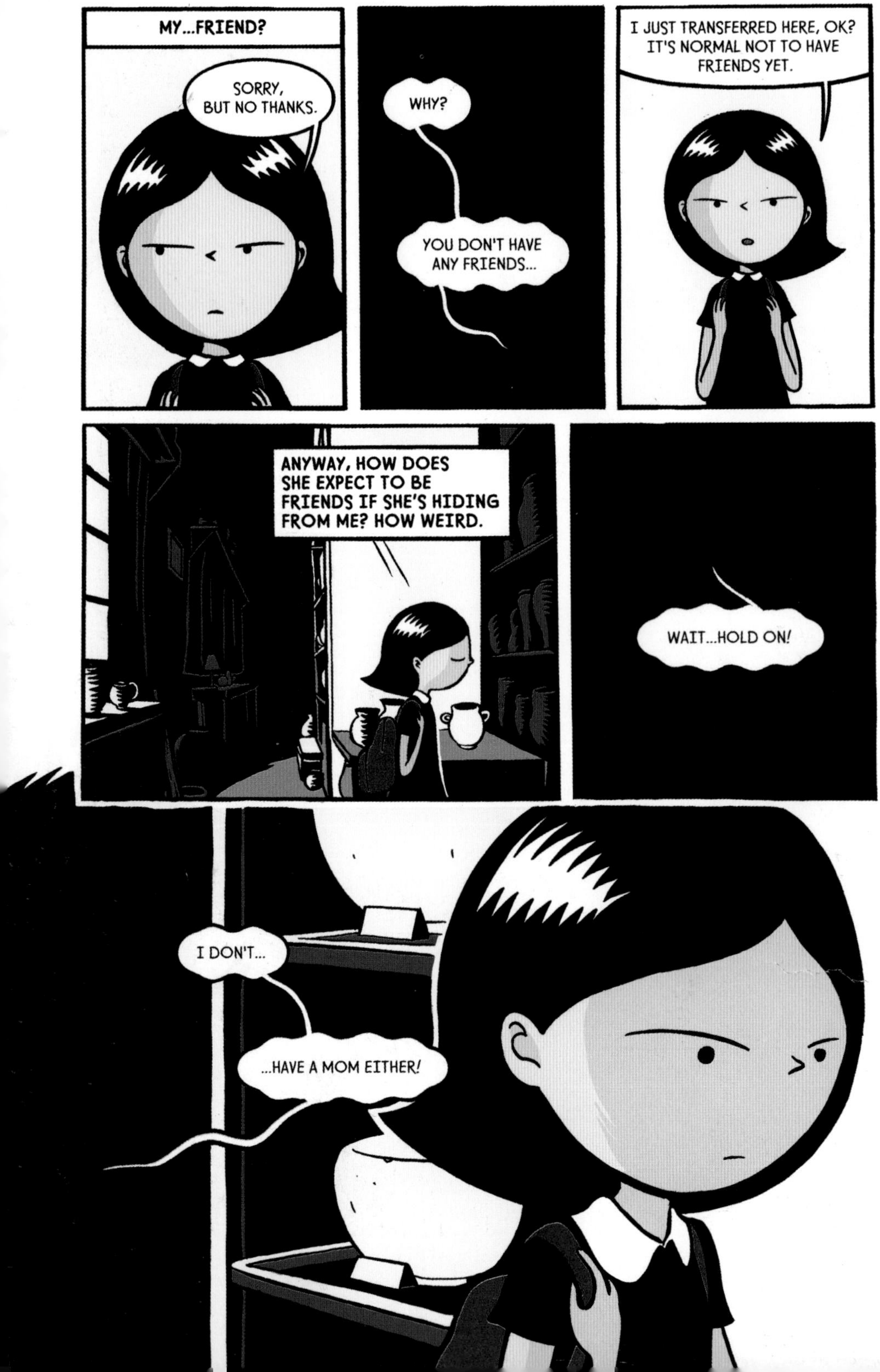
MY...FRIEND?
SORRY, BUT NO THANKS.
WHY?
YOU DON'T HAVE ANY FRIENDS...
I JUST TRANSFERRED HERE, OK? IT'S NORMAL NOT TO HAVE FRIENDS YET.
ANYWAY, HOW DOES SHE EXPECT TO BE FRIENDS IF SHE'S HIDING FROM ME? HOW WEIRD.
WAIT...HOLD ON!
I DON'T...
...HAVE A MOM EITHER!

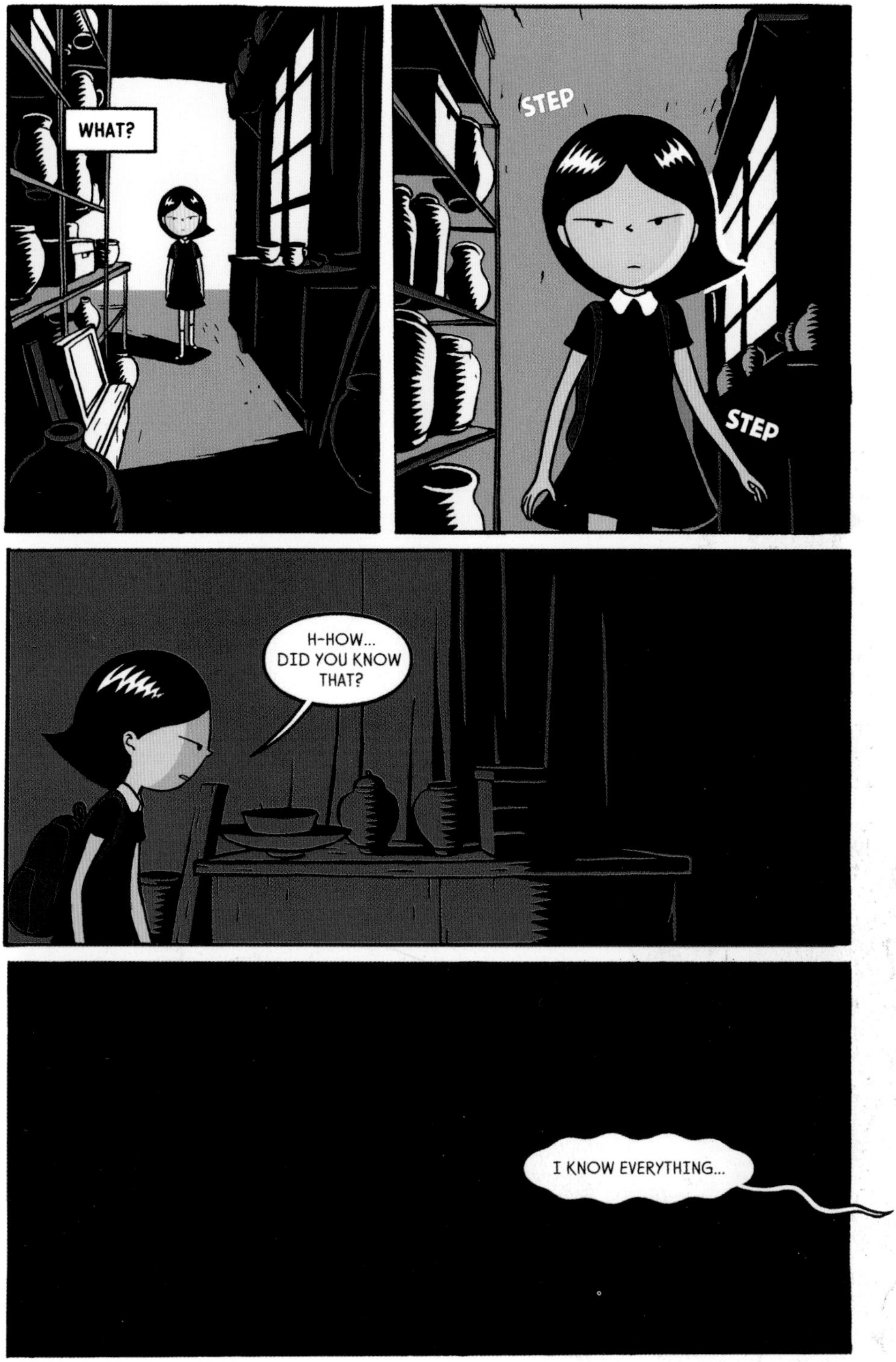
WHAT?
STEP
STEP
H-HOW... DID YOU KNOW THAT?
I KNOW EVERYTHING...

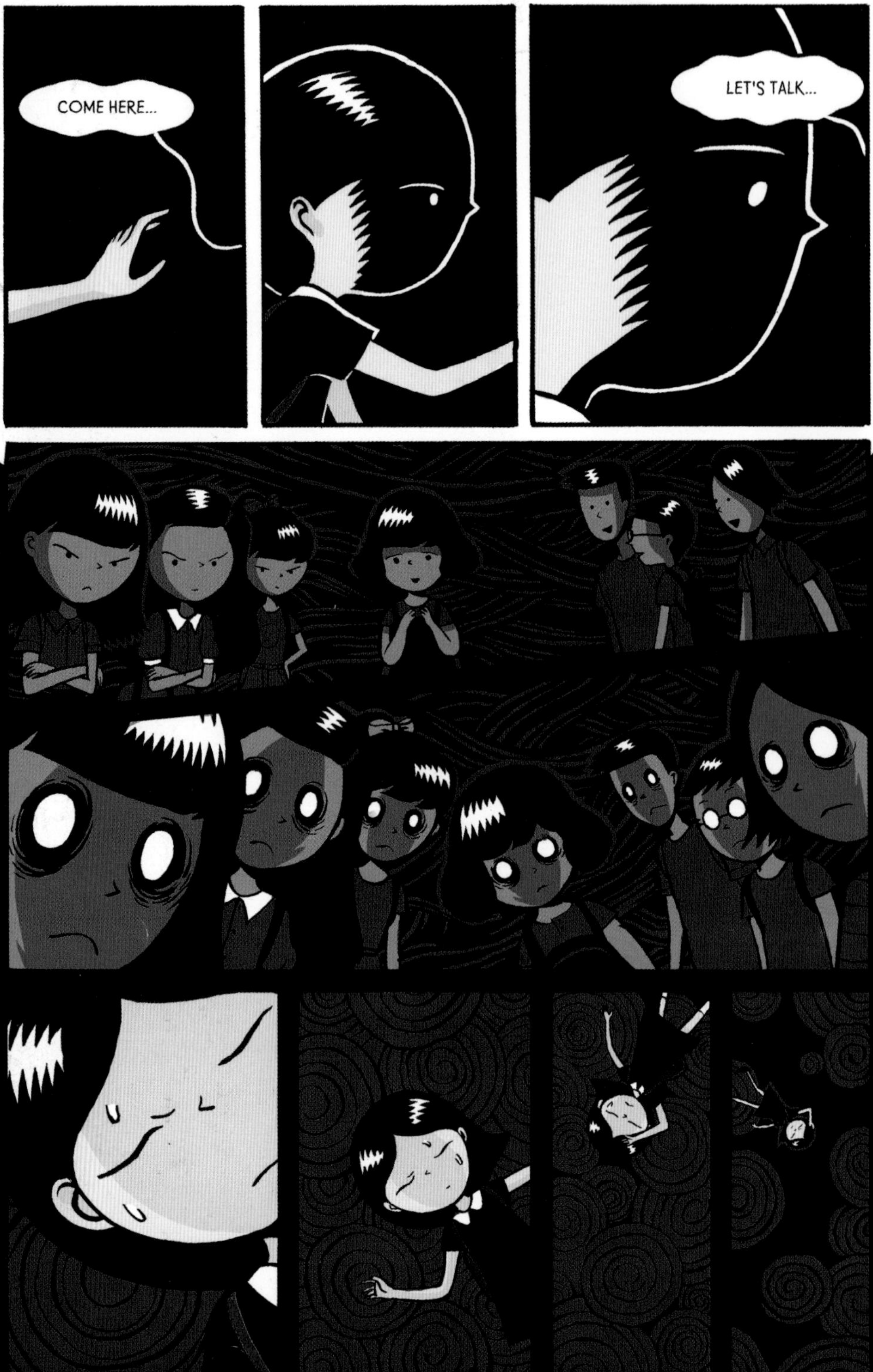
COME HERE...
LET'S TALK...

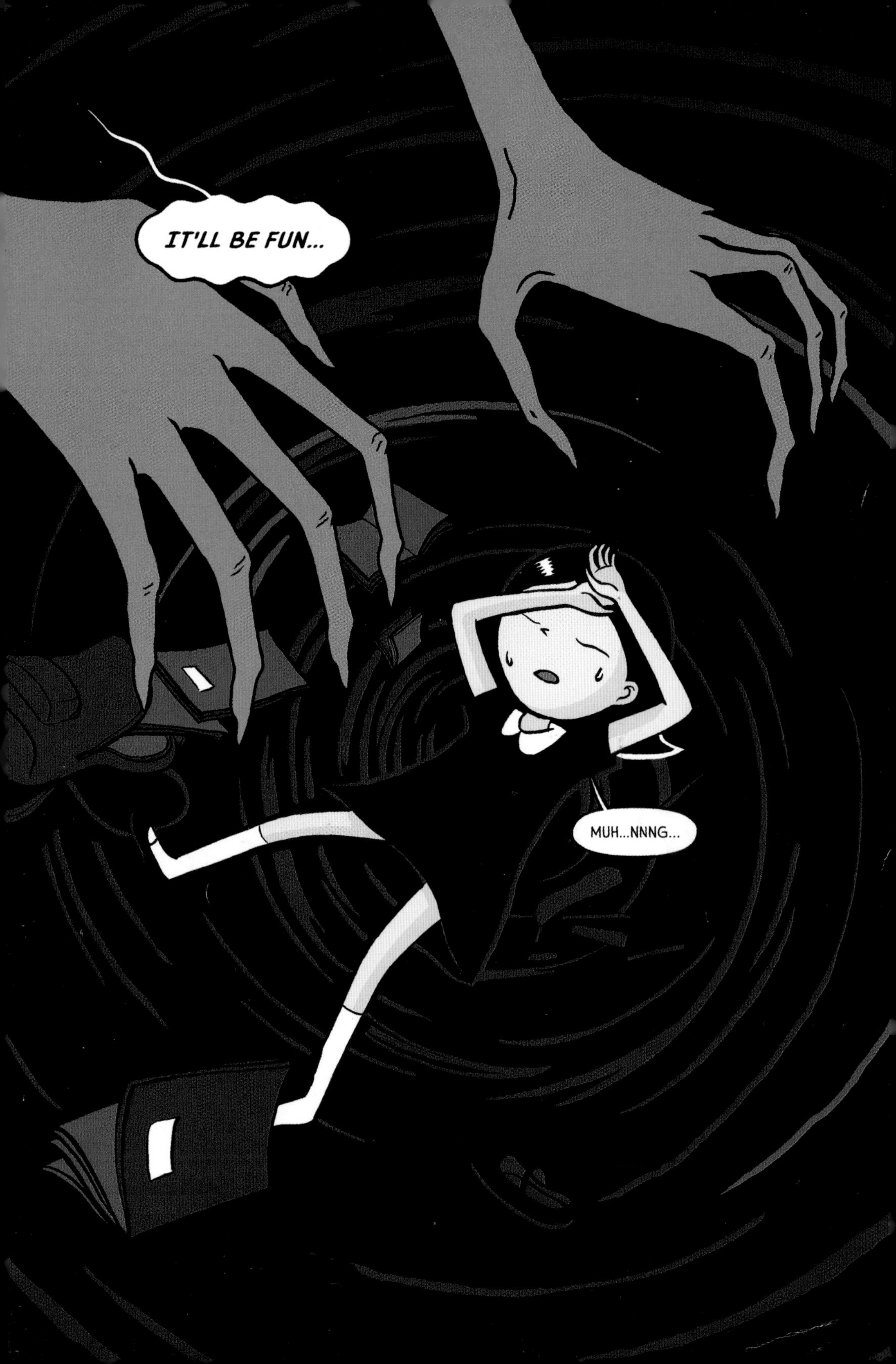
IT'LL BE FUN...
MUH...NNNG...

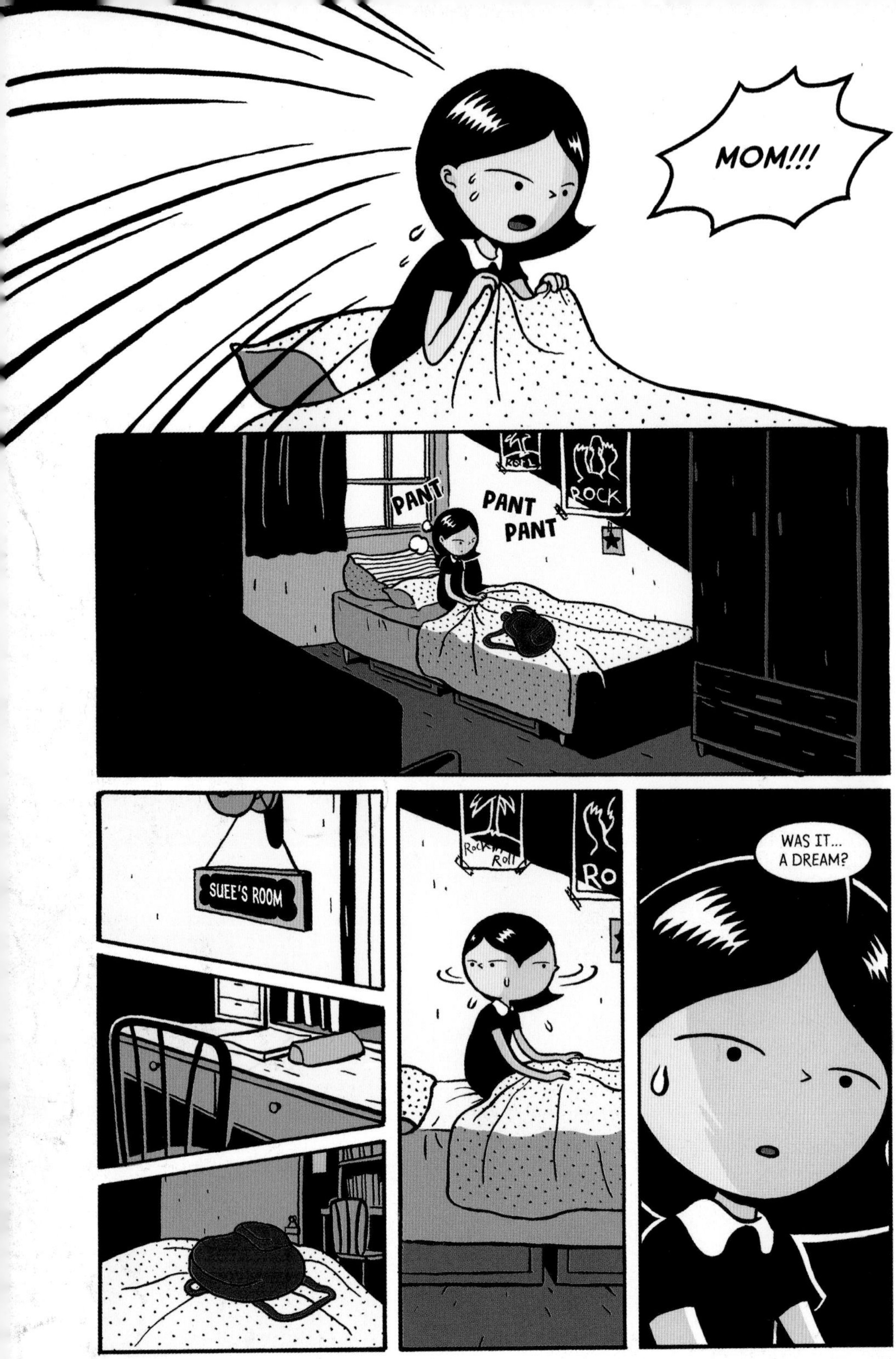
MOM!!!
PANT
PANT
PANT
ROCK
SUEE'S ROOM
WAS IT...
A DREAM?

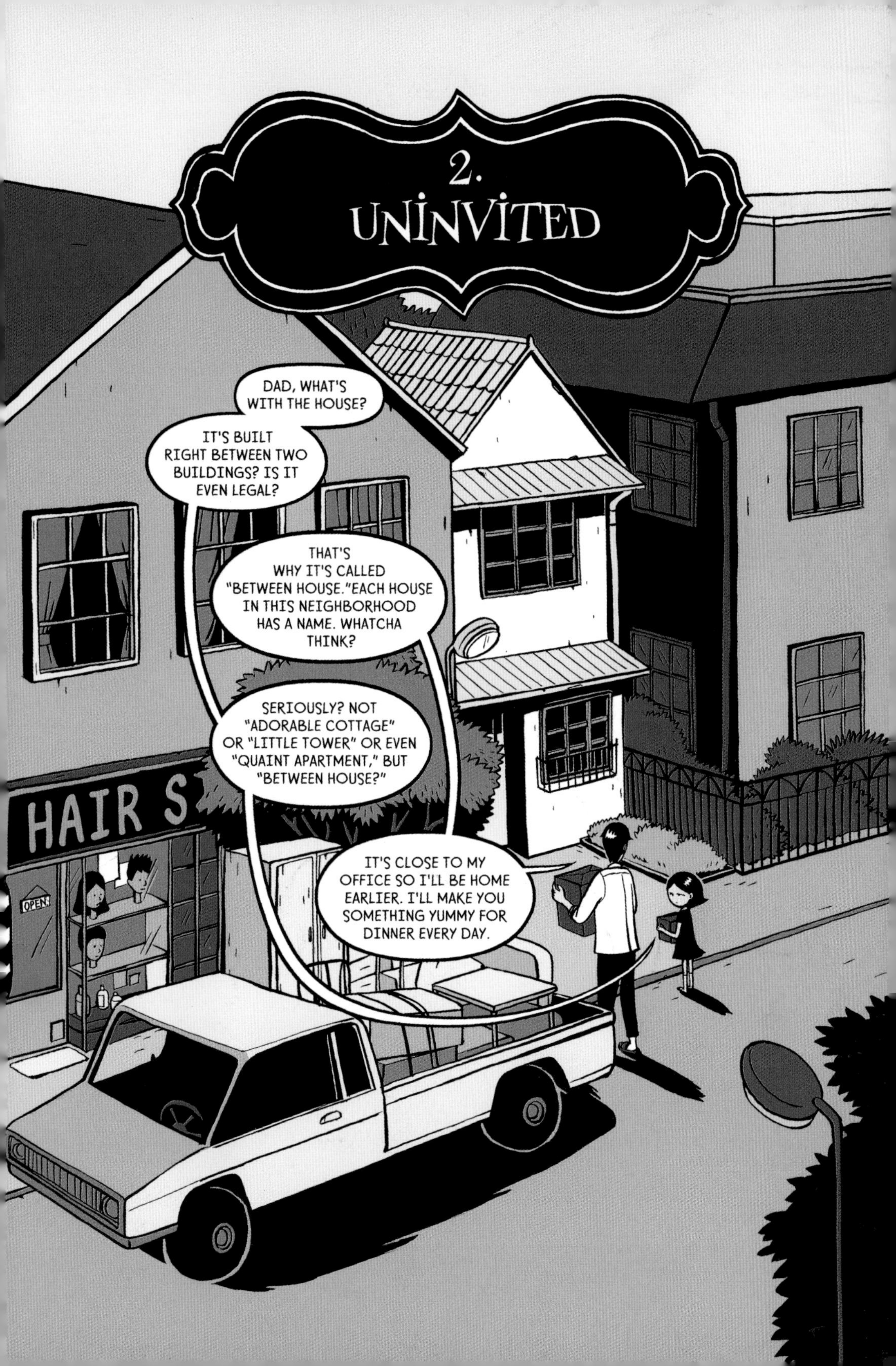
2.
UNINVITED
DAD, WHAT'S WITH THE HOUSE?
IT'S BUILT RIGHT BETWEEN TWO BUILDINGS? IS IT EVEN LEGAL?
THAT'S WHY IT'S CALLED "BETWEEN HOUSE." EACH HOUSE IN THIS NEIGHBORHOOD HAS A NAME. WHATCHA THINK?
SERIOUSLY? NOT "ADORABLE COTTAGE" OR "LITTLE TOWER" OR EVEN "QUAINT APARTMENT," BUT "BETWEEN HOUSE?"
IT'S CLOSE TO MY OFFICE SO I'LL BE HOME EARLIER. I'LL MAKE YOU SOMETHING YUMMY FOR DINNER EVERY DAY.
HAIR S
OPEN

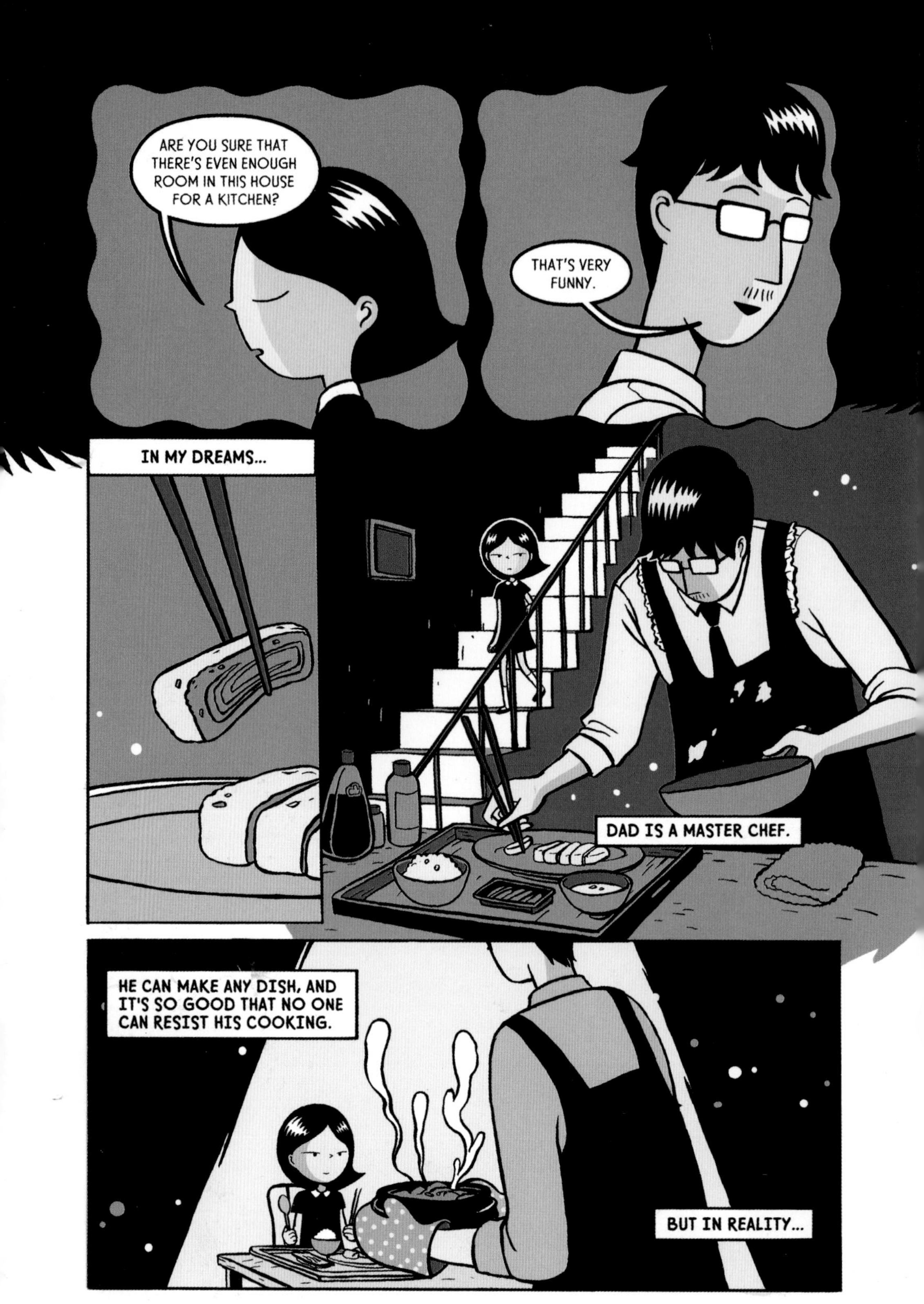
ARE YOU SURE THAT THERE'S EVEN ENOUGH ROOM IN THIS HOUSE FOR A KITCHEN?
THAT'S VERY FUNNY.
IN MY DREAMS...
DAD IS A MASTER CHEF.
HE CAN MAKE ANY DISH, AND IT'S SO GOOD THAT NO ONE CAN RESIST HIS COOKING.
BUT IN REALITY...

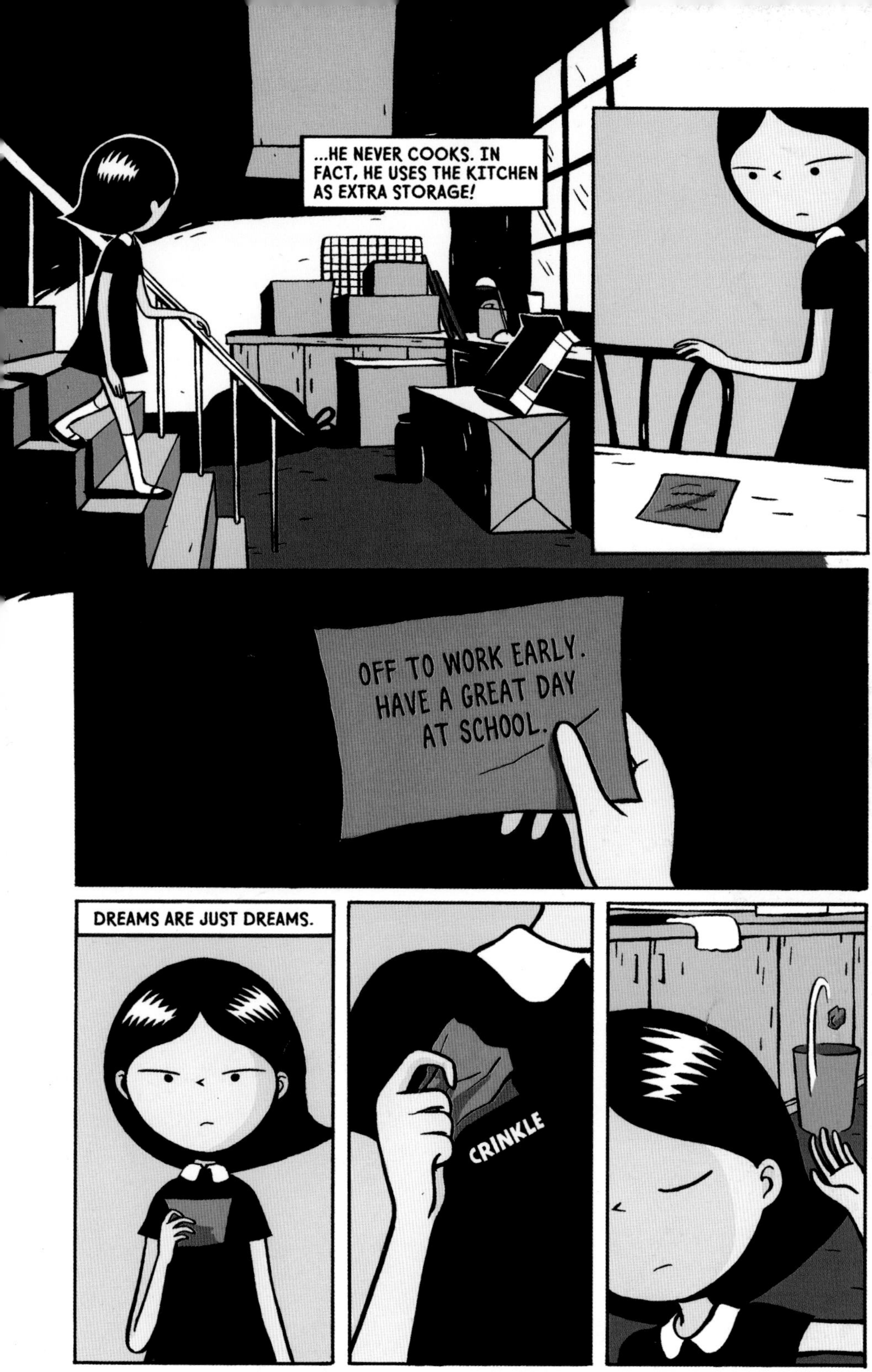

...HE NEVER COOKS. IN FACT, HE USES THE KITCHEN AS EXTRA STORAGE!
OFF TO WORK EARLY. HAVE A GREAT DAY AT SCHOOL.
DREAMS ARE JUST DREAMS.
CRINKLE

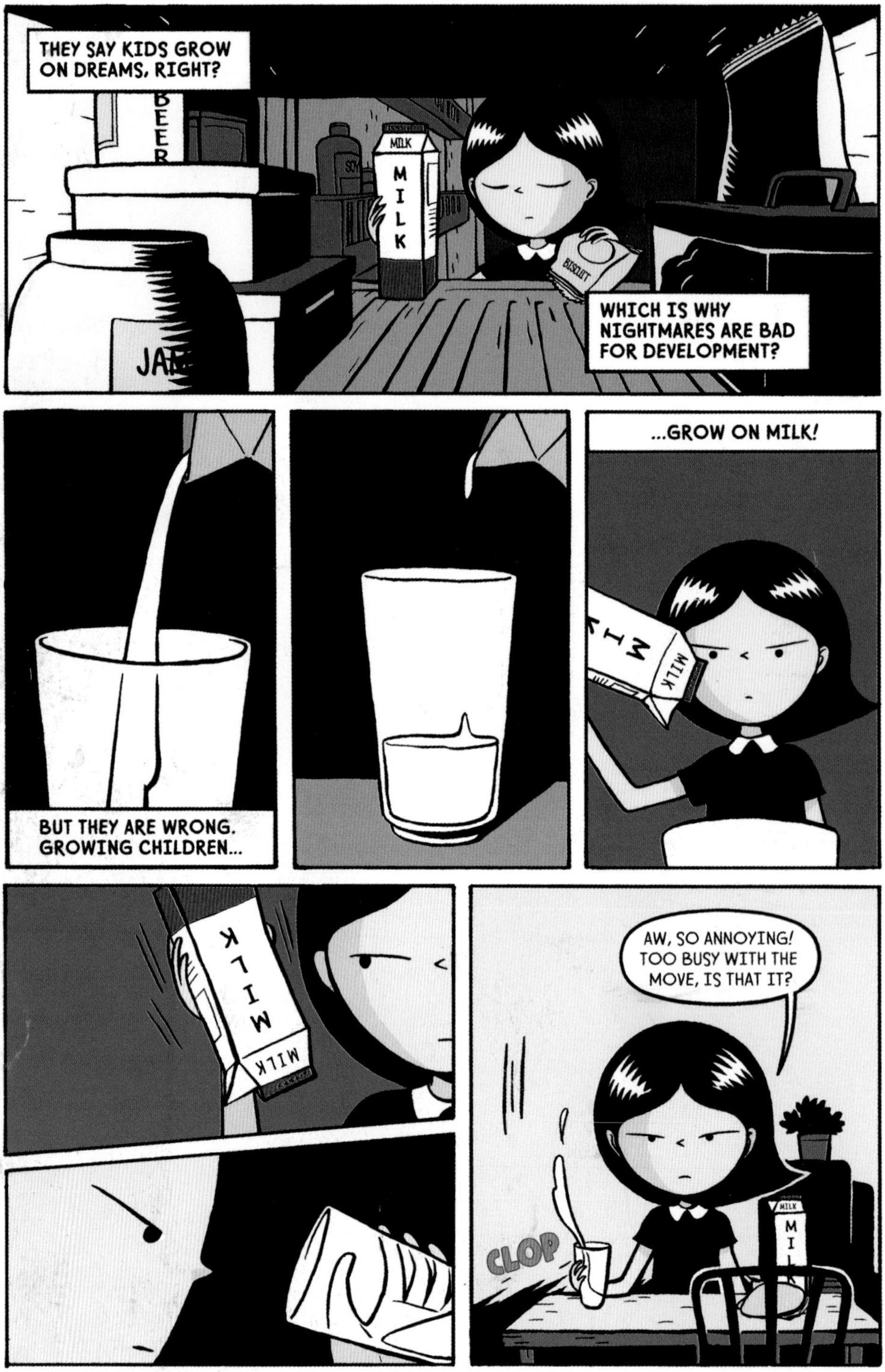
THEY SAY KIDS GROW ON DREAMS, RIGHT?
BEER
MILK
MILK
BISCUIT
JAM
WHICH IS WHY NIGHTMARES ARE BAD FOR DEVELOPMENT?
BUT THEY ARE WRONG. GROWING CHILDREN...
...GROW ON MILK!
MILK
MILK
MILK
MILK
AW, SO ANNOYING! TOO BUSY WITH THE MOVE, IS THAT IT?
CLOP
MILK
MIL

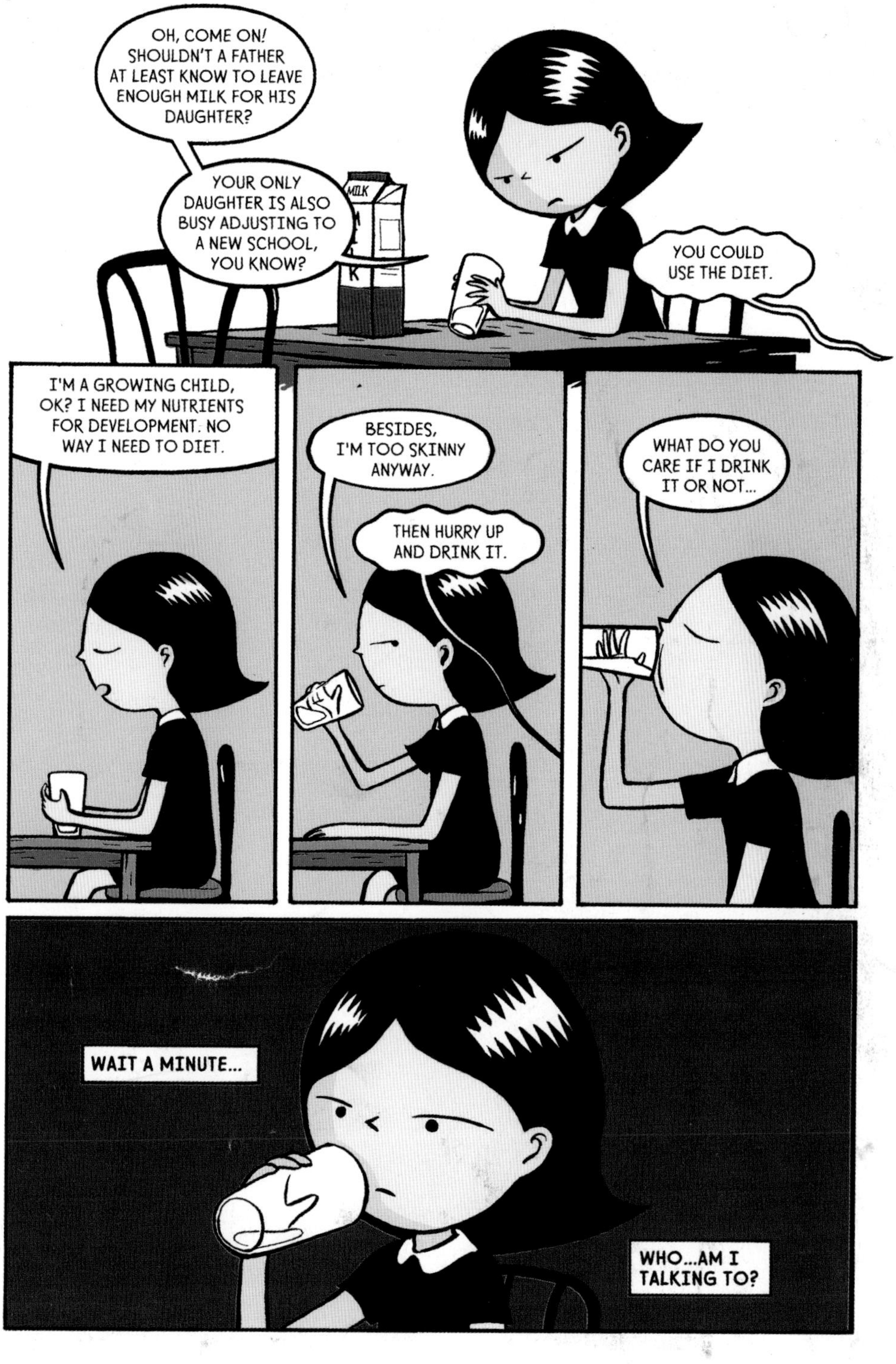
OH, COME ON! SHOULDN'T A FATHER AT LEAST KNOW TO LEAVE ENOUGH MILK FOR HIS DAUGHTER?
YOUR ONLY DAUGHTER IS ALSO BUSY ADJUSTING TO A NEW SCHOOL, YOU KNOW?
MILK
YOU COULD USE THE DIET.
I'M A GROWING CHILD, OK? I NEED MY NUTRIENTS FOR DEVELOPMENT. NO WAY I NEED TO DIET.
BESIDES, I'M TOO SKINNY ANYWAY.
THEN HURRY UP AND DRINK IT.
WHAT DO YOU CARE IF I DRINK IT OR NOT...
WAIT A MINUTE...
WHO...AM I TALKING TO?

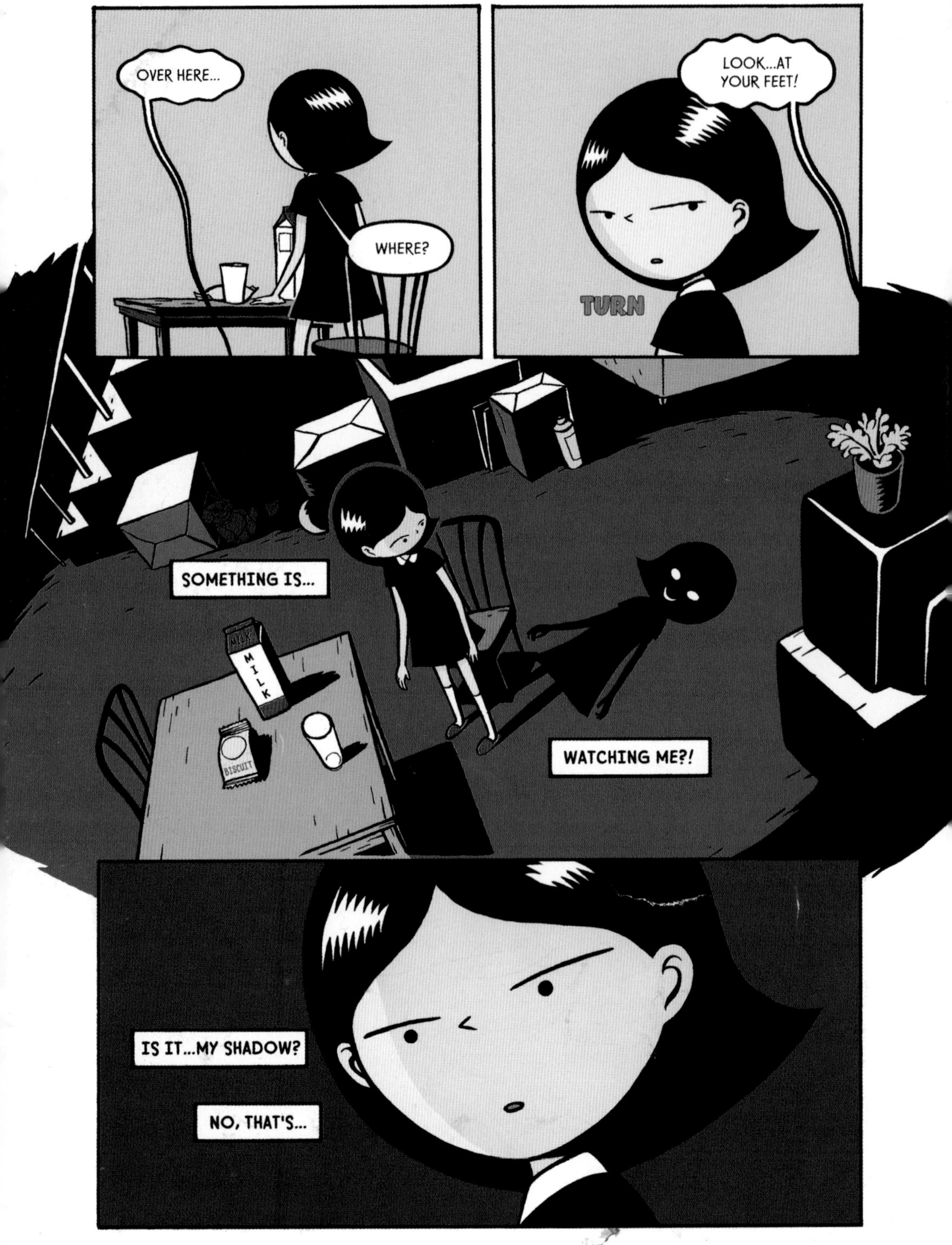
OVER HERE...
WHERE?
LOOK...AT YOUR FEET!
TURN
SOMETHING IS...
MILK
MILK
BISCUIT
WATCHING ME?!
IS IT...MY SHADOW?
NO, THAT'S...

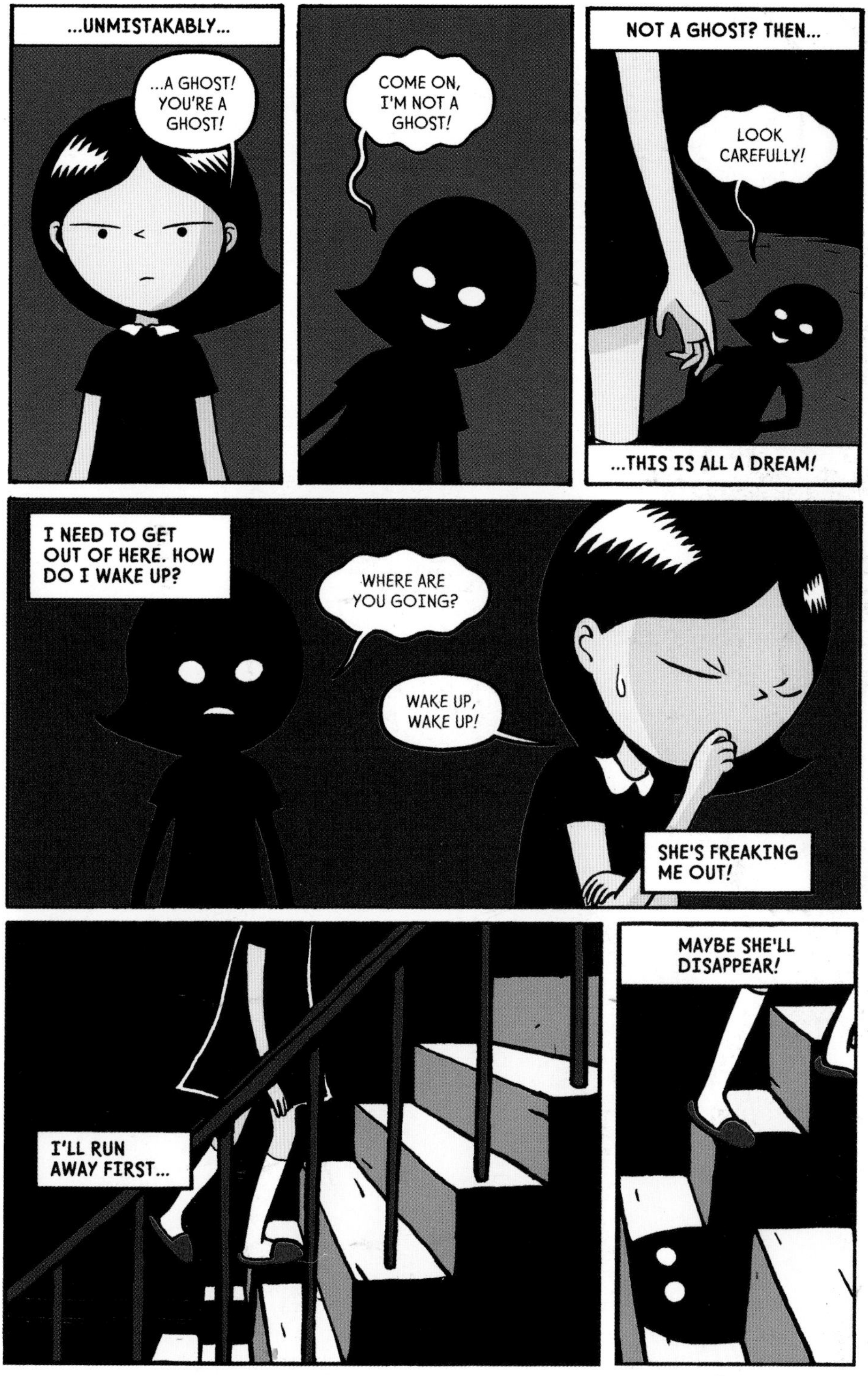
...UNMISTAKABLY...
...A GHOST! YOU'RE A GHOST!
COME ON, I'M NOT A GHOST!
NOT A GHOST? THEN...
LOOK CAREFULLY!
...THIS IS ALL A DREAM!
I NEED TO GET OUT OF HERE. HOW DO I WAKE UP?
WHERE ARE YOU GOING?
WAKE UP, WAKE UP!
SHE'S FREAKING ME OUT!
I'LL RUN AWAY FIRST...
MAYBE SHE'LL DISAPPEAR!

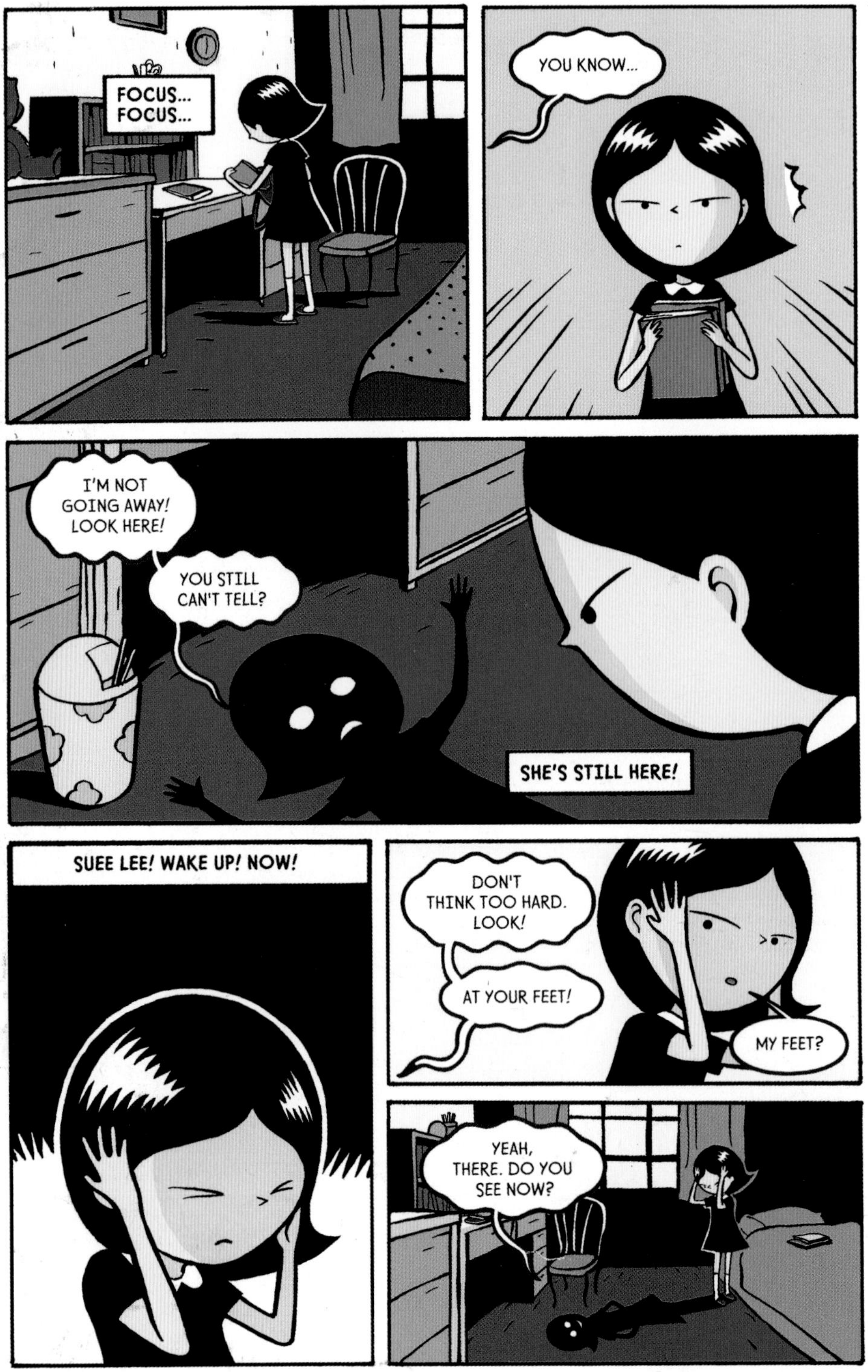
FOCUS...
FOCUS...
YOU KNOW...
I'M NOT GOING AWAY! LOOK HERE!
YOU STILL CAN'T TELL?
SHE'S STILL HERE!
SUEE LEE! WAKE UP! NOW!
DON'T THINK TOO HARD. LOOK!
AT YOUR FEET!
MY FEET?
YEAH, THERE. DO YOU SEE NOW?

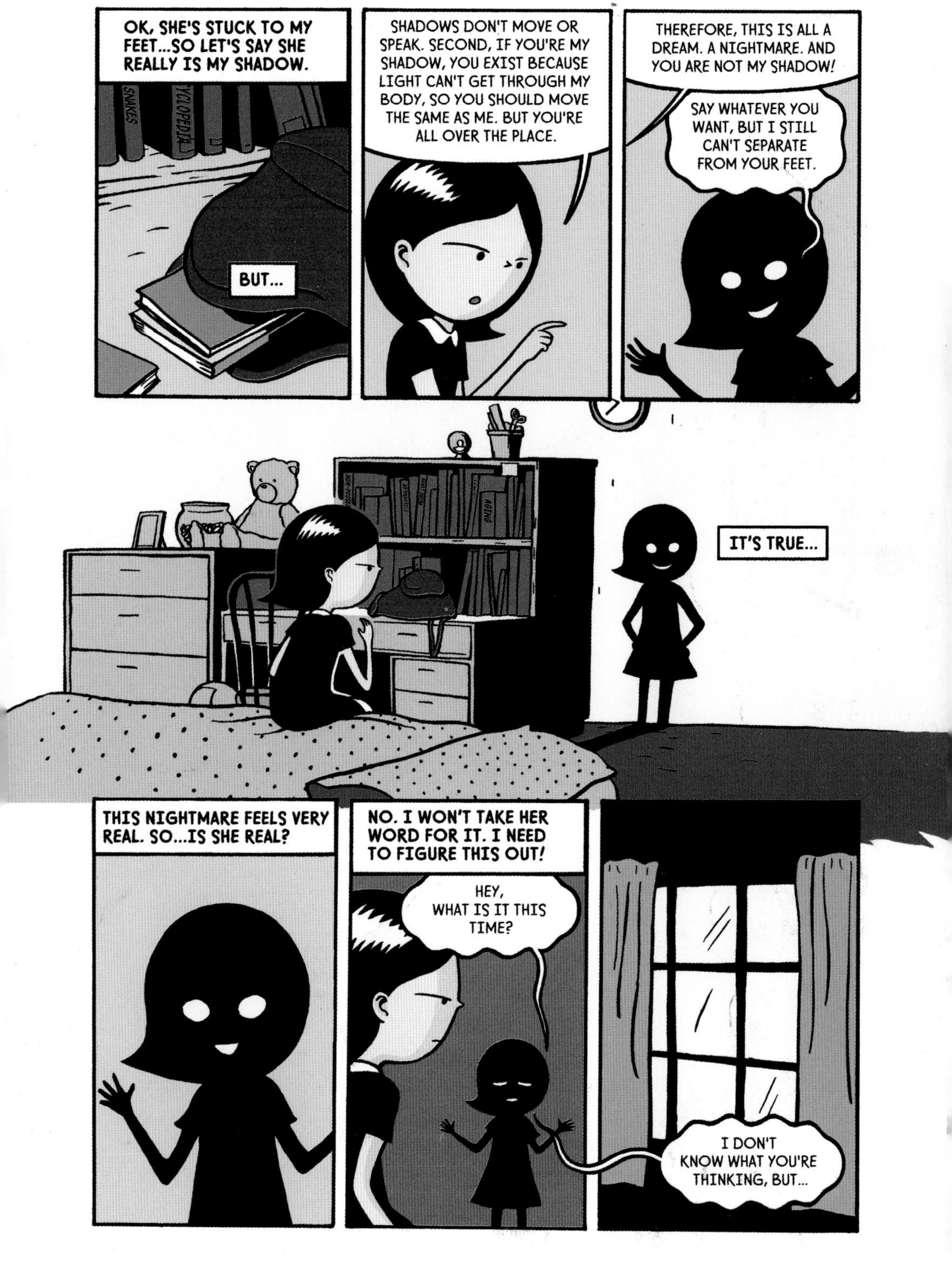
OK, SHE'S STUCK TO MY FEET...SO LET'S SAY SHE REALLY IS MY SHADOW.
BUT...
SHADOWS DON'T MOVE OR SPEAK. SECOND, IF YOU'RE MY SHADOW, YOU EXIST BECAUSE LIGHT CAN'T GET THROUGH MY BODY, SO YOU SHOULD MOVE THE SAME AS ME. BUT YOU'RE ALL OVER THE PLACE.
THEREFORE, THIS IS ALL A DREAM. A NIGHTMARE. AND YOU ARE NOT MY SHADOW!
SAY WHATEVER YOU WANT, BUT I STILL CAN'T SEPARATE FROM YOUR FEET.
IT'S TRUE...
THIS NIGHTMARE FEELS VERY REAL. SO...IS SHE REAL?
NO. I WON'T TAKE HER WORD FOR IT. I NEED TO FIGURE THIS OUT!
HEY, WHAT IS IT THIS TIME?
I DON'T KNOW WHAT YOU'RE THINKING, BUT...

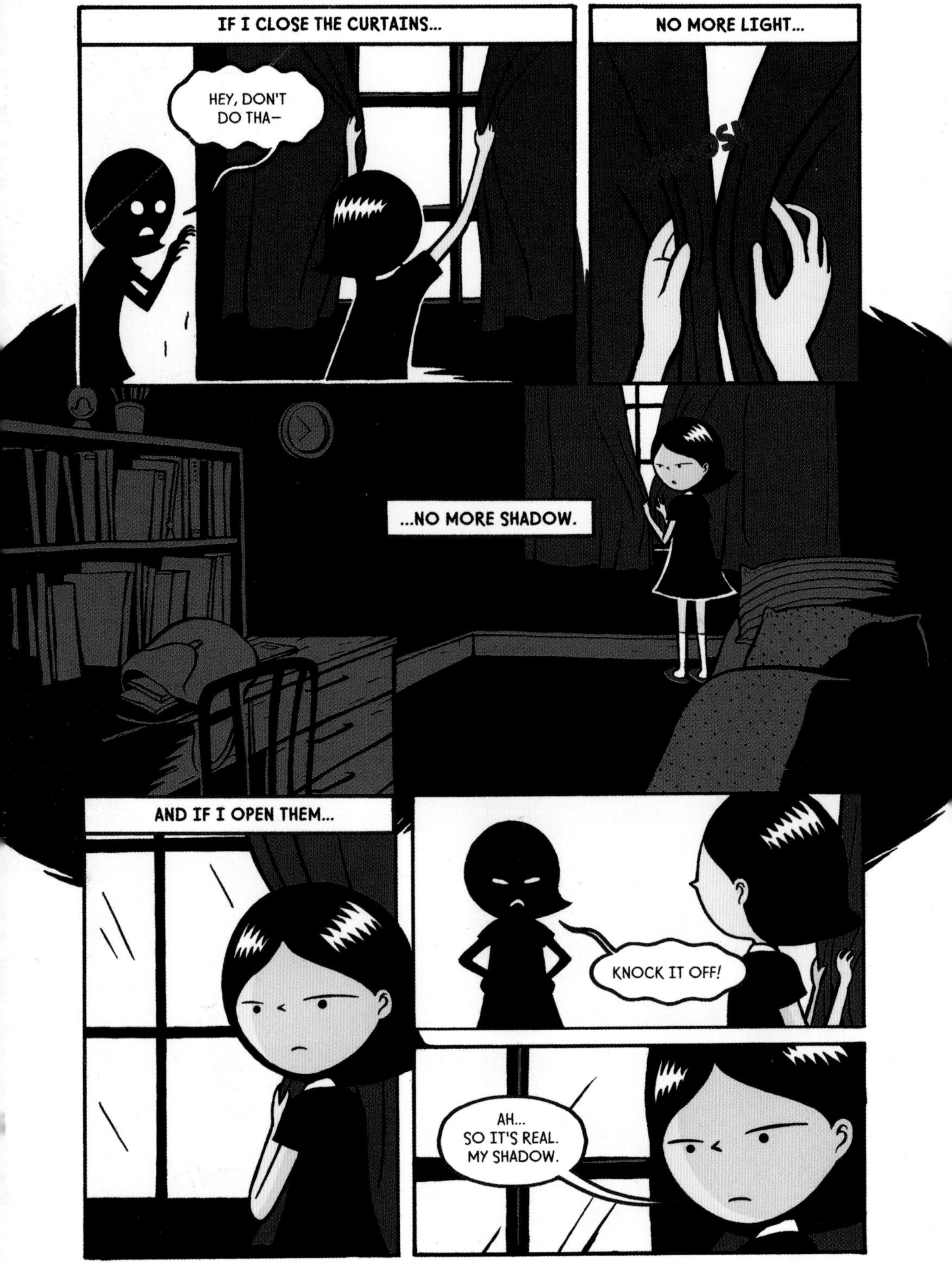
IF I CLOSE THE CURTAINS...
HEY, DON'T DO THA–
NO MORE LIGHT...
...NO MORE SHADOW.
AND IF I OPEN THEM...
KNOCK IT OFF!
AH... SO IT'S REAL. MY SHADOW.

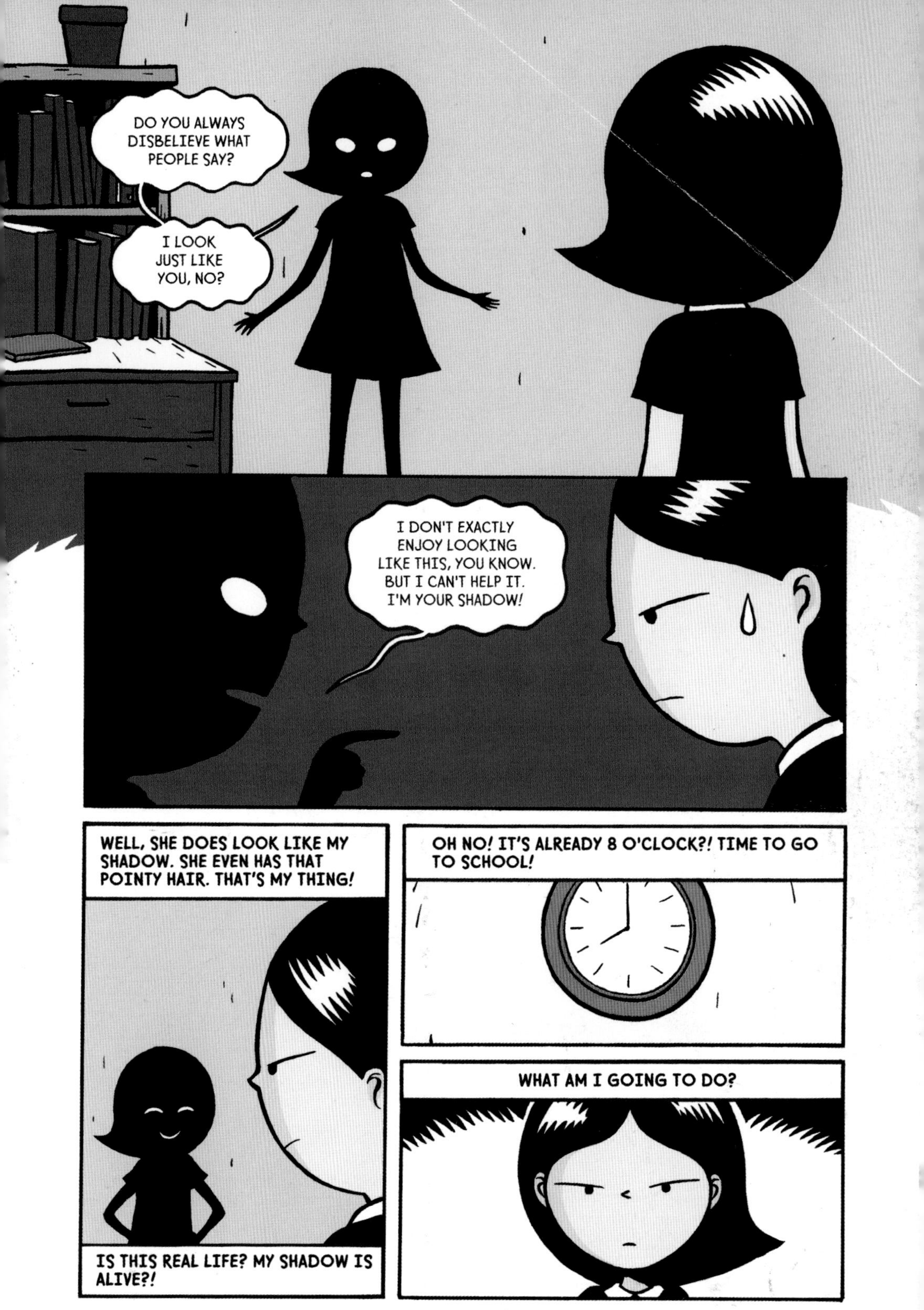
DO YOU ALWAYS DISBELIEVE WHAT PEOPLE SAY?
I LOOK JUST LIKE YOU, NO?
I DON'T EXACTLY ENJOY LOOKING LIKE THIS, YOU KNOW. BUT I CAN'T HELP IT. I'M YOUR SHADOW!
WELL, SHE DOES LOOK LIKE MY SHADOW. SHE EVEN HAS THAT POINTY HAIR. THAT'S MY THING!
IS THIS REAL LIFE? MY SHADOW IS ALIVE?!
OH NO! IT'S ALREADY 8 O'CLOCK?! TIME TO GO TO SCHOOL!
WHAT AM I GOING TO DO?

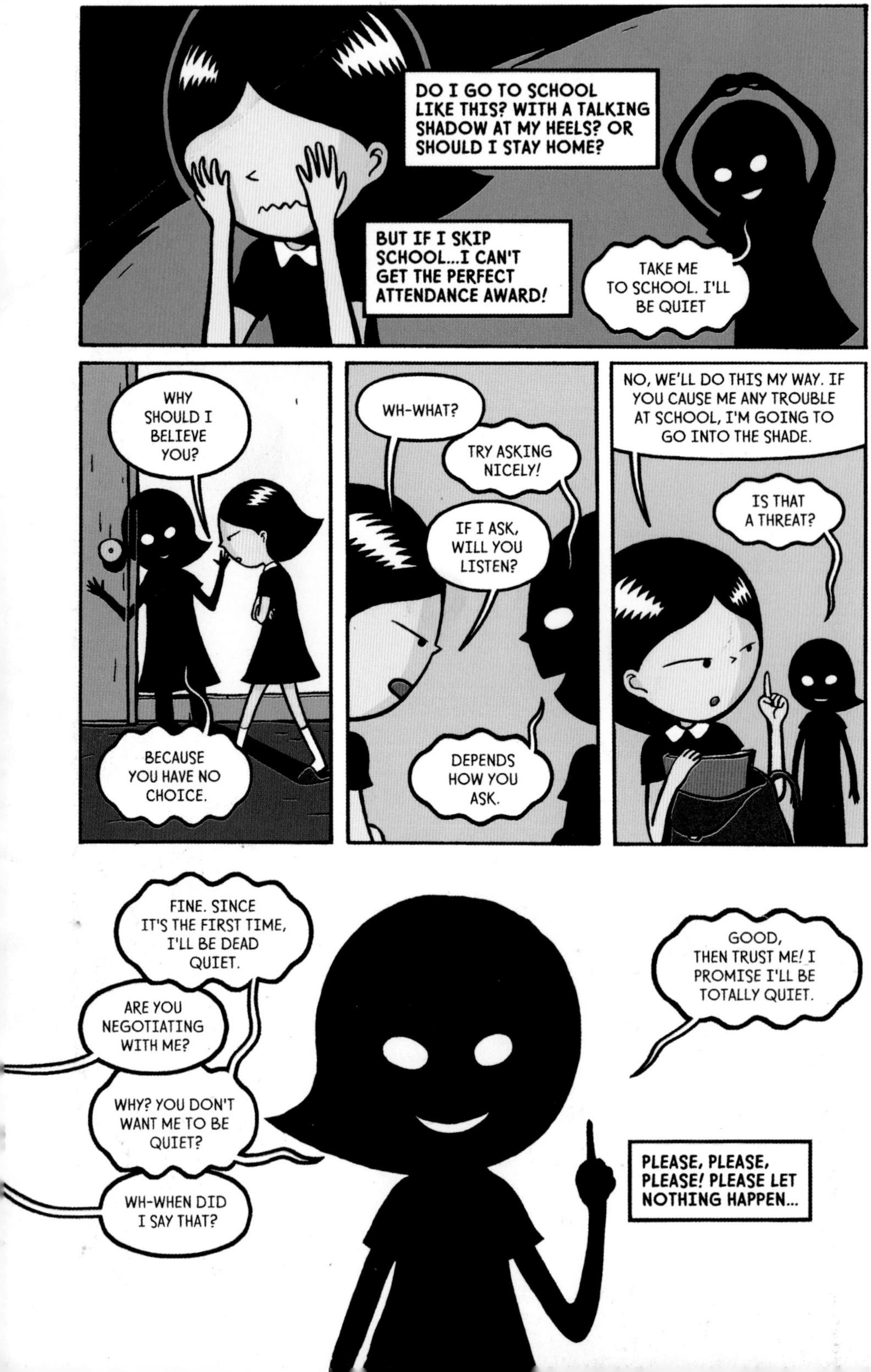

DO I GO TO SCHOOL LIKE THIS? WITH A TALKING SHADOW AT MY HEELS? OR SHOULD I STAY HOME?
BUT IF I SKIP SCHOOL...I CAN'T GET THE PERFECT ATTENDANCE AWARD!
TAKE ME TO SCHOOL. I'LL BE QUIET
WHY SHOULD I BELIEVE YOU?
BECAUSE YOU HAVE NO CHOICE.
WH-WHAT?
TRY ASKING NICELY!
IF I ASK, WILL YOU LISTEN?
DEPENDS HOW YOU ASK.
NO, WE'LL DO THIS MY WAY. IF YOU CAUSE ME ANY TROUBLE AT SCHOOL, I'M GOING TO GO INTO THE SHADE.
IS THAT A THREAT?
GOOD, THEN TRUST ME! I PROMISE I'LL BE TOTALLY QUIET.
ARE YOU NEGOTIATING WITH ME?
FINE. SINCE IT'S THE FIRST TIME, I'LL BE DEAD QUIET.
WHY? YOU DON'T WANT ME TO BE QUIET?
WH-WHEN DID I SAY THAT?
PLEASE, PLEASE, PLEASE! PLEASE LET NOTHING HAPPEN...

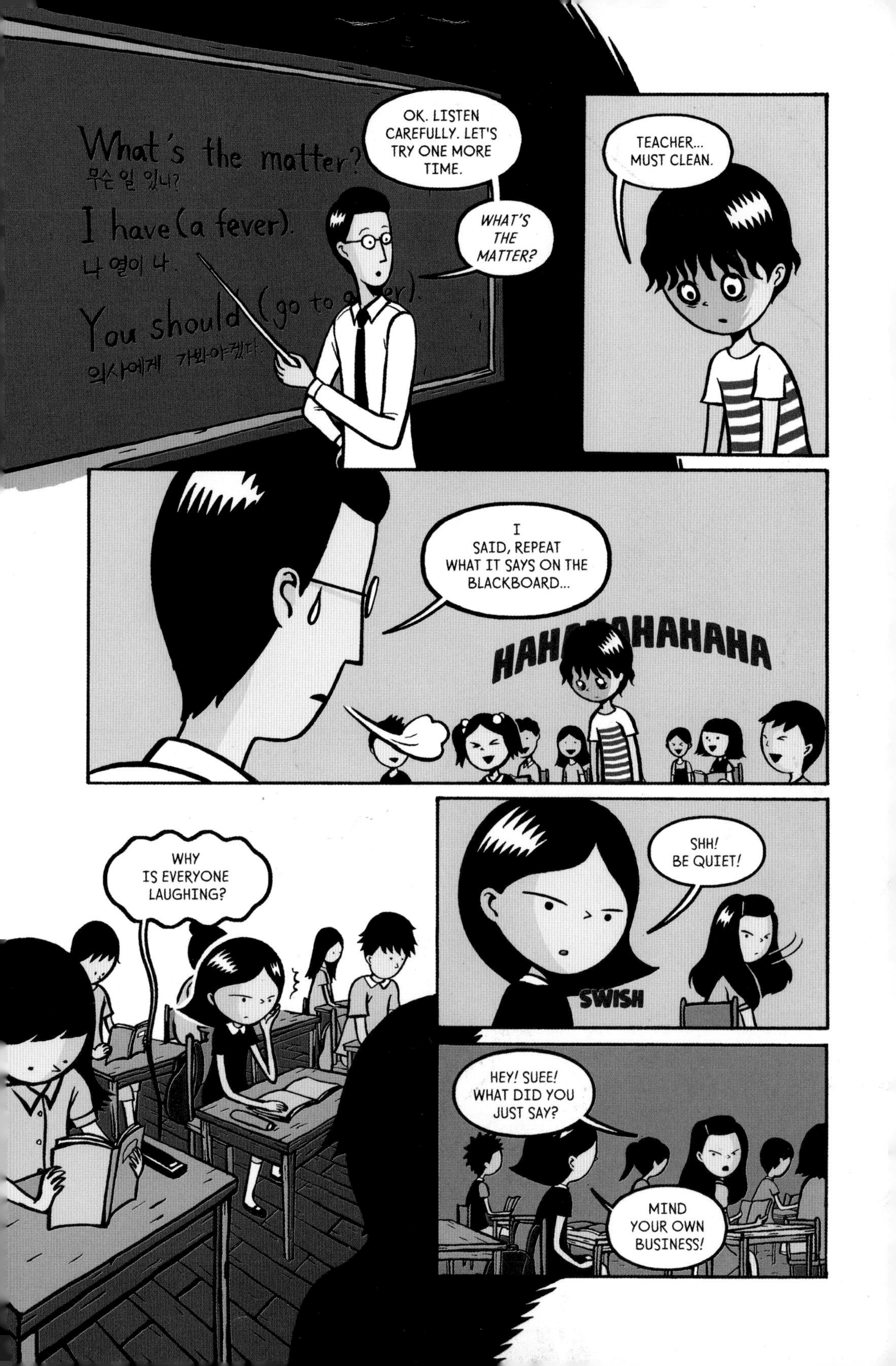
What's the matter?
무슨 일 있니?
I have (a fever).
나 열이 나.
OK. LISTEN CAREFULLY. LET'S TRY ONE MORE TIME.
WHAT'S THE MATTER?
TEACHER... MUST CLEAN.
I SAID, REPEAT WHAT IT SAYS ON THE BLACKBOARD...
WHY IS EVERYONE LAUGHING?
SHH! BE QUIET!
SWISH
HEY! SUEE! WHAT DID YOU JUST SAY?
MIND YOUR OWN BUSINESS!

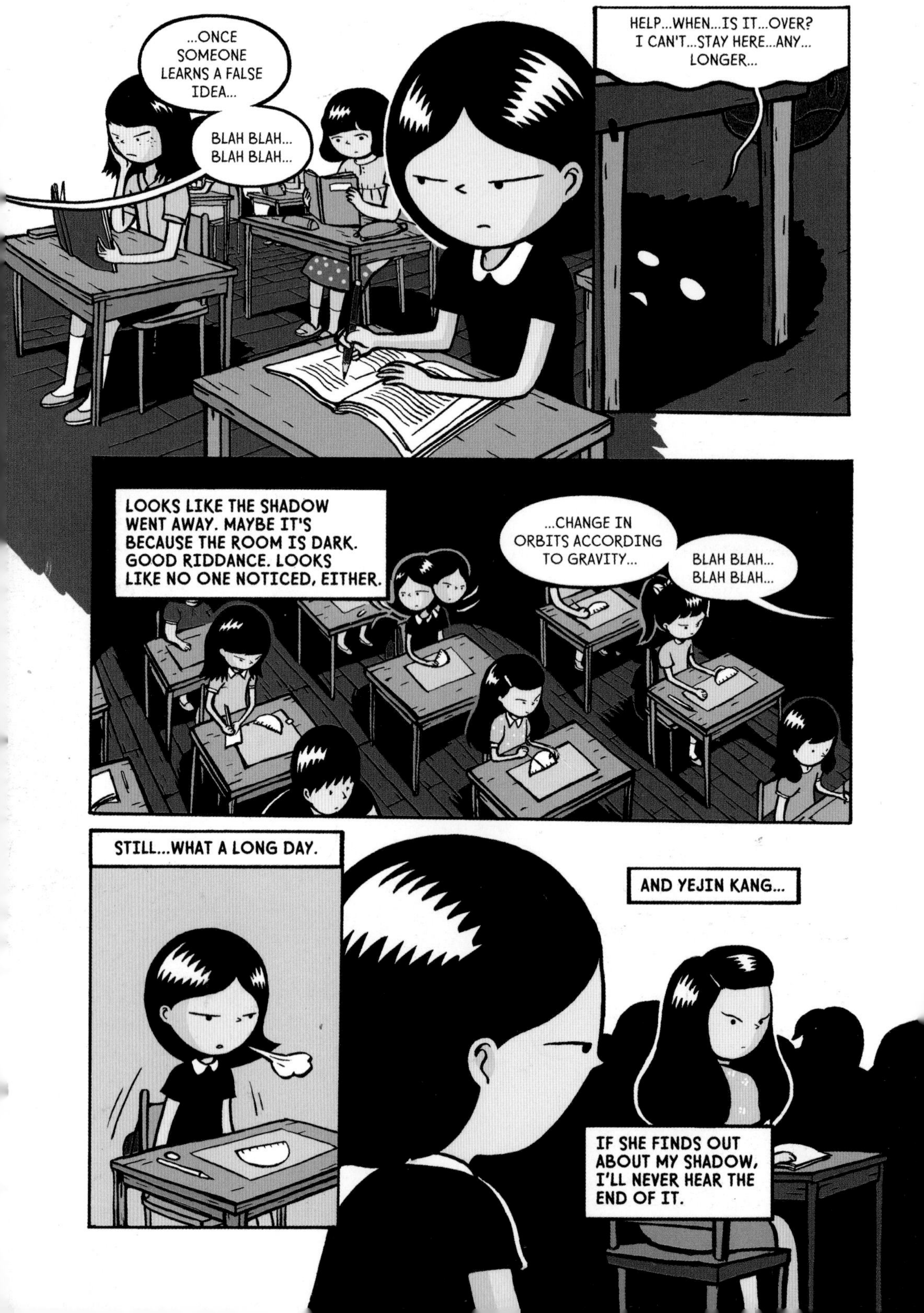
...ONCE SOMEONE LEARNS A FALSE IDEA...
BLAH BLAH... BLAH BLAH...
HELP...WHEN...IS IT...OVER? I CAN'T...STAY HERE...ANY... LONGER...
LOOKS LIKE THE SHADOW WENT AWAY. MAYBE IT'S BECAUSE THE ROOM IS DARK. GOOD RIDDANCE. LOOKS LIKE NO ONE NOTICED, EITHER.
...CHANGE IN ORBITS ACCORDING TO GRAVITY...
BLAH BLAH... BLAH BLAH...
STILL...WHAT A LONG DAY.
AND YEJIN KANG...
IF SHE FINDS OUT ABOUT MY SHADOW, I'LL NEVER HEAR THE END OF IT.

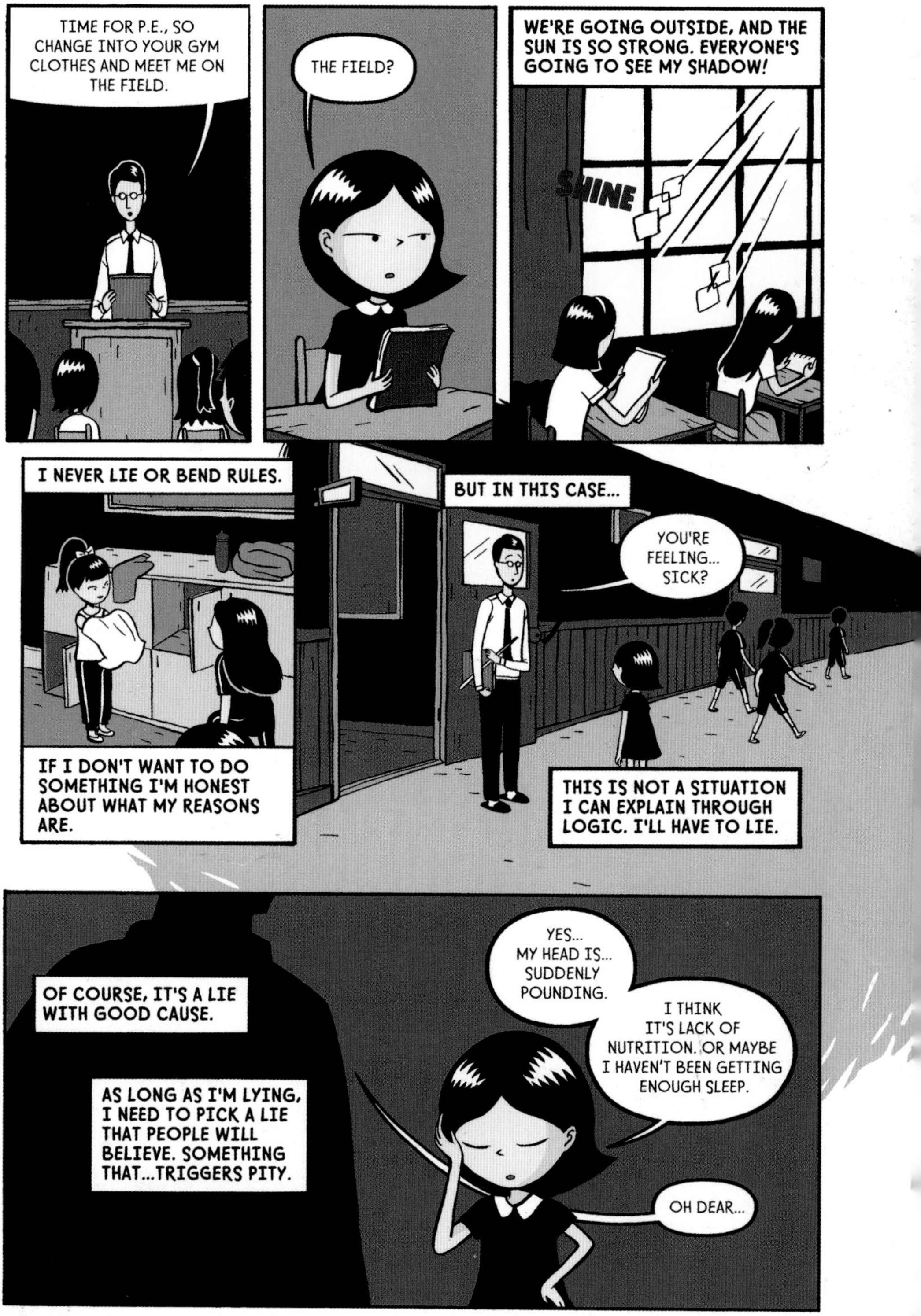
TIME FOR P.E., SO CHANGE INTO YOUR GYM CLOTHES AND MEET ME ON THE FIELD.
THE FIELD?
WE'RE GOING OUTSIDE, AND THE SUN IS SO STRONG. EVERYONE'S GOING TO SEE MY SHADOW!
SHINE
I NEVER LIE OR BEND RULES.
IF I DON'T WANT TO DO SOMETHING I'M HONEST ABOUT WHAT MY REASONS ARE.
BUT IN THIS CASE...
YOU'RE FEELING... SICK?
THIS IS NOT A SITUATION I CAN EXPLAIN THROUGH LOGIC. I'LL HAVE TO LIE.
OF COURSE, IT'S A LIE WITH GOOD CAUSE.
AS LONG AS I'M LYING, I NEED TO PICK A LIE THAT PEOPLE WILL BELIEVE. SOMETHING THAT...TRIGGERS PITY.
YES... MY HEAD IS... SUDDENLY POUNDING.
I THINK IT'S LACK OF NUTRITION. OR MAYBE I HAVEN'T BEEN GETTING ENOUGH SLEEP.
OH DEAR...

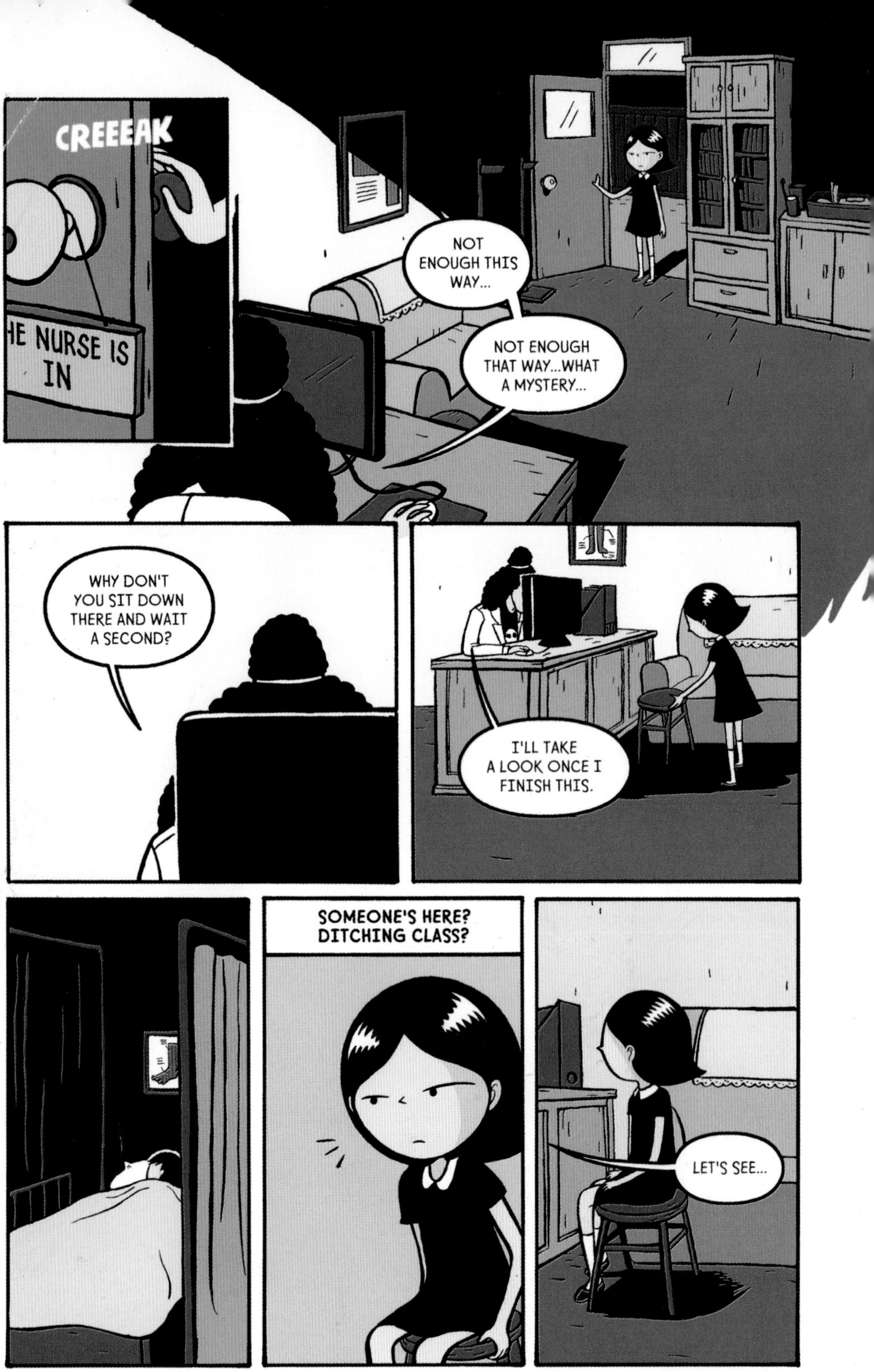
CREEEAK
HE NURSE IS IN
NOT ENOUGH THIS WAY...
NOT ENOUGH THAT WAY...WHAT A MYSTERY...
WHY DON'T YOU SIT DOWN THERE AND WAIT A SECOND?
I'LL TAKE A LOOK ONCE I FINISH THIS.
SOMEONE'S HERE? DITCHING CLASS?
LET'S SEE...

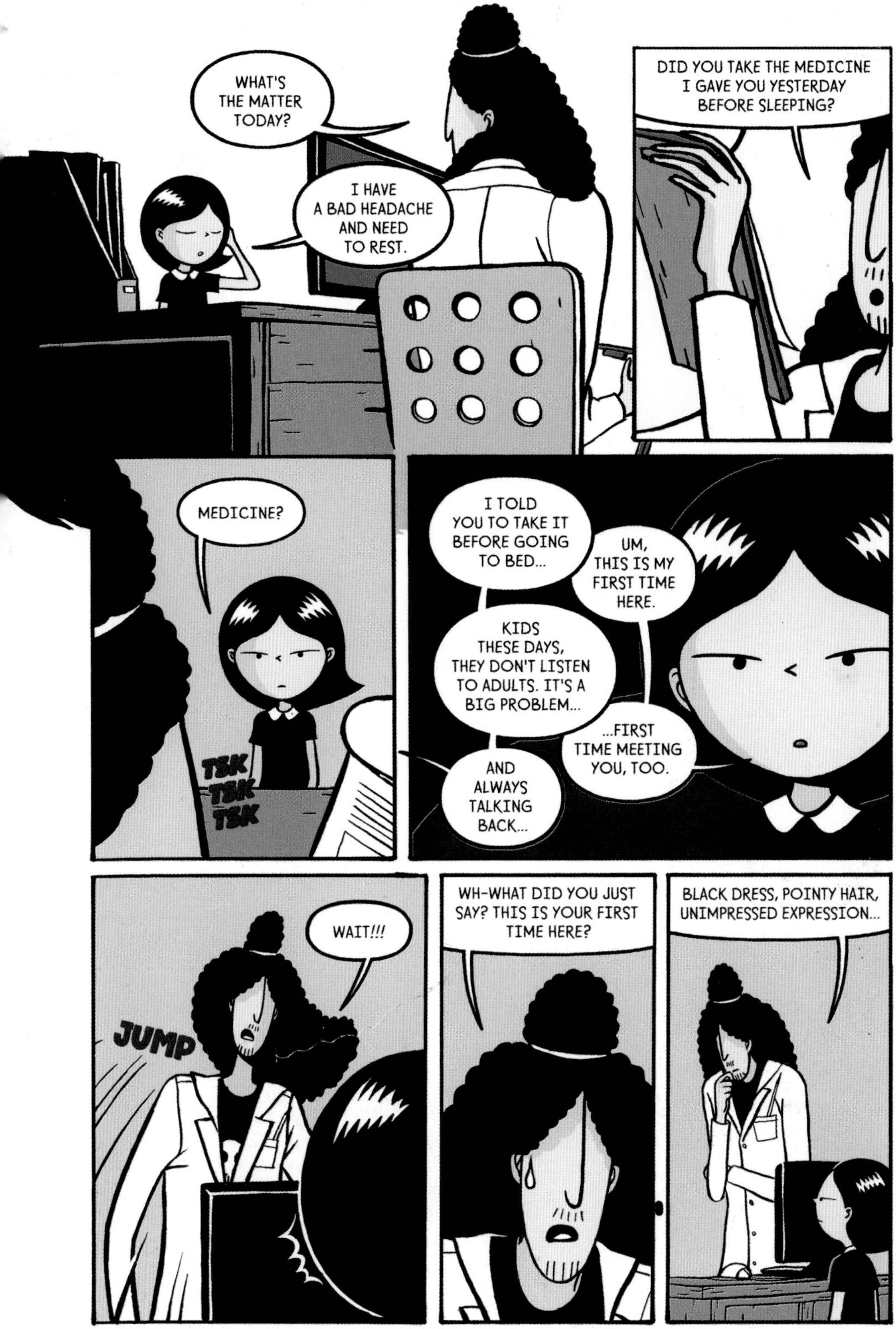
WHAT'S THE MATTER TODAY?
I HAVE A BAD HEADACHE AND NEED TO REST.
DID YOU TAKE THE MEDICINE I GAVE YOU YESTERDAY BEFORE SLEEPING?
MEDICINE?
TSK TSK TSK
I TOLD YOU TO TAKE IT BEFORE GOING TO BED...
UM, THIS IS MY FIRST TIME HERE.
KIDS THESE DAYS, THEY DON'T LISTEN TO ADULTS. IT'S A BIG PROBLEM...
...FIRST TIME MEETING YOU, TOO.
AND ALWAYS TALKING BACK...
WAIT!!!
JUMP
WH-WHAT DID YOU JUST SAY? THIS IS YOUR FIRST TIME HERE?
BLACK DRESS, POINTY HAIR, UNIMPRESSED EXPRESSION...

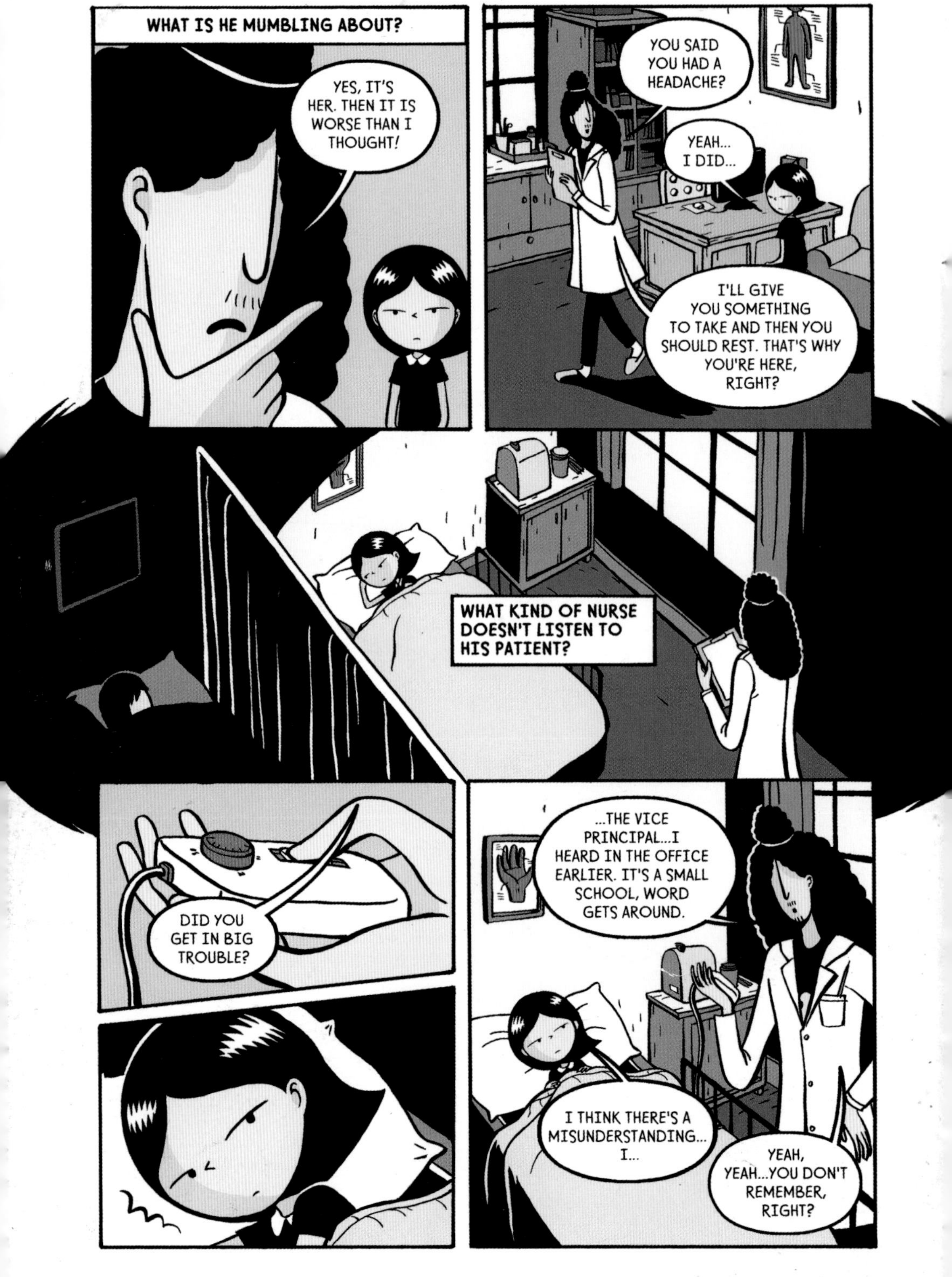

WHAT IS HE MUMBLING ABOUT?
YES, IT'S HER. THEN IT IS WORSE THAN I THOUGHT!
YOU SAID YOU HAD A HEADACHE?
YEAH... I DID...
I'LL GIVE YOU SOMETHING TO TAKE AND THEN YOU SHOULD REST. THAT'S WHY YOU'RE HERE, RIGHT?
WHAT KIND OF NURSE DOESN'T LISTEN TO HIS PATIENT?
DID YOU GET IN BIG TROUBLE?
...THE VICE PRINCIPAL...I HEARD IN THE OFFICE EARLIER. IT'S A SMALL SCHOOL, WORD GETS AROUND.
I THINK THERE'S A MISUNDERSTANDING... I...
YEAH, YEAH...YOU DON'T REMEMBER, RIGHT?

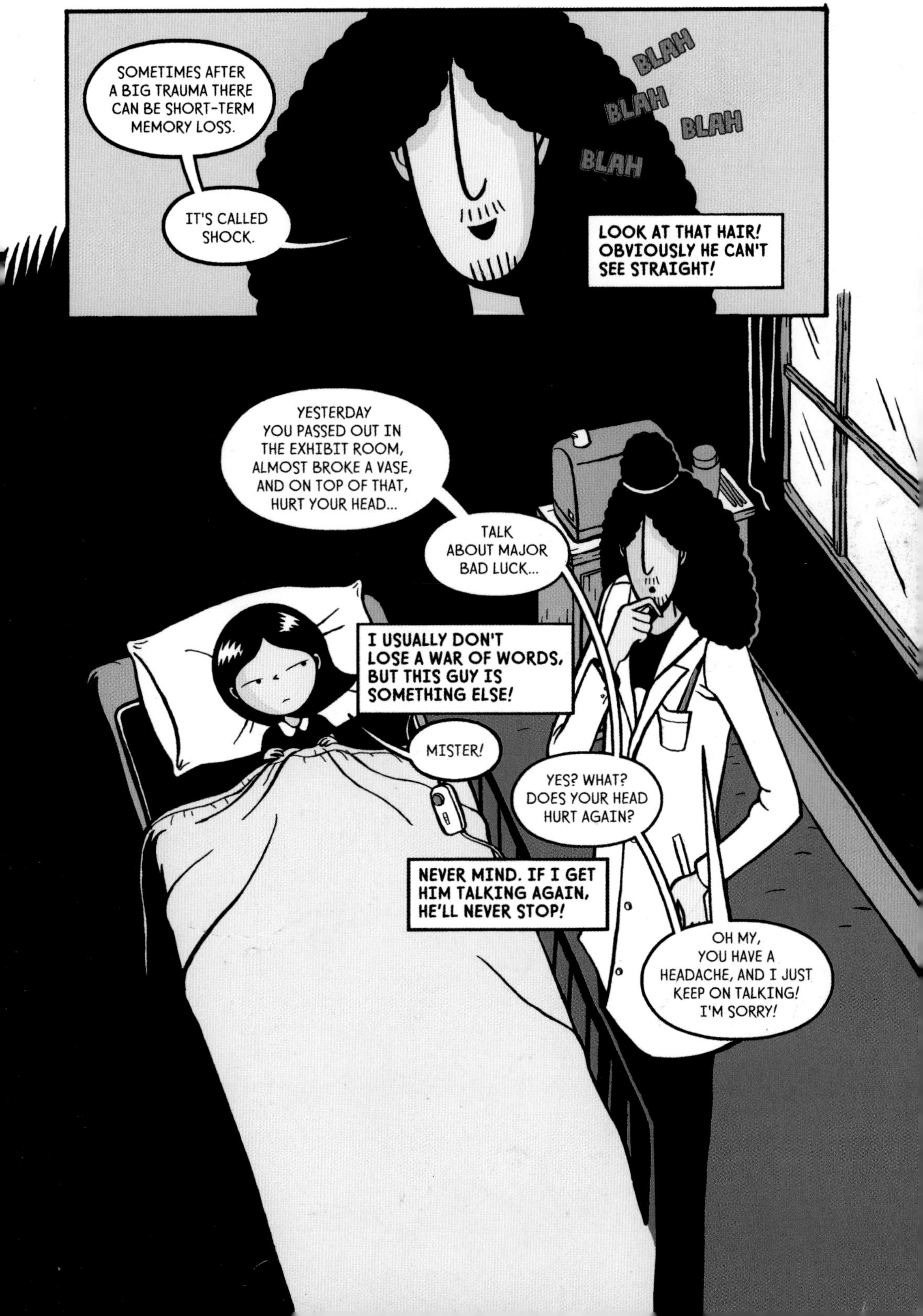
SOMETIMES AFTER A BIG TRAUMA THERE CAN BE SHORT-TERM MEMORY LOSS.
IT'S CALLED SHOCK.
BLAH
BLAH
BLAH
BLAH
LOOK AT THAT HAIR! OBVIOUSLY HE CAN'T SEE STRAIGHT!
YESTERDAY YOU PASSED OUT IN THE EXHIBIT ROOM, ALMOST BROKE A VASE, AND ON TOP OF THAT, HURT YOUR HEAD...
TALK ABOUT MAJOR BAD LUCK...
I USUALLY DON'T LOSE A WAR OF WORDS, BUT THIS GUY IS SOMETHING ELSE!
MISTER!
YES? WHAT? DOES YOUR HEAD HURT AGAIN?
NEVER MIND. IF I GET HIM TALKING AGAIN, HE'LL NEVER STOP!
OH MY, YOU HAVE A HEADACHE, AND I JUST KEEP ON TALKING! I'M SORRY!

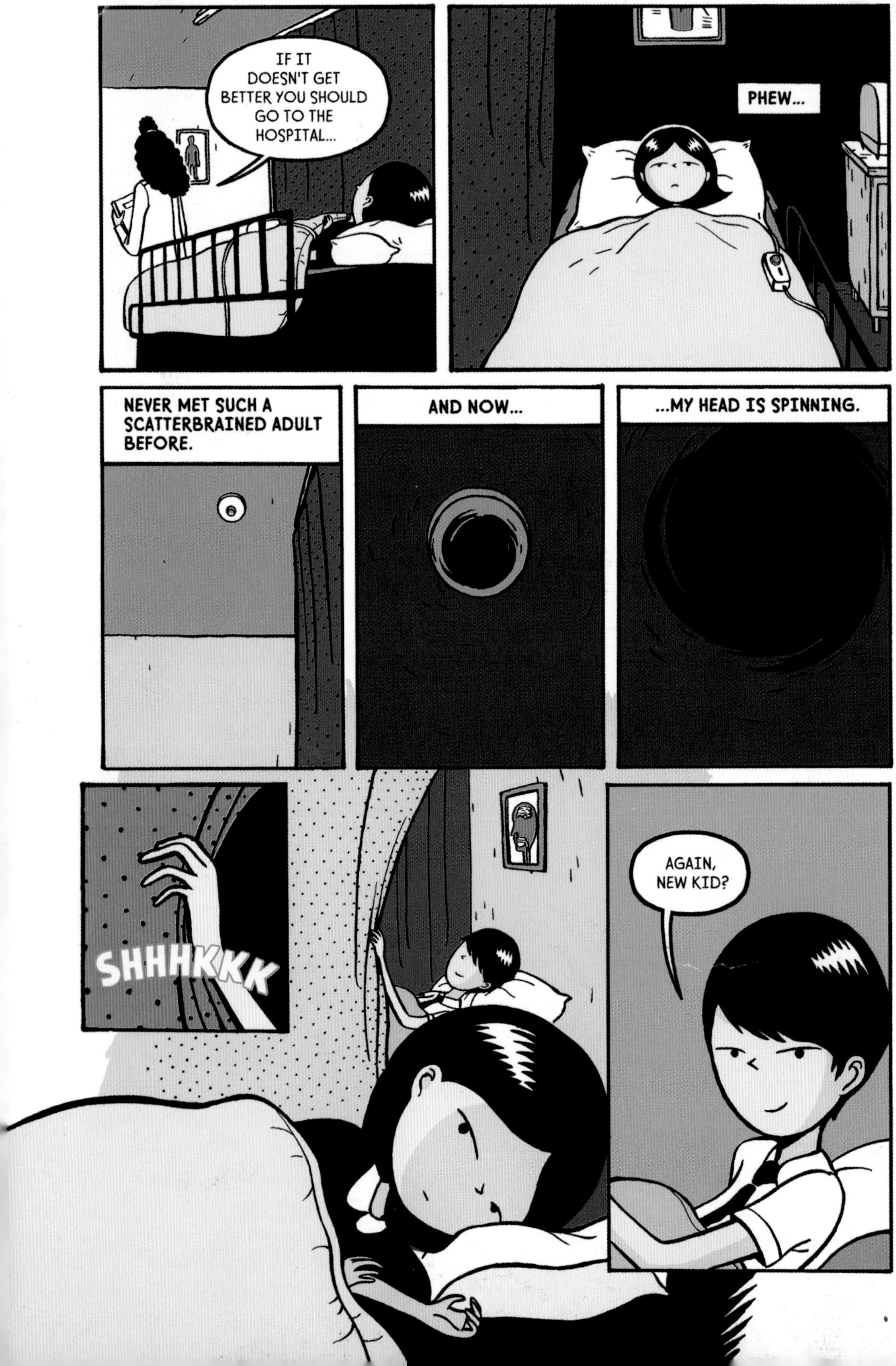
IF IT DOESN'T GET BETTER YOU SHOULD GO TO THE HOSPITAL...
PHEW...
NEVER MET SUCH A SCATTERBRAINED ADULT BEFORE.
AND NOW...
...MY HEAD IS SPINNING.
SHHHKKK
AGAIN, NEW KID?

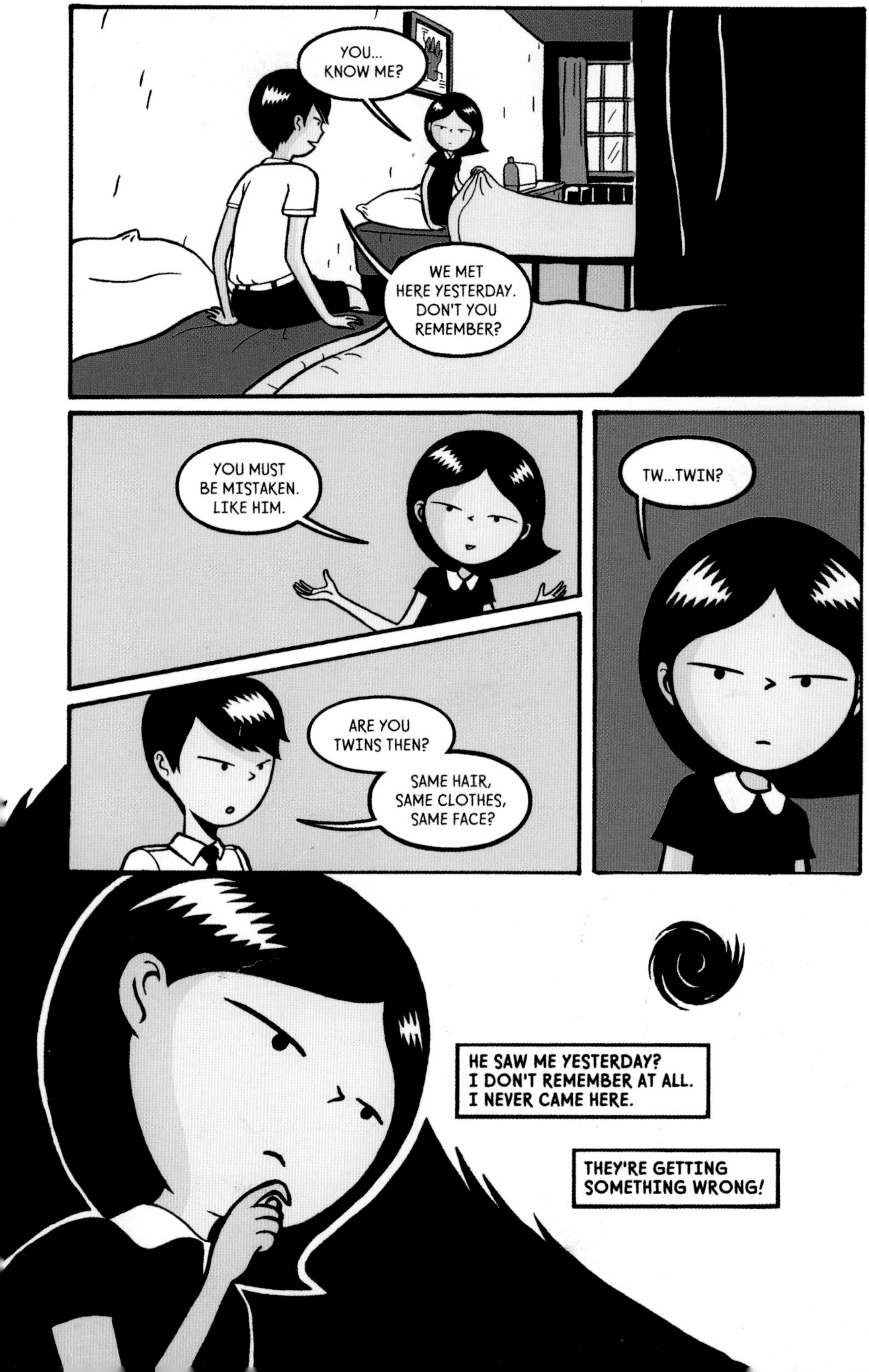
YOU... KNOW ME?
WE MET HERE YESTERDAY. DON'T YOU REMEMBER?
YOU MUST BE MISTAKEN. LIKE HIM.
ARE YOU TWINS THEN?
SAME HAIR, SAME CLOTHES, SAME FACE?
TW...TWIN?
HE SAW ME YESTERDAY? I DON'T REMEMBER AT ALL. I NEVER CAME HERE.
THEY'RE GETTING SOMETHING WRONG!

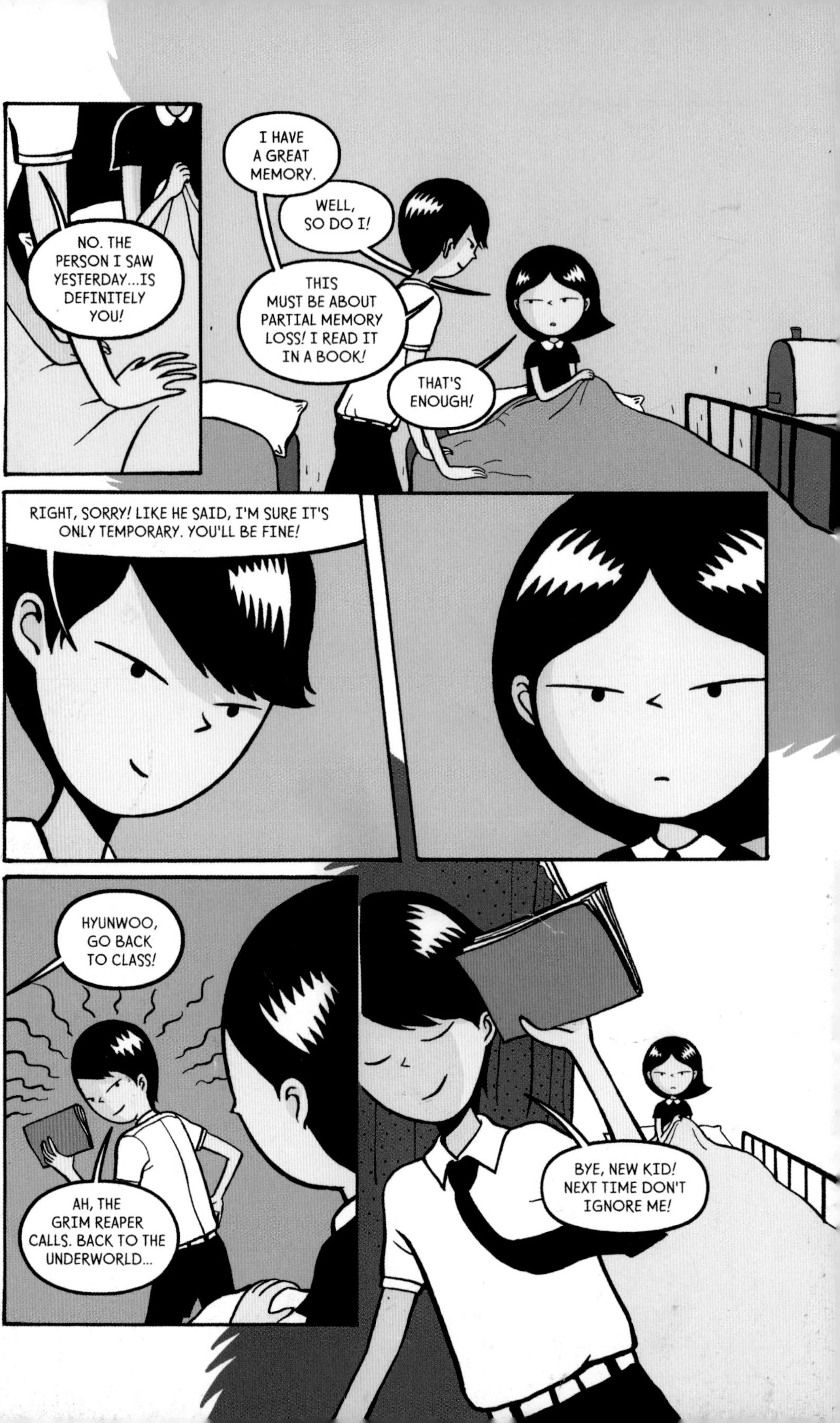
NO. THE PERSON I SAW YESTERDAY...IS DEFINITELY YOU!
I HAVE A GREAT MEMORY.
WELL, SO DO I!
THIS MUST BE ABOUT PARTIAL MEMORY LOSS! I READ IT IN A BOOK!
THAT'S ENOUGH!
RIGHT, SORRY! LIKE HE SAID, I'M SURE IT'S ONLY TEMPORARY. YOU'LL BE FINE!
HYUNWOO, GO BACK TO CLASS!
AH, THE GRIM REAPER CALLS. BACK TO THE UNDERWORLD...
BYE, NEW KID! NEXT TIME DON'T IGNORE ME!

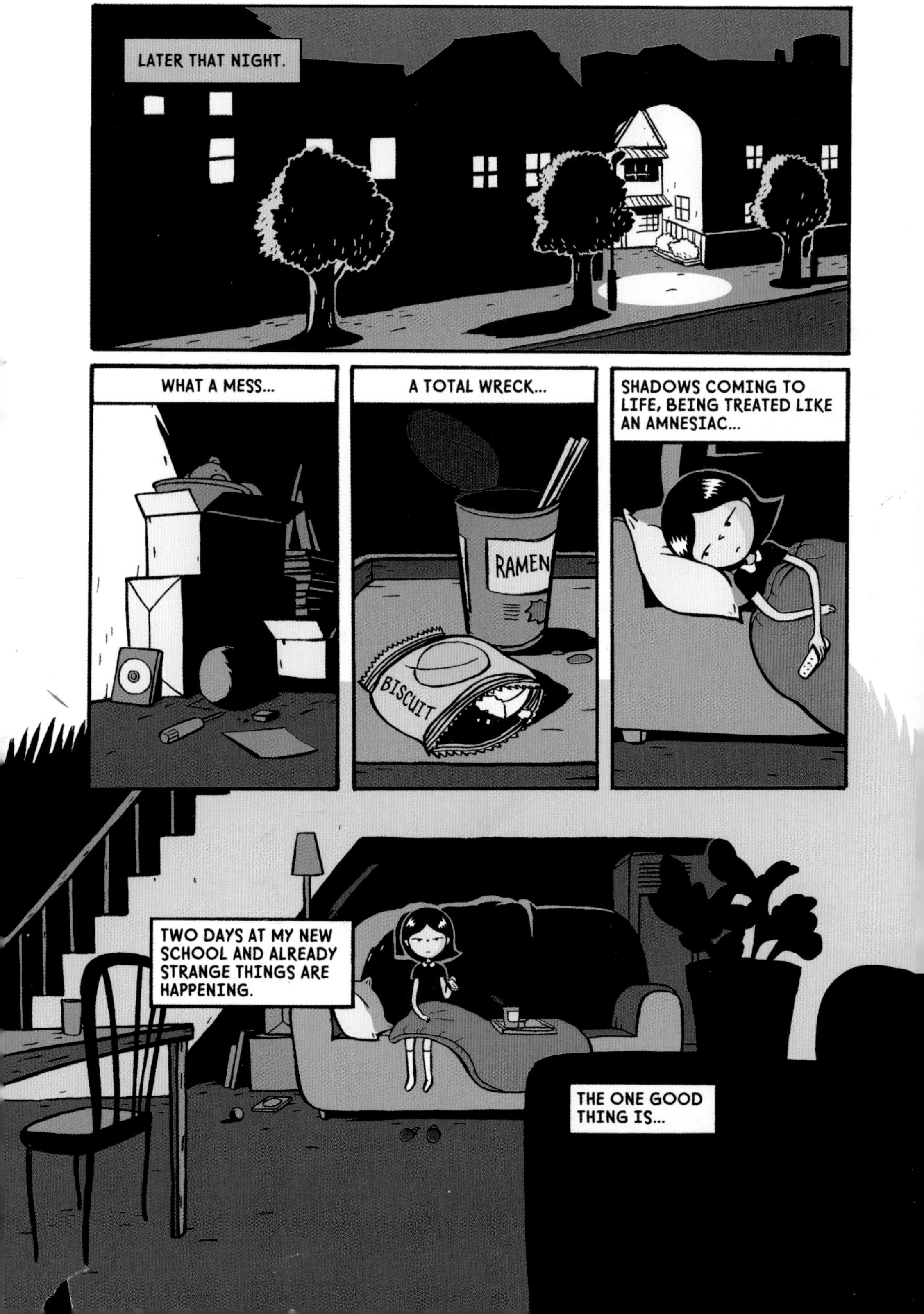
LATER THAT NIGHT.
WHAT A MESS...
A TOTAL WRECK...
RAMEN
BISCUIT
SHADOWS COMING TO LIFE, BEING TREATED LIKE AN AMNESIAC...
TWO DAYS AT MY NEW SCHOOL AND ALREADY STRANGE THINGS ARE HAPPENING.
THE ONE GOOD THING IS...

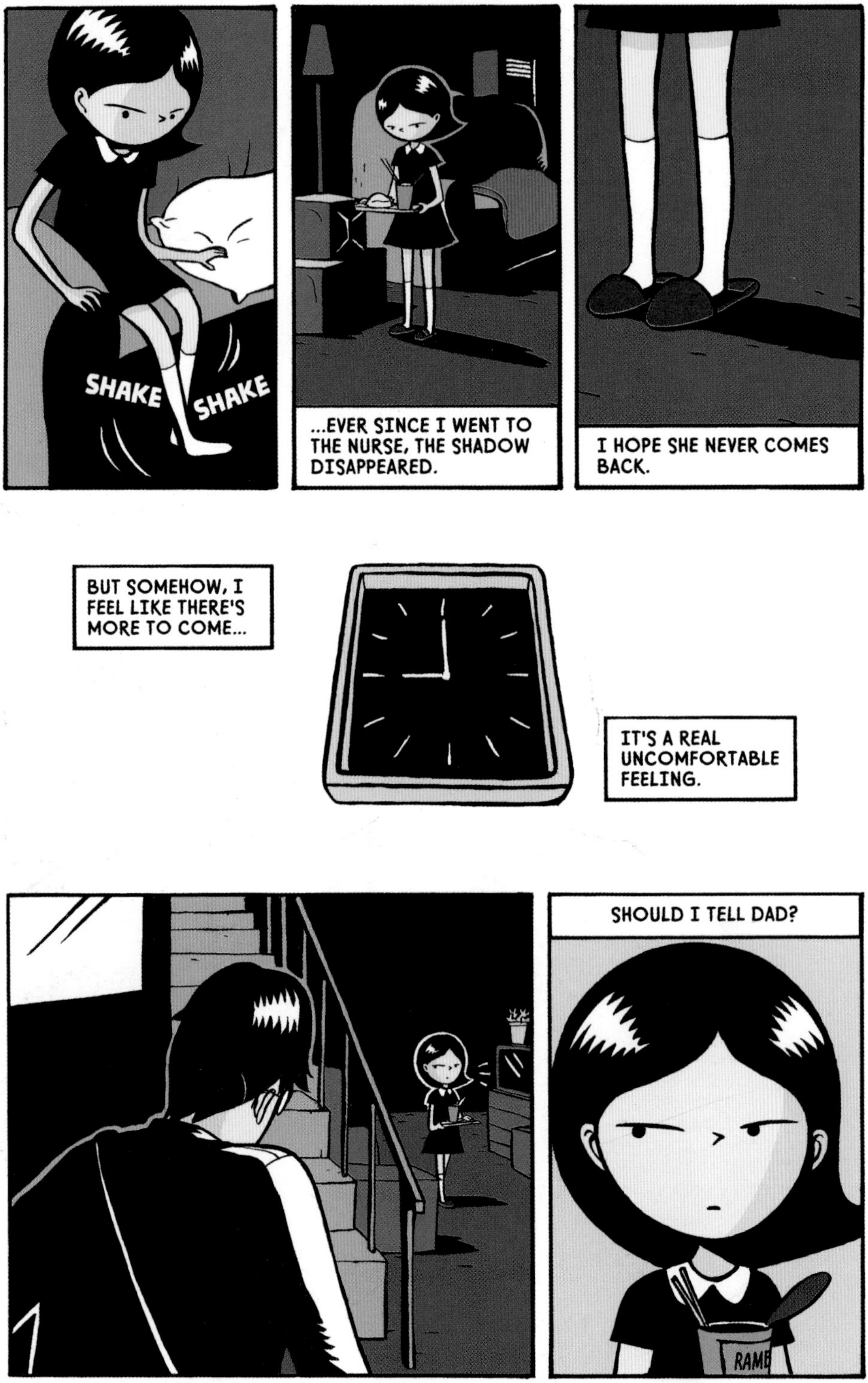
SHAKE
SHAKE
...EVER SINCE I WENT TO THE NURSE, THE SHADOW DISAPPEARED.
I HOPE SHE NEVER COMES BACK.
BUT SOMEHOW, I FEEL LIKE THERE'S MORE TO COME...
IT'S A REAL UNCOMFORTABLE FEELING.
SHOULD I TELL DAD?
RAME

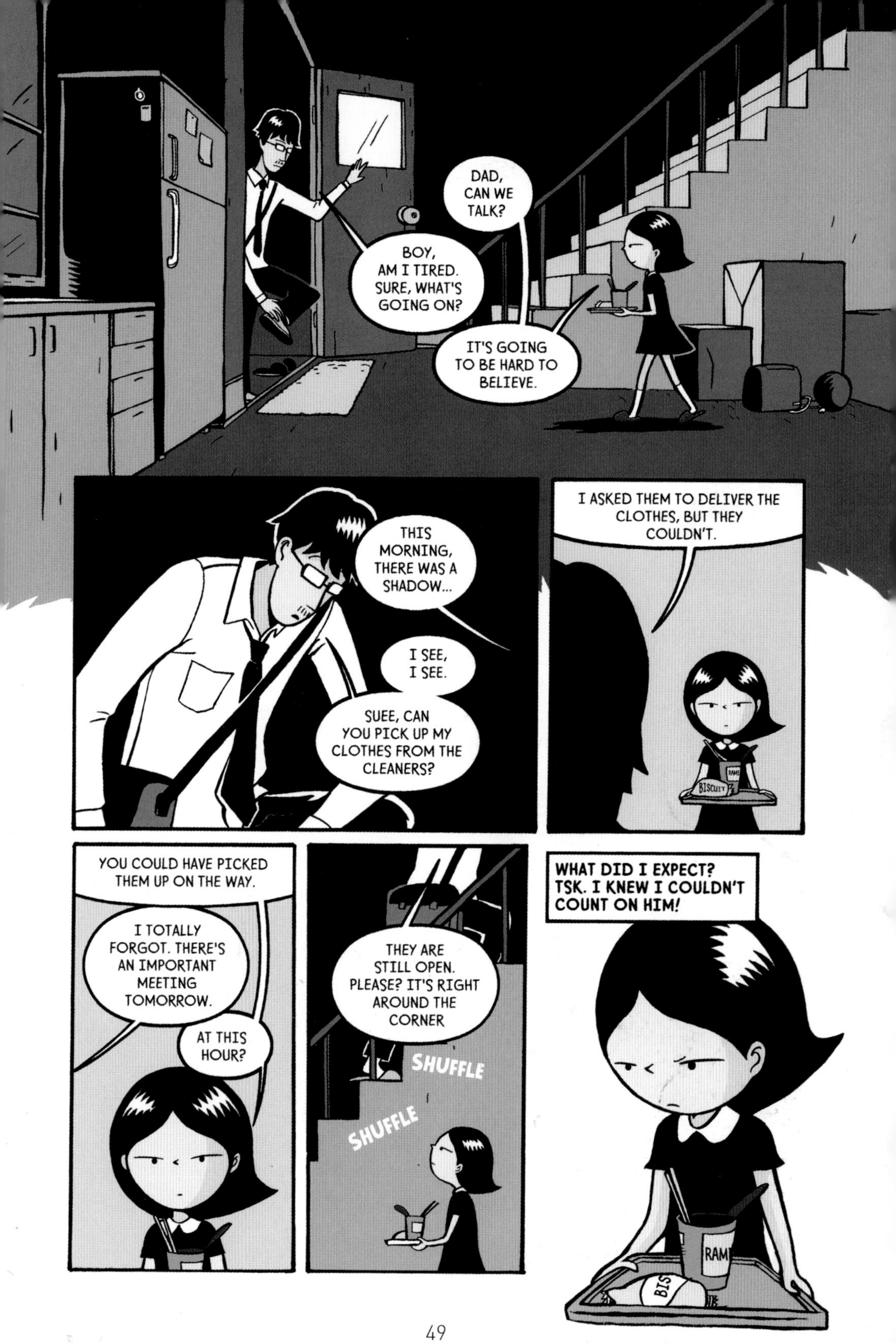
DAD, CAN WE TALK?
BOY, AM I TIRED. SURE, WHAT'S GOING ON?
IT'S GOING TO BE HARD TO BELIEVE.
THIS MORNING, THERE WAS A SHADOW...
I SEE, I SEE.
SUEE, CAN YOU PICK UP MY CLOTHES FROM THE CLEANERS?
I ASKED THEM TO DELIVER THE CLOTHES, BUT THEY COULDN'T.
RAME
BISCUIT
YOU COULD HAVE PICKED THEM UP ON THE WAY.
I TOTALLY FORGOT. THERE'S AN IMPORTANT MEETING TOMORROW.
AT THIS HOUR?
THEY ARE STILL OPEN. PLEASE? IT'S RIGHT AROUND THE CORNER
SHUFFLE
SHUFFLE
WHAT DID I EXPECT? TSK. I KNEW I COULDN'T COUNT ON HIM!
RAM
BIS

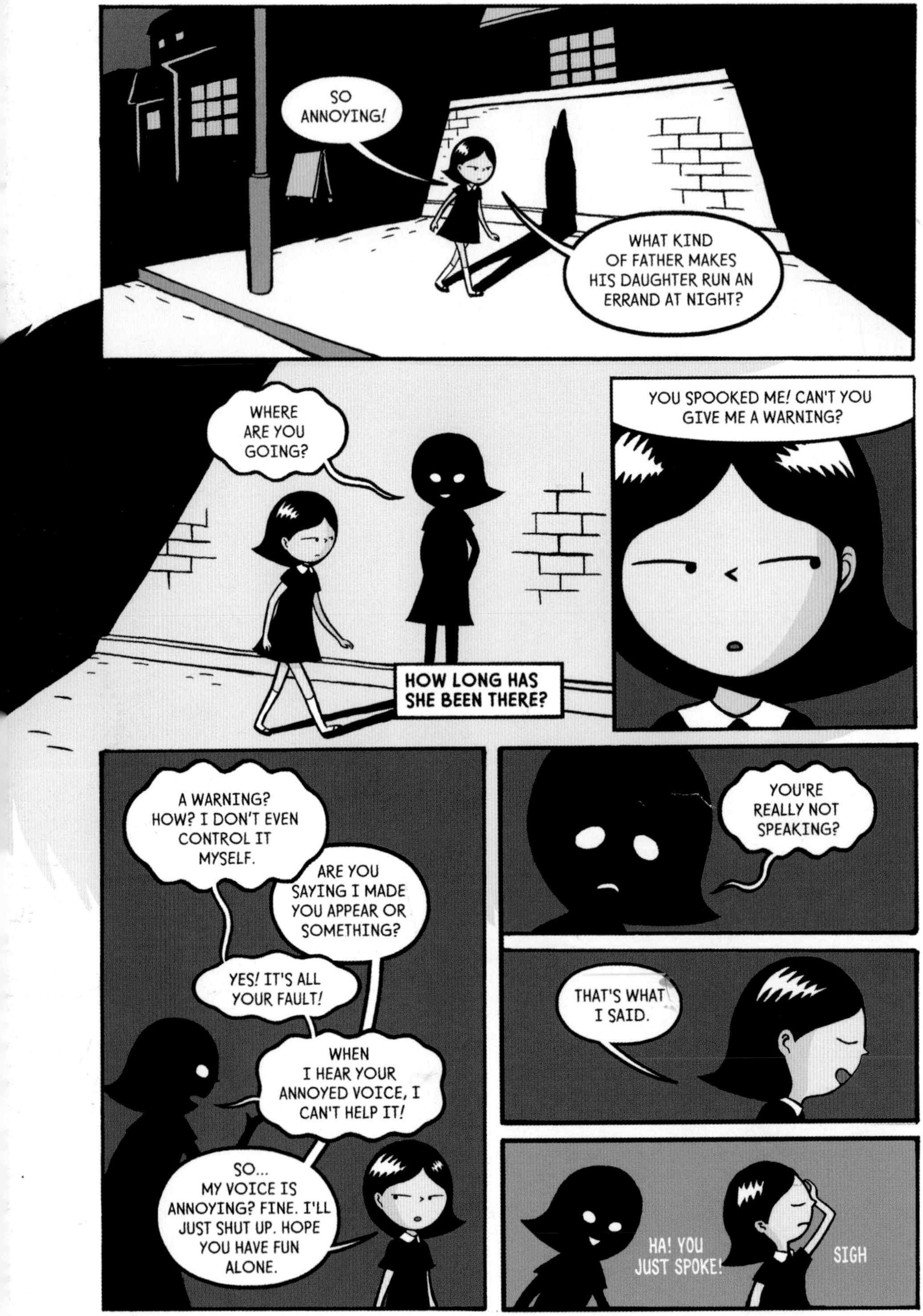
SO ANNOYING!
WHAT KIND OF FATHER MAKES HIS DAUGHTER RUN AN ERRAND AT NIGHT?
WHERE ARE YOU GOING?
HOW LONG HAS SHE BEEN THERE?
YOU SPOOKED ME! CAN'T YOU GIVE ME A WARNING?
A WARNING? HOW? I DON'T EVEN CONTROL IT MYSELF.
ARE YOU SAYING I MADE YOU APPEAR OR SOMETHING?
YES! IT'S ALL YOUR FAULT!
WHEN I HEAR YOUR ANNOYED VOICE, I CAN'T HELP IT!
SO... MY VOICE IS ANNOYING? FINE. I'LL JUST SHUT UP. HOPE YOU HAVE FUN ALONE.
YOU'RE REALLY NOT SPEAKING?
THAT'S WHAT I SAID.
HA! YOU JUST SPOKE!
SIGH

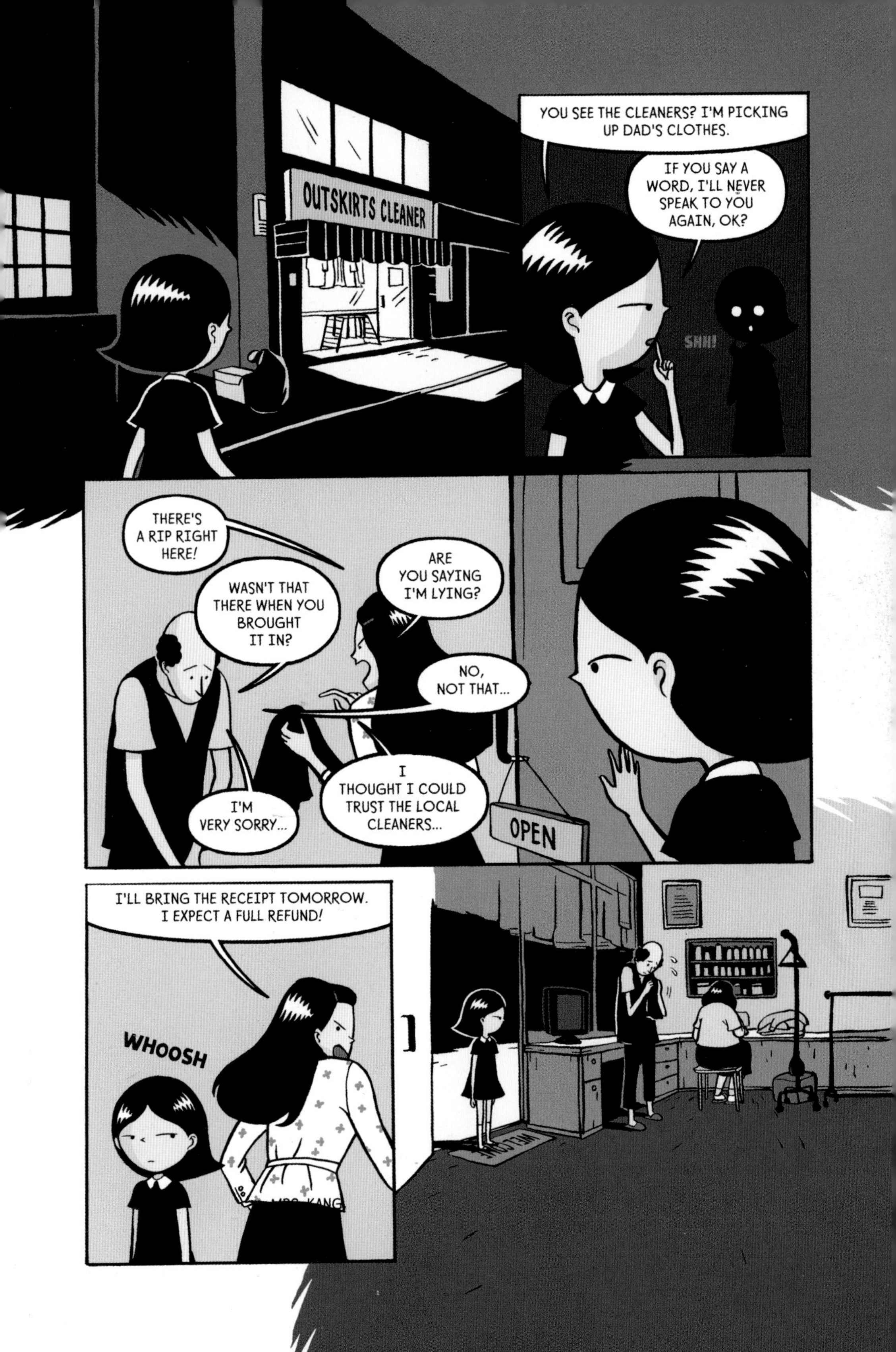
OUTSKIRTS CLEANER
YOU SEE THE CLEANERS? I'M PICKING UP DAD'S CLOTHES.
IF YOU SAY A WORD, I'LL NEVER SPEAK TO YOU AGAIN, OK?
SHH!
THERE'S A RIP RIGHT HERE!
WASN'T THAT THERE WHEN YOU BROUGHT IT IN?
ARE YOU SAYING I'M LYING?
NO, NOT THAT...
I'M VERY SORRY...
I THOUGHT I COULD TRUST THE LOCAL CLEANERS...
OPEN
I'LL BRING THE RECEIPT TOMORROW. I EXPECT A FULL REFUND!
WHOOSH

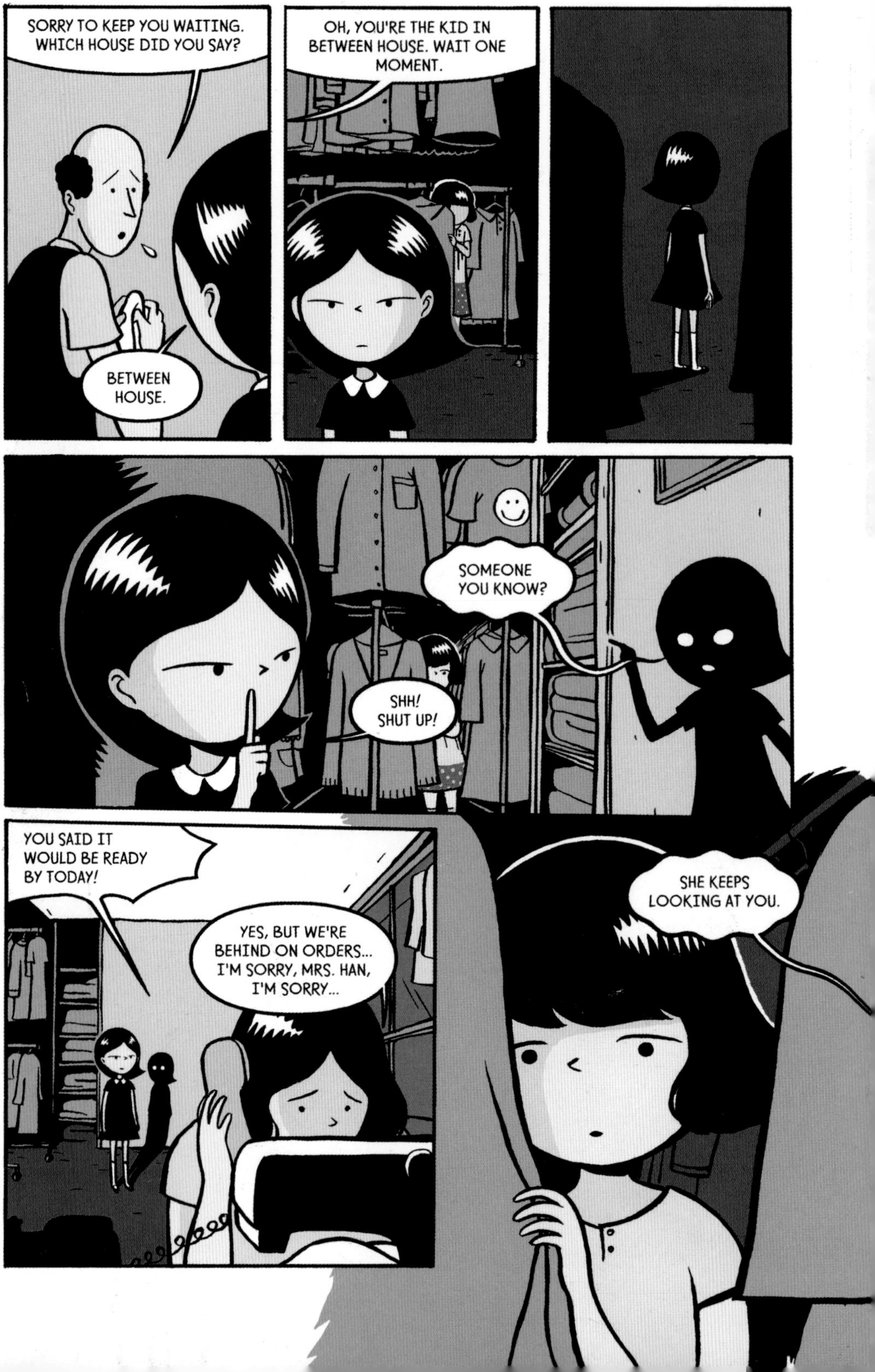
SORRY TO KEEP YOU WAITING. WHICH HOUSE DID YOU SAY?
BETWEEN HOUSE.
OH, YOU'RE THE KID IN BETWEEN HOUSE. WAIT ONE MOMENT.
SOMEONE YOU KNOW?
SHH! SHUT UP!
YOU SAID IT WOULD BE READY BY TODAY!
YES, BUT WE'RE BEHIND ON ORDERS... I'M SORRY, MRS. HAN, I'M SORRY...
SHE KEEPS LOOKING AT YOU.

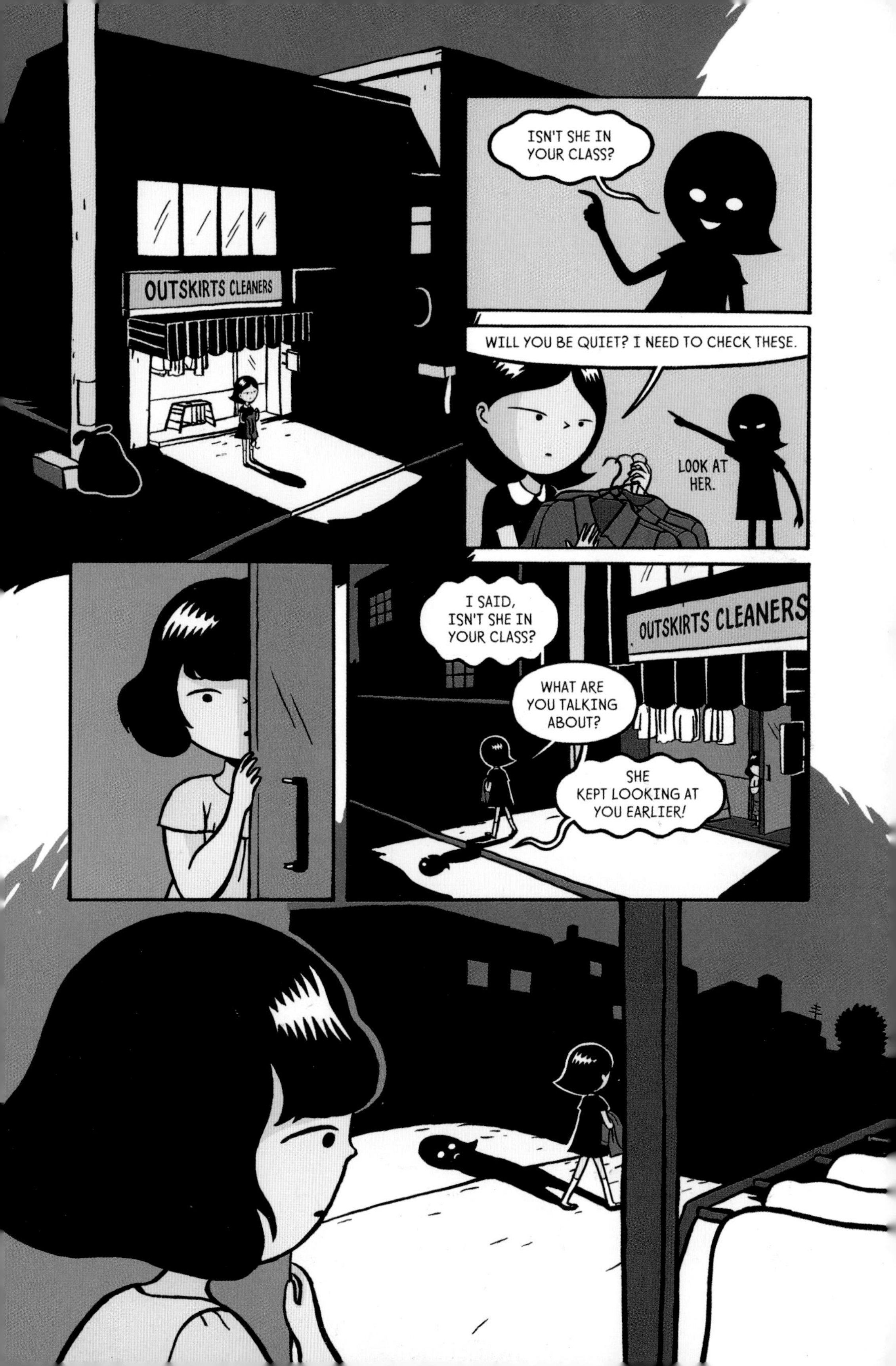
OUTSKIRTS CLEANERS
ISN'T SHE IN YOUR CLASS?
WILL YOU BE QUIET? I NEED TO CHECK THESE.
LOOK AT HER.
I SAID, ISN'T SHE IN YOUR CLASS?
OUTSKIRTS CLEANERS
WHAT ARE YOU TALKING ABOUT?
SHE KEPT LOOKING AT YOU EARLIER!

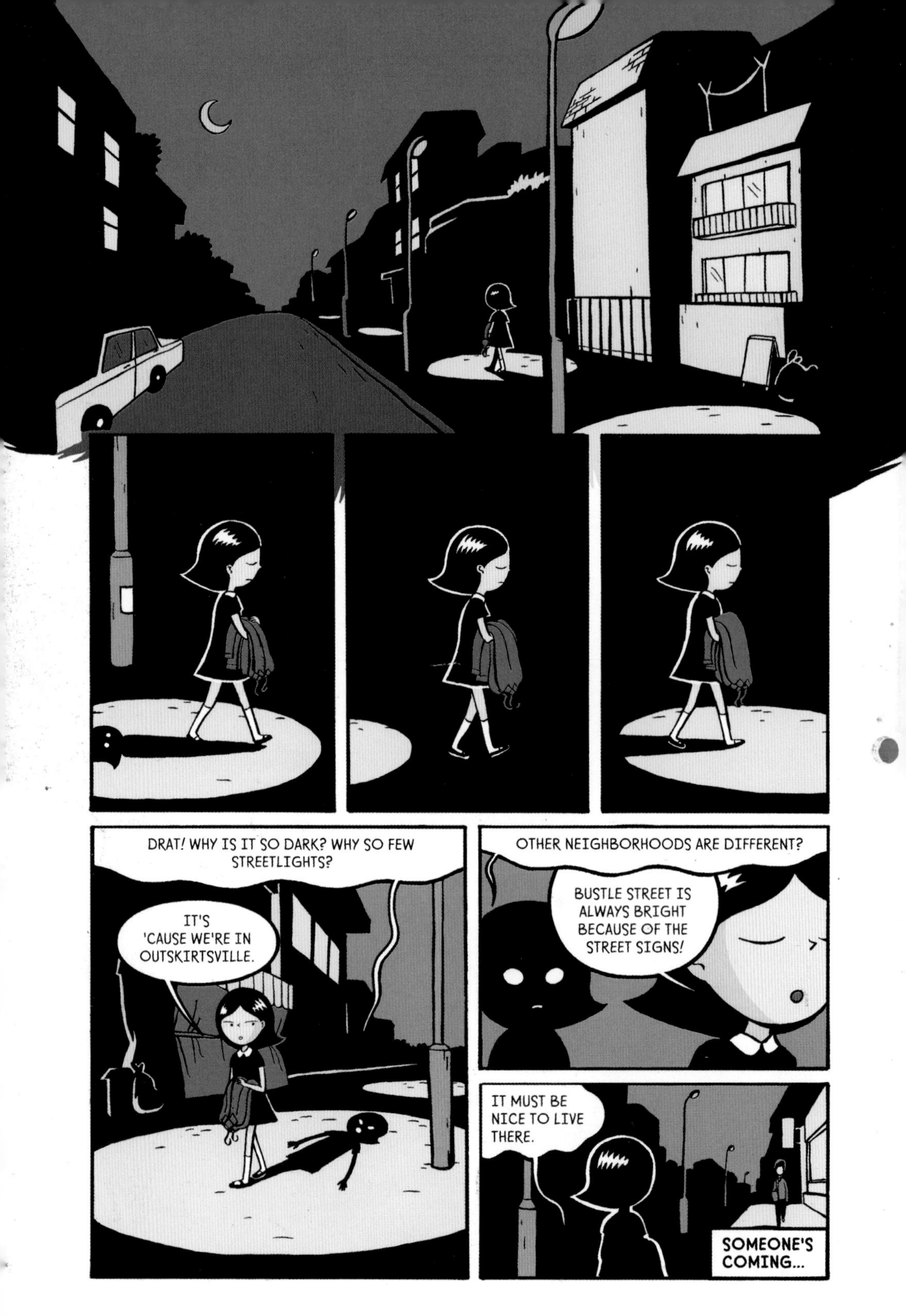
DRAT! WHY IS IT SO DARK? WHY SO FEW STREETLIGHTS?
IT'S 'CAUSE WE'RE IN OUTSKIRTSVILLE.
OTHER NEIGHBORHOODS ARE DIFFERENT?
BUSTLE STREET IS ALWAYS BRIGHT BECAUSE OF THE STREET SIGNS!
IT MUST BE NICE TO LIVE THERE.
SOMEONE'S COMING...

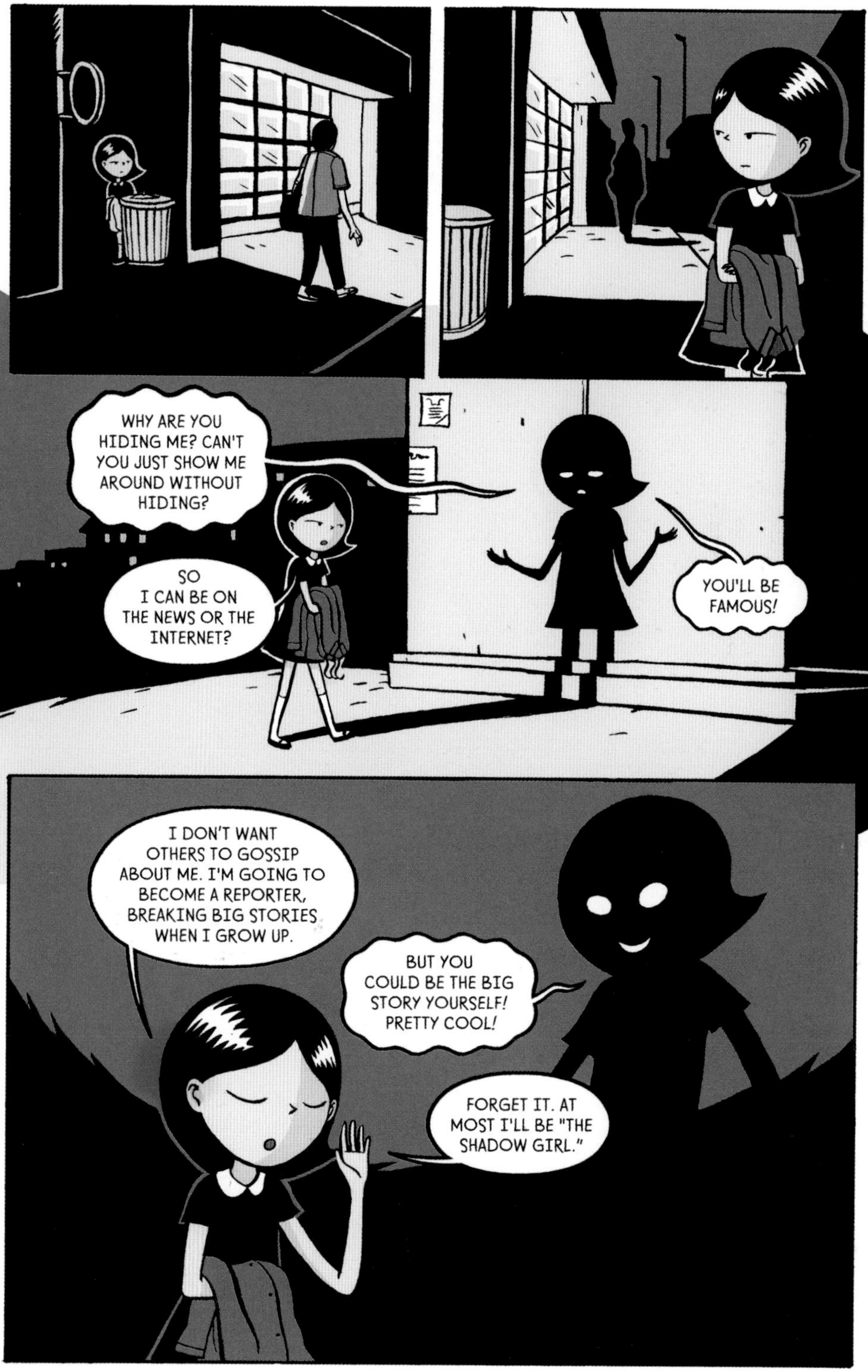
WHY ARE YOU HIDING ME? CAN'T YOU JUST SHOW ME AROUND WITHOUT HIDING?
SO I CAN BE ON THE NEWS OR THE INTERNET?
YOU'LL BE FAMOUS!
I DON'T WANT OTHERS TO GOSSIP ABOUT ME. I'M GOING TO BECOME A REPORTER, BREAKING BIG STORIES WHEN I GROW UP.
BUT YOU COULD BE THE BIG STORY YOURSELF! PRETTY COOL!
FORGET IT. AT MOST I'LL BE "THE SHADOW GIRL."

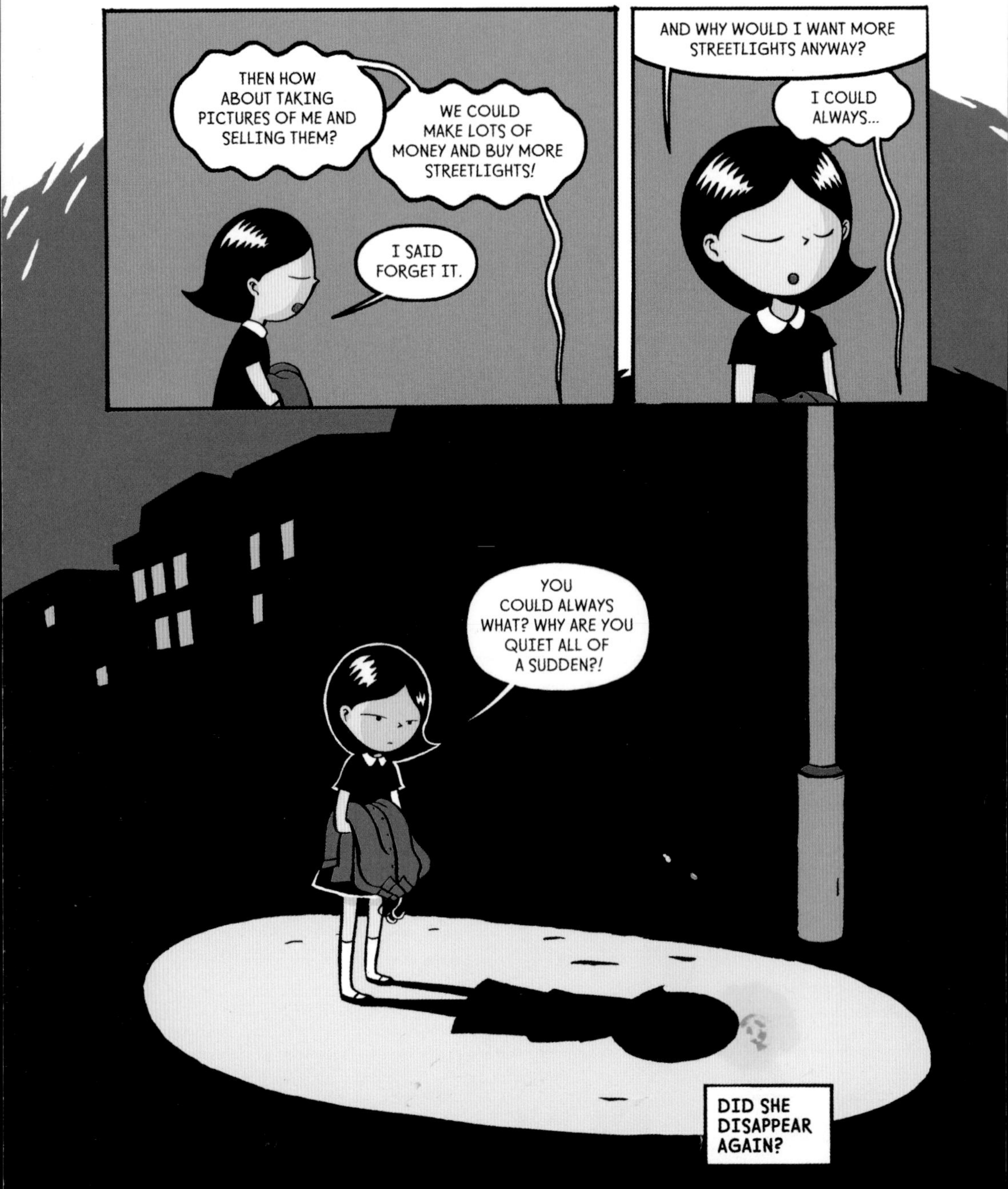
THEN HOW ABOUT TAKING PICTURES OF ME AND SELLING THEM?
WE COULD MAKE LOTS OF MONEY AND BUY MORE STREETLIGHTS!
I SAID FORGET IT.
AND WHY WOULD I WANT MORE STREETLIGHTS ANYWAY?
I COULD ALWAYS...
YOU COULD ALWAYS WHAT? WHY ARE YOU QUIET ALL OF A SUDDEN?!
DID SHE DISAPPEAR AGAIN?

3. FOUND MEMORIES

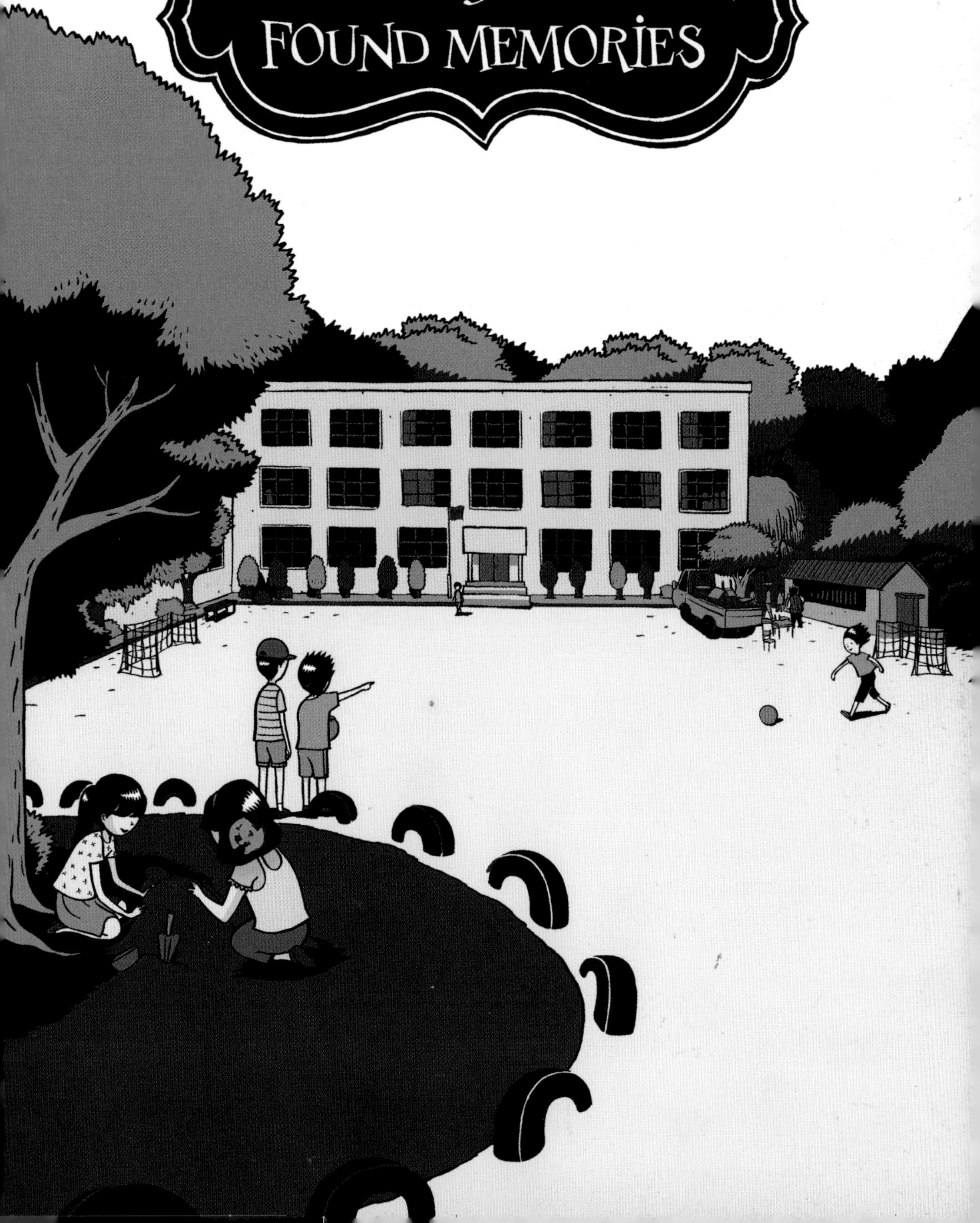

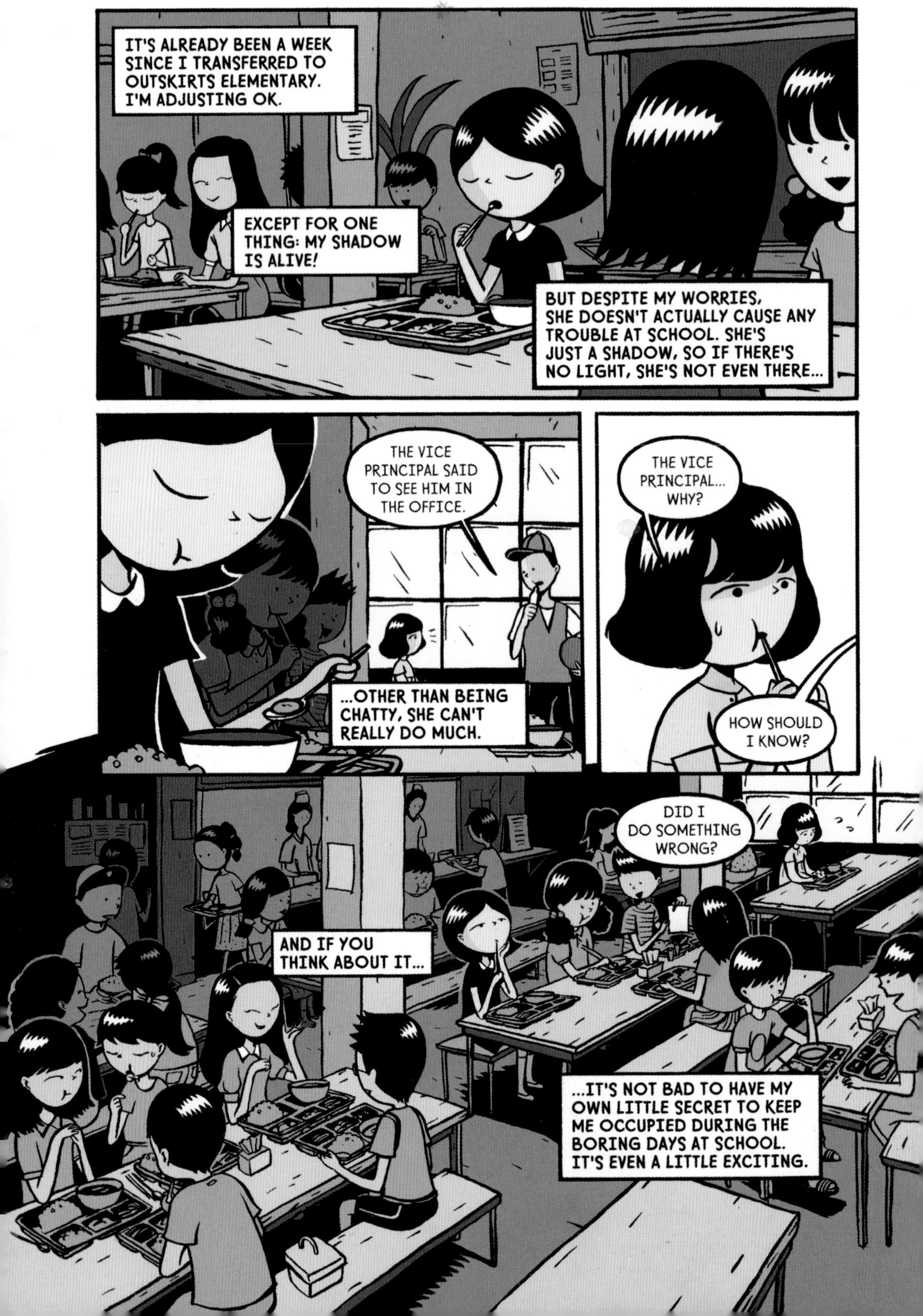
IT'S ALREADY BEEN A WEEK SINCE I TRANSFERRED TO OUTSKIRTS ELEMENTARY. I'M ADJUSTING OK.
EXCEPT FOR ONE THING: MY SHADOW IS ALIVE!
BUT DESPITE MY WORRIES, SHE DOESN'T ACTUALLY CAUSE ANY TROUBLE AT SCHOOL. SHE'S JUST A SHADOW, SO IF THERE'S NO LIGHT, SHE'S NOT EVEN THERE...
THE VICE PRINCIPAL SAID TO SEE HIM IN THE OFFICE.
...OTHER THAN BEING CHATTY, SHE CAN'T REALLY DO MUCH.
THE VICE PRINCIPAL... WHY?
HOW SHOULD I KNOW?
DID I DO SOMETHING WRONG?
AND IF YOU THINK ABOUT IT...
...IT'S NOT BAD TO HAVE MY OWN LITTLE SECRET TO KEEP ME OCCUPIED DURING THE BORING DAYS AT SCHOOL. IT'S EVEN A LITTLE EXCITING.

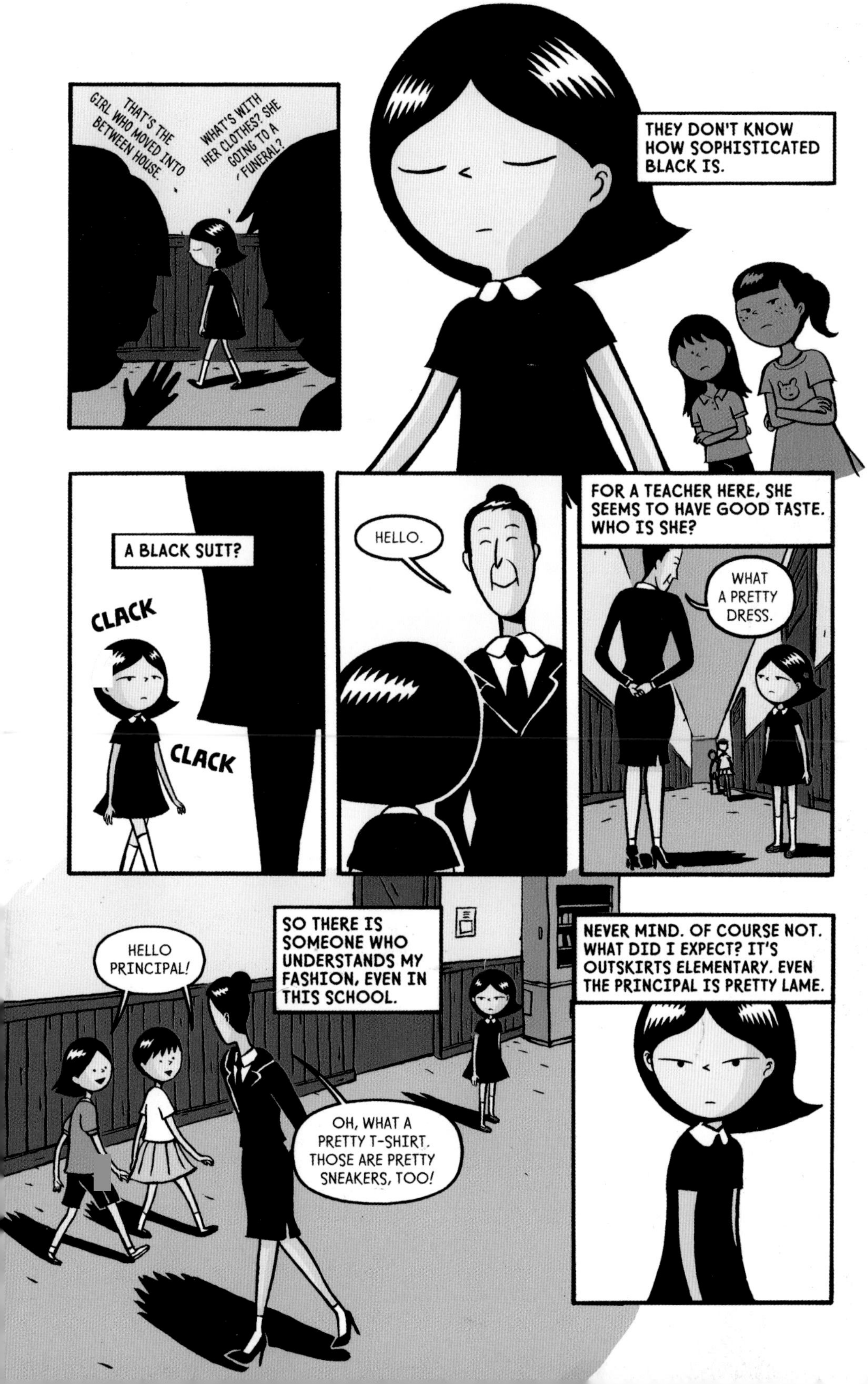
THAT'S THE GIRL WHO MOVED INTO BETWEEN HOUSE.
WHAT'S WITH HER CLOTHES? SHE GOING TO A FUNERAL?
THEY DON'T KNOW HOW SOPHISTICATED BLACK IS.
A BLACK SUIT?
CLACK
CLACK
HELLO.
FOR A TEACHER HERE, SHE SEEMS TO HAVE GOOD TASTE. WHO IS SHE?
WHAT A PRETTY DRESS.
HELLO PRINCIPAL!
SO THERE IS SOMEONE WHO UNDERSTANDS MY FASHION, EVEN IN THIS SCHOOL.
OH, WHAT A PRETTY T-SHIRT. THOSE ARE PRETTY SNEAKERS, TOO!
NEVER MIND. OF COURSE NOT. WHAT DID I EXPECT? IT'S OUTSKIRTS ELEMENTARY. EVEN THE PRINCIPAL IS PRETTY LAME.

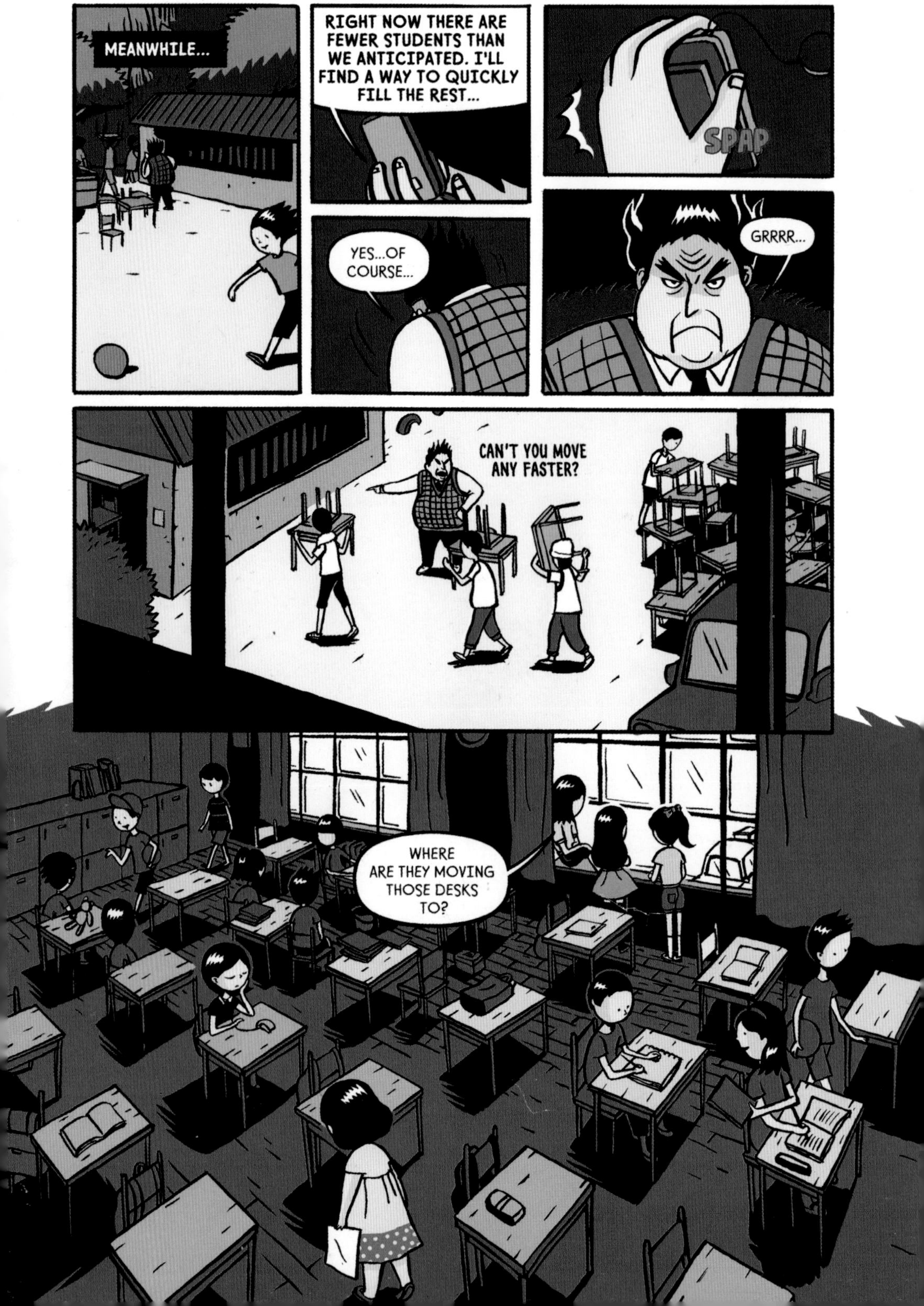
MEANWHILE...
RIGHT NOW THERE ARE FEWER STUDENTS THAN WE ANTICIPATED. I'LL FIND A WAY TO QUICKLY FILL THE REST...
SPAP
YES...OF COURSE...
GRRRR...
CAN'T YOU MOVE ANY FASTER?
WHERE ARE THEY MOVING THOSE DESKS TO?

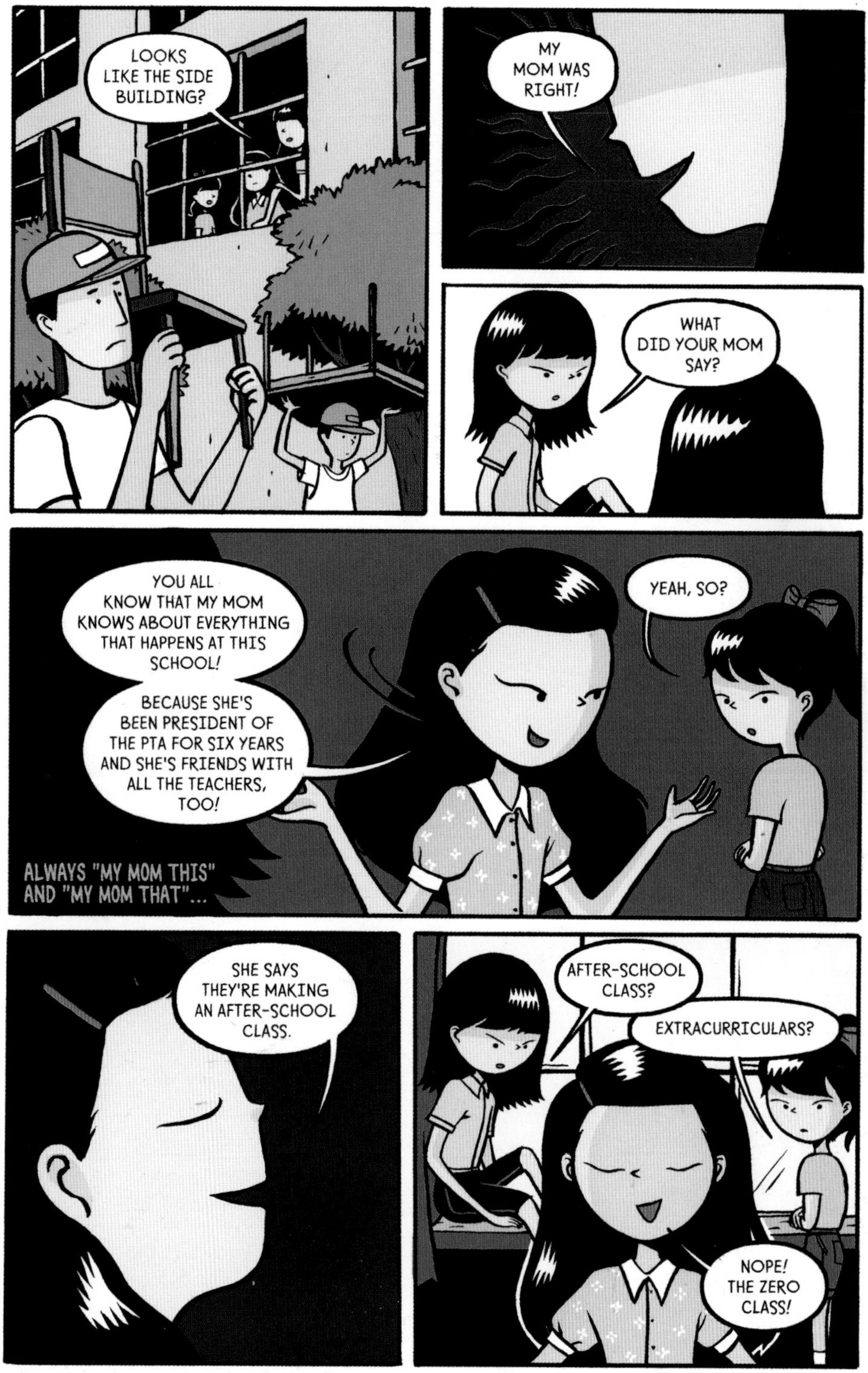
LOOKS LIKE THE SIDE BUILDING?
MY MOM WAS RIGHT!
WHAT DID YOUR MOM SAY?
YOU ALL KNOW THAT MY MOM KNOWS ABOUT EVERYTHING THAT HAPPENS AT THIS SCHOOL!
BECAUSE SHE'S BEEN PRESIDENT OF THE PTA FOR SIX YEARS AND SHE'S FRIENDS WITH ALL THE TEACHERS, TOO!
YEAH, SO?
ALWAYS "MY MOM THIS" AND "MY MOM THAT"...
SHE SAYS THEY'RE MAKING AN AFTER-SCHOOL CLASS.
AFTER-SCHOOL CLASS?
EXTRACURRICULARS?
NOPE! THE ZERO CLASS!

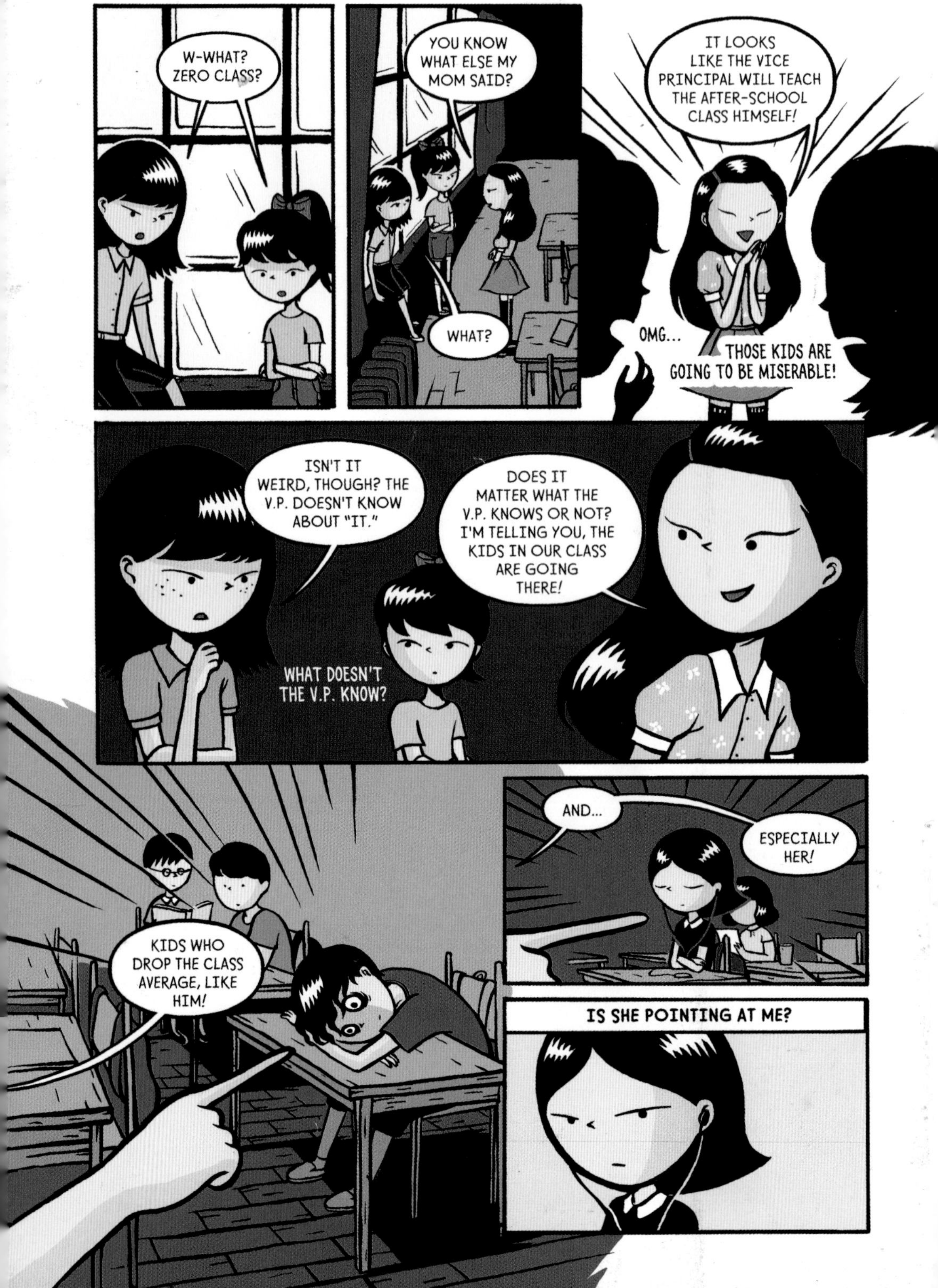
W-WHAT? ZERO CLASS?
YOU KNOW WHAT ELSE MY MOM SAID?
WHAT?
IT LOOKS LIKE THE VICE PRINCIPAL WILL TEACH THE AFTER-SCHOOL CLASS HIMSELF!
OMG...
THOSE KIDS ARE GOING TO BE MISERABLE!
ISN'T IT WEIRD, THOUGH? THE V.P. DOESN'T KNOW ABOUT "IT."
DOES IT MATTER WHAT THE V.P. KNOWS OR NOT? I'M TELLING YOU, THE KIDS IN OUR CLASS ARE GOING THERE!
WHAT DOESN'T THE V.P. KNOW?
KIDS WHO DROP THE CLASS AVERAGE, LIKE HIM!
AND...
ESPECIALLY HER!
IS SHE POINTING AT ME?

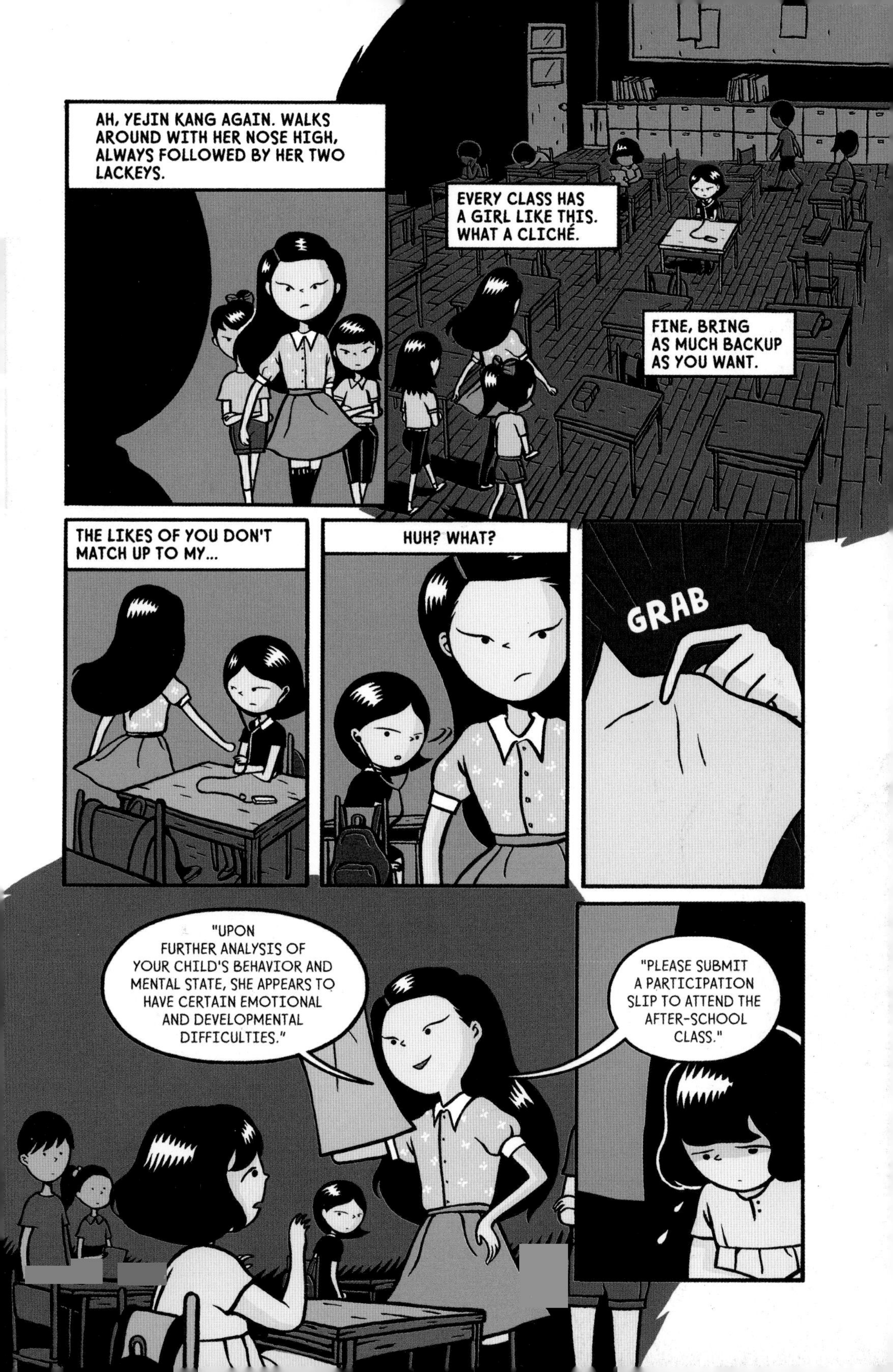
AH, YEJIN KANG AGAIN. WALKS AROUND WITH HER NOSE HIGH, ALWAYS FOLLOWED BY HER TWO LACKEYS.
EVERY CLASS HAS A GIRL LIKE THIS. WHAT A CLICHÉ.
FINE, BRING AS MUCH BACKUP AS YOU WANT.
THE LIKES OF YOU DON'T MATCH UP TO MY...
HUH? WHAT?
GRAB
"UPON FURTHER ANALYSIS OF YOUR CHILD'S BEHAVIOR AND MENTAL STATE, SHE APPEARS TO HAVE CERTAIN EMOTIONAL AND DEVELOPMENTAL DIFFICULTIES."
"PLEASE SUBMIT A PARTICIPATION SLIP TO ATTEND THE AFTER-SCHOOL CLASS."

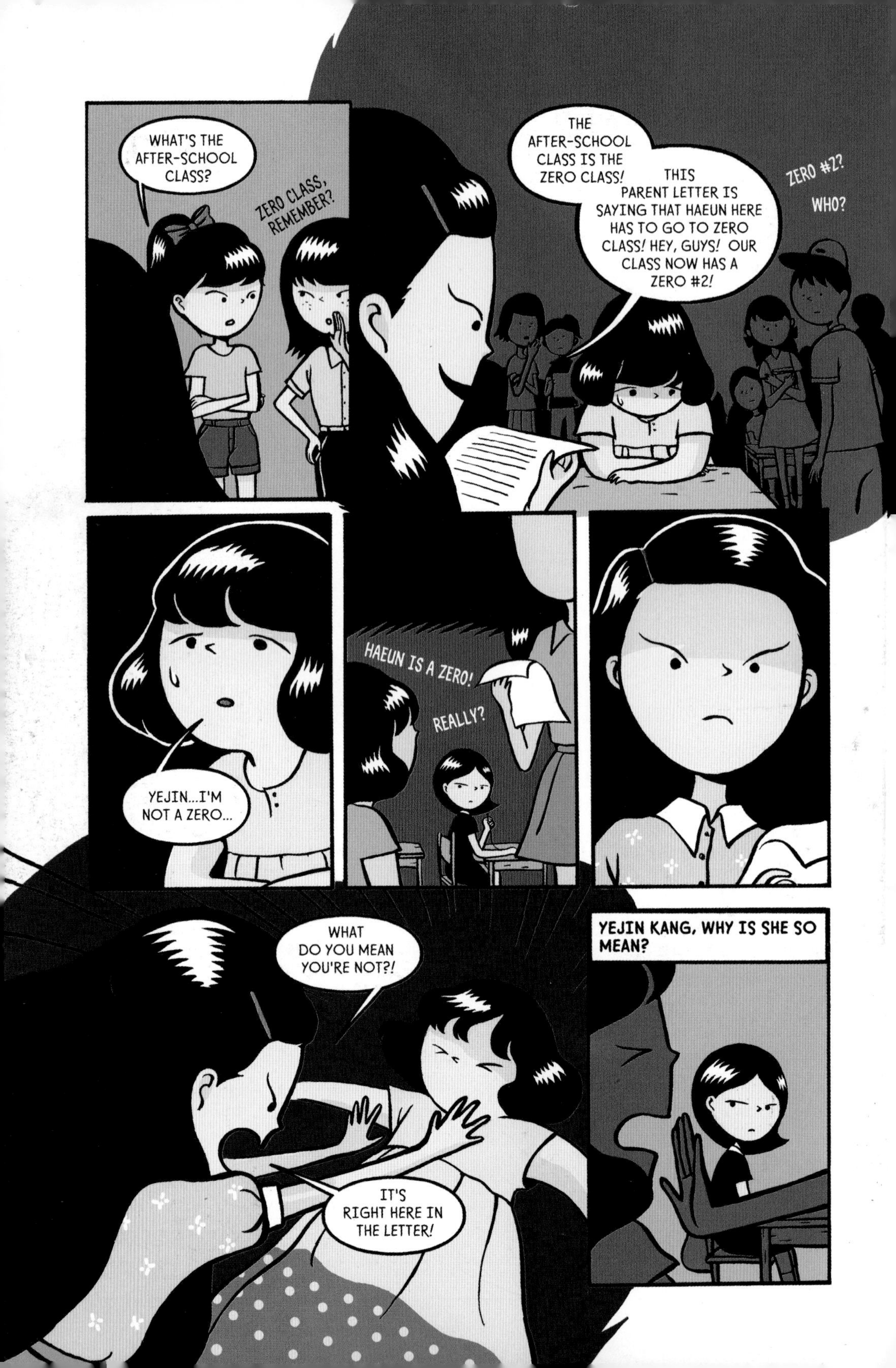
WHAT'S THE AFTER-SCHOOL CLASS?
ZERO CLASS, REMEMBER?
THE AFTER-SCHOOL CLASS IS THE ZERO CLASS!
THIS PARENT LETTER IS SAYING THAT HAEUN HERE HAS TO GO TO ZERO CLASS! HEY, GUYS! OUR CLASS NOW HAS A ZERO #2!
ZERO #2?
WHO?
YEJIN...I'M NOT A ZERO...
HAEUN IS A ZERO!
REALLY?
WHAT DO YOU MEAN YOU'RE NOT?!
IT'S RIGHT HERE IN THE LETTER!
YEJIN KANG, WHY IS SHE SO MEAN?

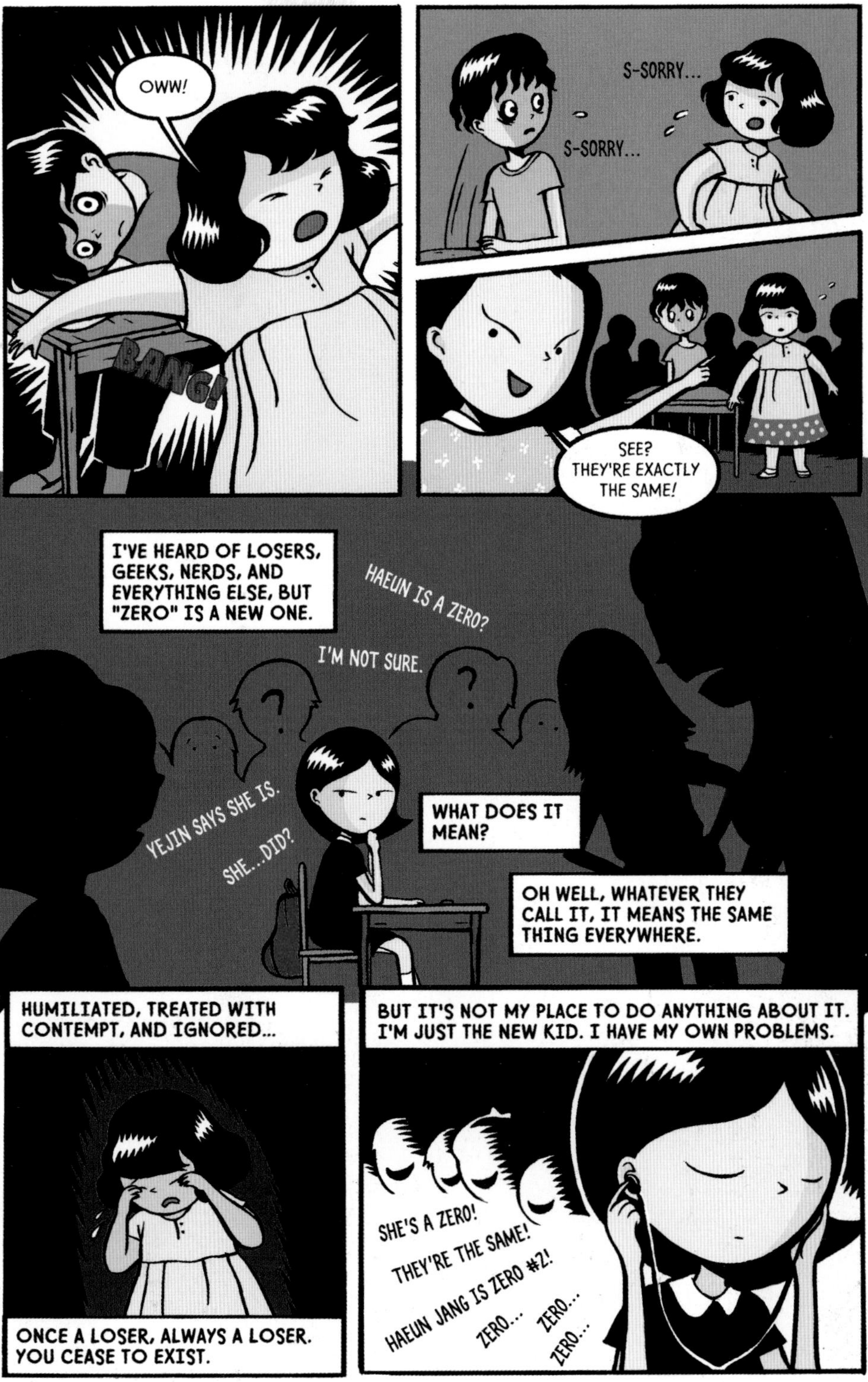
OWW!
BANG!
S-SORRY...
S-SORRY...
SEE? THEY'RE EXACTLY THE SAME!
I'VE HEARD OF LOSERS, GEEKS, NERDS, AND EVERYTHING ELSE, BUT "ZERO" IS A NEW ONE.
HAEUN IS A ZERO?
I'M NOT SURE.
YEJIN SAYS SHE IS.
SHE...DID?
WHAT DOES IT MEAN?
OH WELL, WHATEVER THEY CALL IT, IT MEANS THE SAME THING EVERYWHERE.
HUMILIATED, TREATED WITH CONTEMPT, AND IGNORED...
ONCE A LOSER, ALWAYS A LOSER. YOU CEASE TO EXIST.
BUT IT'S NOT MY PLACE TO DO ANYTHING ABOUT IT. I'M JUST THE NEW KID. I HAVE MY OWN PROBLEMS.
SHE'S A ZERO!
THEY'RE THE SAME!
HAEUN JANG IS ZERO #2!
ZERO...
ZERO...
ZERO...

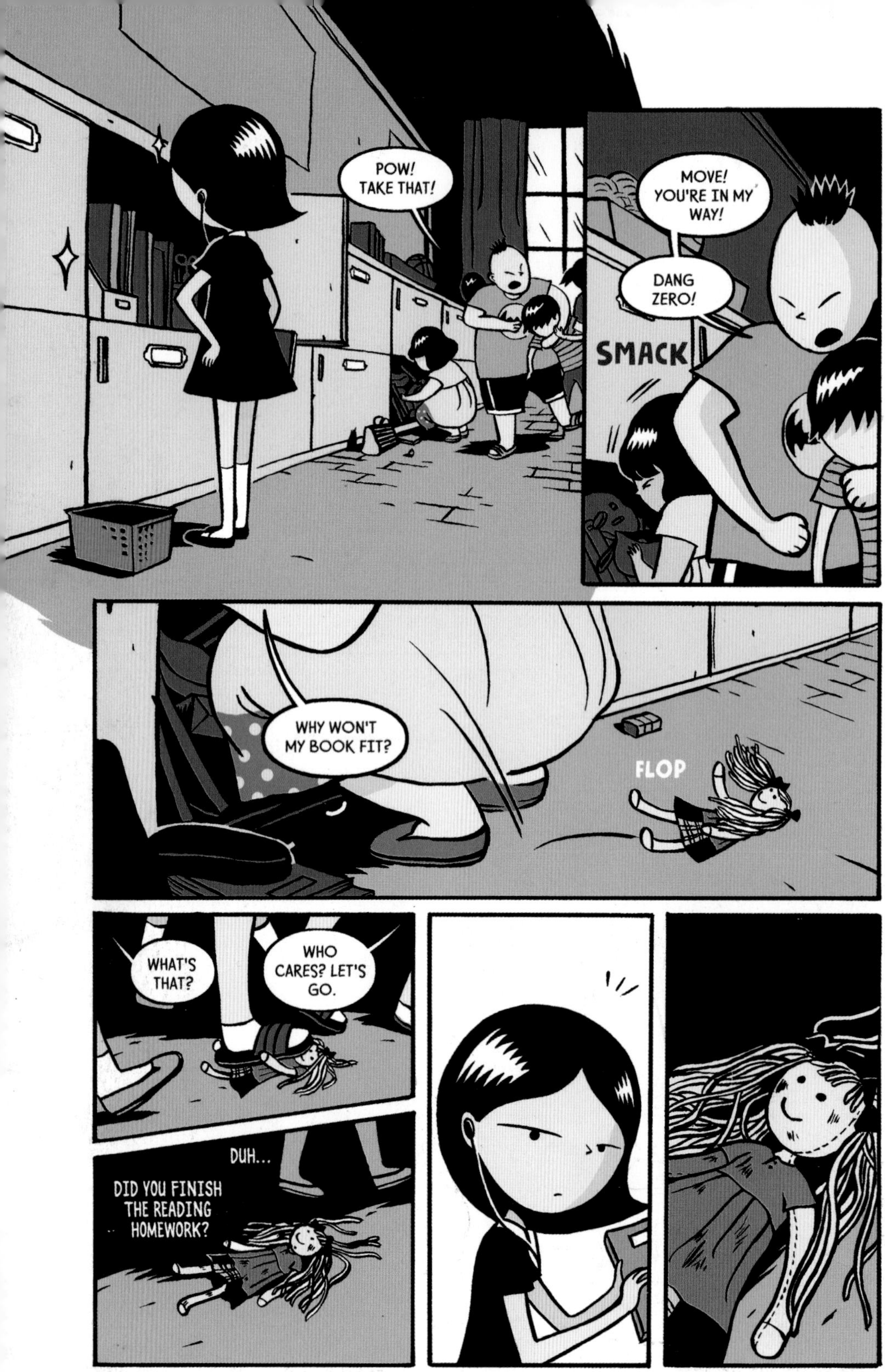
POW! TAKE THAT!
MOVE! YOU'RE IN MY WAY!
DANG ZERO!
SMACK
WHY WON'T MY BOOK FIT?
FLOP
WHAT'S THAT?
WHO CARES? LET'S GO.
DUH...
DID YOU FINISH THE READING HOMEWORK?

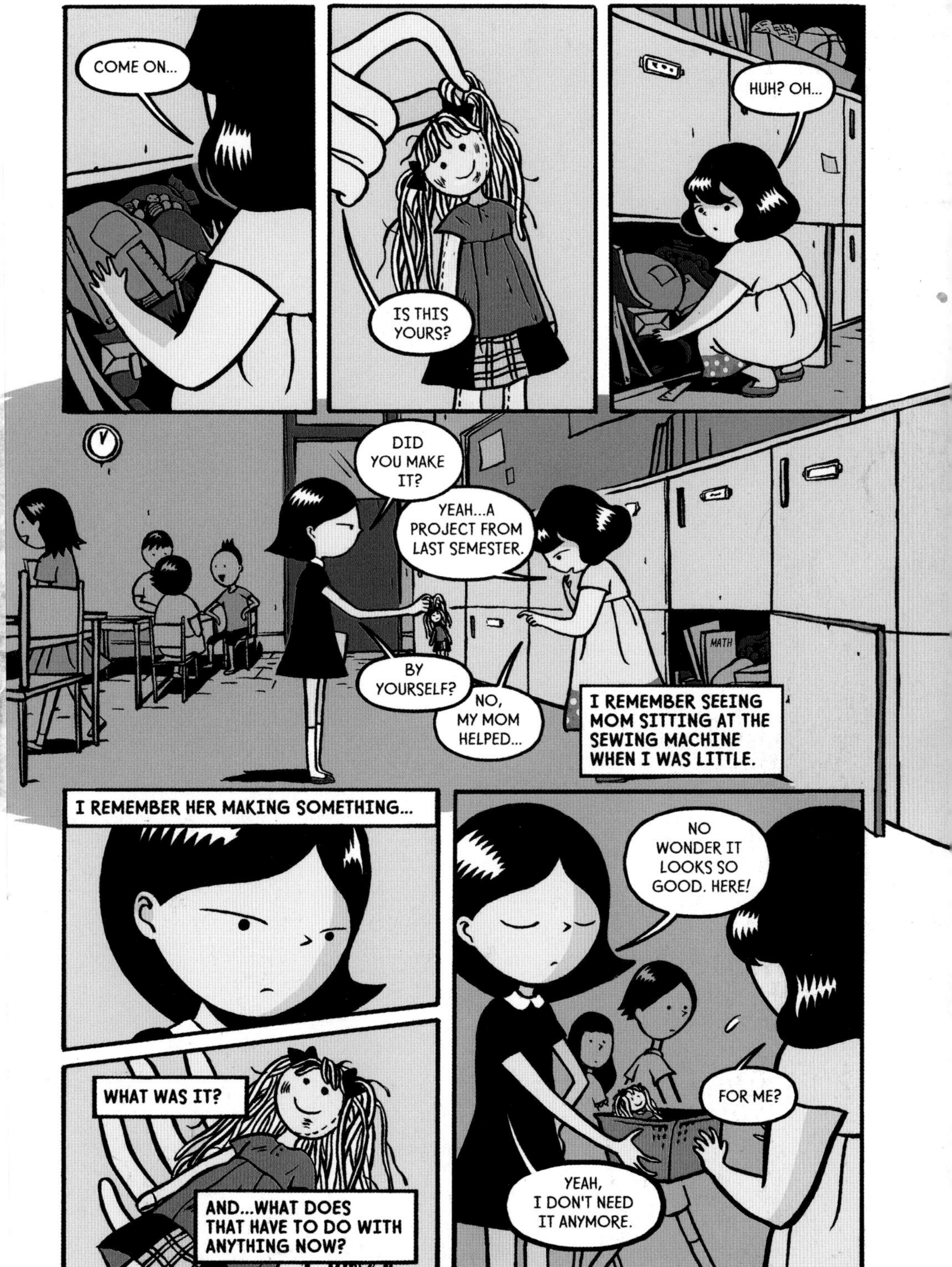
COME ON...
IS THIS YOURS?
HUH? OH...
DID YOU MAKE IT?
YEAH...A PROJECT FROM LAST SEMESTER.
BY YOURSELF?
NO, MY MOM HELPED...
MATH
I REMEMBER SEEING MOM SITTING AT THE SEWING MACHINE WHEN I WAS LITTLE.
I REMEMBER HER MAKING SOMETHING...
WHAT WAS IT?
AND...WHAT DOES THAT HAVE TO DO WITH ANYTHING NOW?
NO WONDER IT LOOKS SO GOOD. HERE!
FOR ME?
YEAH, I DON'T NEED IT ANYMORE.

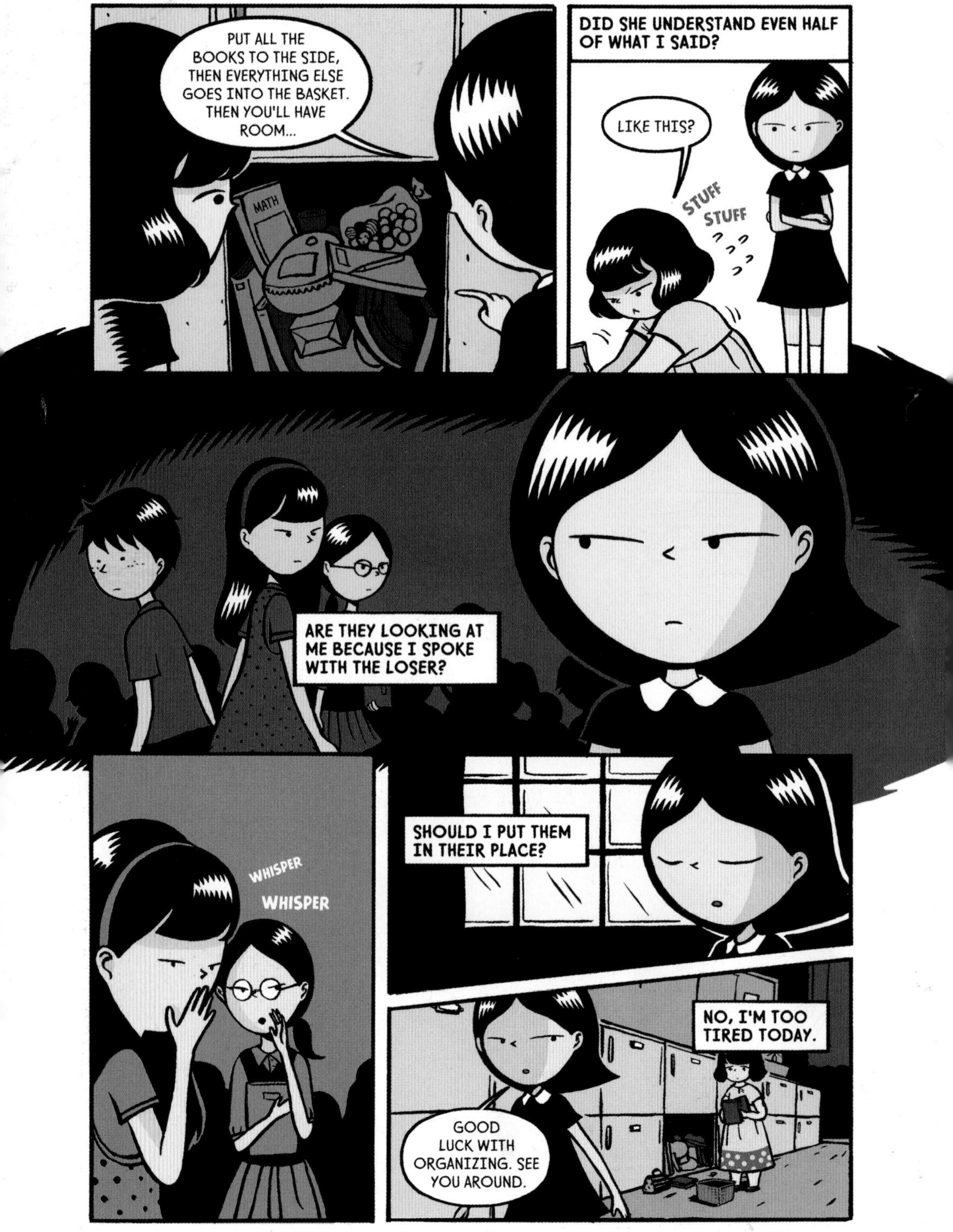
PUT ALL THE BOOKS TO THE SIDE, THEN EVERYTHING ELSE GOES INTO THE BASKET. THEN YOU'LL HAVE ROOM...
MATH
DID SHE UNDERSTAND EVEN HALF OF WHAT I SAID?
LIKE THIS?
STUFF
STUFF
ARE THEY LOOKING AT ME BECAUSE I SPOKE WITH THE LOSER?
WHISPER
WHISPER
SHOULD I PUT THEM IN THEIR PLACE?
NO, I'M TOO TIRED TODAY.
GOOD LUCK WITH ORGANIZING. SEE YOU AROUND.

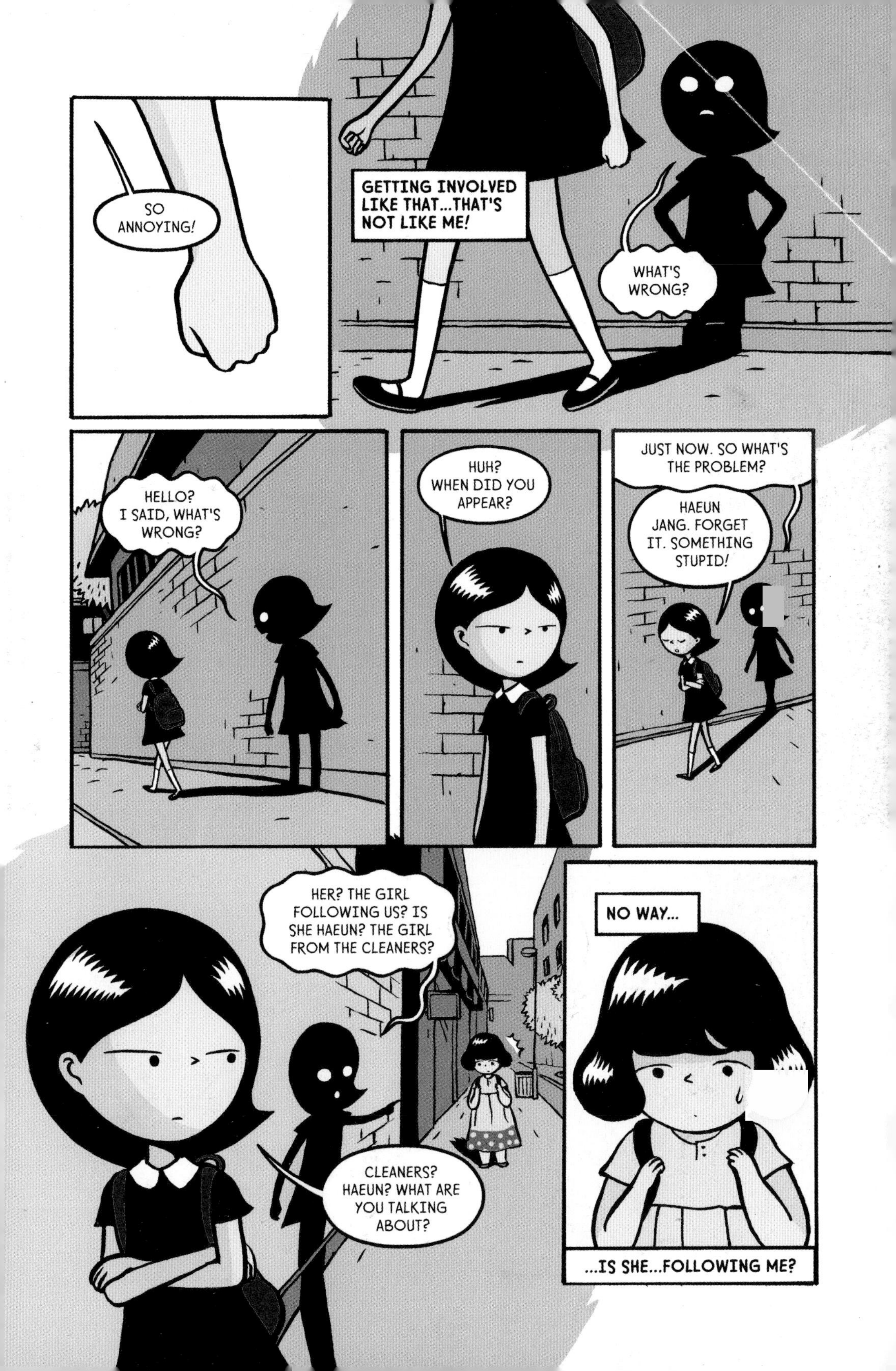
SO ANNOYING!
GETTING INVOLVED LIKE THAT...THAT'S NOT LIKE ME!
WHAT'S WRONG?
HELLO? I SAID, WHAT'S WRONG?
HUH? WHEN DID YOU APPEAR?
JUST NOW. SO WHAT'S THE PROBLEM?
HAEUN JANG. FORGET IT. SOMETHING STUPID!
HER? THE GIRL FOLLOWING US? IS SHE HAEUN? THE GIRL FROM THE CLEANERS?
CLEANERS? HAEUN? WHAT ARE YOU TALKING ABOUT?
NO WAY...
...IS SHE...FOLLOWING ME?

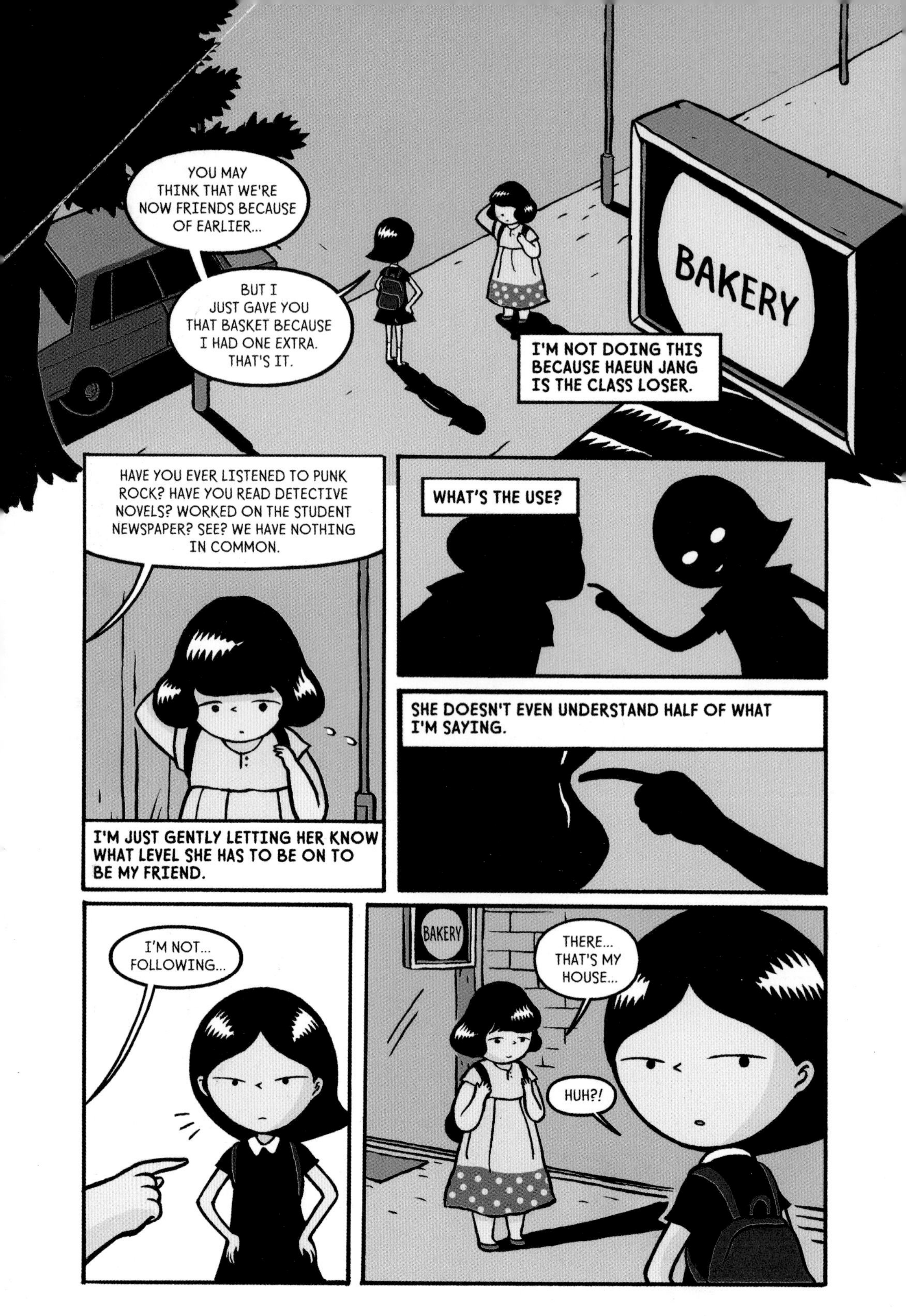
YOU MAY THINK THAT WE'RE NOW FRIENDS BECAUSE OF EARLIER...
BUT I JUST GAVE YOU THAT BASKET BECAUSE I HAD ONE EXTRA. THAT'S IT.
BAKERY
I'M NOT DOING THIS BECAUSE HAEUN JANG IS THE CLASS LOSER.
HAVE YOU EVER LISTENED TO PUNK ROCK? HAVE YOU READ DETECTIVE NOVELS? WORKED ON THE STUDENT NEWSPAPER? SEE? WE HAVE NOTHING IN COMMON.
I'M JUST GENTLY LETTING HER KNOW WHAT LEVEL SHE HAS TO BE ON TO BE MY FRIEND.
WHAT'S THE USE?
SHE DOESN'T EVEN UNDERSTAND HALF OF WHAT I'M SAYING.
I'M NOT... FOLLOWING...
BAKERY
THERE... THAT'S MY HOUSE...
HUH?!

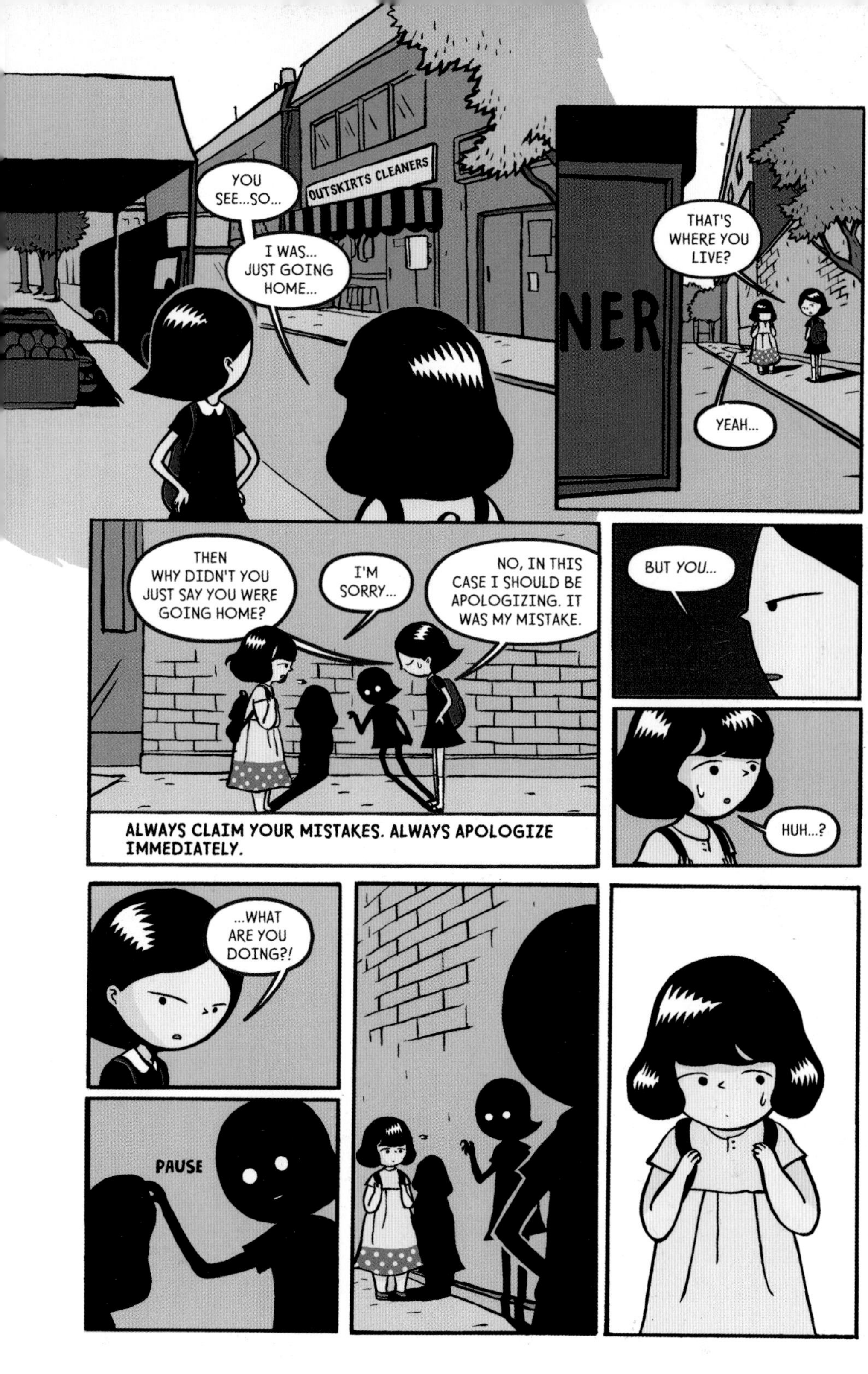

YOU SEE...SO...
I WAS... JUST GOING HOME...
OUTSKIRTS CLEANERS
NER
THAT'S WHERE YOU LIVE?
YEAH...
THEN WHY DIDN'T YOU JUST SAY YOU WERE GOING HOME?
I'M SORRY...
NO, IN THIS CASE I SHOULD BE APOLOGIZING. IT WAS MY MISTAKE.
ALWAYS CLAIM YOUR MISTAKES. ALWAYS APOLOGIZE IMMEDIATELY.
BUT YOU...
HUH...?
...WHAT ARE YOU DOING?!
PAUSE

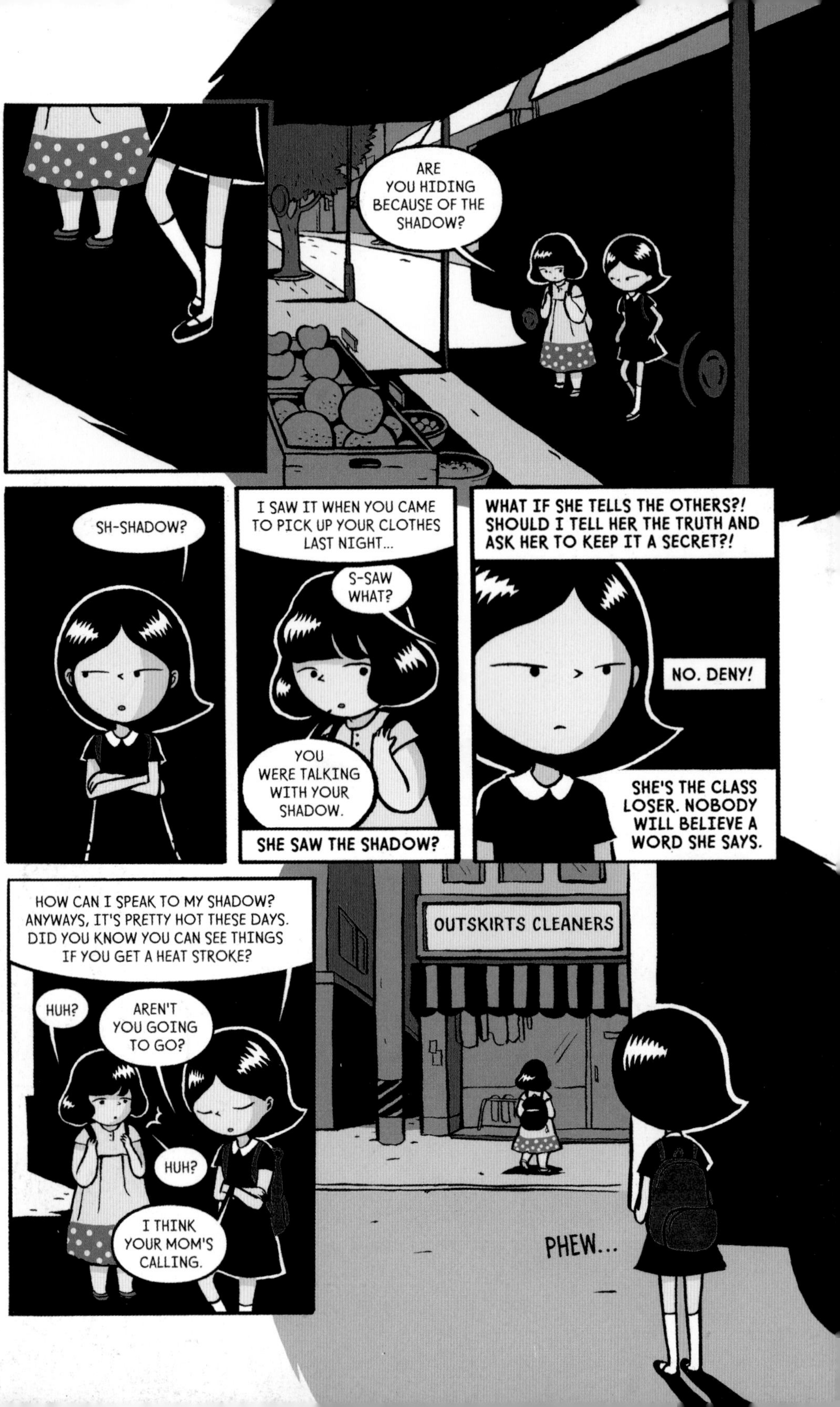
ARE YOU HIDING BECAUSE OF THE SHADOW?
SH-SHADOW?
I SAW IT WHEN YOU CAME TO PICK UP YOUR CLOTHES LAST NIGHT...
S-SAW WHAT?
YOU WERE TALKING WITH YOUR SHADOW.
SHE SAW THE SHADOW?
WHAT IF SHE TELLS THE OTHERS?! SHOULD I TELL HER THE TRUTH AND ASK HER TO KEEP IT A SECRET?!
NO. DENY!
SHE'S THE CLASS LOSER. NOBODY WILL BELIEVE A WORD SHE SAYS.
HOW CAN I SPEAK TO MY SHADOW? ANYWAYS, IT'S PRETTY HOT THESE DAYS. DID YOU KNOW YOU CAN SEE THINGS IF YOU GET A HEAT STROKE?
HUH?
AREN'T YOU GOING TO GO?
HUH?
I THINK YOUR MOM'S CALLING.
OUTSKIRTS CLEANERS
PHEW...

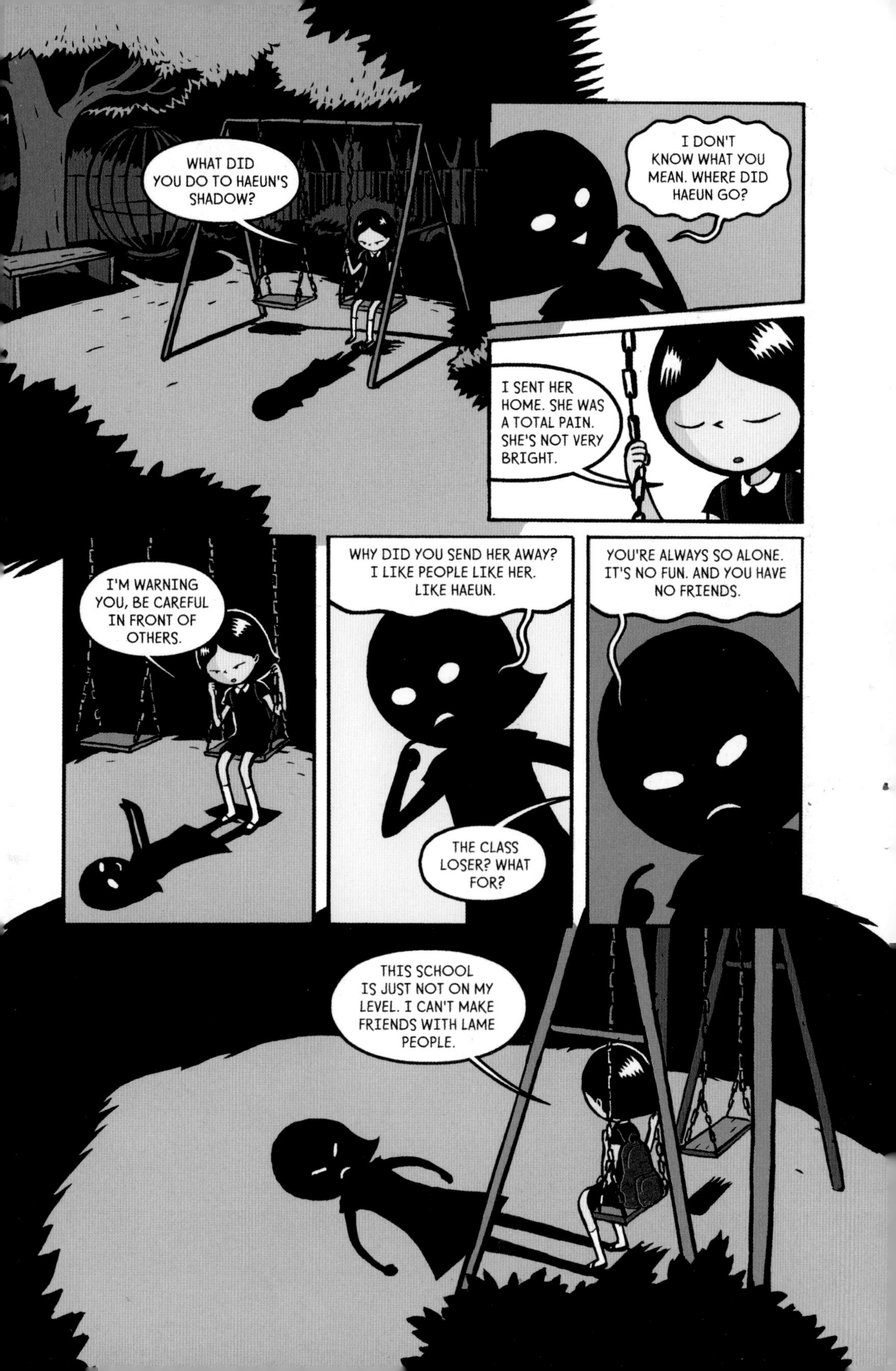
WHAT DID YOU DO TO HAEUN'S SHADOW?
I DON'T KNOW WHAT YOU MEAN. WHERE DID HAEUN GO?
I SENT HER HOME. SHE WAS A TOTAL PAIN. SHE'S NOT VERY BRIGHT.
I'M WARNING YOU, BE CAREFUL IN FRONT OF OTHERS.
WHY DID YOU SEND HER AWAY? I LIKE PEOPLE LIKE HER. LIKE HAEUN.
THE CLASS LOSER? WHAT FOR?
YOU'RE ALWAYS SO ALONE. IT'S NO FUN. AND YOU HAVE NO FRIENDS.
THIS SCHOOL IS JUST NOT ON MY LEVEL. I CAN'T MAKE FRIENDS WITH LAME PEOPLE.

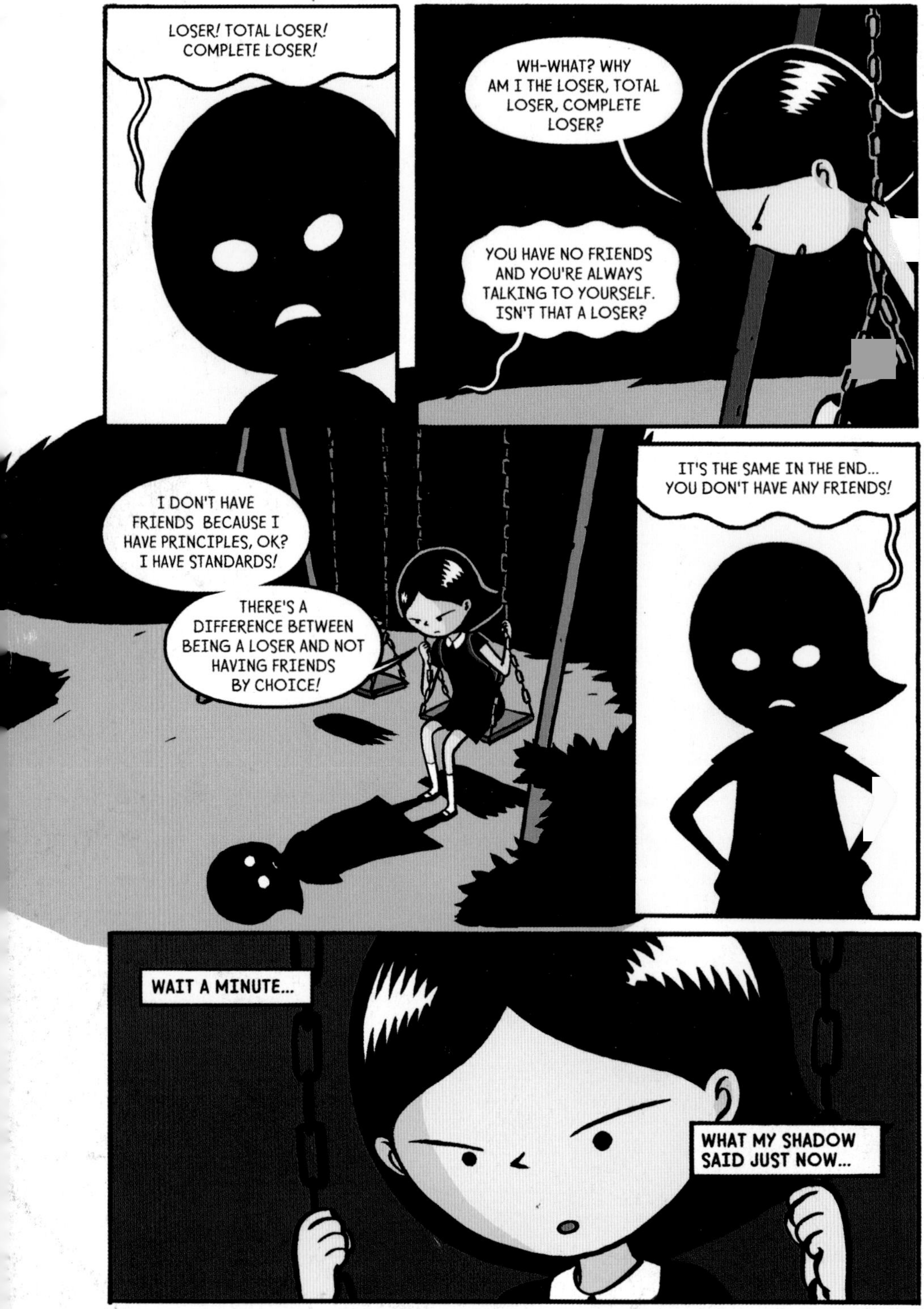

LOSER! TOTAL LOSER! COMPLETE LOSER!
WH-WHAT? WHY AM I THE LOSER, TOTAL LOSER, COMPLETE LOSER?
YOU HAVE NO FRIENDS AND YOU'RE ALWAYS TALKING TO YOURSELF. ISN'T THAT A LOSER?
I DON'T HAVE FRIENDS BECAUSE I HAVE PRINCIPLES, OK? I HAVE STANDARDS!
THERE'S A DIFFERENCE BETWEEN BEING A LOSER AND NOT HAVING FRIENDS BY CHOICE!
IT'S THE SAME IN THE END... YOU DON'T HAVE ANY FRIENDS!
WAIT A MINUTE...
WHAT MY SHADOW SAID JUST NOW...

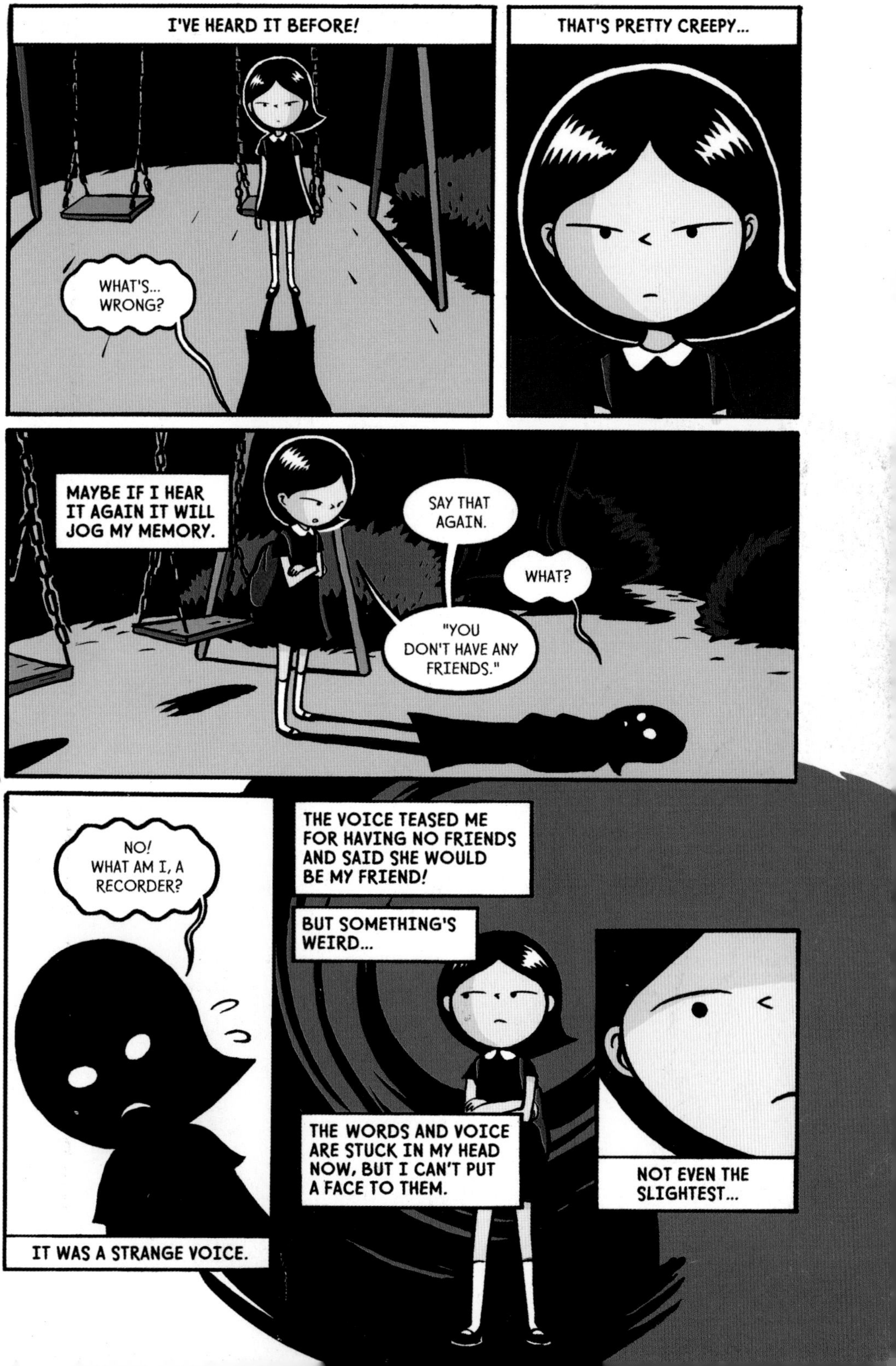
I'VE HEARD IT BEFORE!
WHAT'S... WRONG?
THAT'S PRETTY CREEPY...
MAYBE IF I HEAR IT AGAIN IT WILL JOG MY MEMORY.
SAY THAT AGAIN.
WHAT?
"YOU DON'T HAVE ANY FRIENDS."
NO! WHAT AM I, A RECORDER?
IT WAS A STRANGE VOICE.
THE VOICE TEASED ME FOR HAVING NO FRIENDS AND SAID SHE WOULD BE MY FRIEND!
BUT SOMETHING'S WEIRD...
THE WORDS AND VOICE ARE STUCK IN MY HEAD NOW, BUT I CAN'T PUT A FACE TO THEM.
NOT EVEN THE SLIGHTEST...

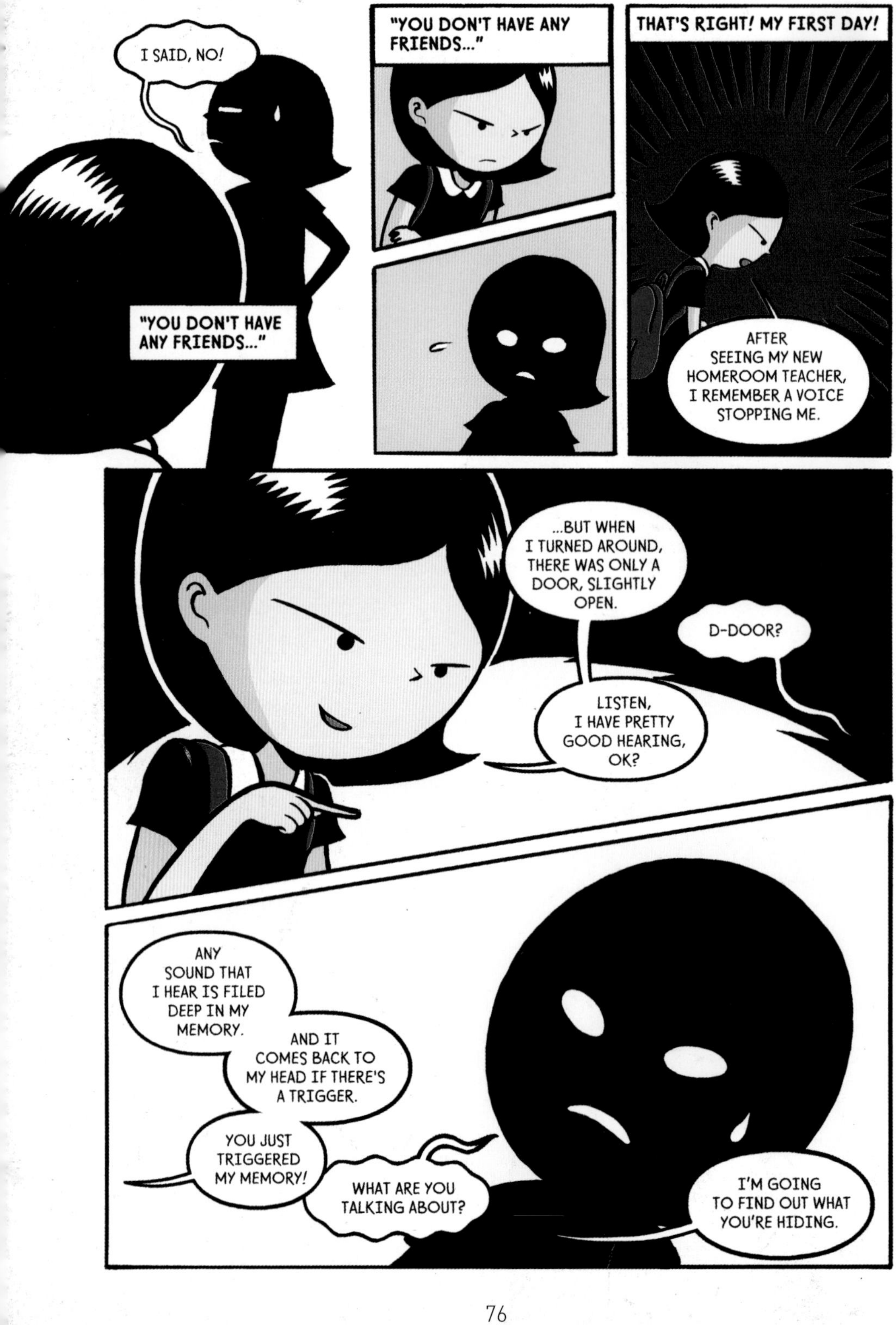
I SAID, NO!
"YOU DON'T HAVE ANY FRIENDS..."
"YOU DON'T HAVE ANY FRIENDS..."
THAT'S RIGHT! MY FIRST DAY!
AFTER SEEING MY NEW HOMEROOM TEACHER, I REMEMBER A VOICE STOPPING ME.
...BUT WHEN I TURNED AROUND, THERE WAS ONLY A DOOR, SLIGHTLY OPEN.
D-DOOR?
LISTEN, I HAVE PRETTY GOOD HEARING, OK?
ANY SOUND THAT I HEAR IS FILED DEEP IN MY MEMORY.
AND IT COMES BACK TO MY HEAD IF THERE'S A TRIGGER.
YOU JUST TRIGGERED MY MEMORY!
WHAT ARE YOU TALKING ABOUT?
I'M GOING TO FIND OUT WHAT YOU'RE HIDING.

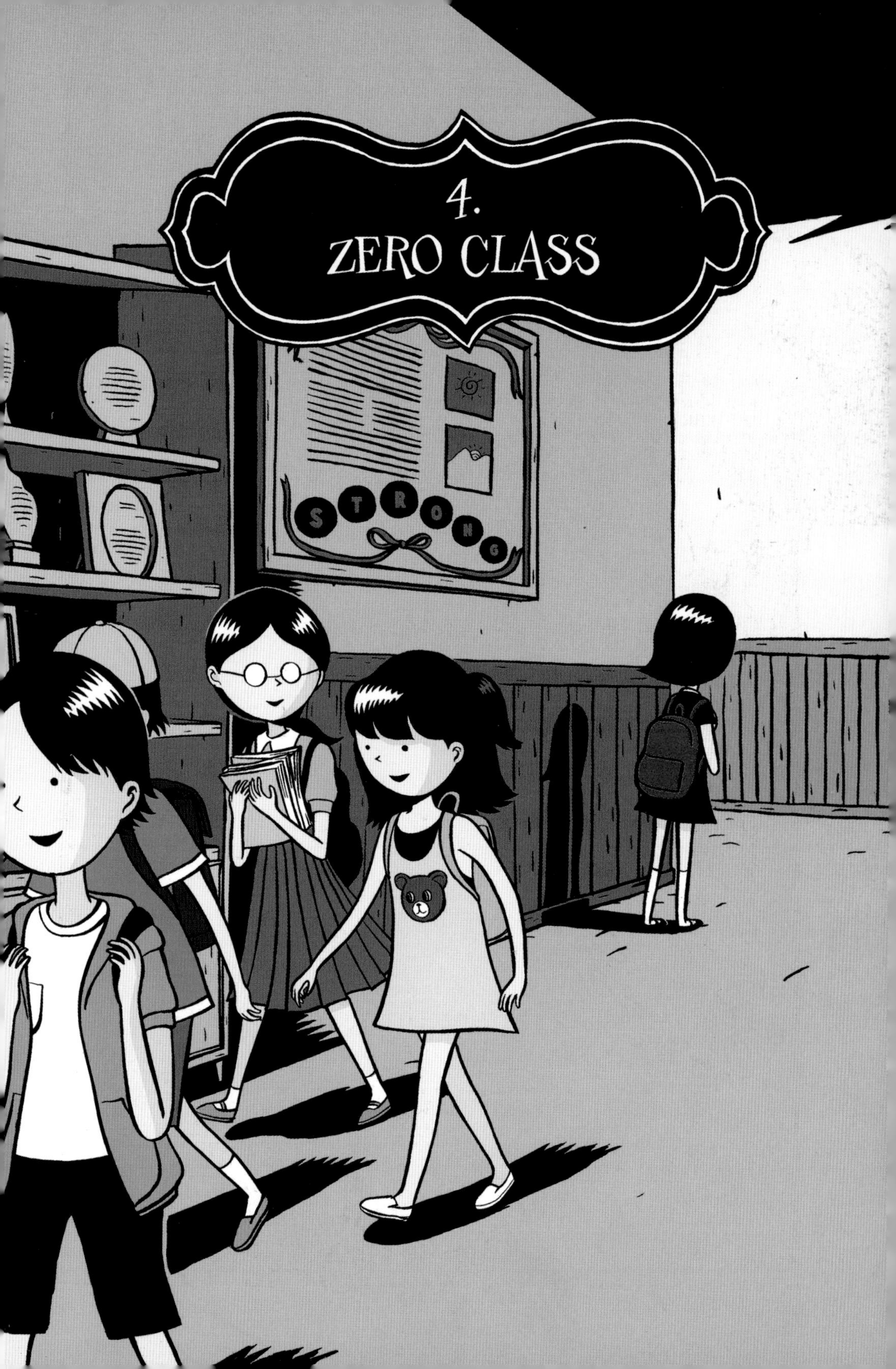
4.
ZERO CLASS
STRONG

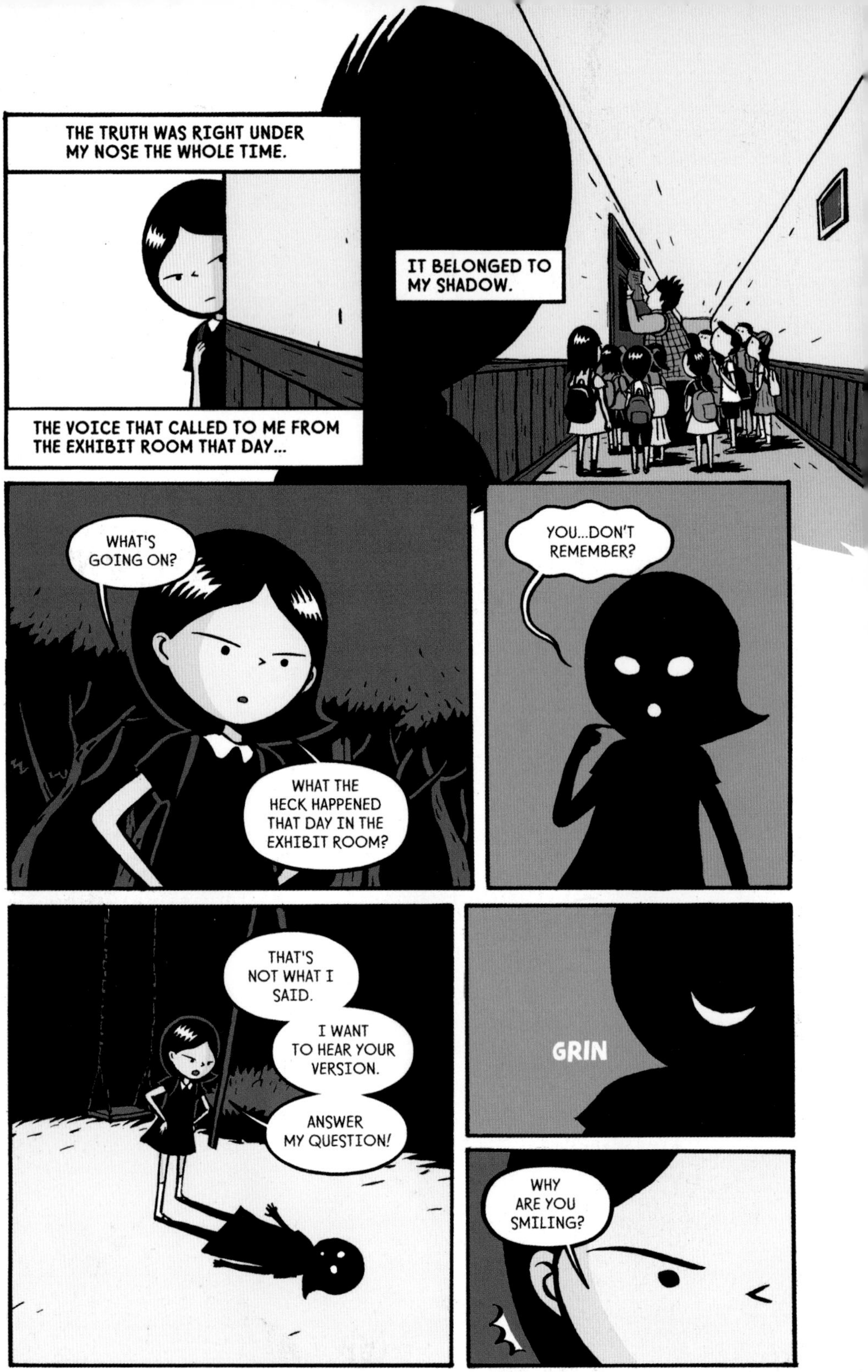
THE TRUTH WAS RIGHT UNDER MY NOSE THE WHOLE TIME.
IT BELONGED TO MY SHADOW.
THE VOICE THAT CALLED TO ME FROM THE EXHIBIT ROOM THAT DAY...
WHAT'S GOING ON?
WHAT THE HECK HAPPENED THAT DAY IN THE EXHIBIT ROOM?
YOU...DON'T REMEMBER?
THAT'S NOT WHAT I SAID.
I WANT TO HEAR YOUR VERSION.
ANSWER MY QUESTION!
GRIN
WHY ARE YOU SMILING?

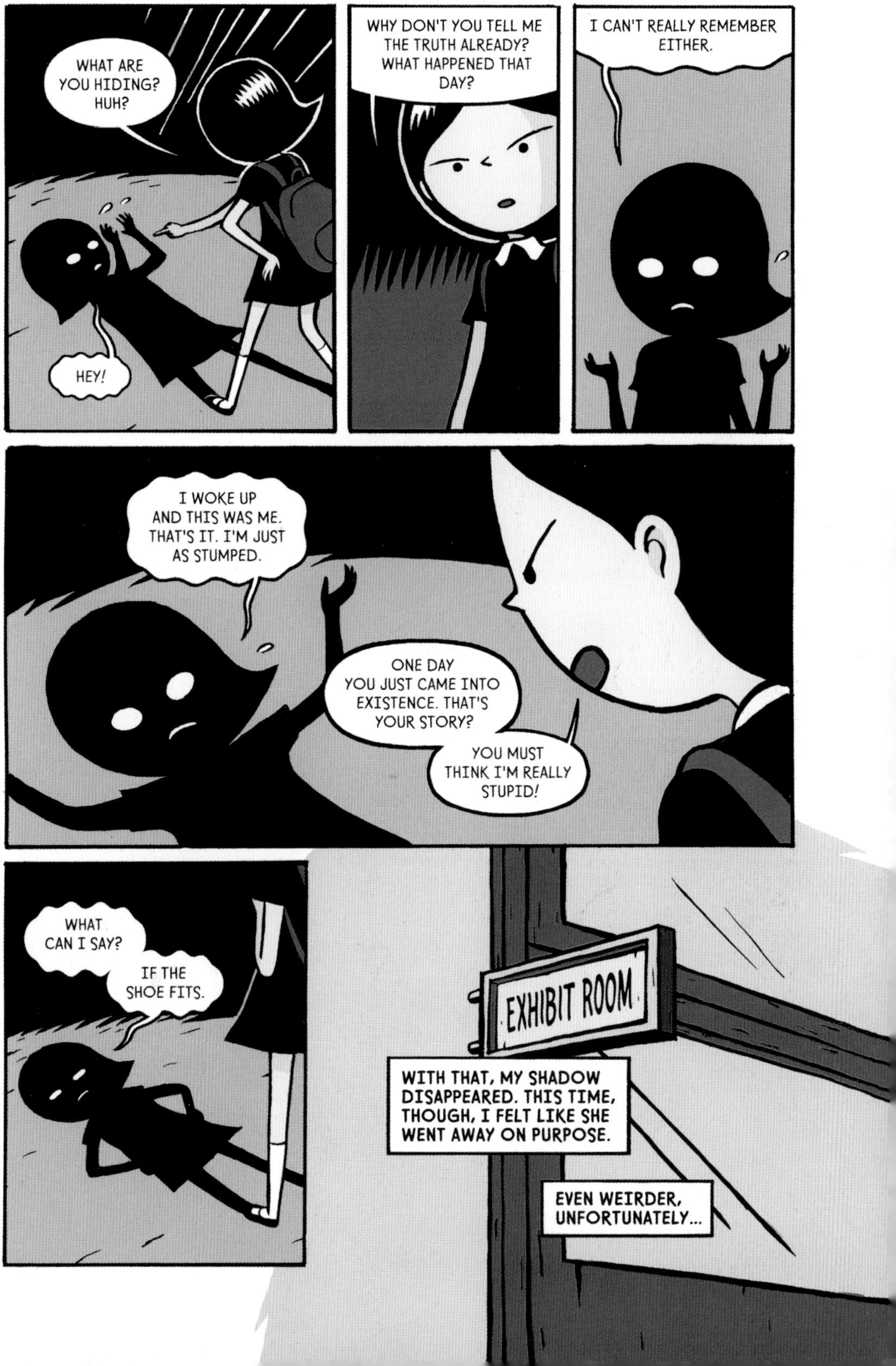
WHAT ARE YOU HIDING? HUH?
HEY!
WHY DON'T YOU TELL ME THE TRUTH ALREADY? WHAT HAPPENED THAT DAY?
I CAN'T REALLY REMEMBER EITHER.
I WOKE UP AND THIS WAS ME. THAT'S IT. I'M JUST AS STUMPED.
ONE DAY YOU JUST CAME INTO EXISTENCE. THAT'S YOUR STORY?
YOU MUST THINK I'M REALLY STUPID!
WHAT CAN I SAY?
IF THE SHOE FITS.
EXHIBIT ROOM
WITH THAT, MY SHADOW DISAPPEARED. THIS TIME, THOUGH, I FELT LIKE SHE WENT AWAY ON PURPOSE.
EVEN WEIRDER, UNFORTUNATELY...

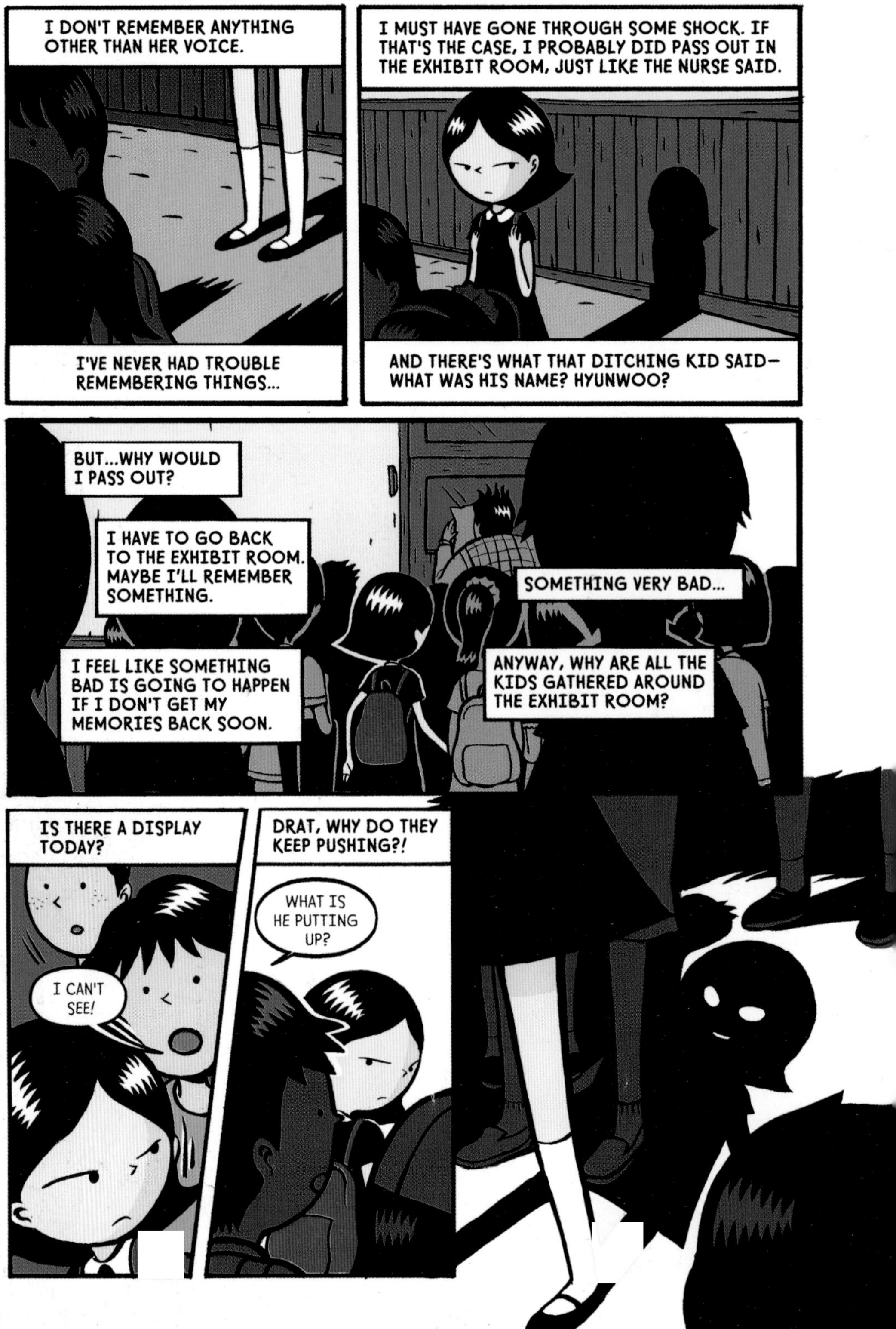

I DON'T REMEMBER ANYTHING OTHER THAN HER VOICE.
I'VE NEVER HAD TROUBLE REMEMBERING THINGS...
I MUST HAVE GONE THROUGH SOME SHOCK. IF THAT'S THE CASE, I PROBABLY DID PASS OUT IN THE EXHIBIT ROOM, JUST LIKE THE NURSE SAID.
AND THERE'S WHAT THAT DITCHING KID SAID—WHAT WAS HIS NAME? HYUNWOO?
BUT...WHY WOULD I PASS OUT?
I HAVE TO GO BACK TO THE EXHIBIT ROOM. MAYBE I'LL REMEMBER SOMETHING.
I FEEL LIKE SOMETHING BAD IS GOING TO HAPPEN IF I DON'T GET MY MEMORIES BACK SOON.
SOMETHING VERY BAD...
ANYWAY, WHY ARE ALL THE KIDS GATHERED AROUND THE EXHIBIT ROOM?
IS THERE A DISPLAY TODAY?
I CAN'T SEE!
DRAT, WHY DO THEY KEEP PUSHING?!
WHAT IS HE PUTTING UP?

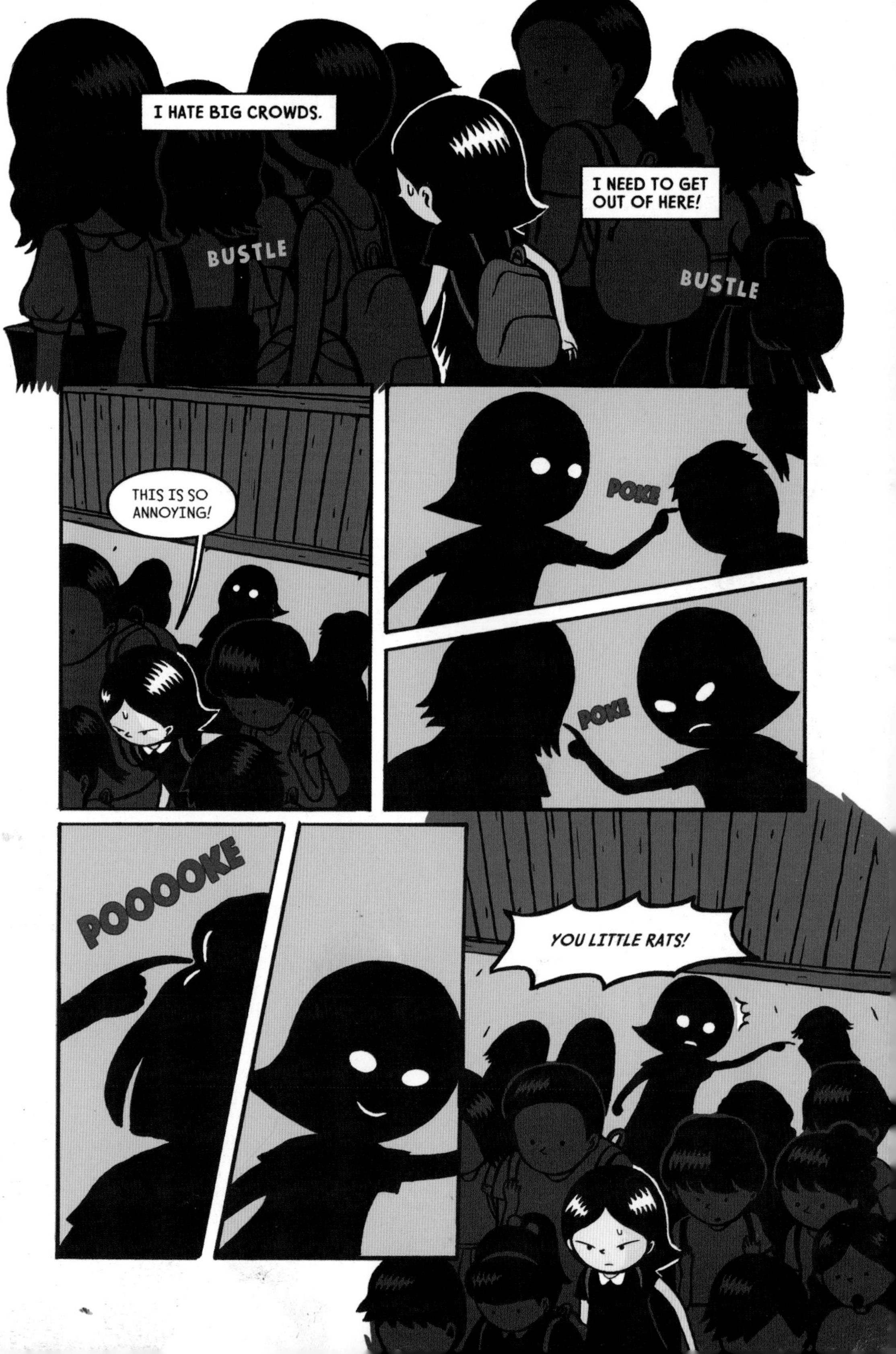
I HATE BIG CROWDS.
BUSTLE
I NEED TO GET OUT OF HERE!
BUSTLE
THIS IS SO ANNOYING!
POKE
POKE
POOOOKE
YOU LITTLE RATS!

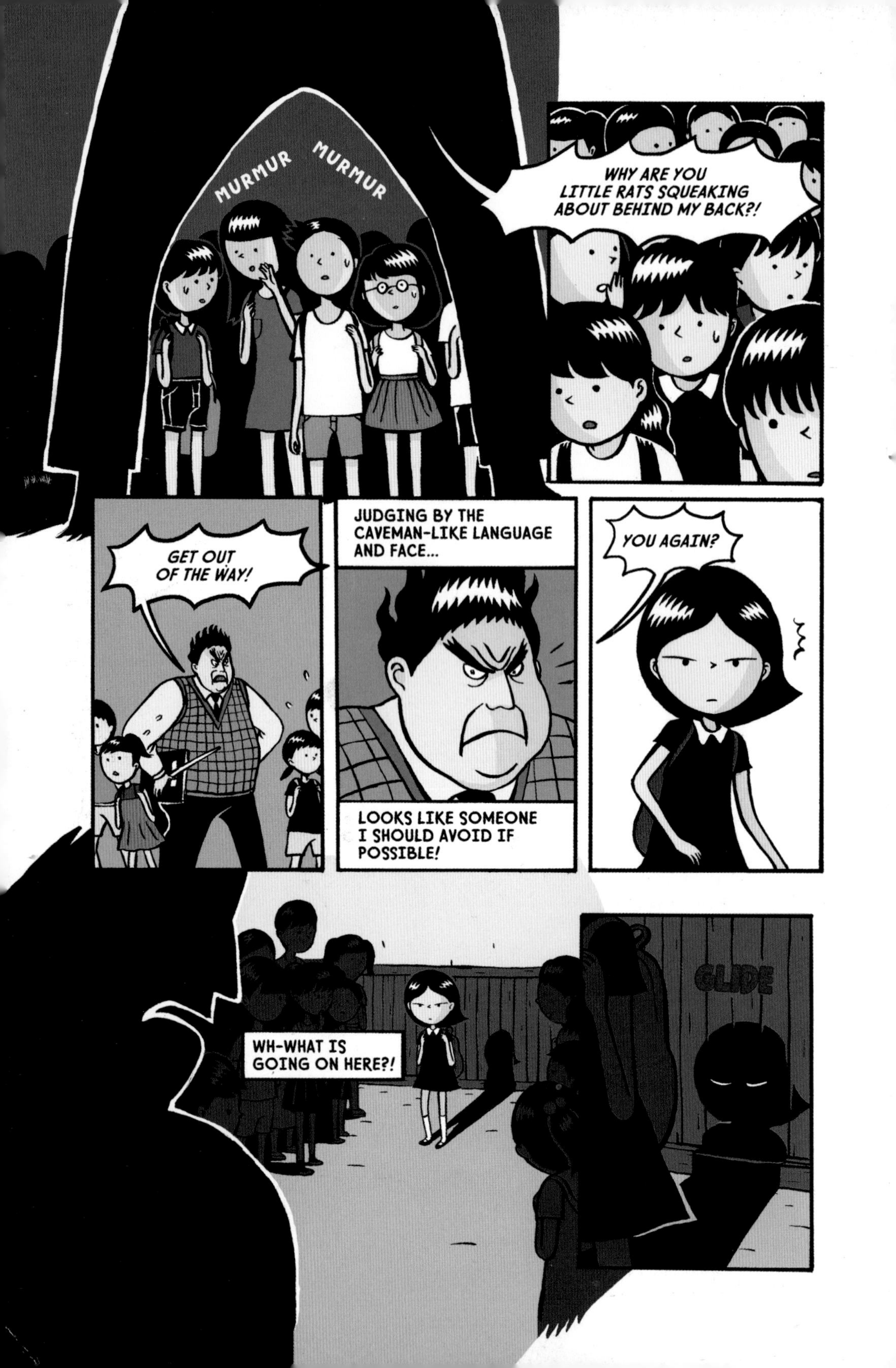
MURMUR MURMUR
WHY ARE YOU LITTLE RATS SQUEAKING ABOUT BEHIND MY BACK?!
GET OUT OF THE WAY!
JUDGING BY THE CAVEMAN-LIKE LANGUAGE AND FACE...
LOOKS LIKE SOMEONE I SHOULD AVOID IF POSSIBLE!
YOU AGAIN?
WH-WHAT IS GOING ON HERE?!
GLIDE

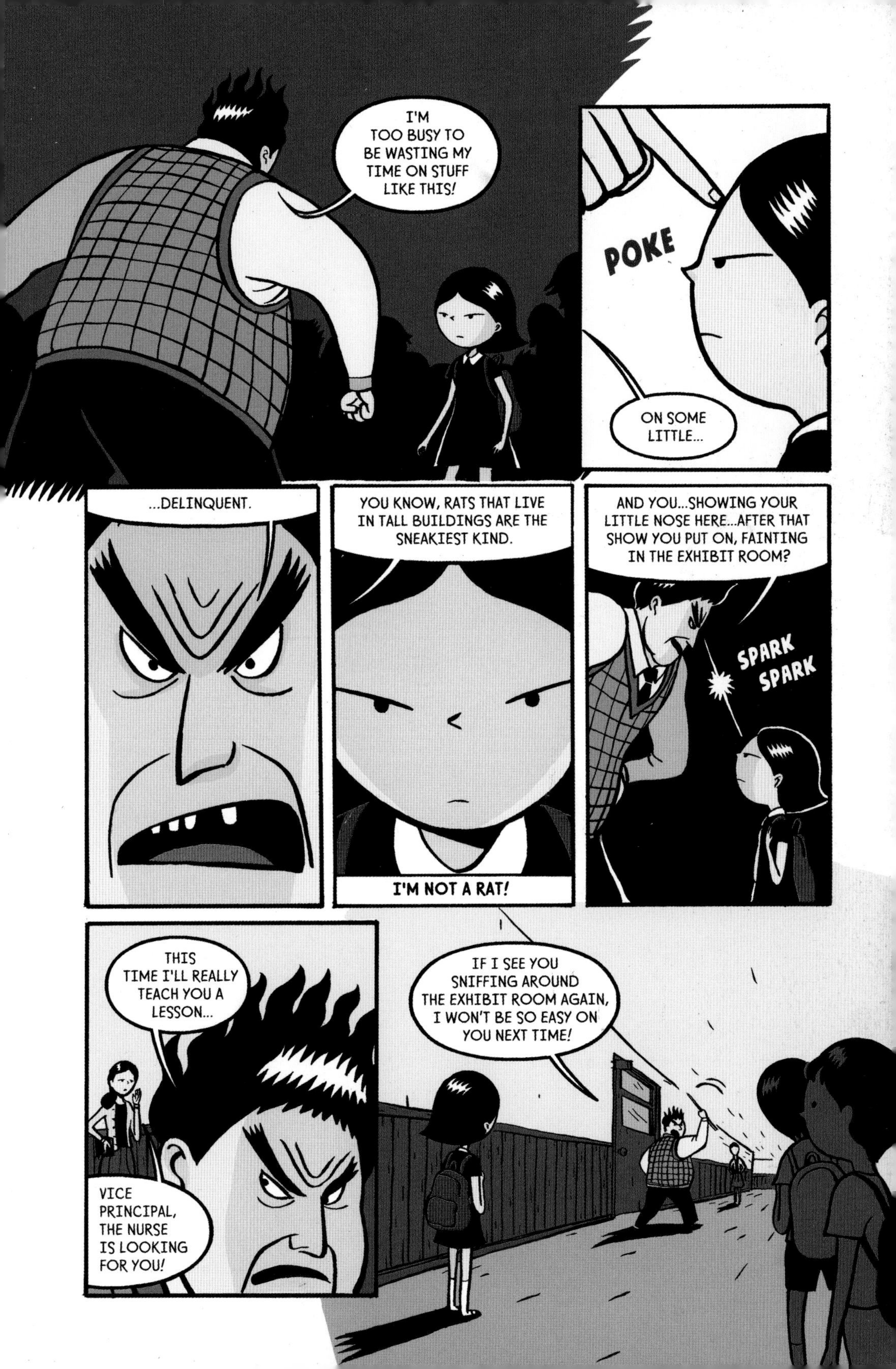
I'M TOO BUSY TO BE WASTING MY TIME ON STUFF LIKE THIS!
POKE
ON SOME LITTLE...
...DELINQUENT.
YOU KNOW, RATS THAT LIVE IN TALL BUILDINGS ARE THE SNEAKIEST KIND.
I'M NOT A RAT!
AND YOU...SHOWING YOUR LITTLE NOSE HERE...AFTER THAT SHOW YOU PUT ON, FAINTING IN THE EXHIBIT ROOM?
SPARK SPARK
THIS TIME I'LL REALLY TEACH YOU A LESSON...
VICE PRINCIPAL, THE NURSE IS LOOKING FOR YOU!
IF I SEE YOU SNIFFING AROUND THE EXHIBIT ROOM AGAIN, I WON'T BE SO EASY ON YOU NEXT TIME!

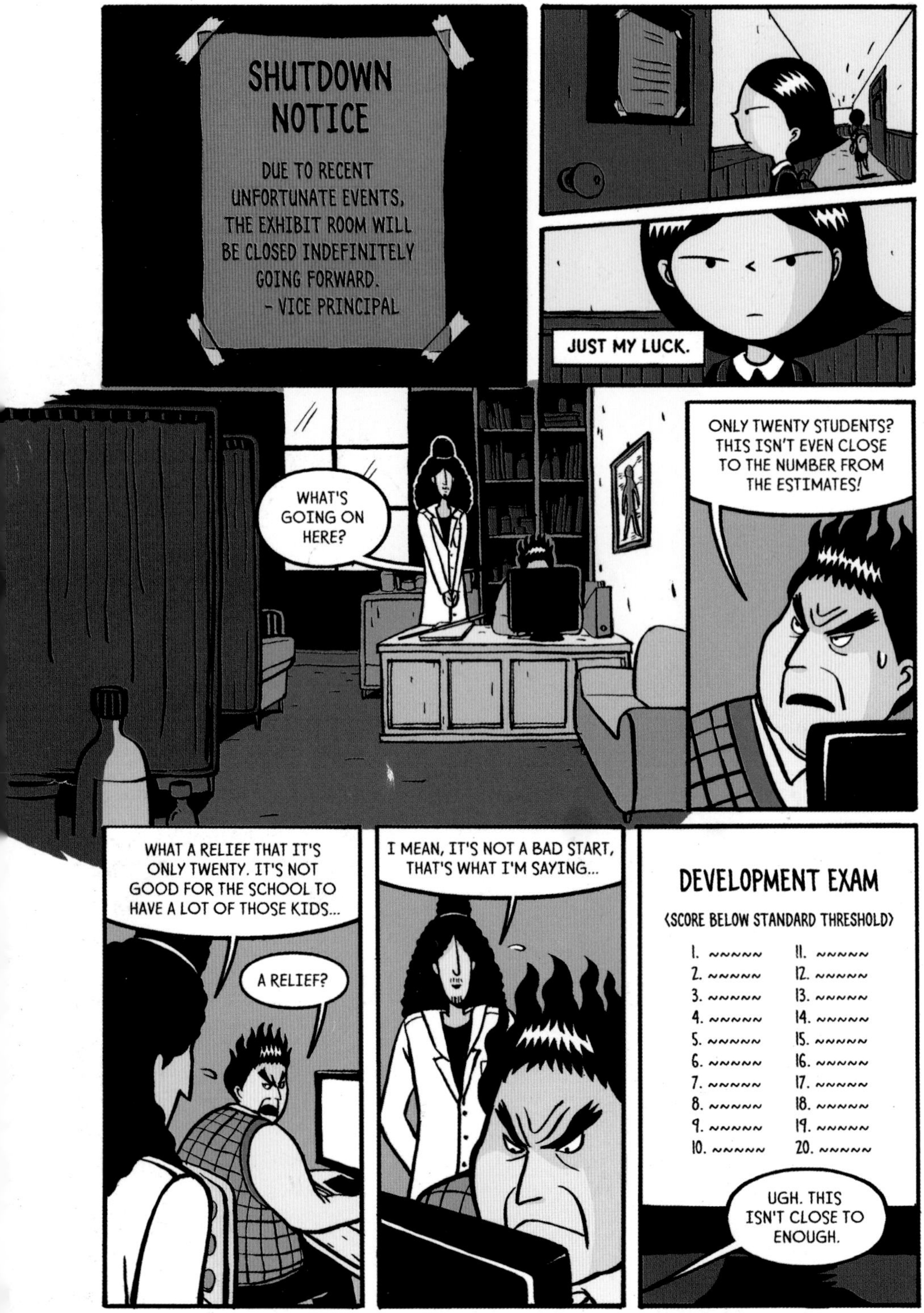
SHUTDOWN NOTICE
DUE TO RECENT UNFORTUNATE EVENTS, THE EXHIBIT ROOM WILL BE CLOSED INDEFINITELY GOING FORWARD. - VICE PRINCIPAL
JUST MY LUCK.
WHAT'S GOING ON HERE?
ONLY TWENTY STUDENTS? THIS ISN'T EVEN CLOSE TO THE NUMBER FROM THE ESTIMATES!
WHAT A RELIEF THAT IT'S ONLY TWENTY. IT'S NOT GOOD FOR THE SCHOOL TO HAVE A LOT OF THOSE KIDS...
A RELIEF?
I MEAN, IT'S NOT A BAD START, THAT'S WHAT I'M SAYING...
DEVELOPMENT EXAM
⟨SCORE BELOW STANDARD THRESHOLD⟩
1. ~~~~~
2. ~~~~~
3. ~~~~~
4. ~~~~~
5. ~~~~~
6. ~~~~~
7. ~~~~~
8. ~~~~~
9. ~~~~~
10. ~~~~~
11. ~~~~~
12. ~~~~~
13. ~~~~~
14. ~~~~~
15. ~~~~~
16. ~~~~~
17. ~~~~~
18. ~~~~~
19. ~~~~~
20. ~~~~~
UGH. THIS ISN'T CLOSE TO ENOUGH.

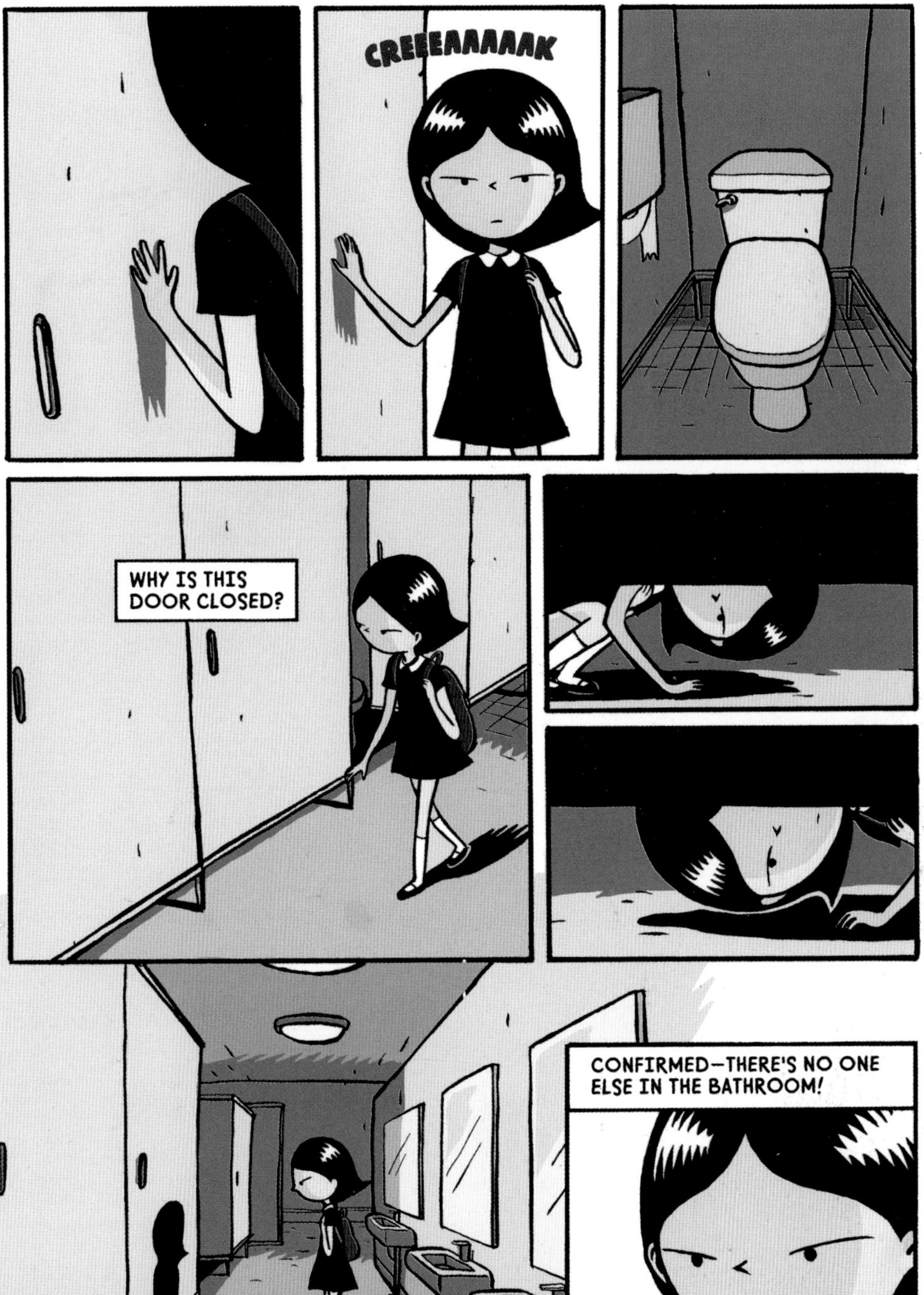
CREEEAAAAAK
WHY IS THIS DOOR CLOSED?
CONFIRMED—THERE'S NO ONE ELSE IN THE BATHROOM!

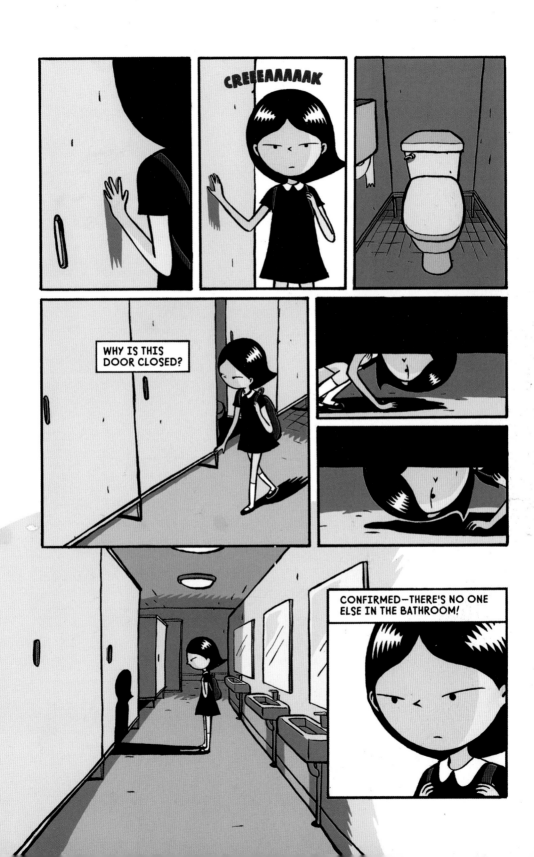

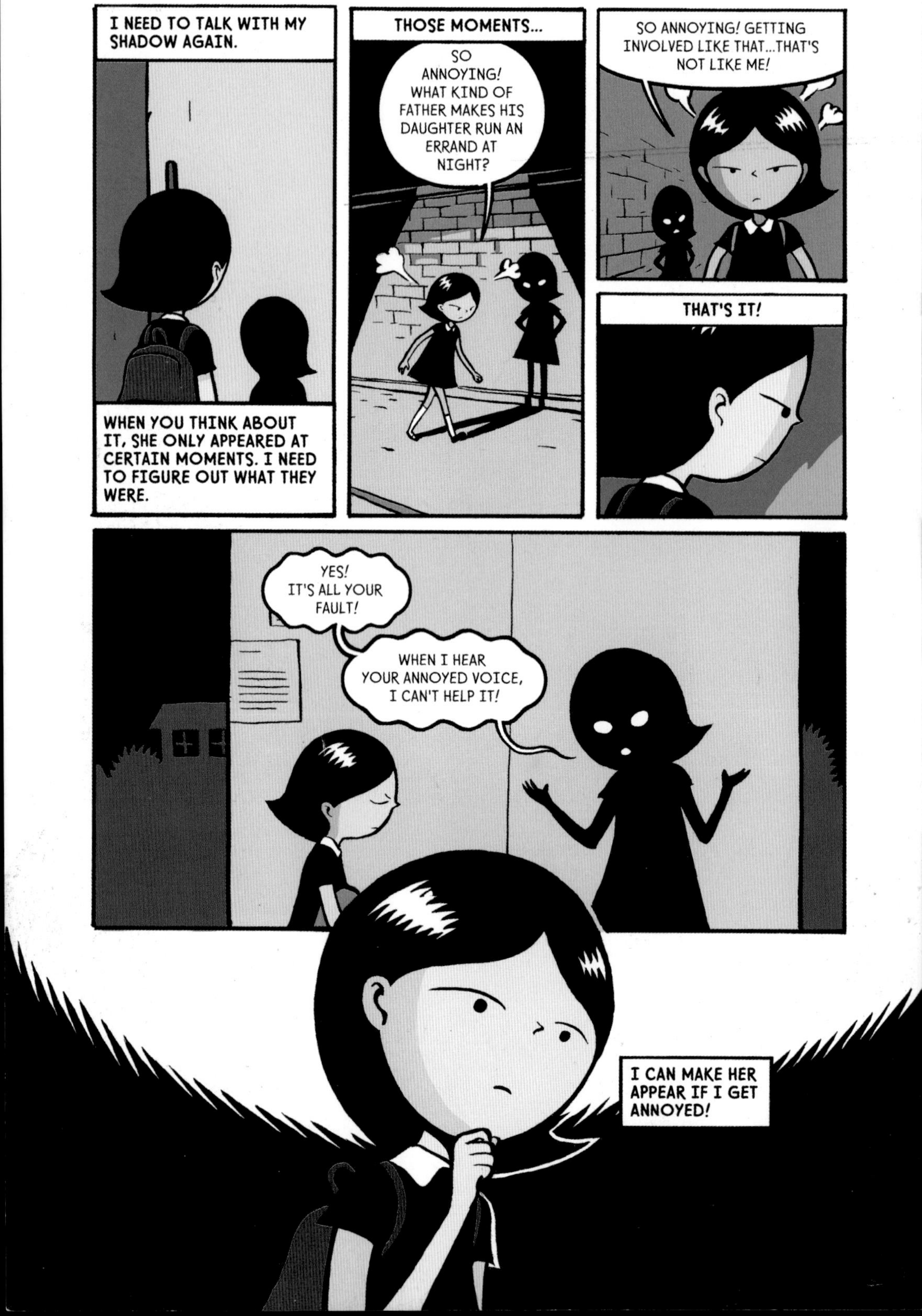

I NEED TO TALK WITH MY SHADOW AGAIN.
WHEN YOU THINK ABOUT IT, SHE ONLY APPEARED AT CERTAIN MOMENTS. I NEED TO FIGURE OUT WHAT THEY WERE.
THOSE MOMENTS...
SO ANNOYING! WHAT KIND OF FATHER MAKES HIS DAUGHTER RUN AN ERRAND AT NIGHT?
SO ANNOYING! GETTING INVOLVED LIKE THAT...THAT'S NOT LIKE ME!
THAT'S IT!
YES! IT'S ALL YOUR FAULT!
WHEN I HEAR YOUR ANNOYED VOICE, I CAN'T HELP IT!
I CAN MAKE HER APPEAR IF I GET ANNOYED!

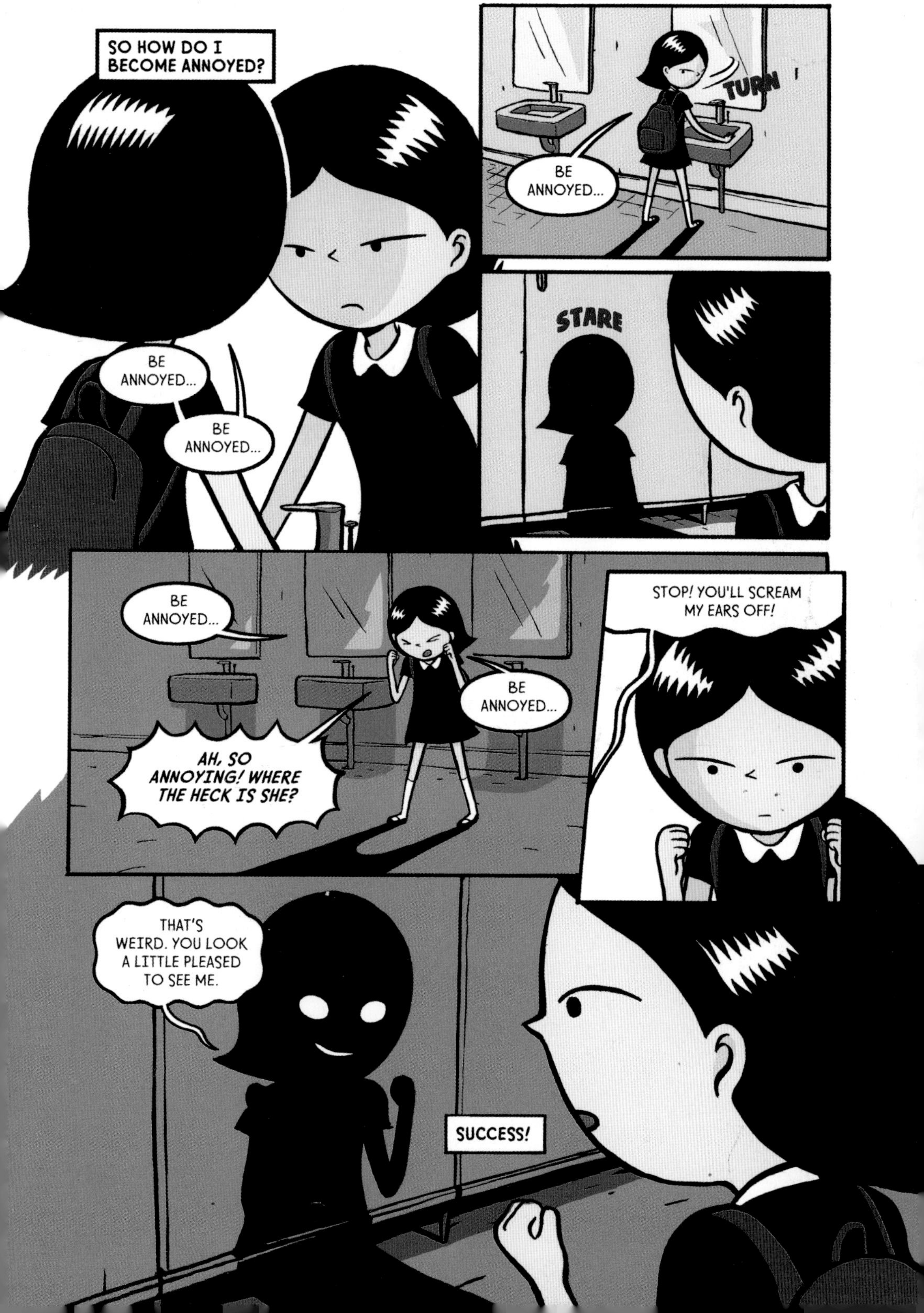
SO HOW DO I BECOME ANNOYED?
BE ANNOYED...
BE ANNOYED...
BE ANNOYED...
TURN
STARE
BE ANNOYED...
BE ANNOYED...
AH, SO ANNOYING! WHERE THE HECK IS SHE?
STOP! YOU'LL SCREAM MY EARS OFF!
THAT'S WEIRD. YOU LOOK A LITTLE PLEASED TO SEE ME.
SUCCESS!

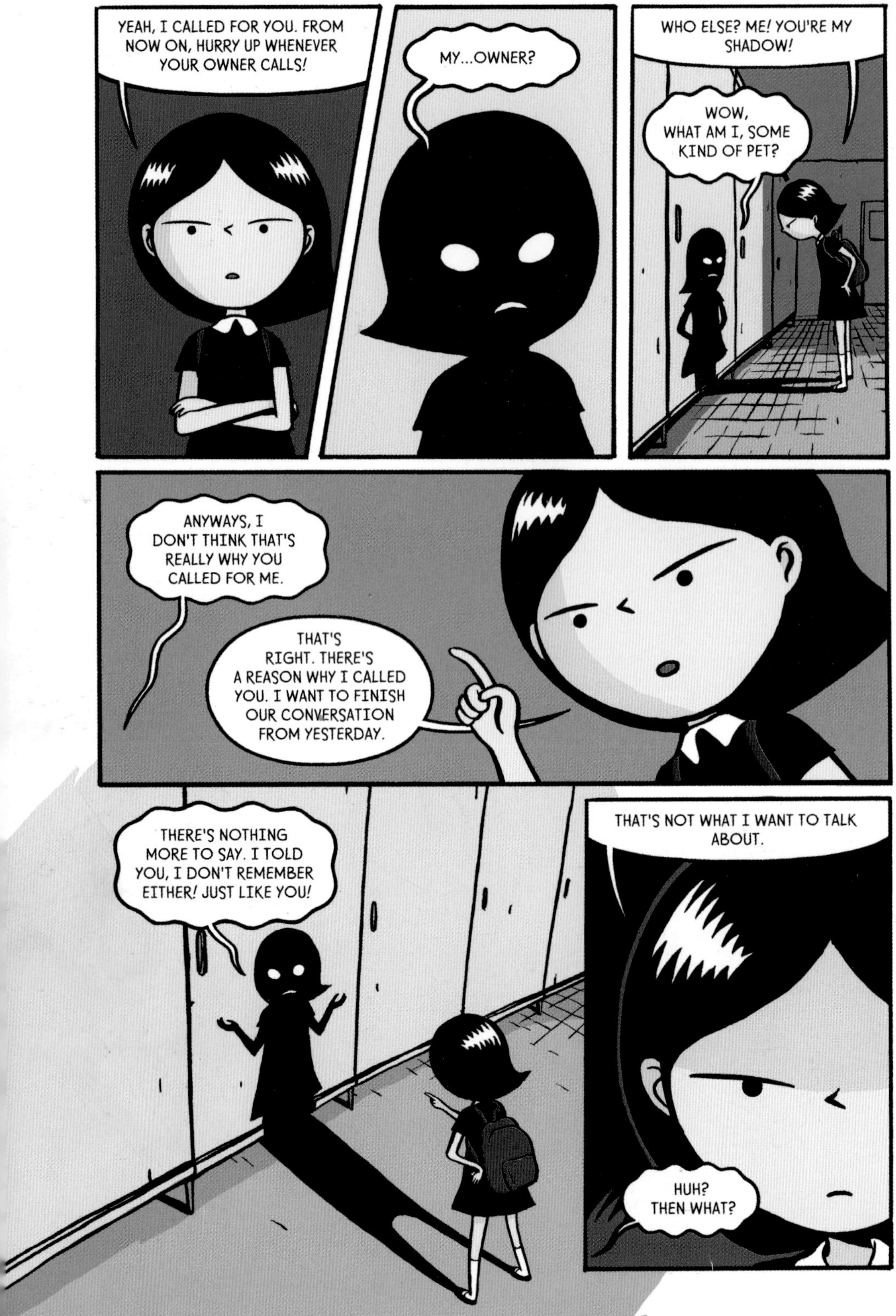
YEAH, I CALLED FOR YOU. FROM NOW ON, HURRY UP WHENEVER YOUR OWNER CALLS!
MY...OWNER?
WHO ELSE? ME! YOU'RE MY SHADOW!
WOW, WHAT AM I, SOME KIND OF PET?
ANYWAYS, I DON'T THINK THAT'S REALLY WHY YOU CALLED FOR ME.
THAT'S RIGHT. THERE'S A REASON WHY I CALLED YOU. I WANT TO FINISH OUR CONVERSATION FROM YESTERDAY.
THERE'S NOTHING MORE TO SAY. I TOLD YOU, I DON'T REMEMBER EITHER! JUST LIKE YOU!
THAT'S NOT WHAT I WANT TO TALK ABOUT.
HUH? THEN WHAT?

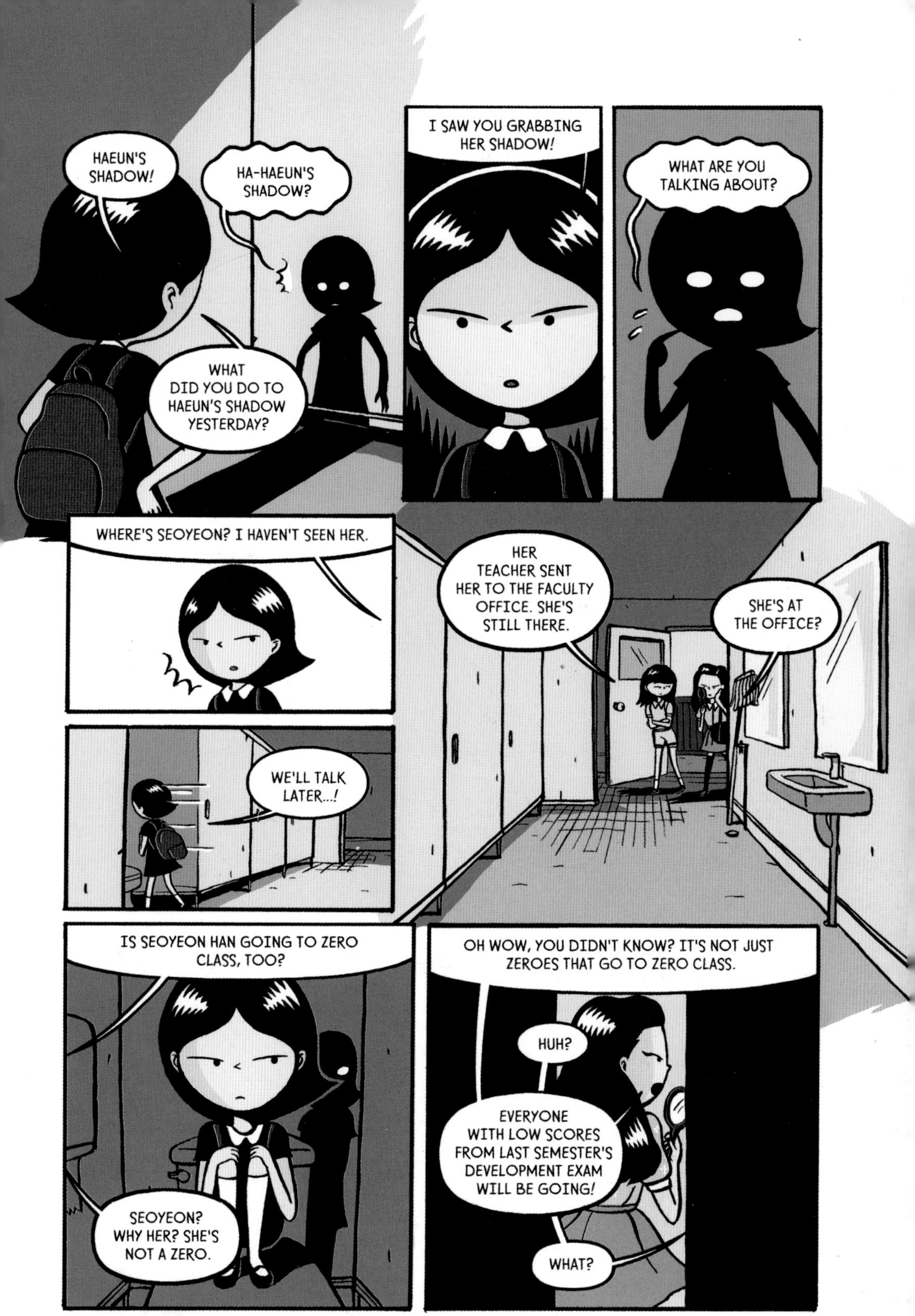
HAEUN'S SHADOW!
HA-HAEUN'S SHADOW?
WHAT DID YOU DO TO HAEUN'S SHADOW YESTERDAY?
I SAW YOU GRABBING HER SHADOW!
WHAT ARE YOU TALKING ABOUT?
WHERE'S SEOYEON? I HAVEN'T SEEN HER.
HER TEACHER SENT HER TO THE FACULTY OFFICE. SHE'S STILL THERE.
SHE'S AT THE OFFICE?
WE'LL TALK LATER...!
IS SEOYEON HAN GOING TO ZERO CLASS, TOO?
SEOYEON? WHY HER? SHE'S NOT A ZERO.
OH WOW, YOU DIDN'T KNOW? IT'S NOT JUST ZEROES THAT GO TO ZERO CLASS.
HUH?
EVERYONE WITH LOW SCORES FROM LAST SEMESTER'S DEVELOPMENT EXAM WILL BE GOING!
WHAT?

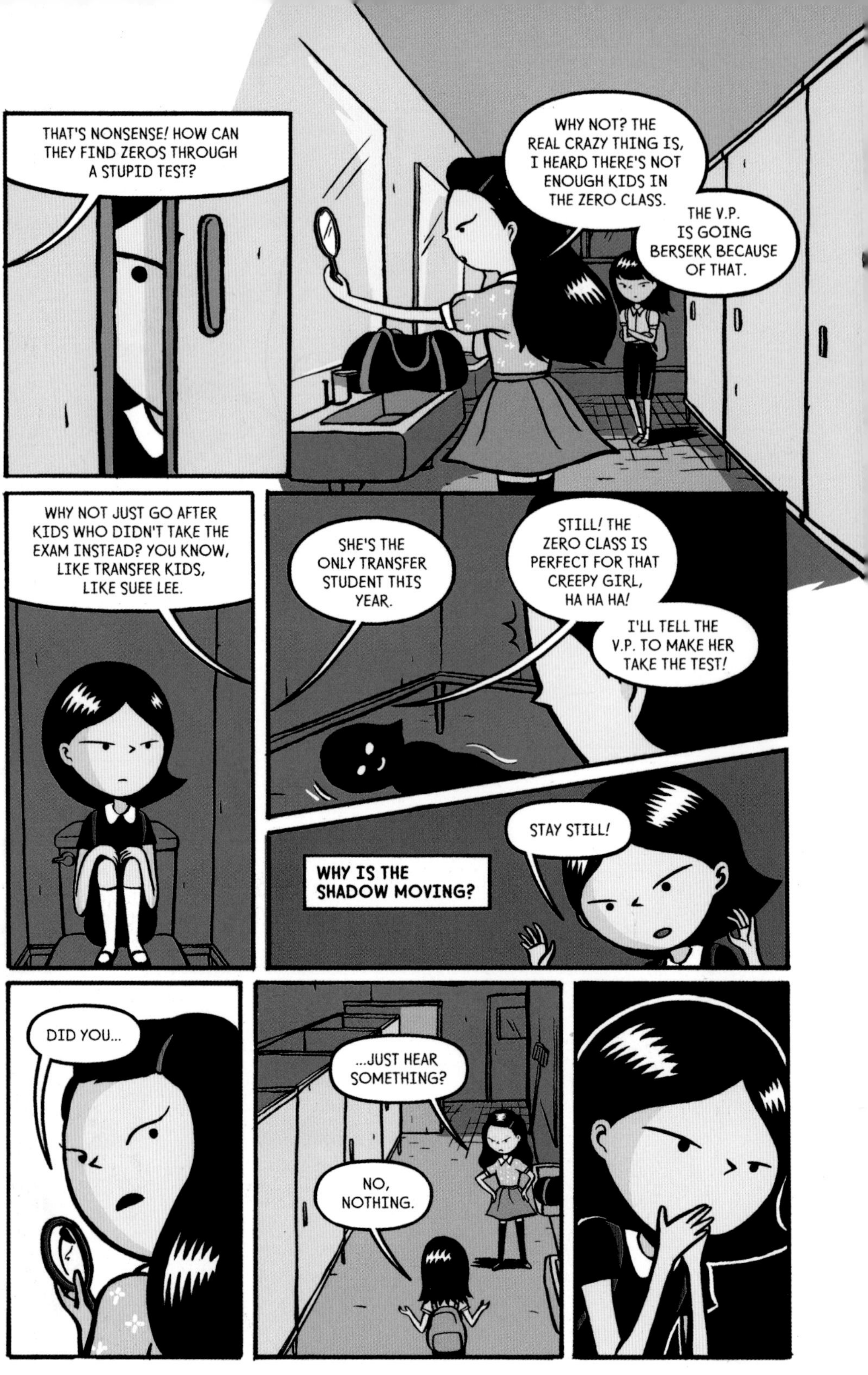
THAT'S NONSENSE! HOW CAN THEY FIND ZEROS THROUGH A STUPID TEST?
WHY NOT? THE REAL CRAZY THING IS, I HEARD THERE'S NOT ENOUGH KIDS IN THE ZERO CLASS.
THE V.P. IS GOING BERSERK BECAUSE OF THAT.
WHY NOT JUST GO AFTER KIDS WHO DIDN'T TAKE THE EXAM INSTEAD? YOU KNOW, LIKE TRANSFER KIDS, LIKE SUEE LEE.
SHE'S THE ONLY TRANSFER STUDENT THIS YEAR.
STILL! THE ZERO CLASS IS PERFECT FOR THAT CREEPY GIRL, HA HA HA!
I'LL TELL THE V.P. TO MAKE HER TAKE THE TEST!
WHY IS THE SHADOW MOVING?
STAY STILL!
DID YOU...
...JUST HEAR SOMETHING?
NO, NOTHING.

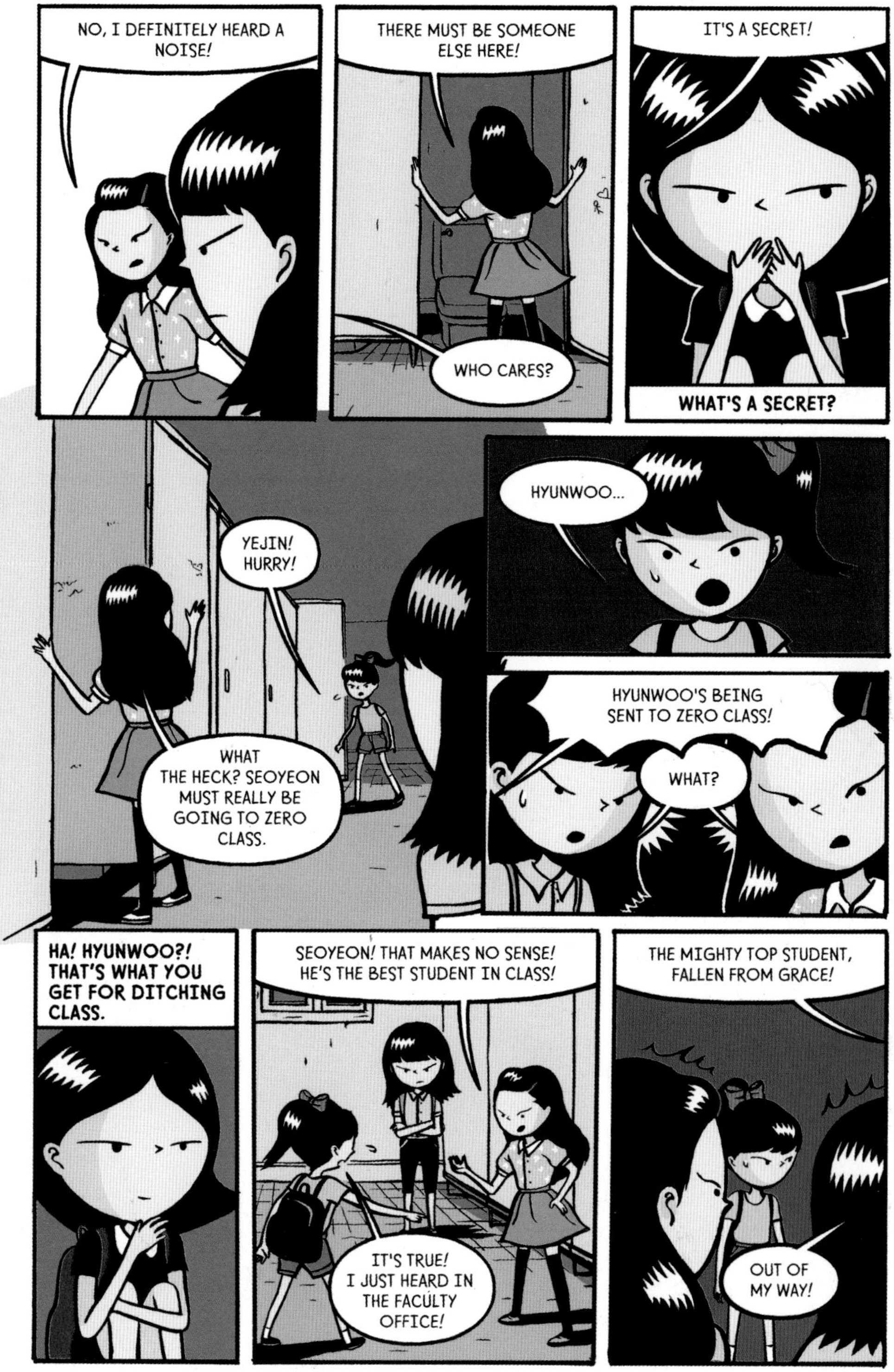
NO, I DEFINITELY HEARD A NOISE!
THERE MUST BE SOMEONE ELSE HERE!
WHO CARES?
IT'S A SECRET!
WHAT'S A SECRET?
YEJIN! HURRY!
WHAT THE HECK? SEOYEON MUST REALLY BE GOING TO ZERO CLASS.
HYUNWOO...
HYUNWOO'S BEING SENT TO ZERO CLASS!
WHAT?
HA! HYUNWOO?! THAT'S WHAT YOU GET FOR DITCHING CLASS.
SEOYEON! THAT MAKES NO SENSE! HE'S THE BEST STUDENT IN CLASS!
IT'S TRUE! I JUST HEARD IN THE FACULTY OFFICE!
THE MIGHTY TOP STUDENT, FALLEN FROM GRACE!
OUT OF MY WAY!

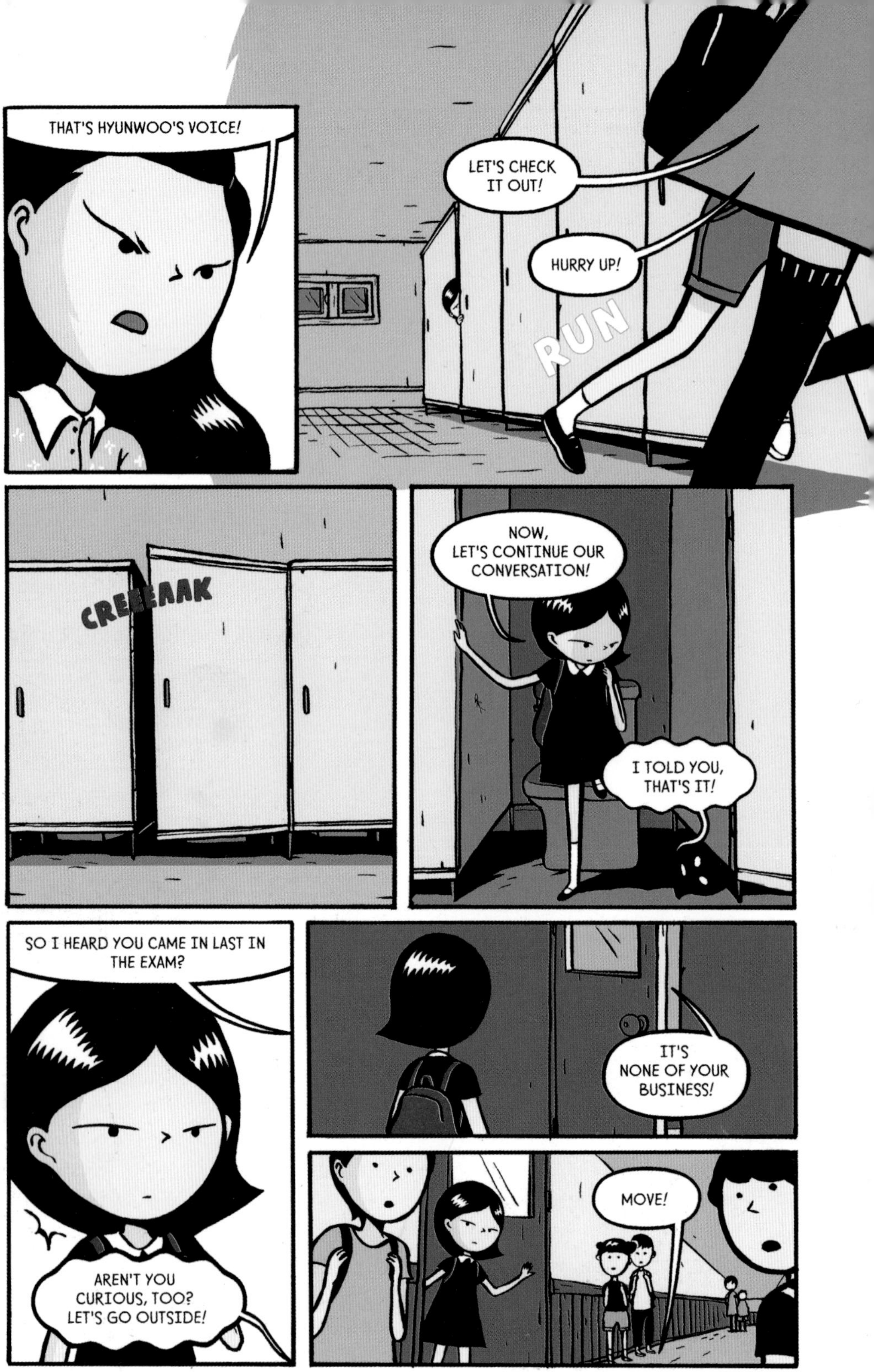
THAT'S HYUNWOO'S VOICE!
LET'S CHECK IT OUT!
HURRY UP!
RUN
CREEEAAK
NOW, LET'S CONTINUE OUR CONVERSATION!
I TOLD YOU, THAT'S IT!
SO I HEARD YOU CAME IN LAST IN THE EXAM?
AREN'T YOU CURIOUS, TOO? LET'S GO OUTSIDE!
IT'S NONE OF YOUR BUSINESS!
MOVE!

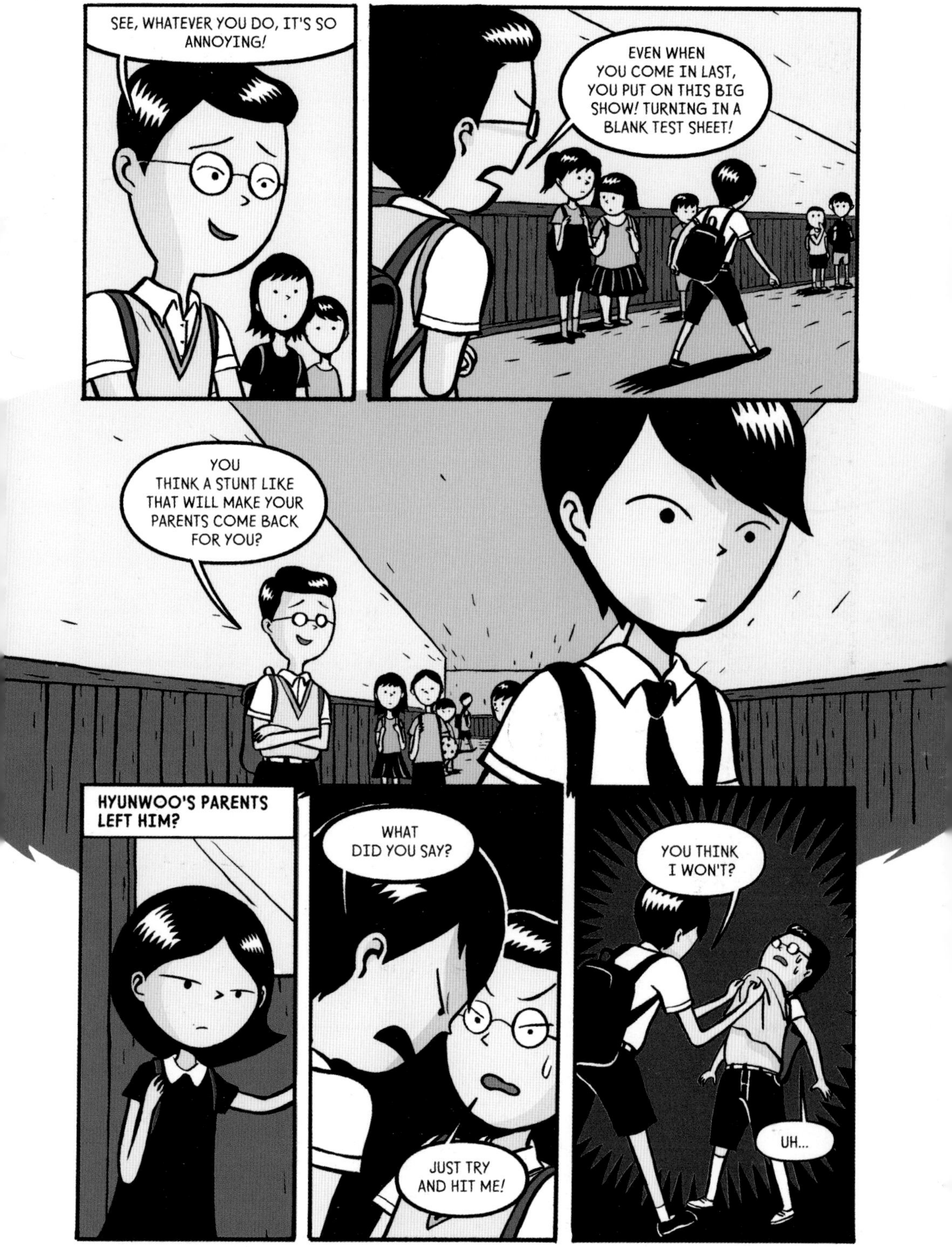
SEE, WHATEVER YOU DO, IT'S SO ANNOYING!
EVEN WHEN YOU COME IN LAST, YOU PUT ON THIS BIG SHOW! TURNING IN A BLANK TEST SHEET!
YOU THINK A STUNT LIKE THAT WILL MAKE YOUR PARENTS COME BACK FOR YOU?
HYUNWOO'S PARENTS LEFT HIM?
WHAT DID YOU SAY?
JUST TRY AND HIT ME!
YOU THINK I WON'T?
UH...

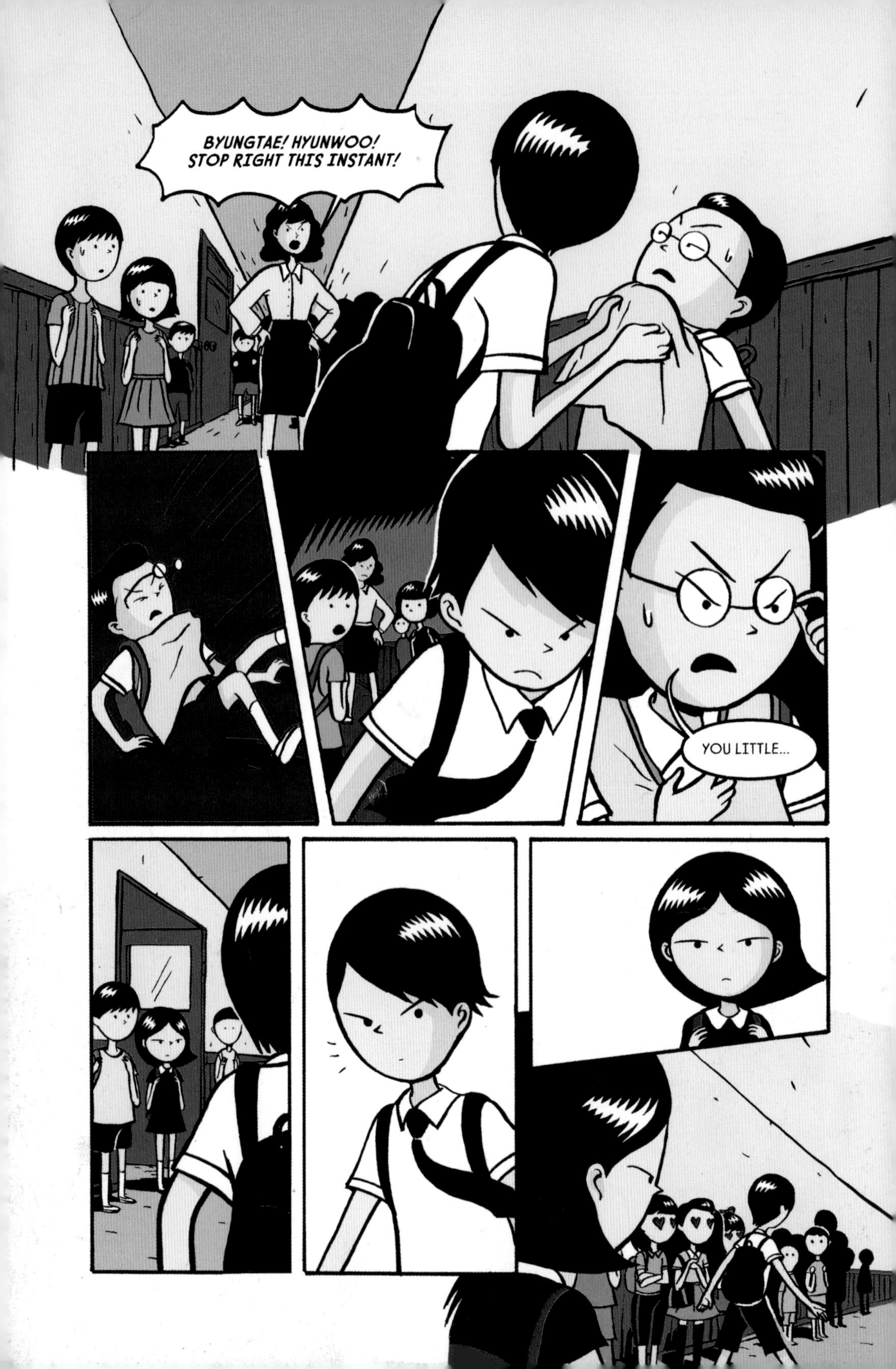
BYUNGTAE! HYUNWOO! STOP RIGHT THIS INSTANT!
YOU LITTLE...

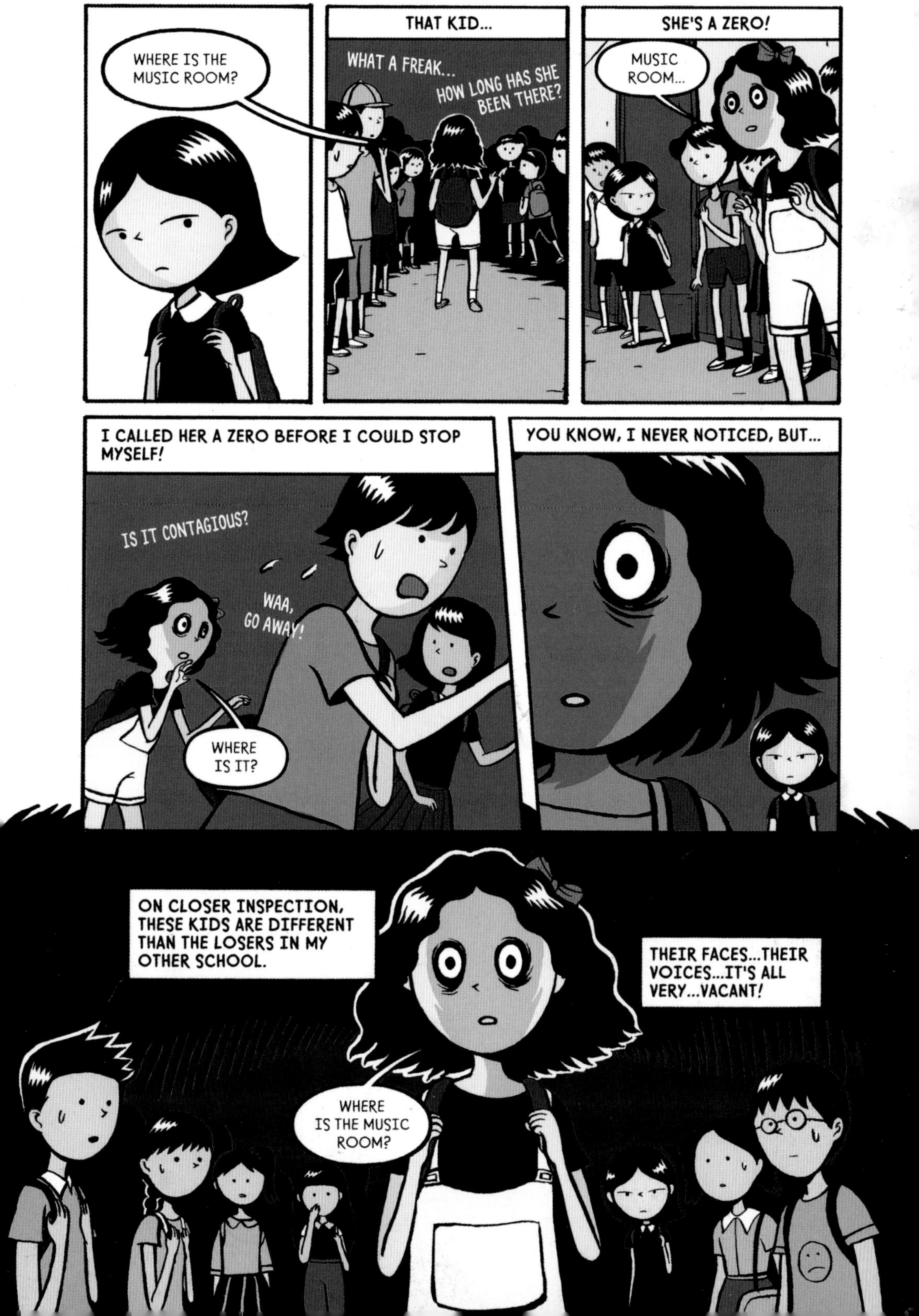
WHERE IS THE MUSIC ROOM?
THAT KID...
WHAT A FREAK...
HOW LONG HAS SHE BEEN THERE?
SHE'S A ZERO!
MUSIC ROOM...
I CALLED HER A ZERO BEFORE I COULD STOP MYSELF!
IS IT CONTAGIOUS?
WAA, GO AWAY!
WHERE IS IT?
YOU KNOW, I NEVER NOTICED, BUT...
ON CLOSER INSPECTION, THESE KIDS ARE DIFFERENT THAN THE LOSERS IN MY OTHER SCHOOL.
THEIR FACES...THEIR VOICES...IT'S ALL VERY...VACANT!
WHERE IS THE MUSIC ROOM?

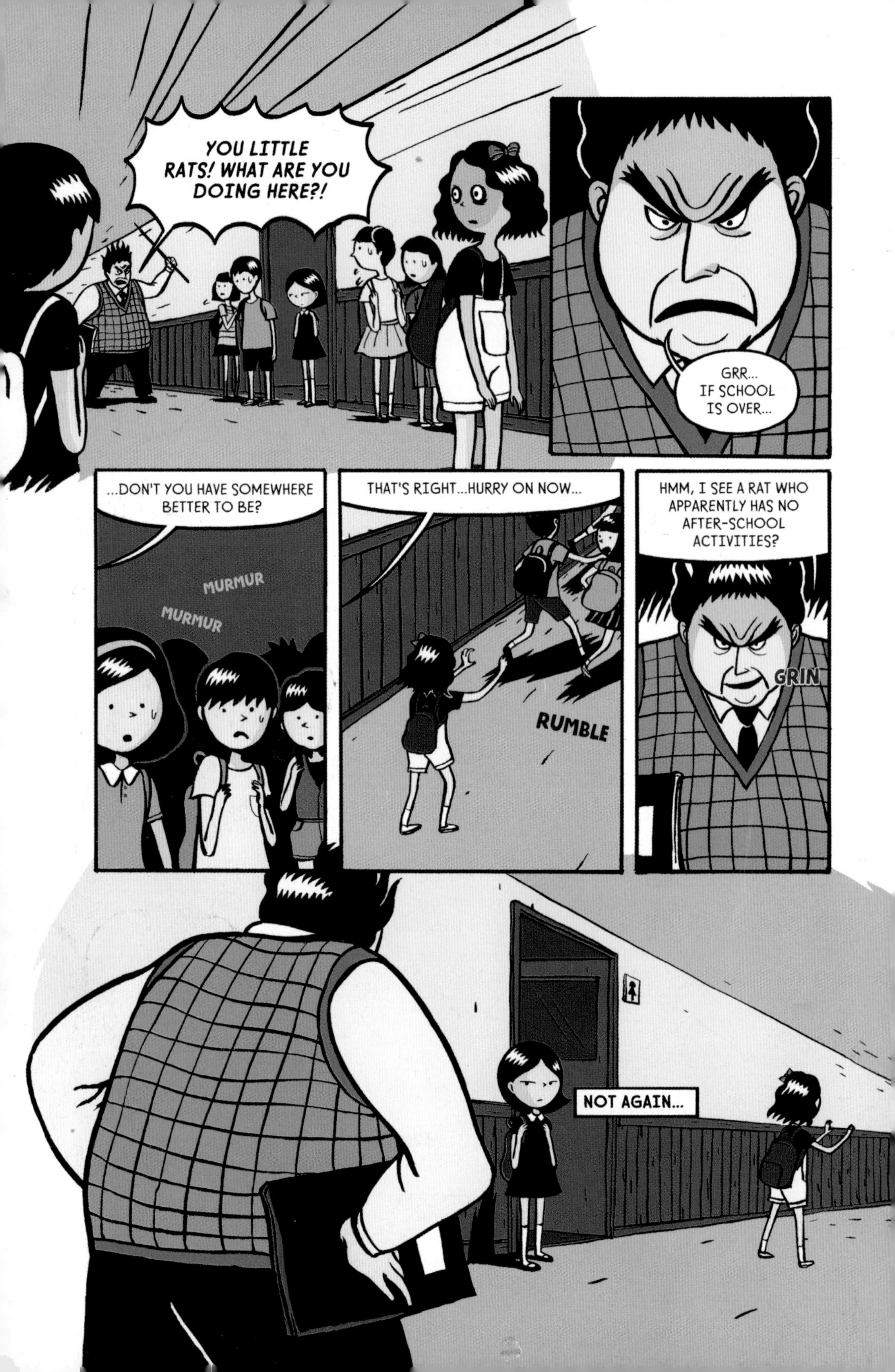

YOU LITTLE RATS! WHAT ARE YOU DOING HERE?!
GRR... IF SCHOOL IS OVER...
...DON'T YOU HAVE SOMEWHERE BETTER TO BE?
MURMUR
MURMUR
THAT'S RIGHT...HURRY ON NOW...
RUMBLE
HMM, I SEE A RAT WHO APPARENTLY HAS NO AFTER-SCHOOL ACTIVITIES?
GRIN
NOT AGAIN...

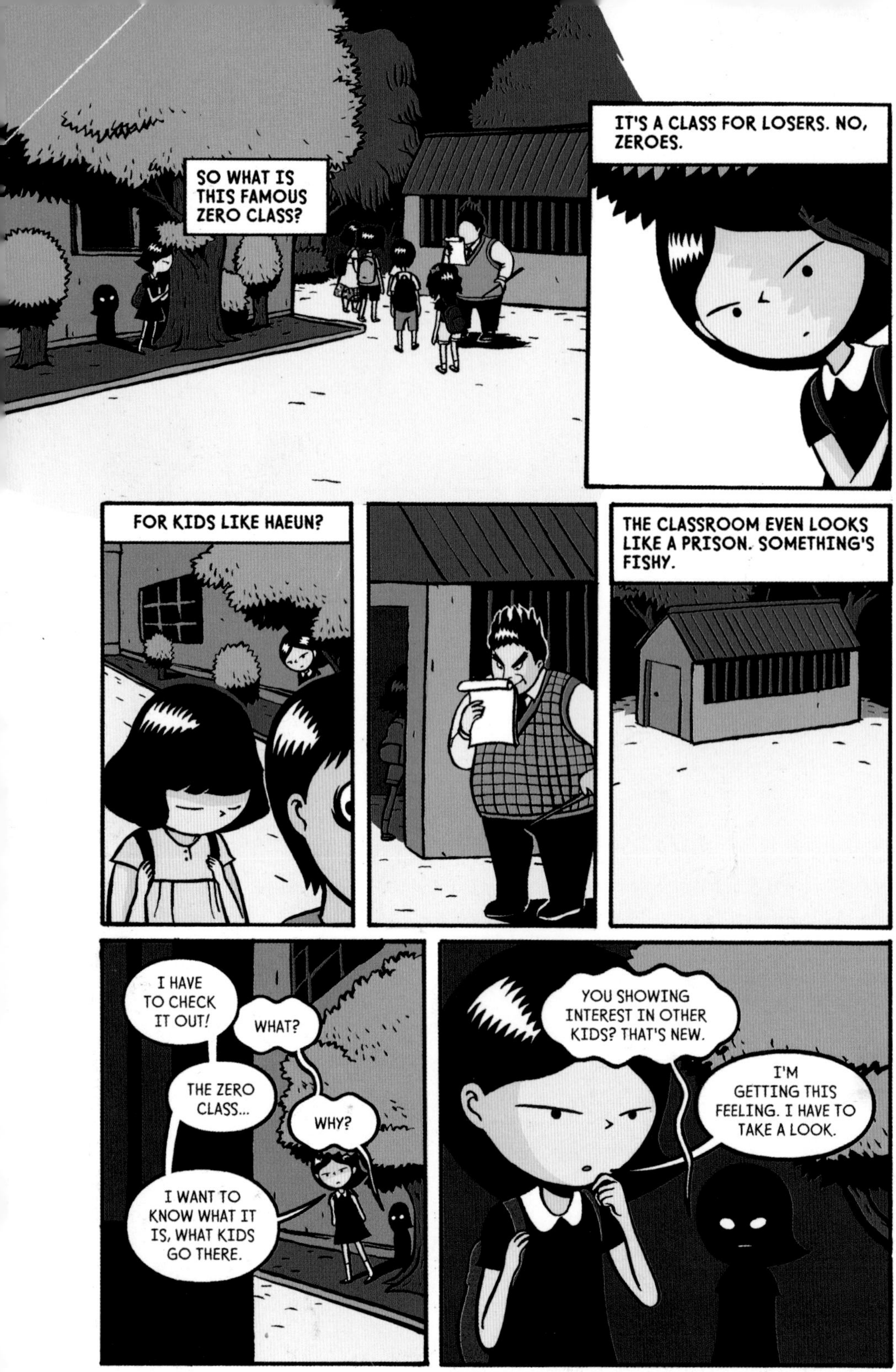
SO WHAT IS THIS FAMOUS ZERO CLASS?
IT'S A CLASS FOR LOSERS. NO, ZEROES.
FOR KIDS LIKE HAEUN?
THE CLASSROOM EVEN LOOKS LIKE A PRISON. SOMETHING'S FISHY.
I HAVE TO CHECK IT OUT!
WHAT?
THE ZERO CLASS...
WHY?
I WANT TO KNOW WHAT IT IS, WHAT KIDS GO THERE.
YOU SHOWING INTEREST IN OTHER KIDS? THAT'S NEW.
I'M GETTING THIS FEELING. I HAVE TO TAKE A LOOK.

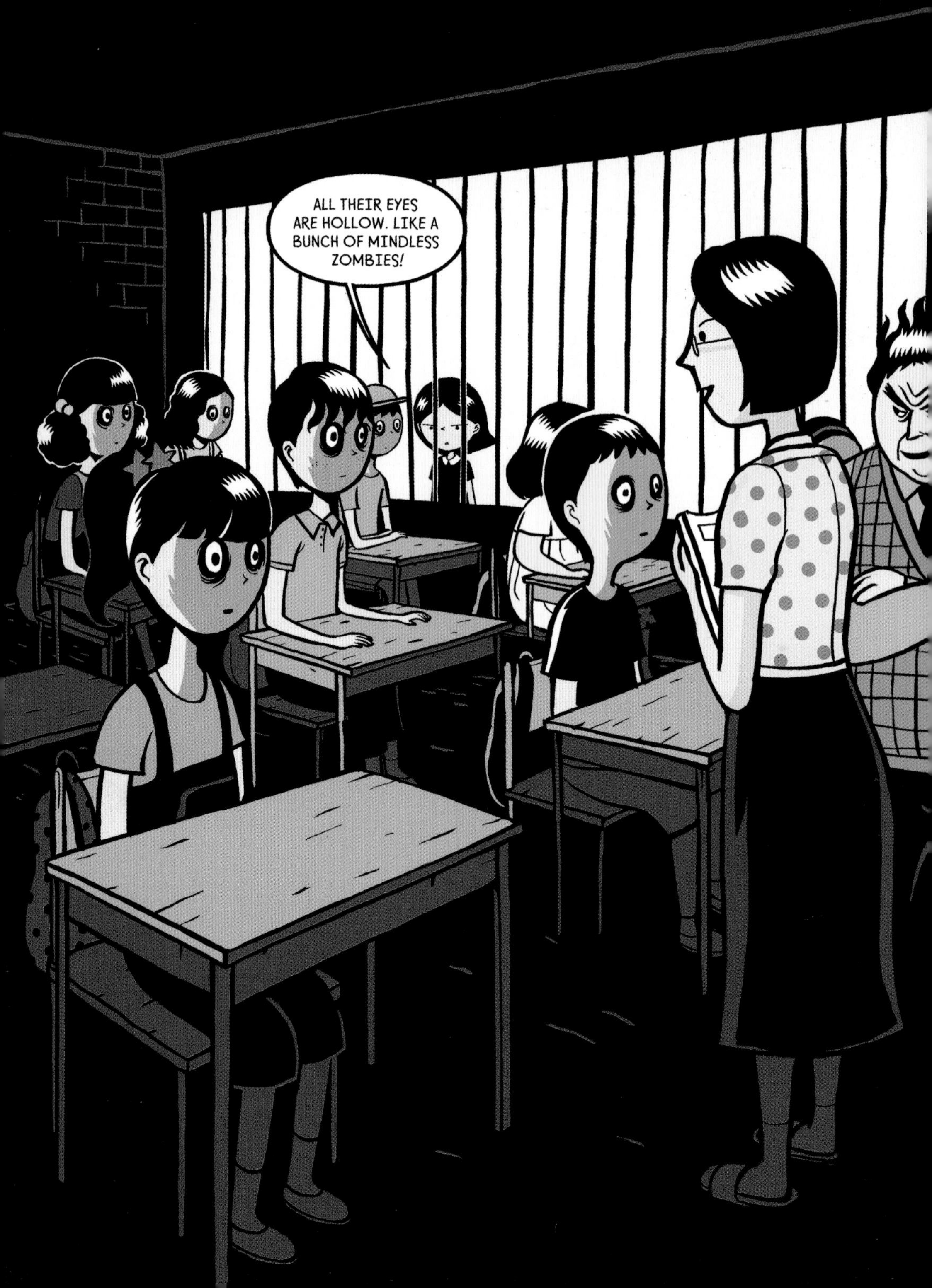
ALL THEIR EYES ARE HOLLOW. LIKE A BUNCH OF MINDLESS ZOMBIES!

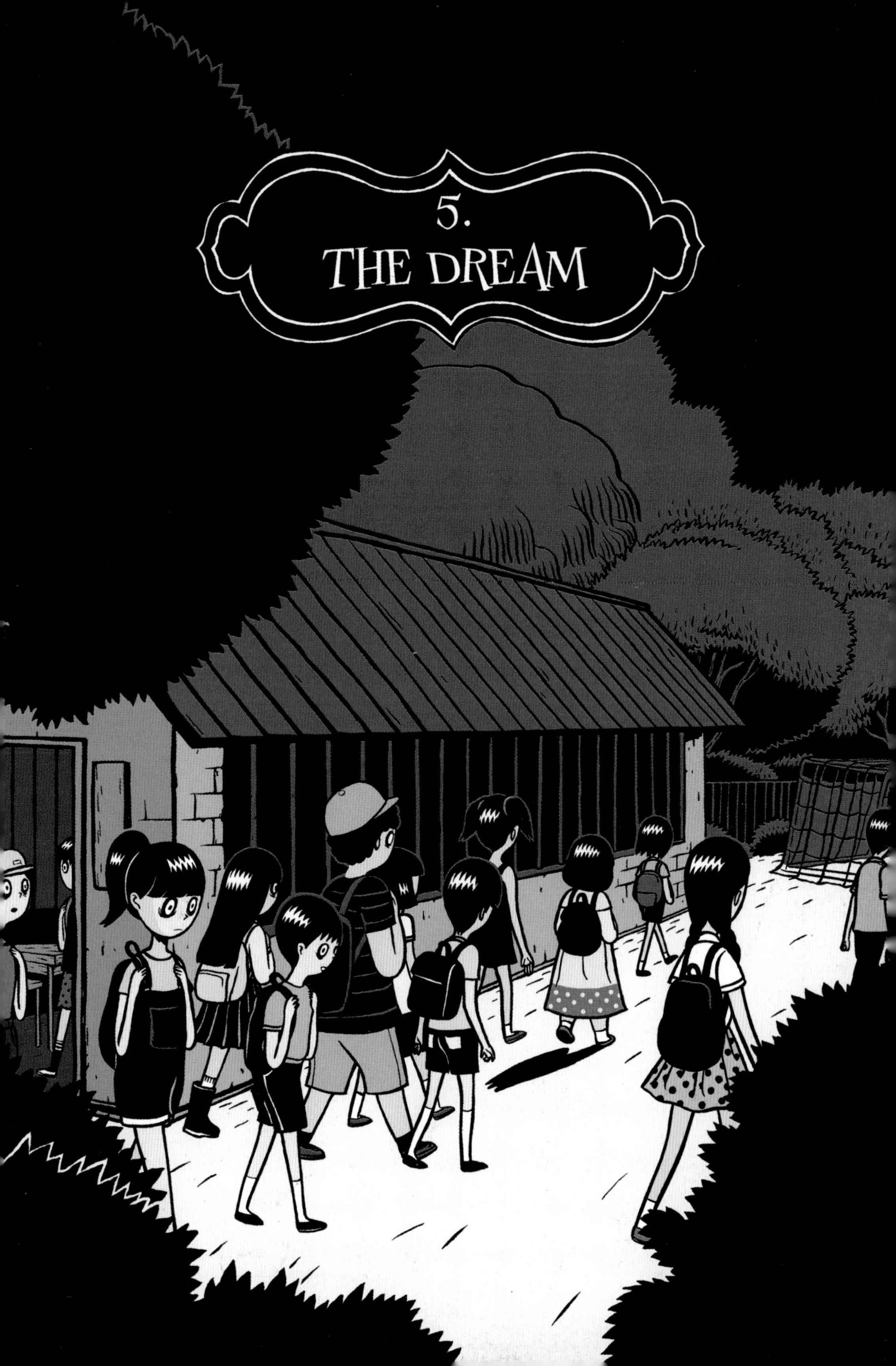
5.
THE DREAM

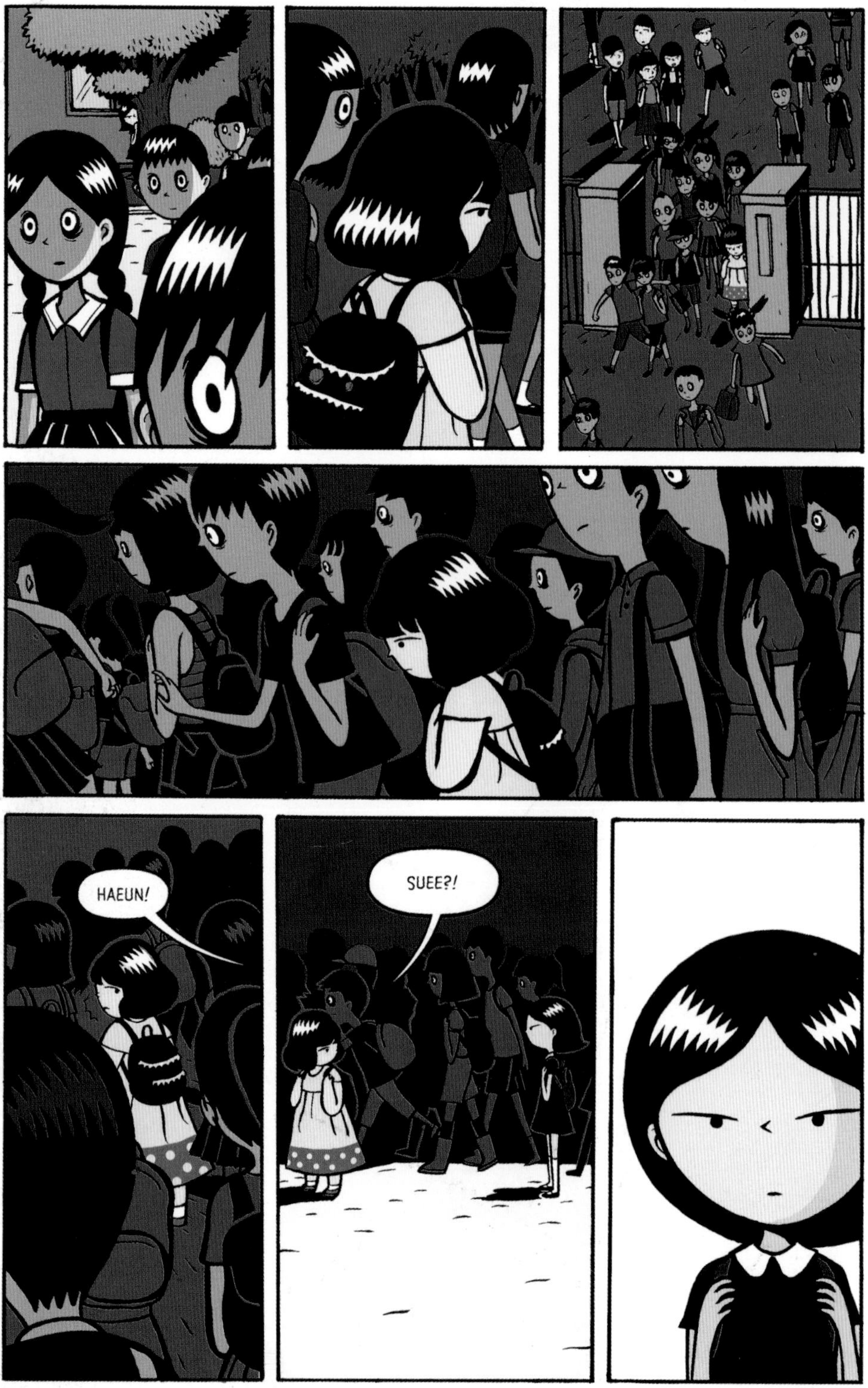
HAEUN!
SUEE?!

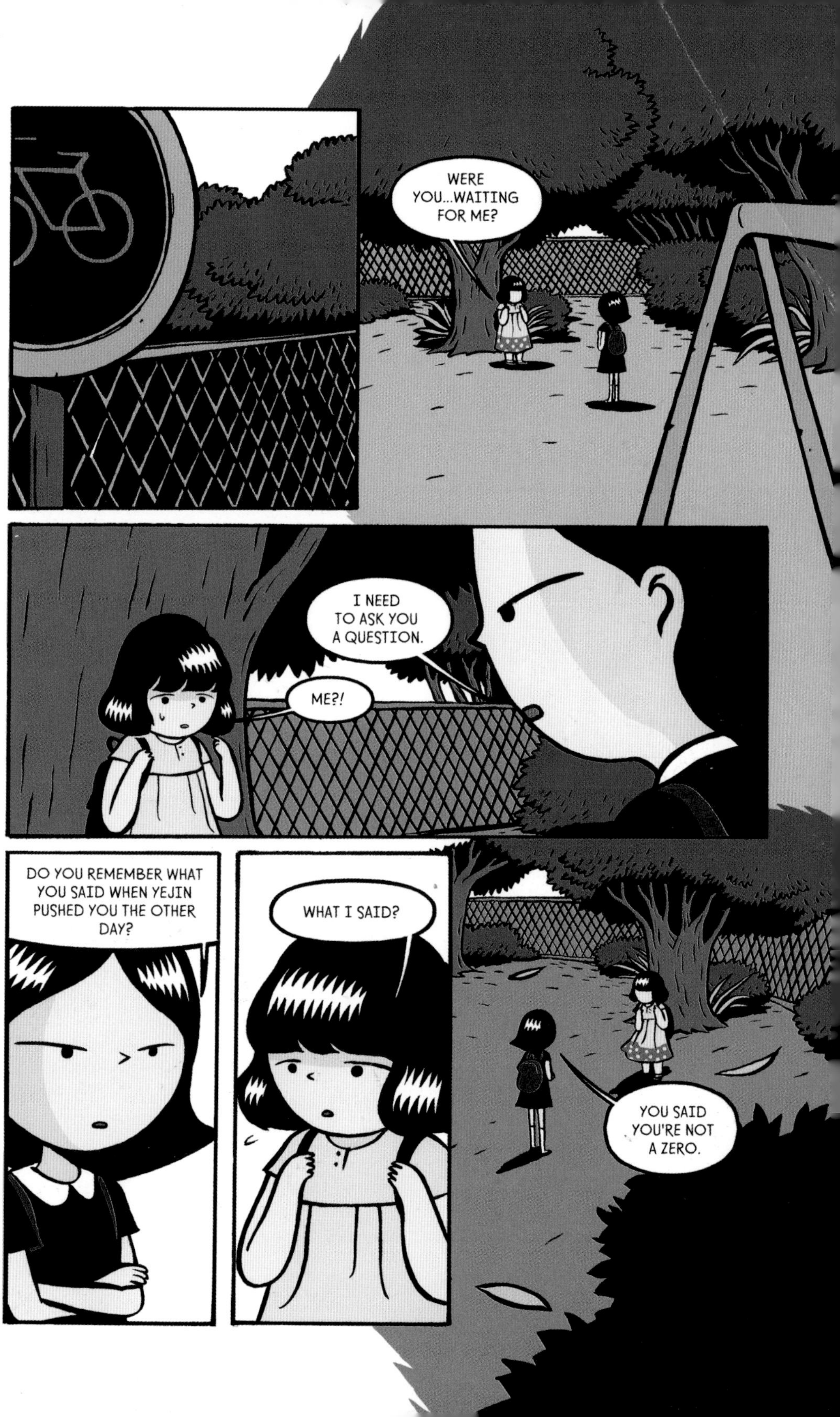
WERE YOU...WAITING FOR ME?
I NEED TO ASK YOU A QUESTION.
ME?!
DO YOU REMEMBER WHAT YOU SAID WHEN YEJIN PUSHED YOU THE OTHER DAY?
WHAT I SAID?
YOU SAID YOU'RE NOT A ZERO.

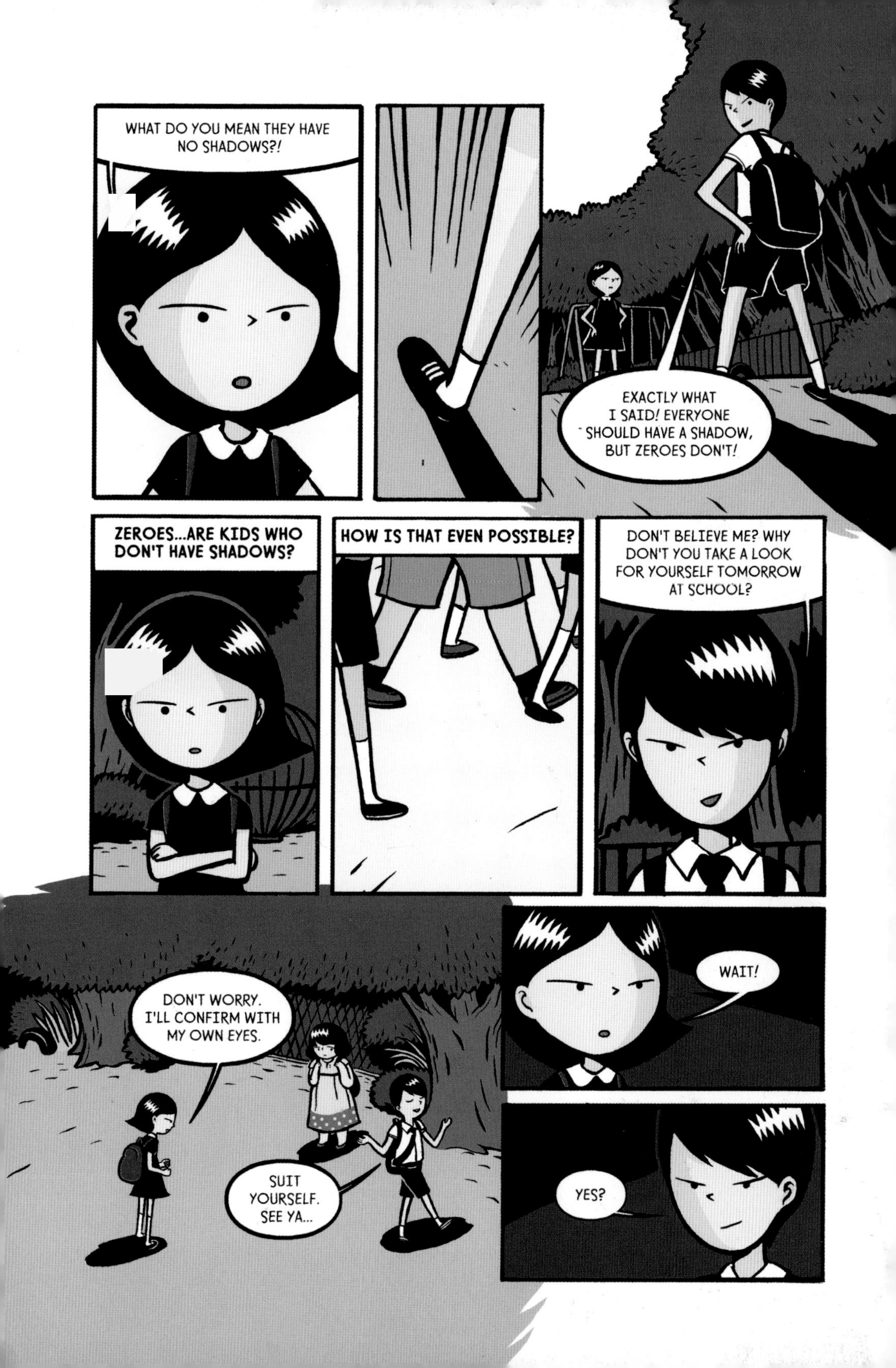
WHAT DO YOU MEAN THEY HAVE NO SHADOWS?!
EXACTLY WHAT I SAID! EVERYONE SHOULD HAVE A SHADOW, BUT ZEROES DON'T!
ZEROES...ARE KIDS WHO DON'T HAVE SHADOWS?
HOW IS THAT EVEN POSSIBLE?
DON'T BELIEVE ME? WHY DON'T YOU TAKE A LOOK FOR YOURSELF TOMORROW AT SCHOOL?
DON'T WORRY. I'LL CONFIRM WITH MY OWN EYES.
SUIT YOURSELF. SEE YA...
WAIT!
YES?

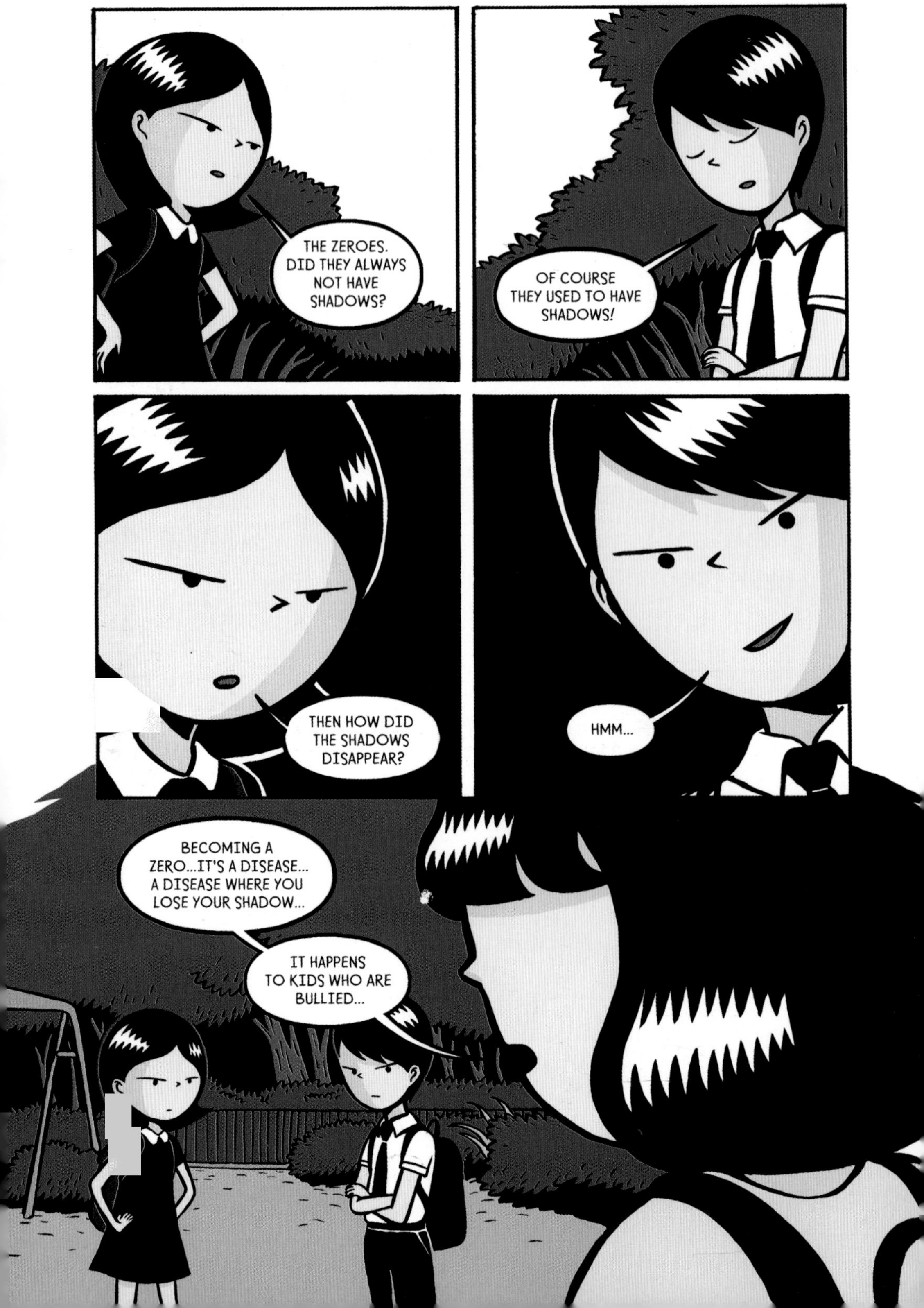
THE ZEROES. DID THEY ALWAYS NOT HAVE SHADOWS?
OF COURSE THEY USED TO HAVE SHADOWS!
THEN HOW DID THE SHADOWS DISAPPEAR?
HMM...
BECOMING A ZERO...IT'S A DISEASE... A DISEASE WHERE YOU LOSE YOUR SHADOW...
IT HAPPENS TO KIDS WHO ARE BULLIED...

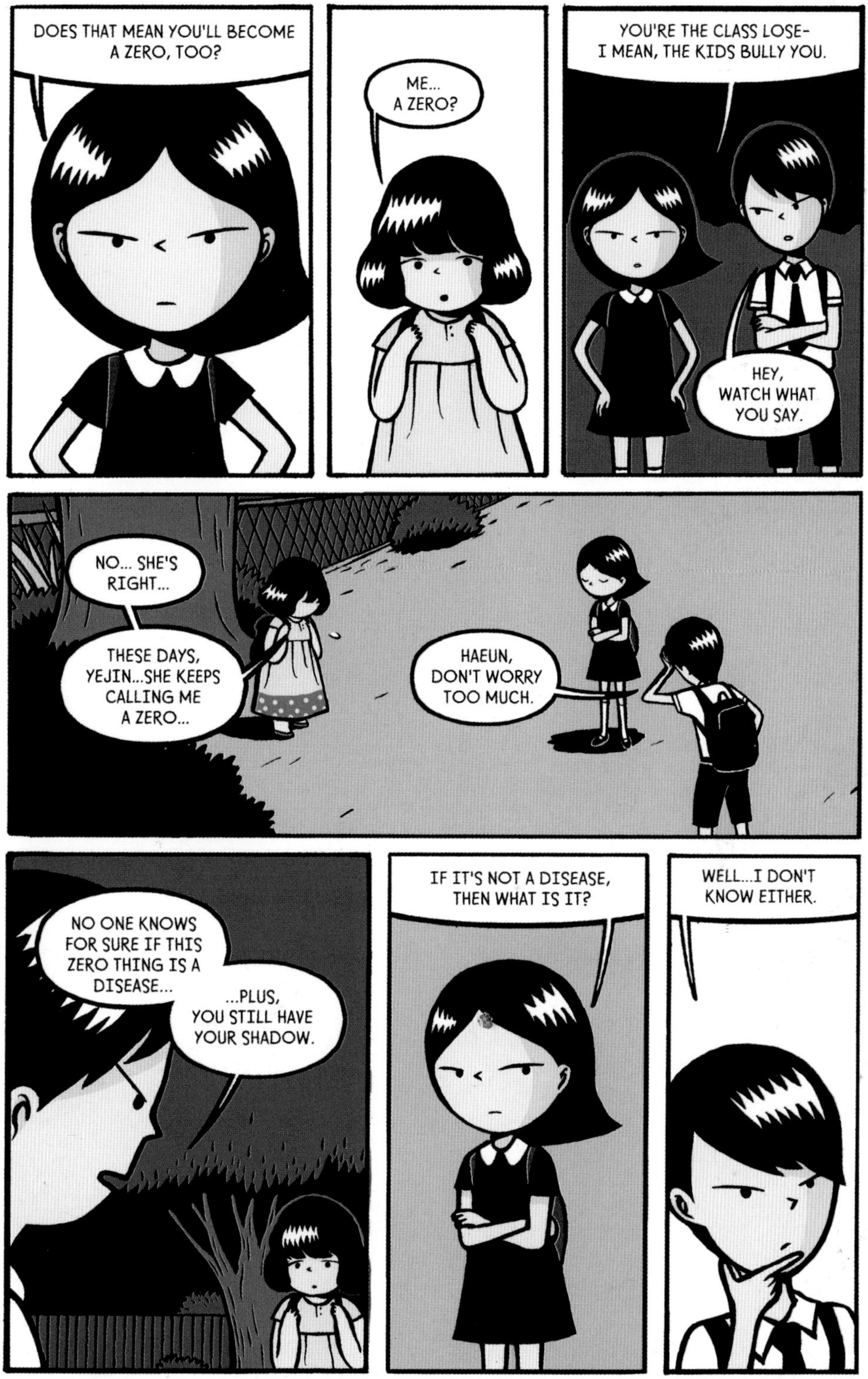
DOES THAT MEAN YOU'LL BECOME A ZERO, TOO?
ME... A ZERO?
YOU'RE THE CLASS LOSE- I MEAN, THE KIDS BULLY YOU.
HEY, WATCH WHAT YOU SAY.
NO... SHE'S RIGHT...
THESE DAYS, YEJIN...SHE KEEPS CALLING ME A ZERO...
HAEUN, DON'T WORRY TOO MUCH.
NO ONE KNOWS FOR SURE IF THIS ZERO THING IS A DISEASE...
...PLUS, YOU STILL HAVE YOUR SHADOW.
IF IT'S NOT A DISEASE, THEN WHAT IS IT?
WELL...I DON'T KNOW EITHER.

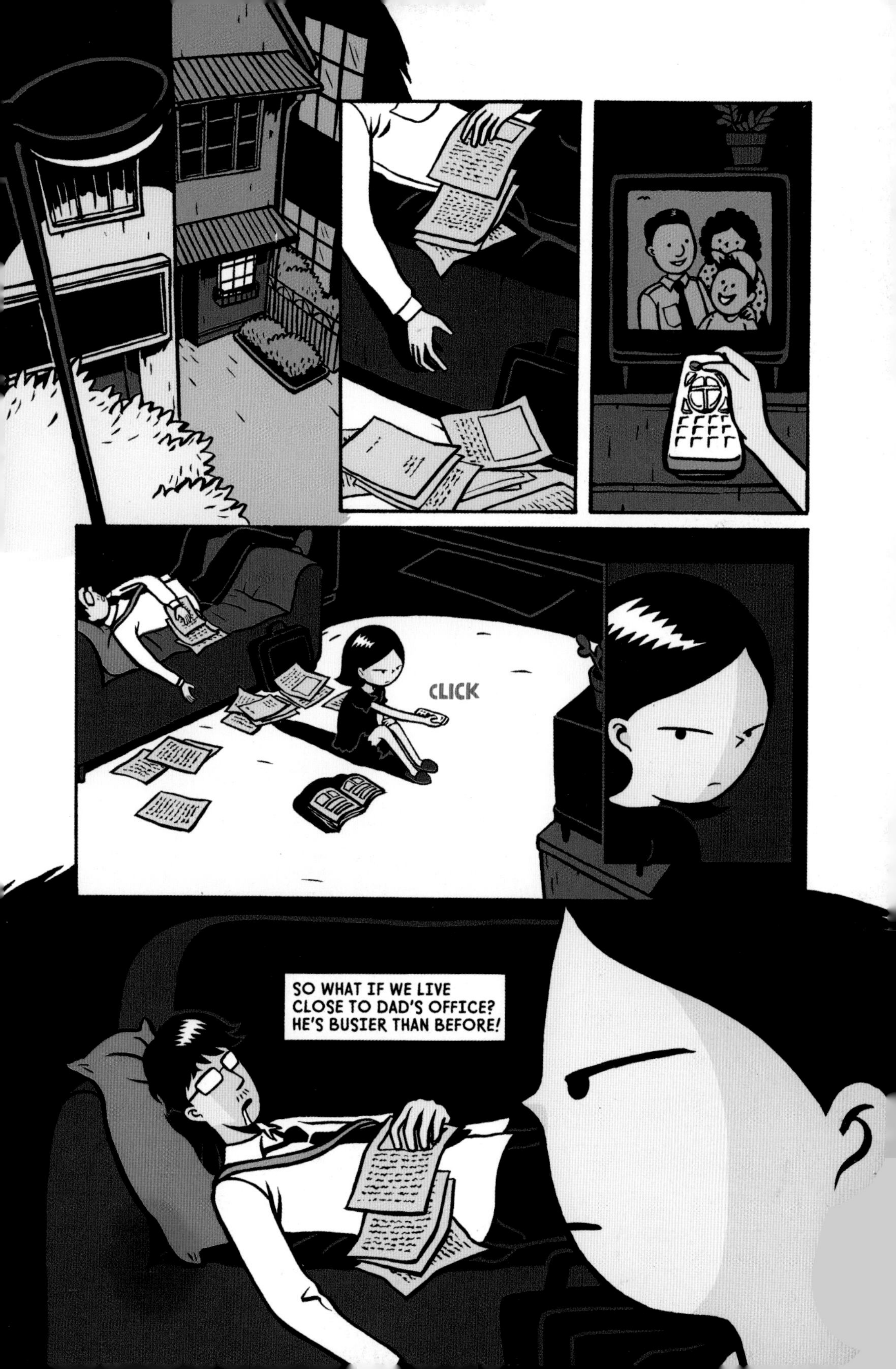
CLICK
SO WHAT IF WE LIVE CLOSE TO DAD'S OFFICE? HE'S BUSIER THAN BEFORE!

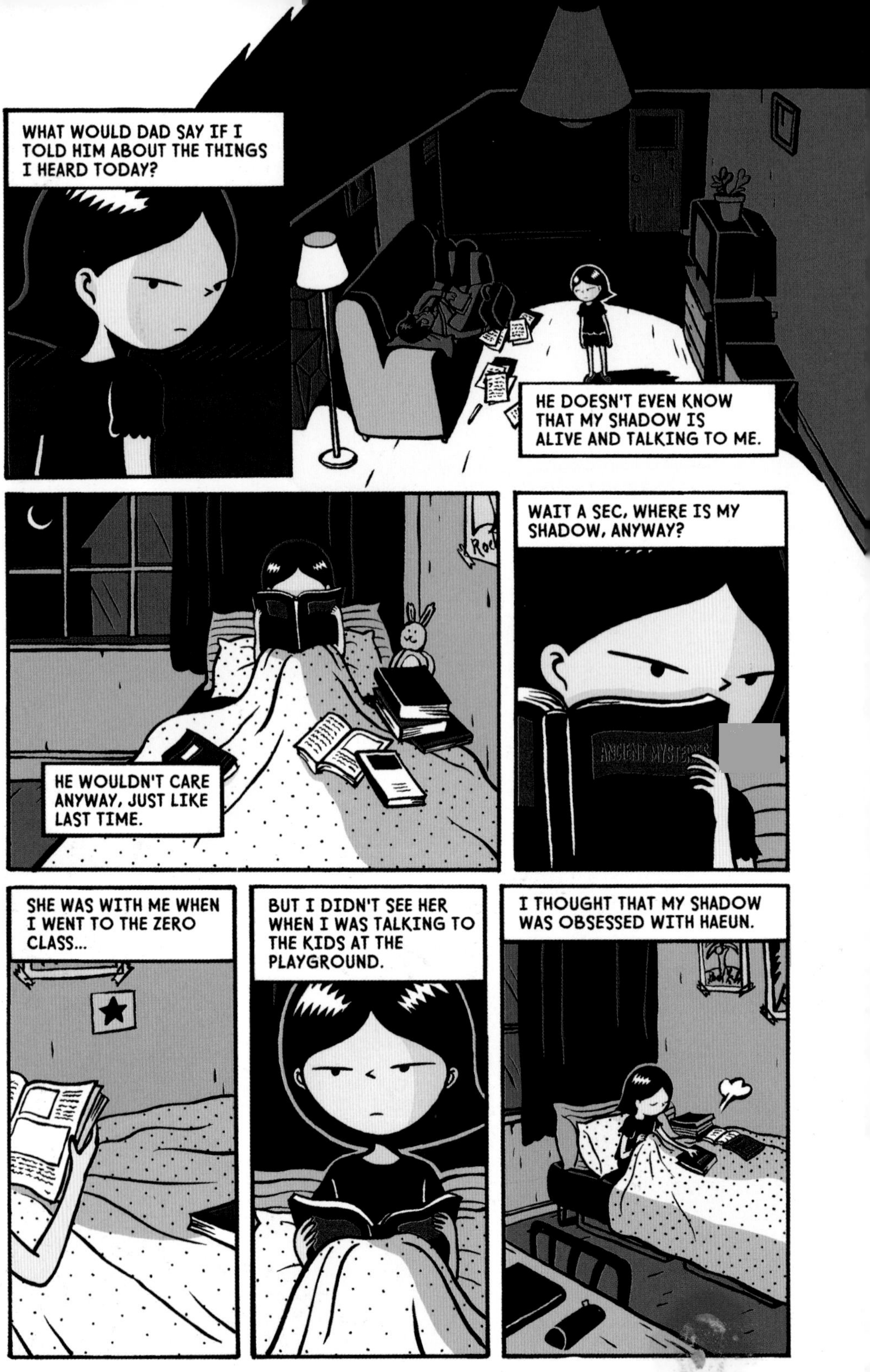
WHAT WOULD DAD SAY IF I TOLD HIM ABOUT THE THINGS I HEARD TODAY?
HE DOESN'T EVEN KNOW THAT MY SHADOW IS ALIVE AND TALKING TO ME.
HE WOULDN'T CARE ANYWAY, JUST LIKE LAST TIME.
WAIT A SEC, WHERE IS MY SHADOW, ANYWAY?
ANCIENT MYSTERIES
SHE WAS WITH ME WHEN I WENT TO THE ZERO CLASS...
BUT I DIDN'T SEE HER WHEN I WAS TALKING TO THE KIDS AT THE PLAYGROUND.
I THOUGHT THAT MY SHADOW WAS OBSESSED WITH HAEUN.

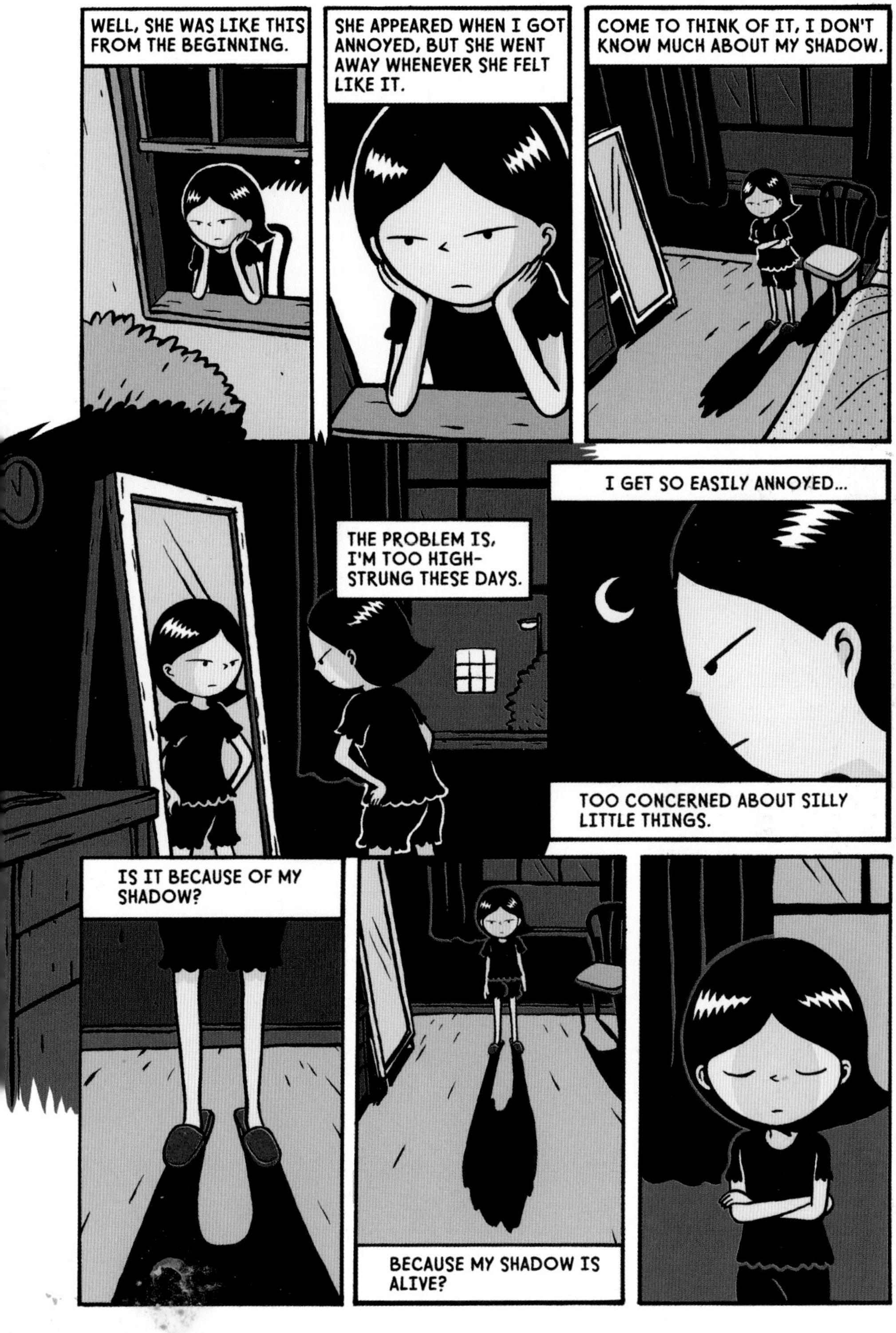

WELL, SHE WAS LIKE THIS FROM THE BEGINNING.
SHE APPEARED WHEN I GOT ANNOYED, BUT SHE WENT AWAY WHENEVER SHE FELT LIKE IT.
COME TO THINK OF IT, I DON'T KNOW MUCH ABOUT MY SHADOW.
THE PROBLEM IS, I'M TOO HIGH-STRUNG THESE DAYS.
I GET SO EASILY ANNOYED...
TOO CONCERNED ABOUT SILLY LITTLE THINGS.
IS IT BECAUSE OF MY SHADOW?
BECAUSE MY SHADOW IS ALIVE?

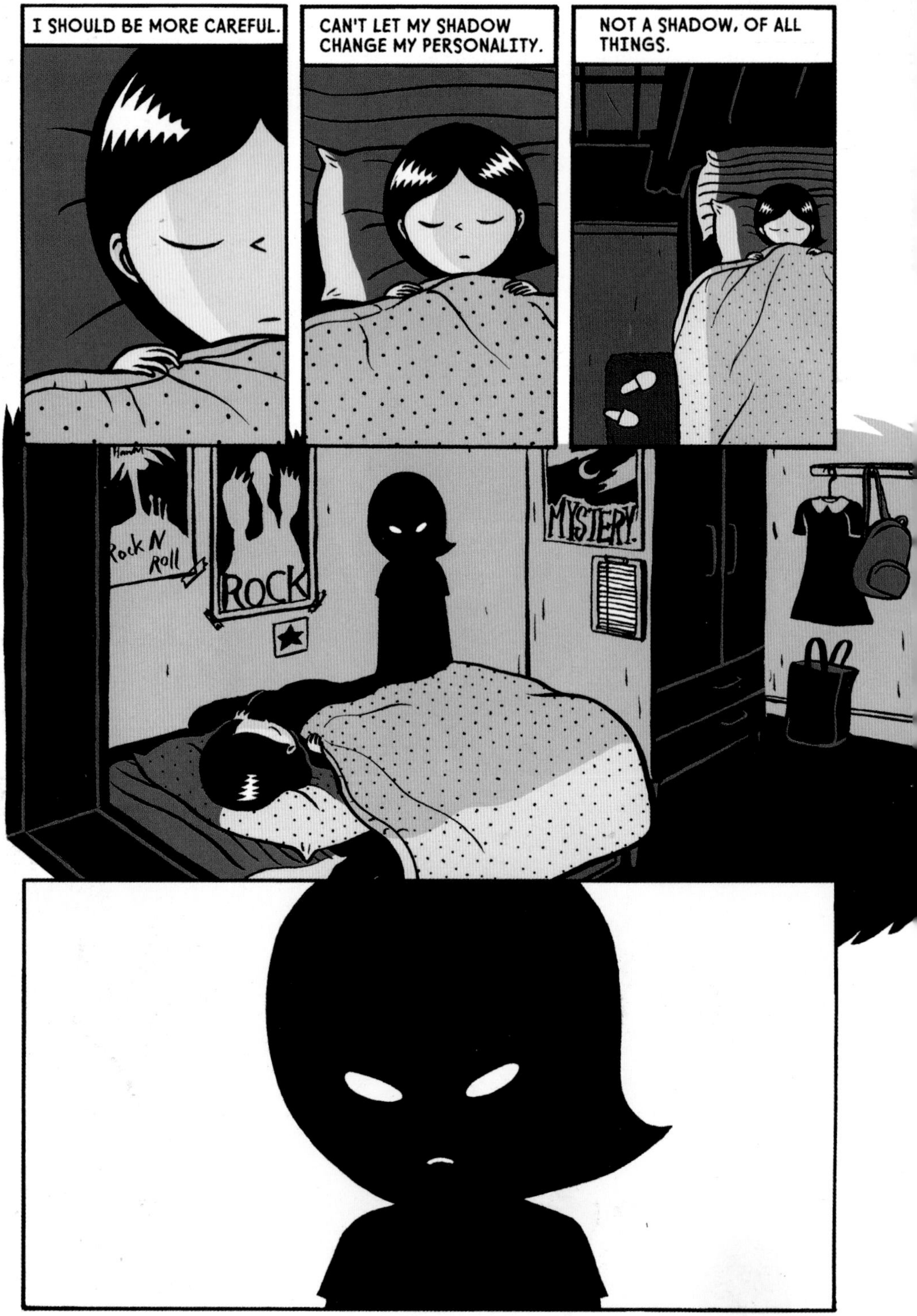
I SHOULD BE MORE CAREFUL.
CAN'T LET MY SHADOW CHANGE MY PERSONALITY.
NOT A SHADOW, OF ALL THINGS.
Rock N Roll
ROCK
MYSTERY

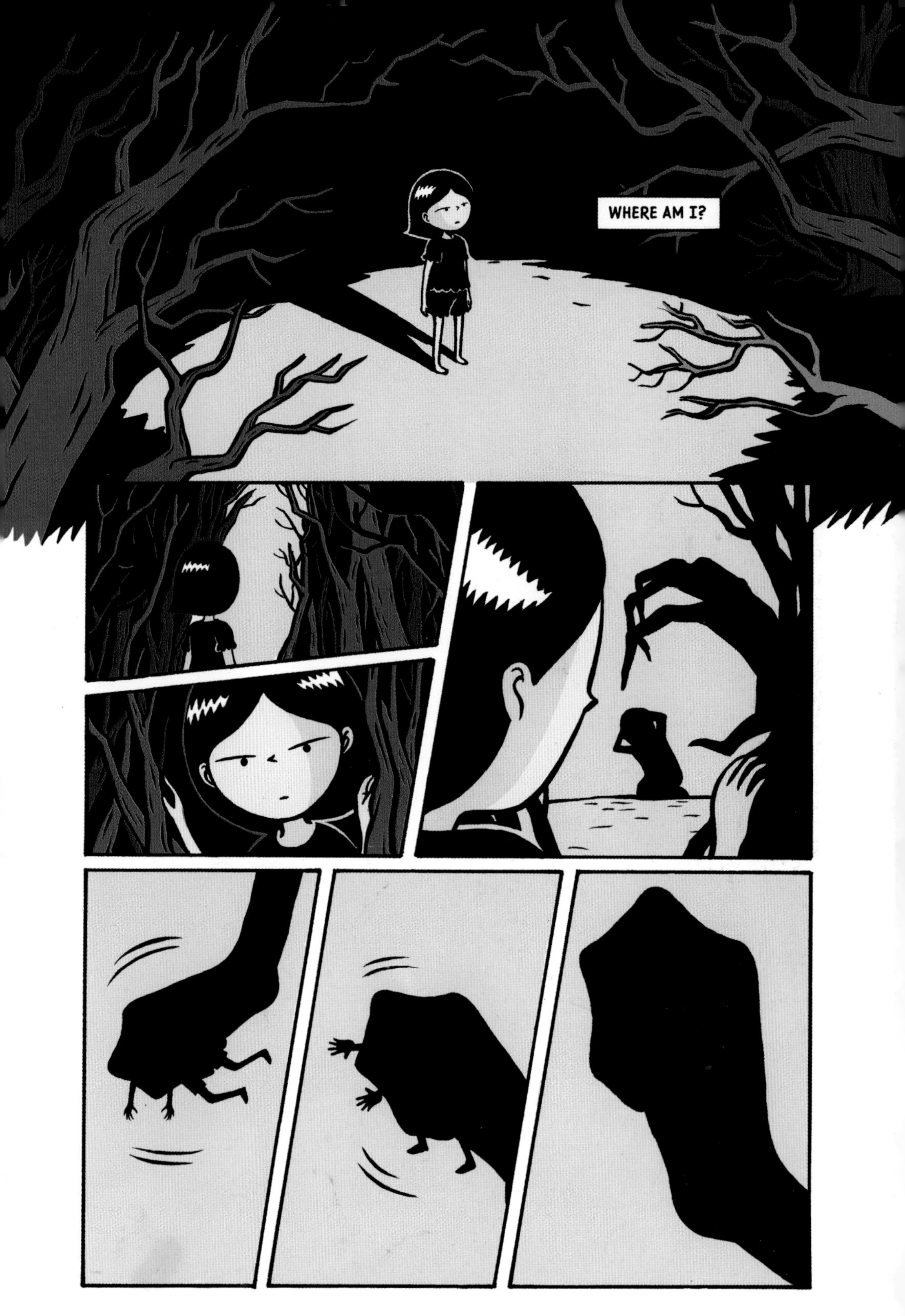
WHERE AM I?

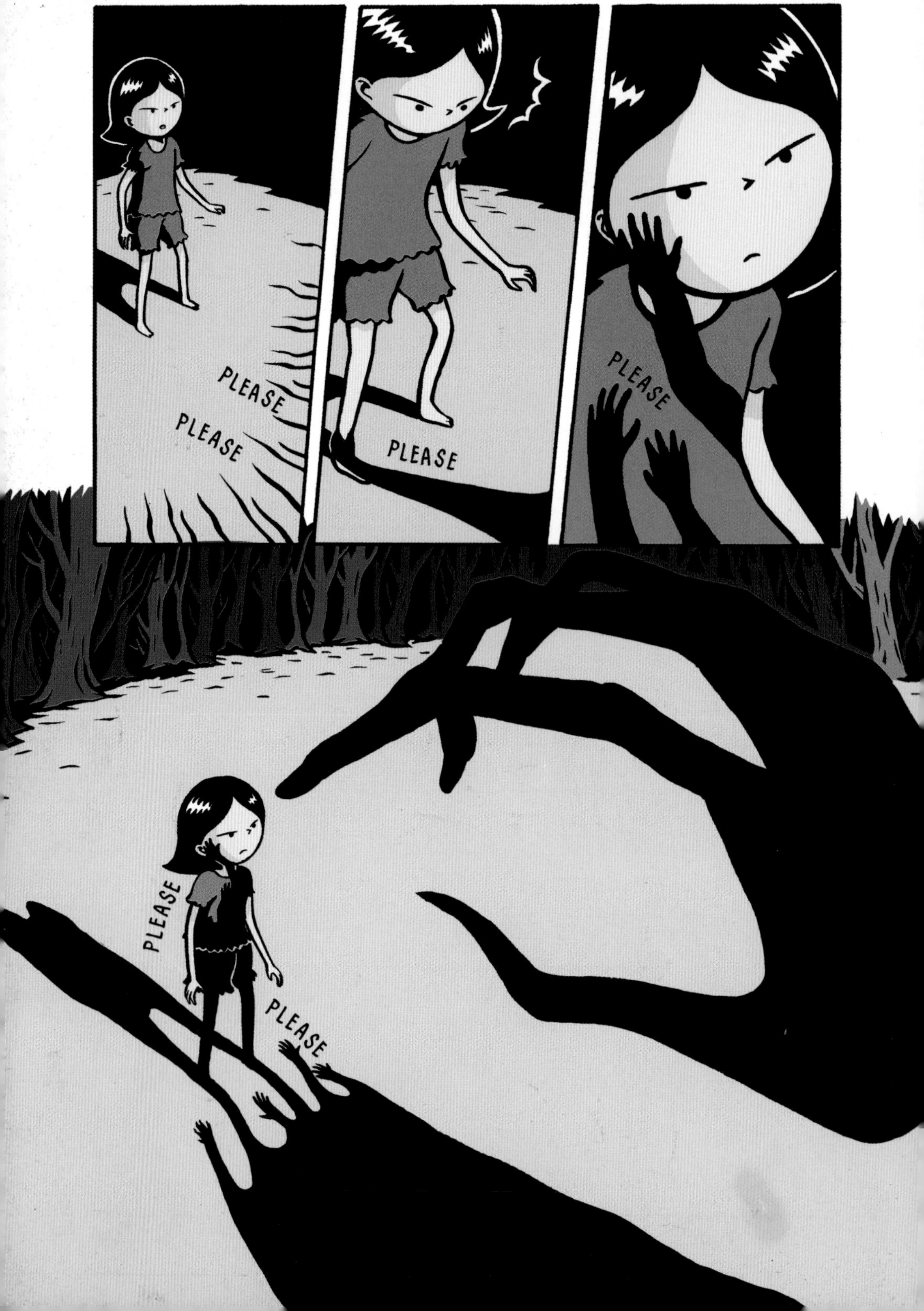
PLEASE
PLEASE
PLEASE
PLEASE
PLEASE
PLEASE

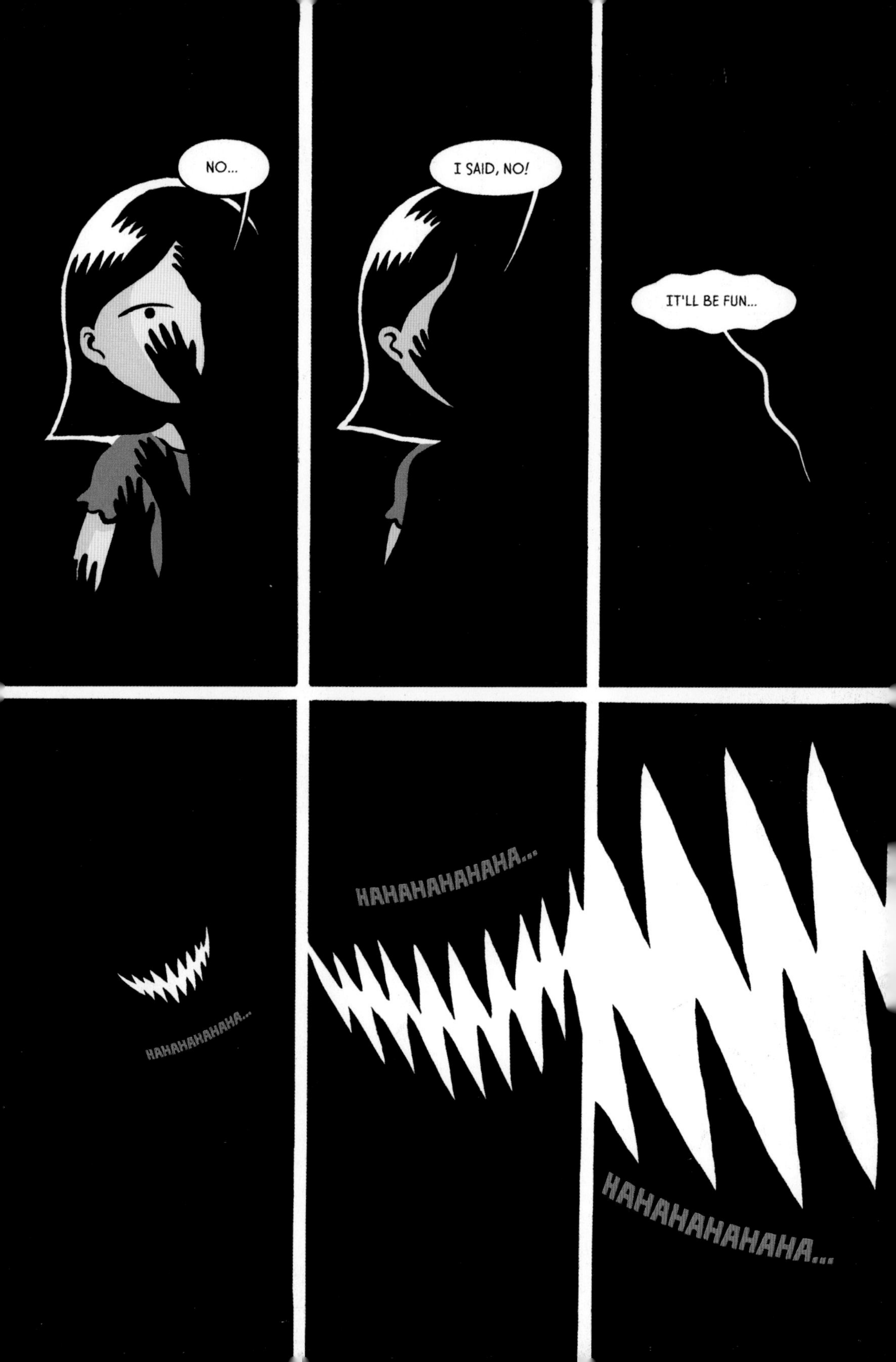
NO...
I SAID, NO!
IT'LL BE FUN...
HAHAHAHAHAHA...
HAHAHAHAHAHA...
HAHAHAHAHAHA...

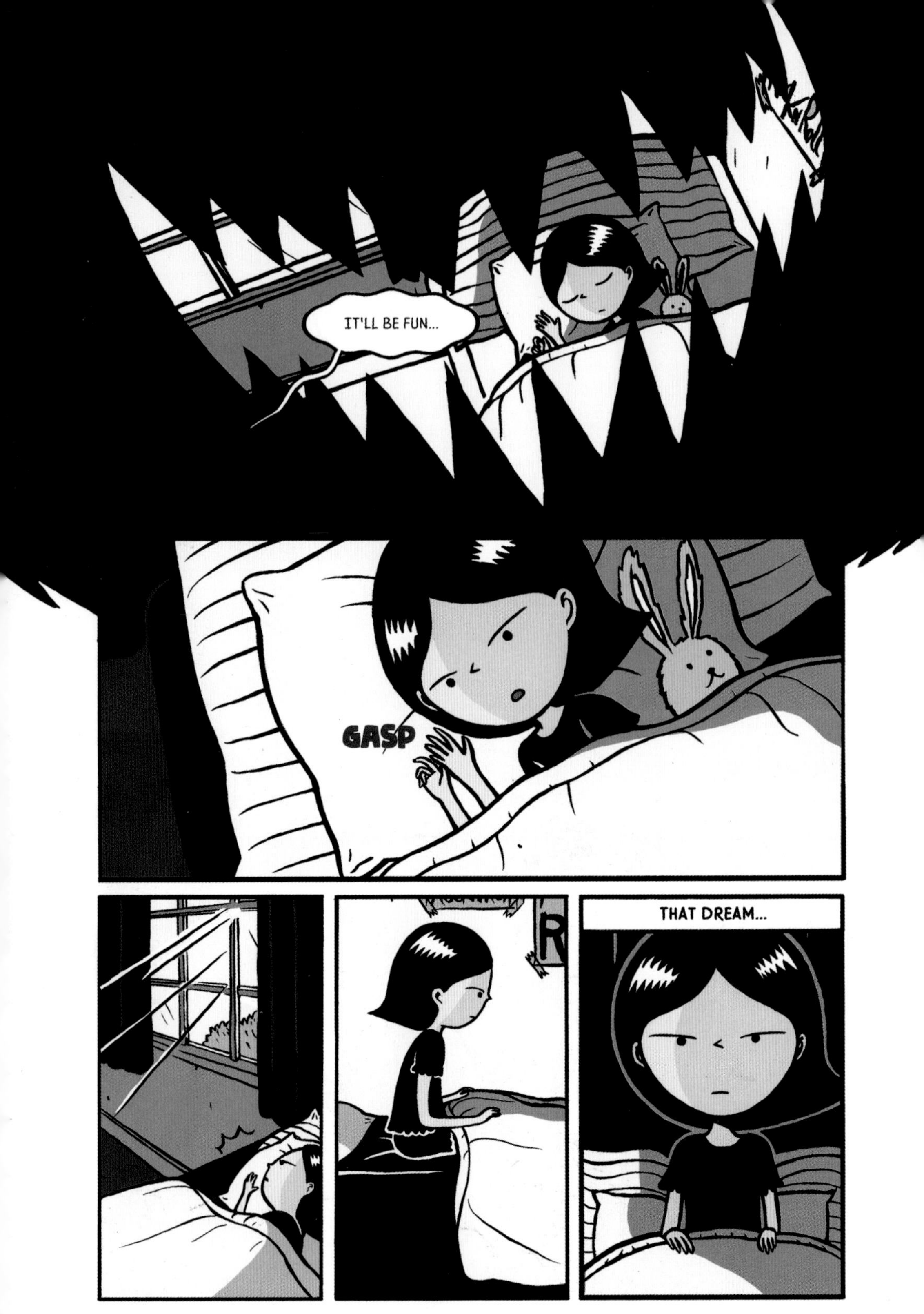
IT'LL BE FUN...
GASP
THAT DREAM...

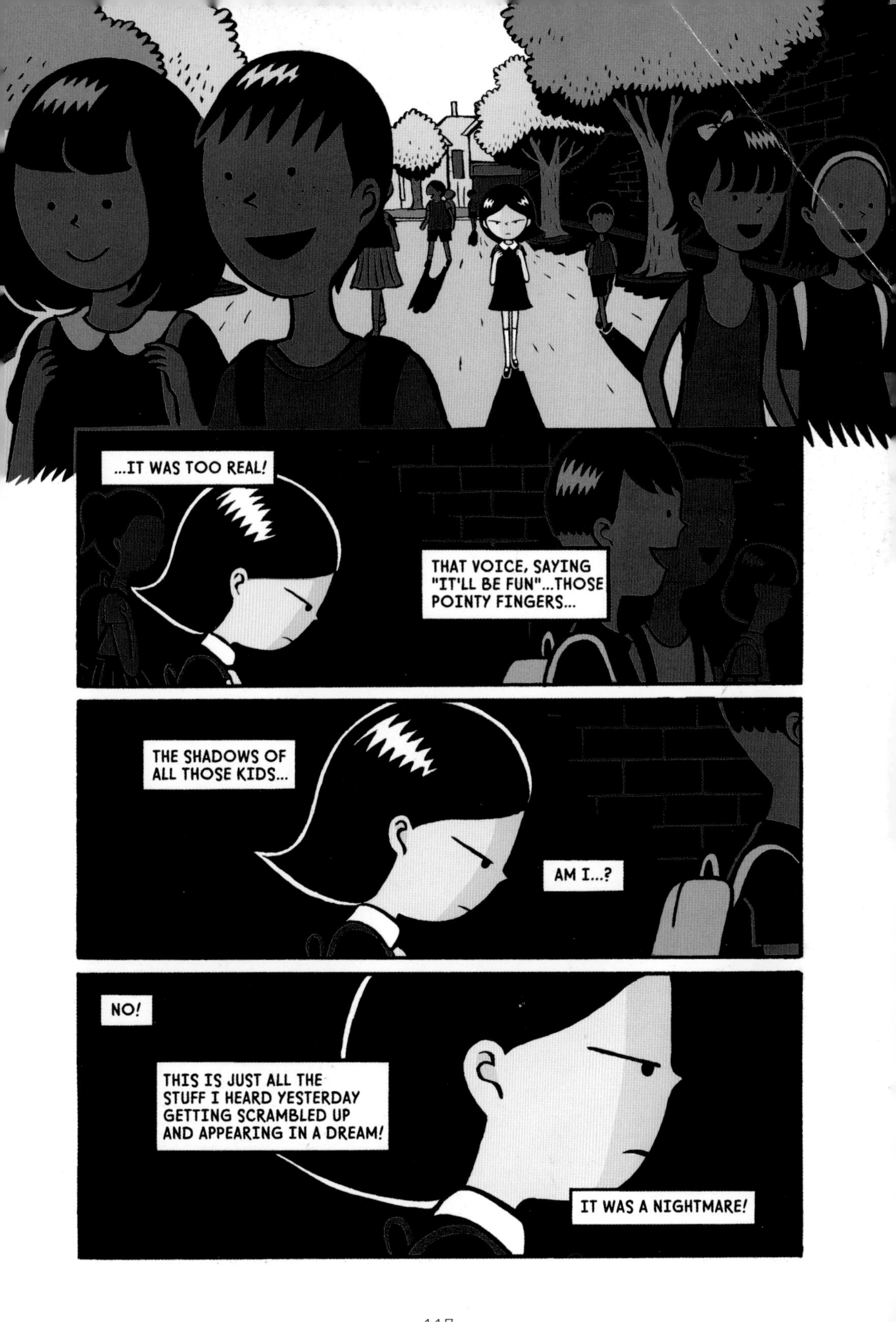
...IT WAS TOO REAL!
THAT VOICE, SAYING "IT'LL BE FUN"...THOSE POINTY FINGERS...
THE SHADOWS OF ALL THOSE KIDS...
AM I...?
NO!
THIS IS JUST ALL THE STUFF I HEARD YESTERDAY GETTING SCRAMBLED UP AND APPEARING IN A DREAM!
IT WAS A NIGHTMARE!

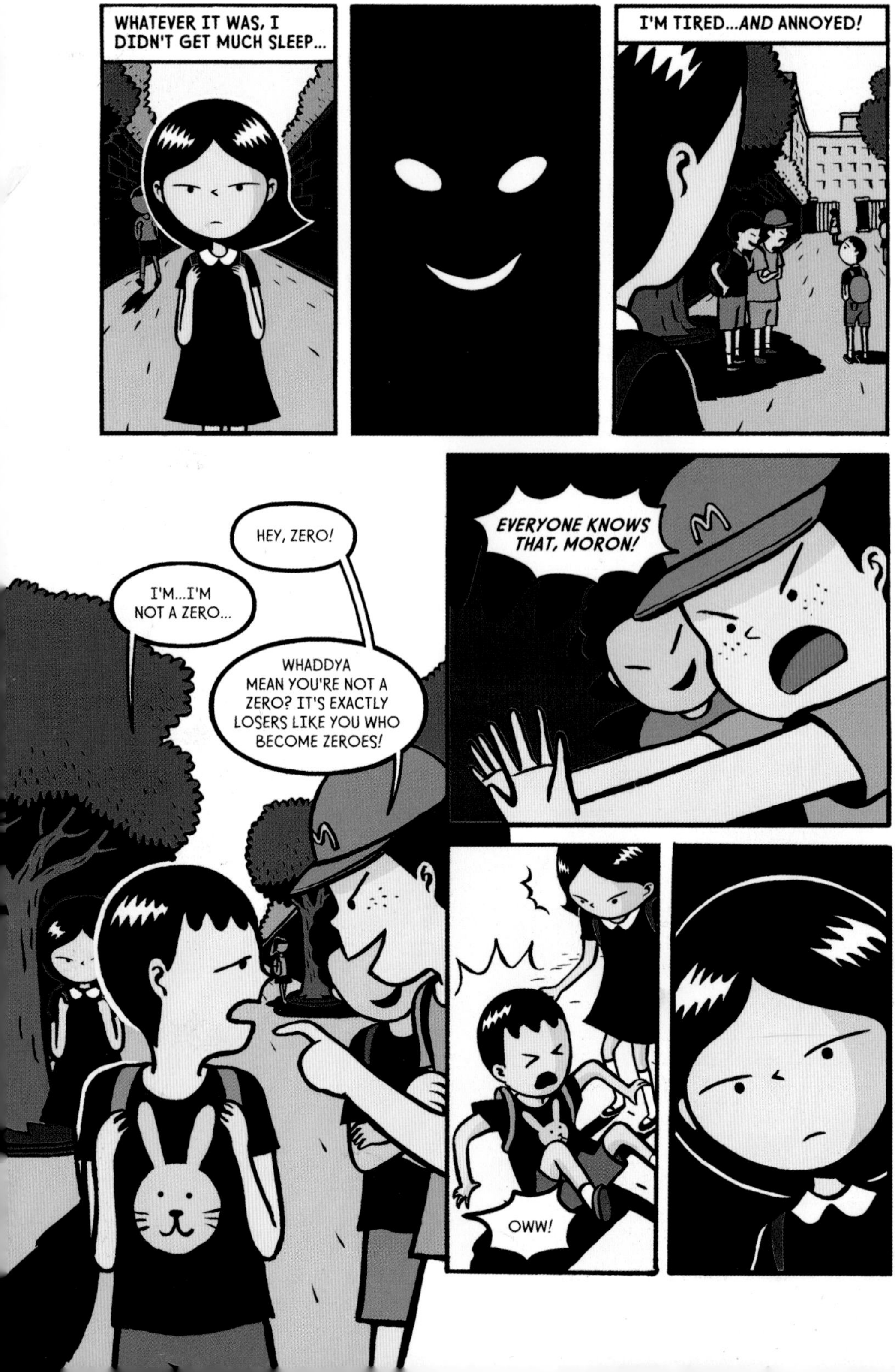
WHATEVER IT WAS, I DIDN'T GET MUCH SLEEP...
I'M TIRED...AND ANNOYED!
HEY, ZERO!
I'M...I'M NOT A ZERO...
WHADDYA MEAN YOU'RE NOT A ZERO? IT'S EXACTLY LOSERS LIKE YOU WHO BECOME ZEROES!
EVERYONE KNOWS THAT, MORON!
OWW!

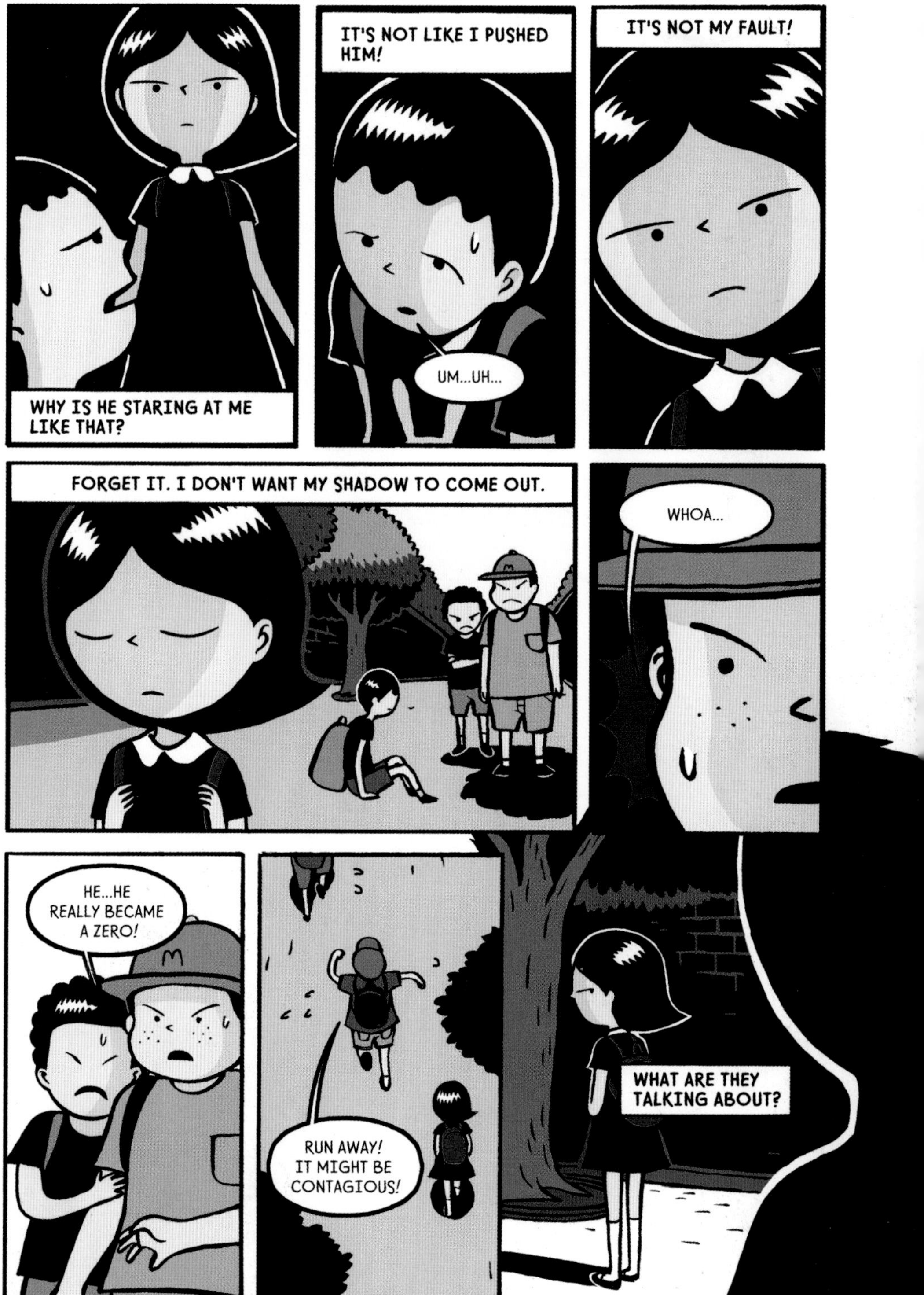
WHY IS HE STARING AT ME LIKE THAT?
IT'S NOT LIKE I PUSHED HIM!
UM...UH...
IT'S NOT MY FAULT!
FORGET IT. I DON'T WANT MY SHADOW TO COME OUT.
WHOA...
HE...HE REALLY BECAME A ZERO!
RUN AWAY! IT MIGHT BE CONTAGIOUS!
WHAT ARE THEY TALKING ABOUT?

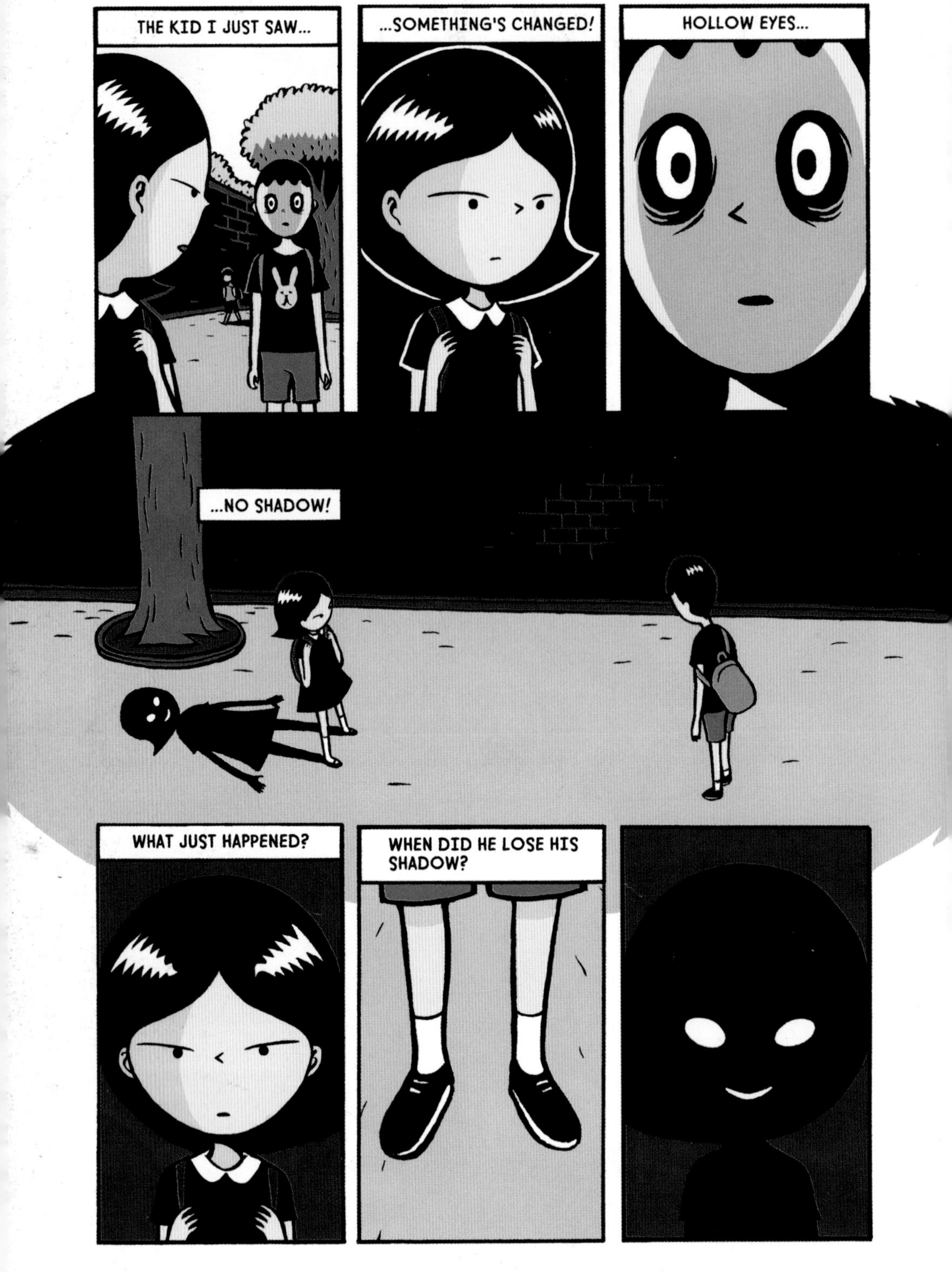
THE KID I JUST SAW...
...SOMETHING'S CHANGED!
HOLLOW EYES...
...NO SHADOW!
WHAT JUST HAPPENED?
WHEN DID HE LOSE HIS SHADOW?

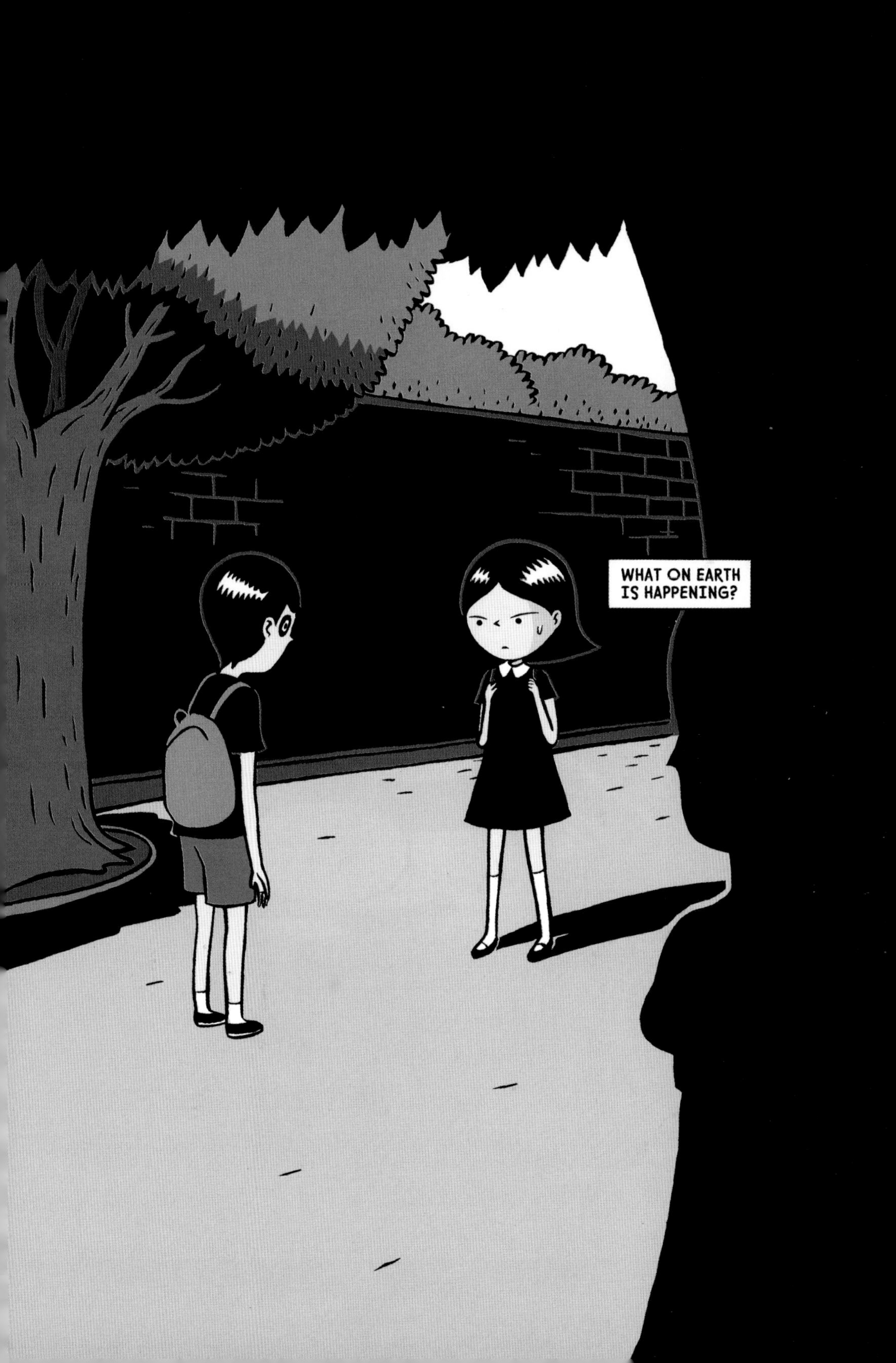
WHAT ON EARTH
IS HAPPENING?

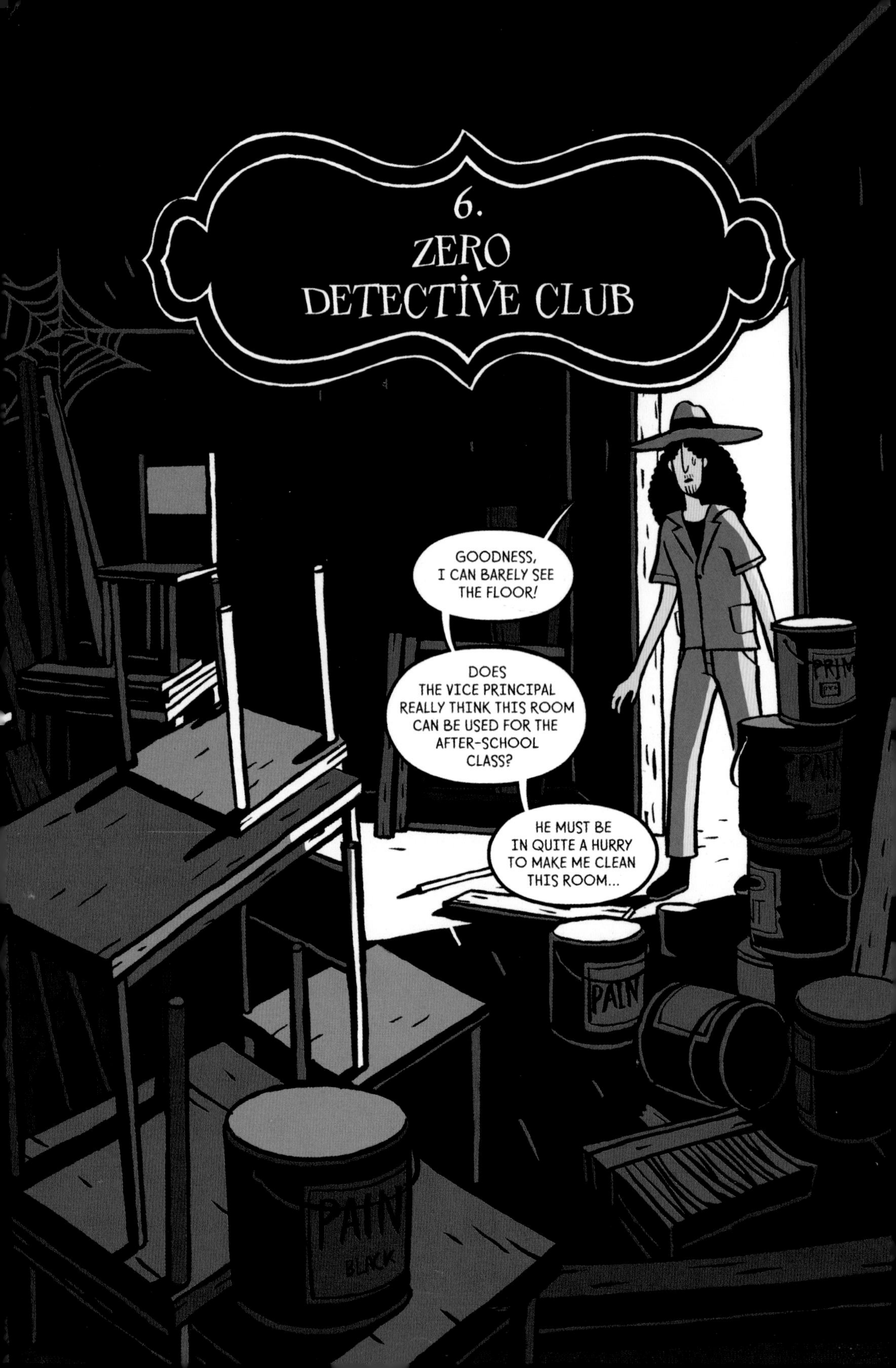
6.
ZERO
DETECTIVE CLUB
GOODNESS, I CAN BARELY SEE THE FLOOR!
DOES THE VICE PRINCIPAL REALLY THINK THIS ROOM CAN BE USED FOR THE AFTER-SCHOOL CLASS?
HE MUST BE IN QUITE A HURRY TO MAKE ME CLEAN THIS ROOM...

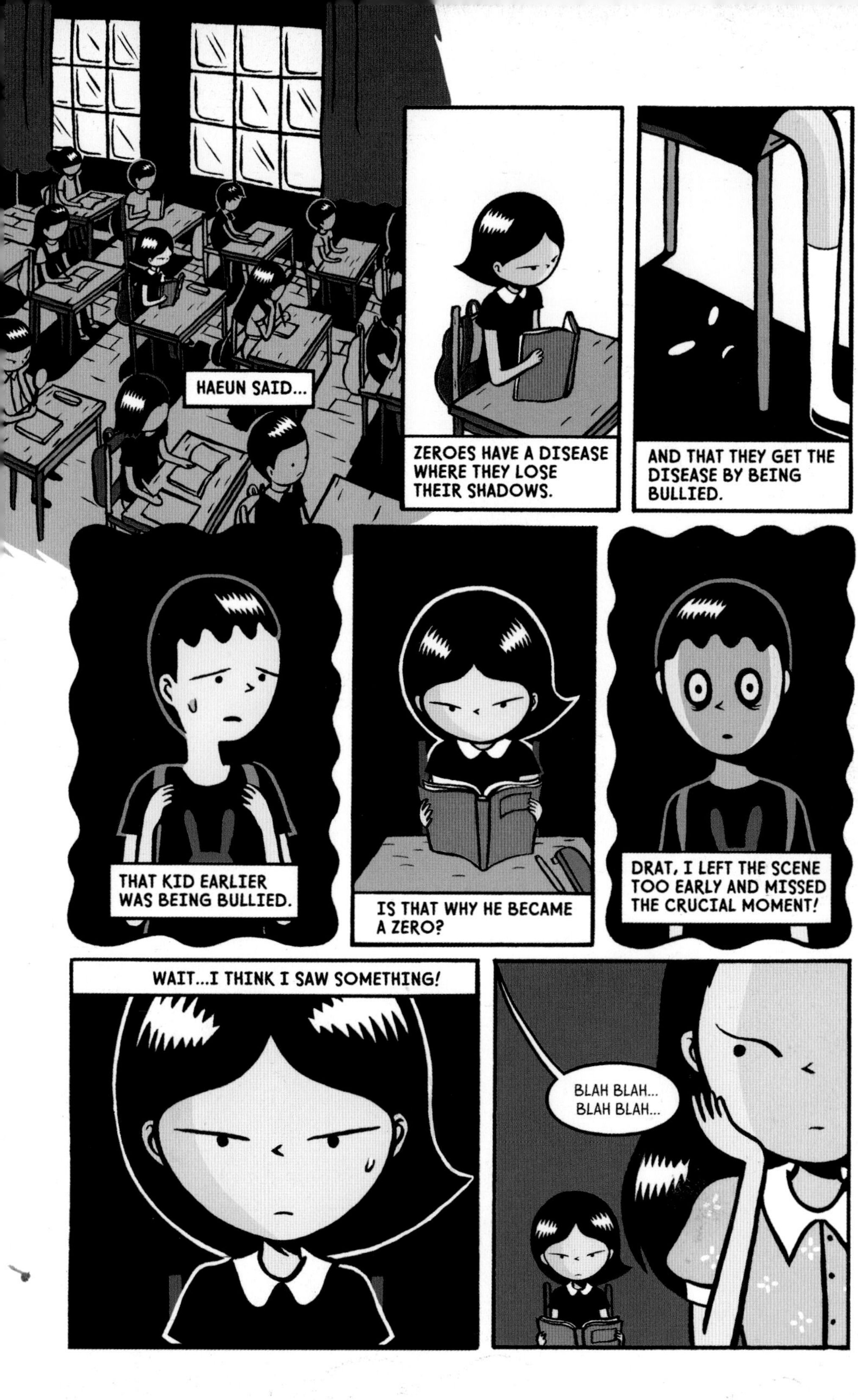
HAEUN SAID...
ZEROES HAVE A DISEASE WHERE THEY LOSE THEIR SHADOWS.
AND THAT THEY GET THE DISEASE BY BEING BULLIED.
THAT KID EARLIER WAS BEING BULLIED.
IS THAT WHY HE BECAME A ZERO?
DRAT, I LEFT THE SCENE TOO EARLY AND MISSED THE CRUCIAL MOMENT!
WAIT...I THINK I SAW SOMETHING!
BLAH BLAH... BLAH BLAH...

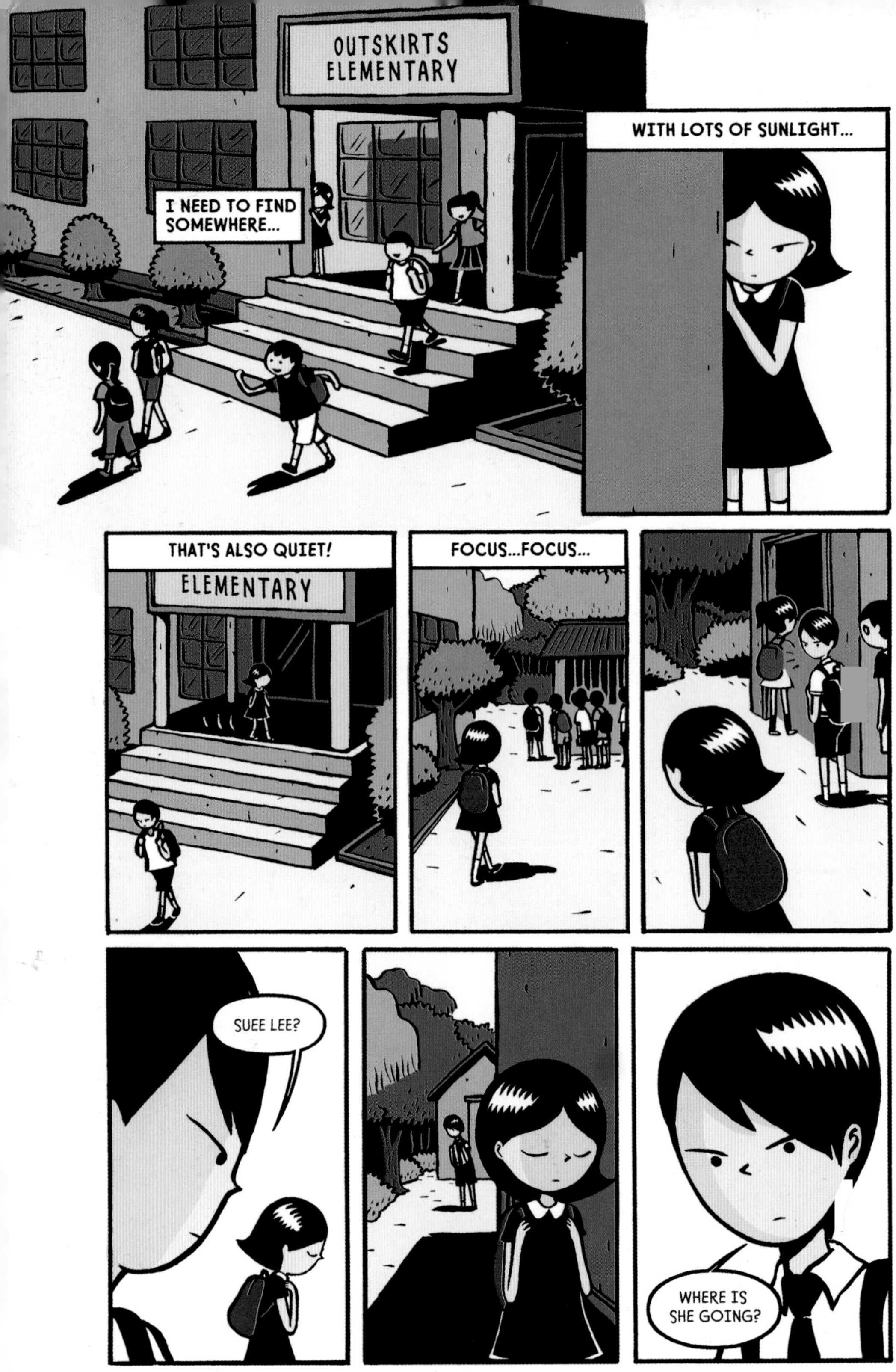
OUTSKIRTS ELEMENTARY
I NEED TO FIND SOMEWHERE...
WITH LOTS OF SUNLIGHT...
THAT'S ALSO QUIET!
ELEMENTARY
FOCUS...FOCUS...
SUEE LEE?
WHERE IS SHE GOING?

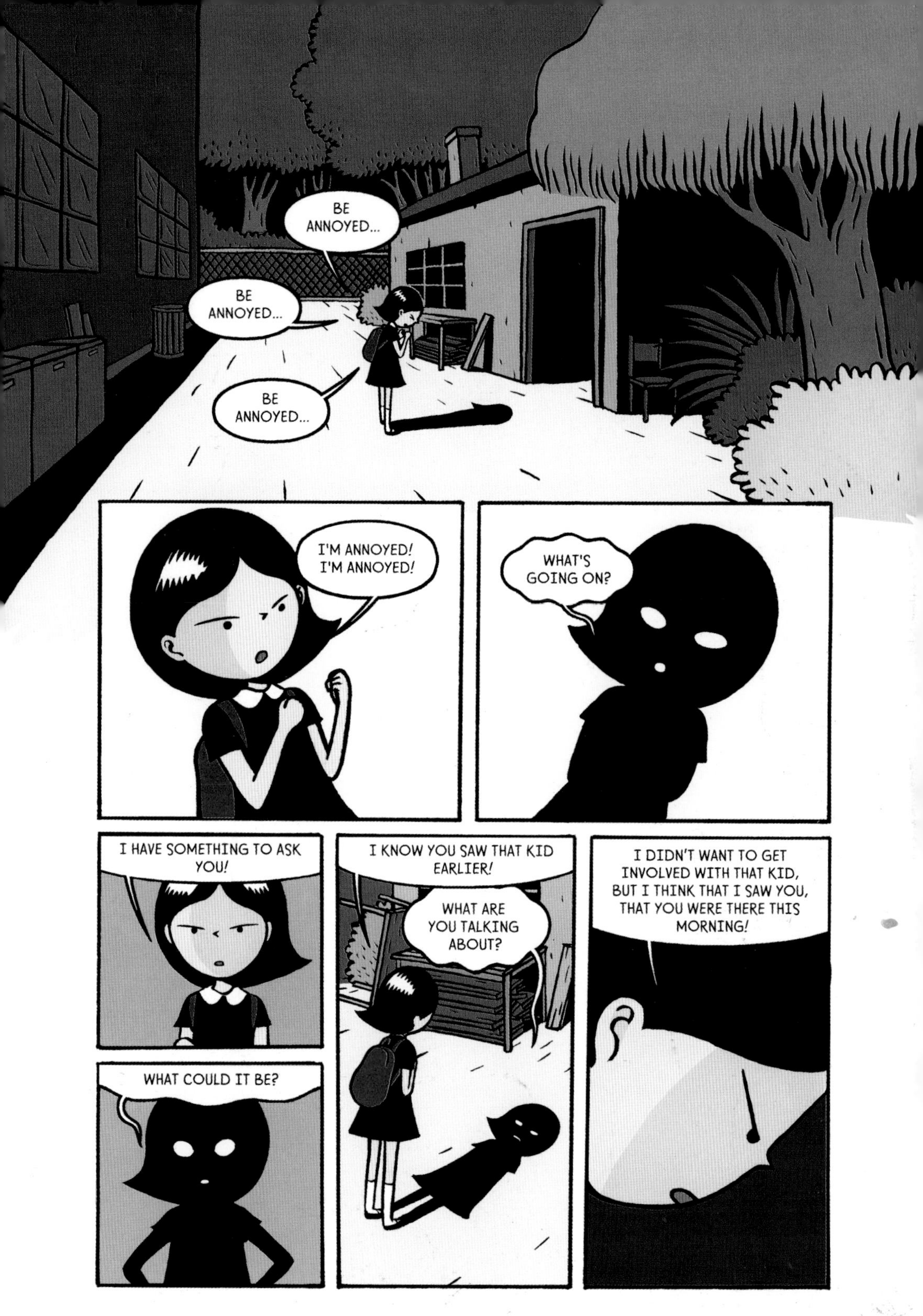
BE ANNOYED...
BE ANNOYED...
BE ANNOYED...
I'M ANNOYED! I'M ANNOYED!
WHAT'S GOING ON?
I HAVE SOMETHING TO ASK YOU!
WHAT COULD IT BE?
I KNOW YOU SAW THAT KID EARLIER!
WHAT ARE YOU TALKING ABOUT?
I DIDN'T WANT TO GET INVOLVED WITH THAT KID, BUT I THINK THAT I SAW YOU, THAT YOU WERE THERE THIS MORNING!

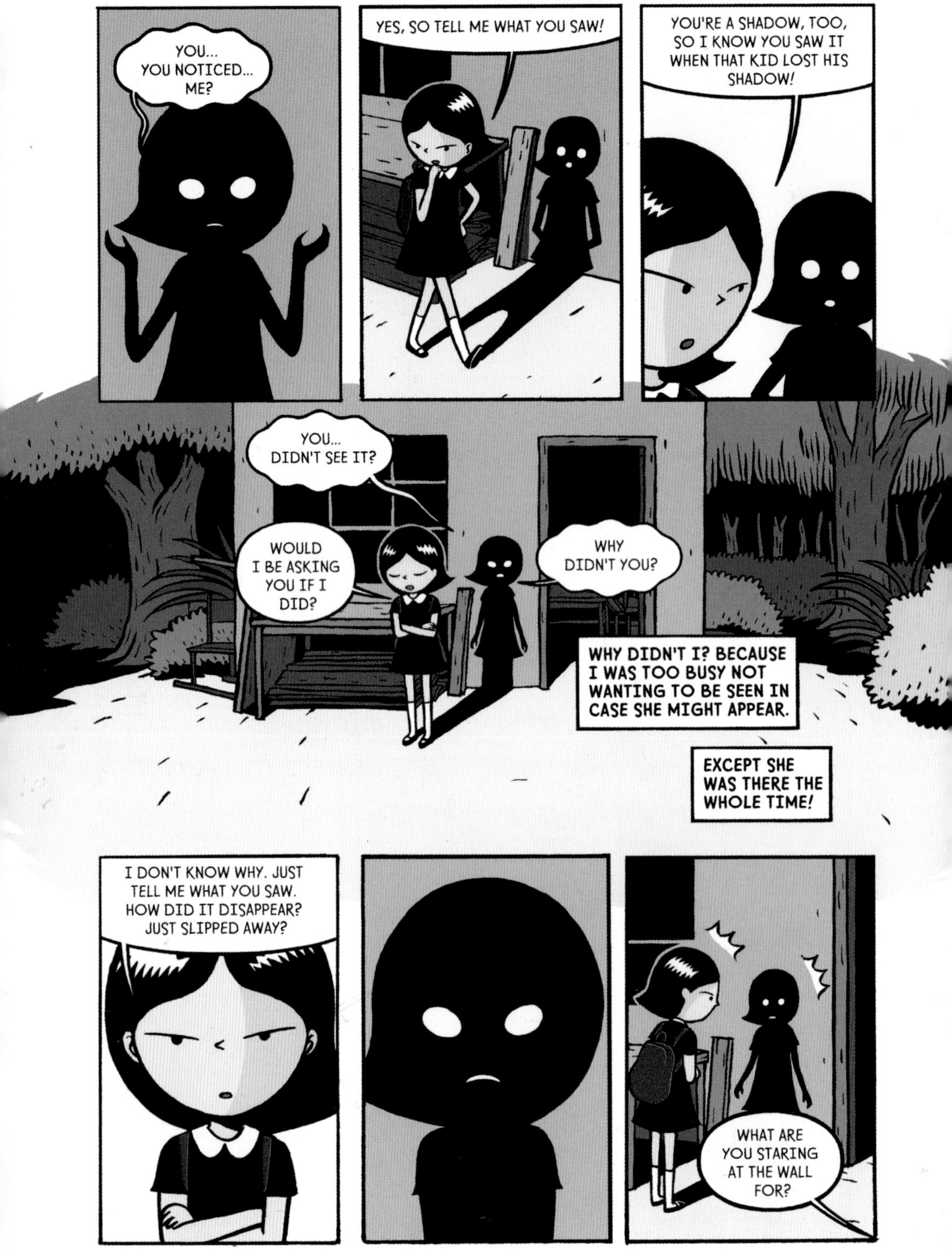

YOU... YOU NOTICED... ME?
YES, SO TELL ME WHAT YOU SAW!
YOU'RE A SHADOW, TOO, SO I KNOW YOU SAW IT WHEN THAT KID LOST HIS SHADOW!
YOU... DIDN'T SEE IT?
WOULD I BE ASKING YOU IF I DID?
WHY DIDN'T YOU?
WHY DIDN'T I? BECAUSE I WAS TOO BUSY NOT WANTING TO BE SEEN IN CASE SHE MIGHT APPEAR.
EXCEPT SHE WAS THERE THE WHOLE TIME!
I DON'T KNOW WHY. JUST TELL ME WHAT YOU SAW. HOW DID IT DISAPPEAR? JUST SLIPPED AWAY?
WHAT ARE YOU STARING AT THE WALL FOR?

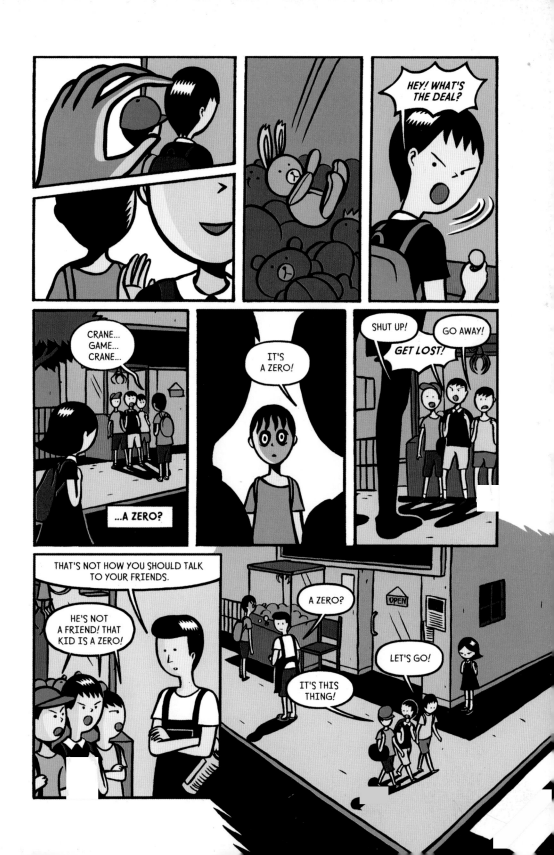

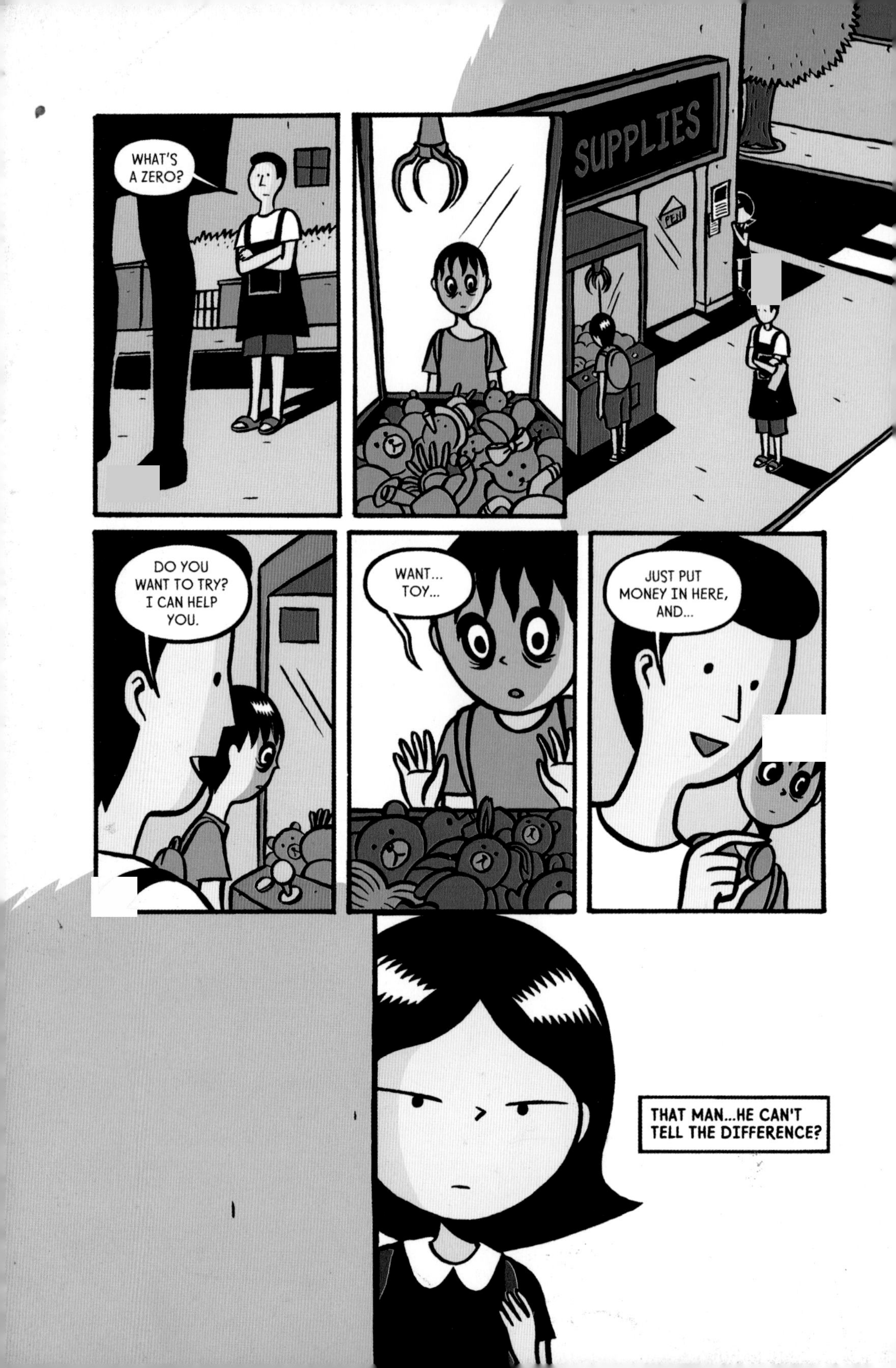
WHAT'S A ZERO?
SUPPLIES
DO YOU WANT TO TRY? I CAN HELP YOU.
WANT... TOY...
JUST PUT MONEY IN HERE, AND...
THAT MAN...HE CAN'T TELL THE DIFFERENCE?

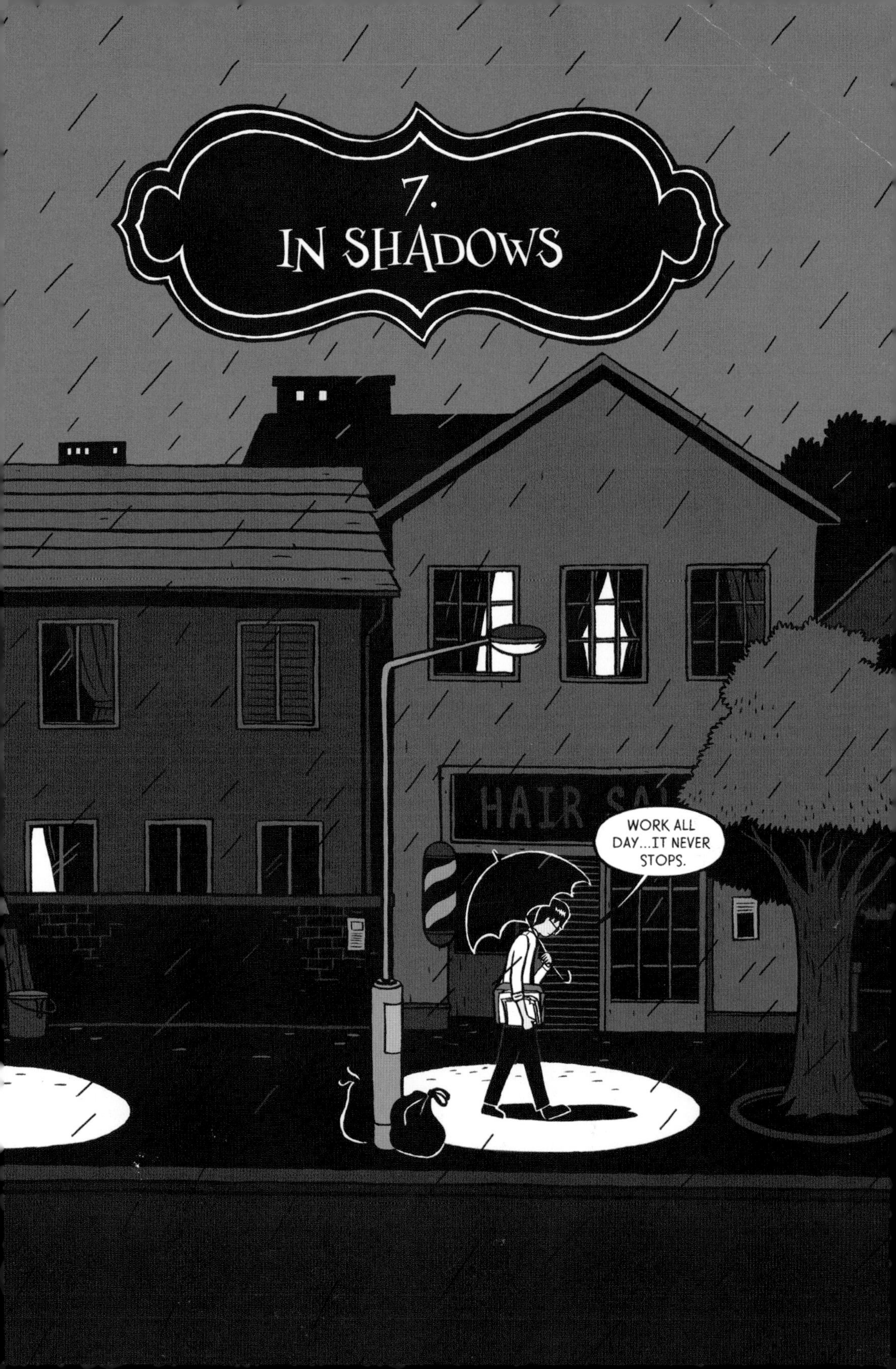
7.
IN SHADOWS
WORK ALL DAY...IT NEVER STOPS.

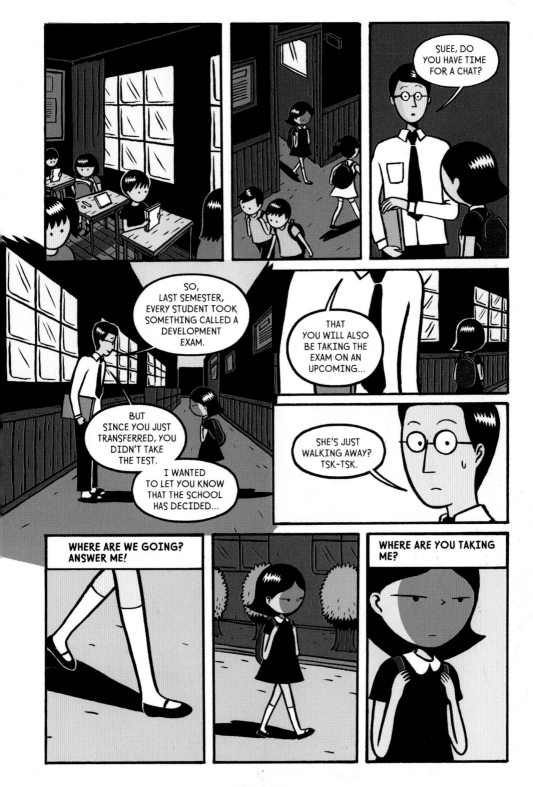

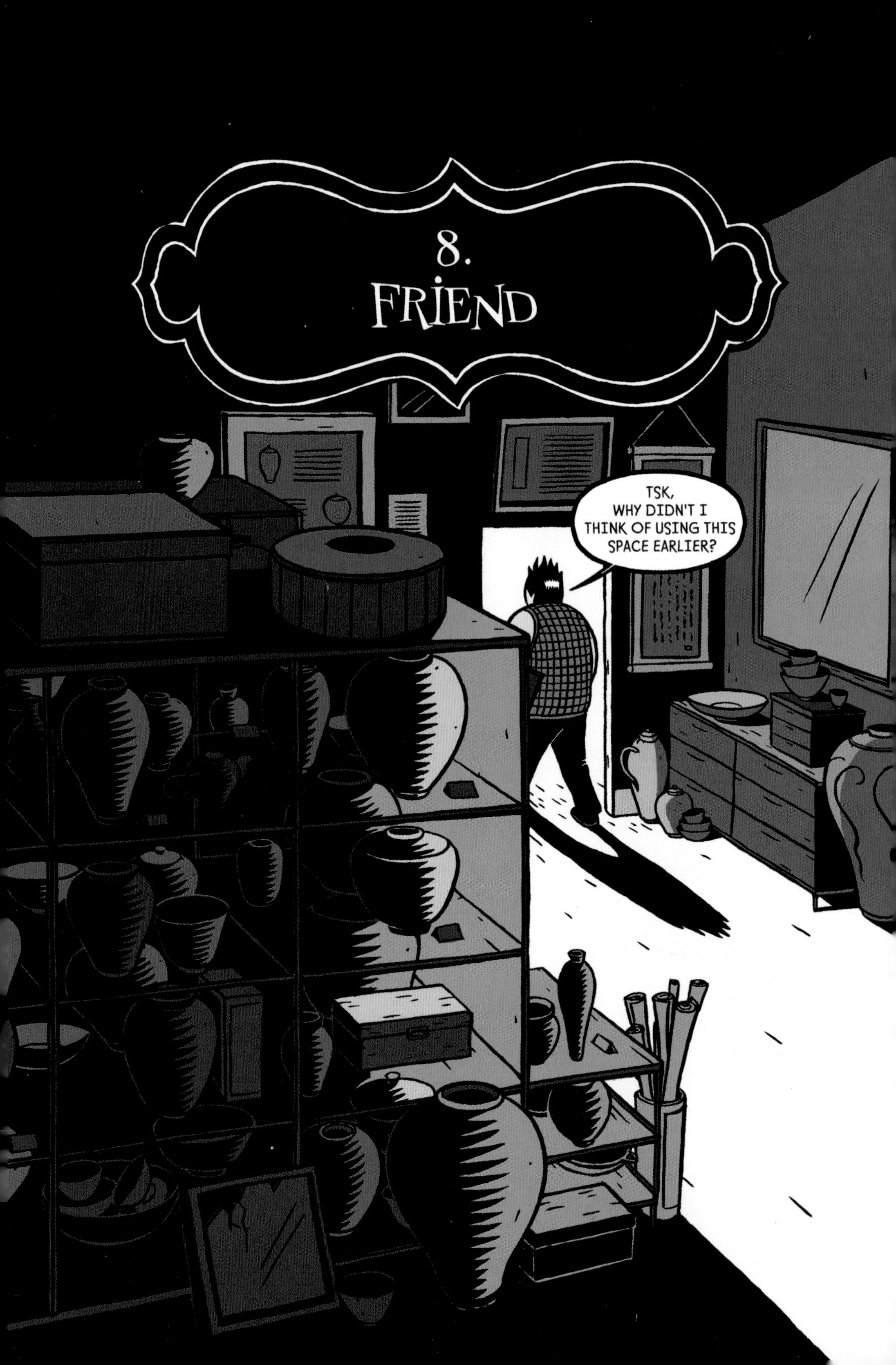
8.
FRIEND
TSK, WHY DIDN'T I THINK OF USING THIS SPACE EARLIER?

167

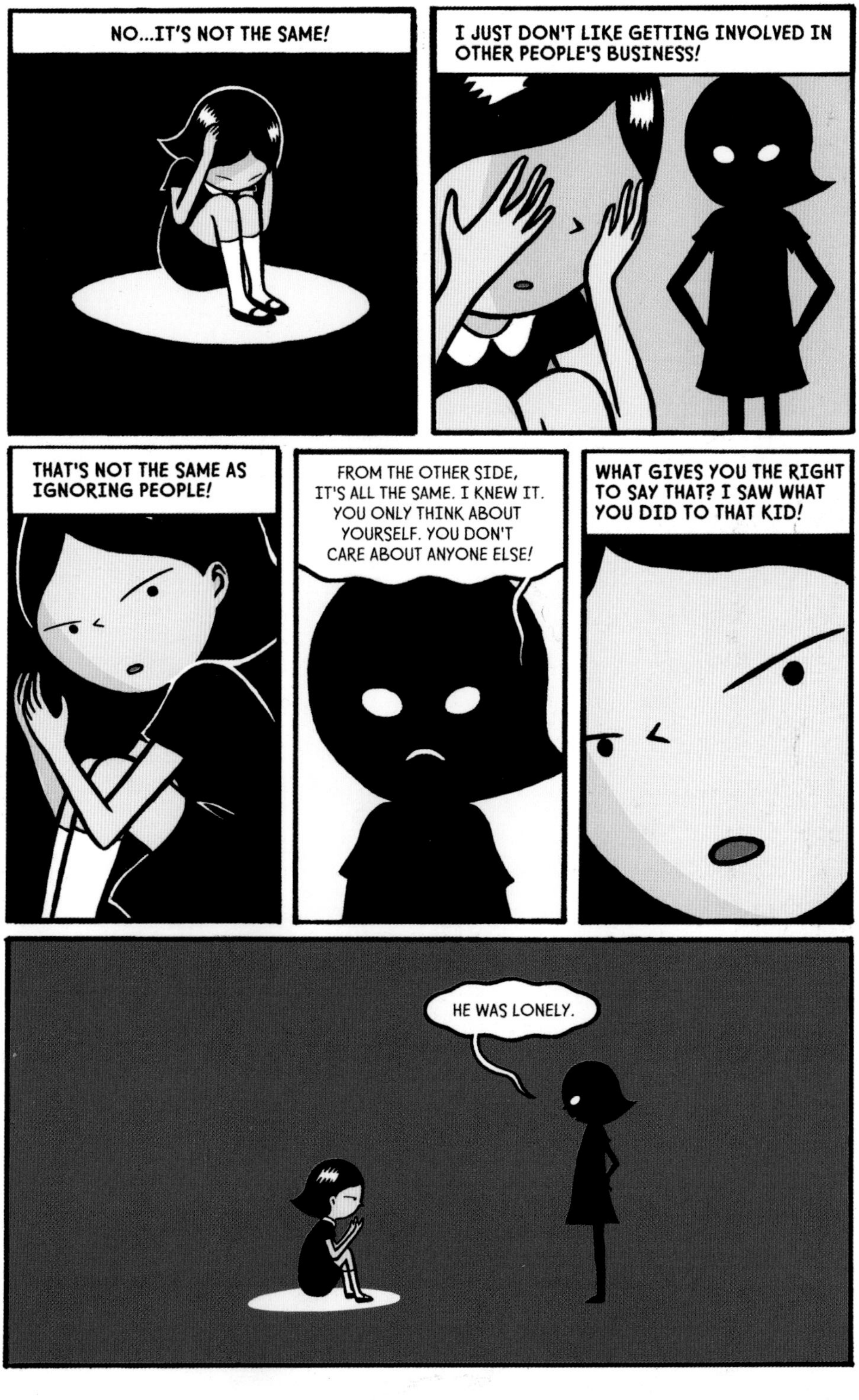
NO...IT'S NOT THE SAME!
I JUST DON'T LIKE GETTING INVOLVED IN OTHER PEOPLE'S BUSINESS!
THAT'S NOT THE SAME AS IGNORING PEOPLE!
FROM THE OTHER SIDE, IT'S ALL THE SAME. I KNEW IT. YOU ONLY THINK ABOUT YOURSELF. YOU DON'T CARE ABOUT ANYONE ELSE!
WHAT GIVES YOU THE RIGHT TO SAY THAT? I SAW WHAT YOU DID TO THAT KID!
HE WAS LONELY.

172

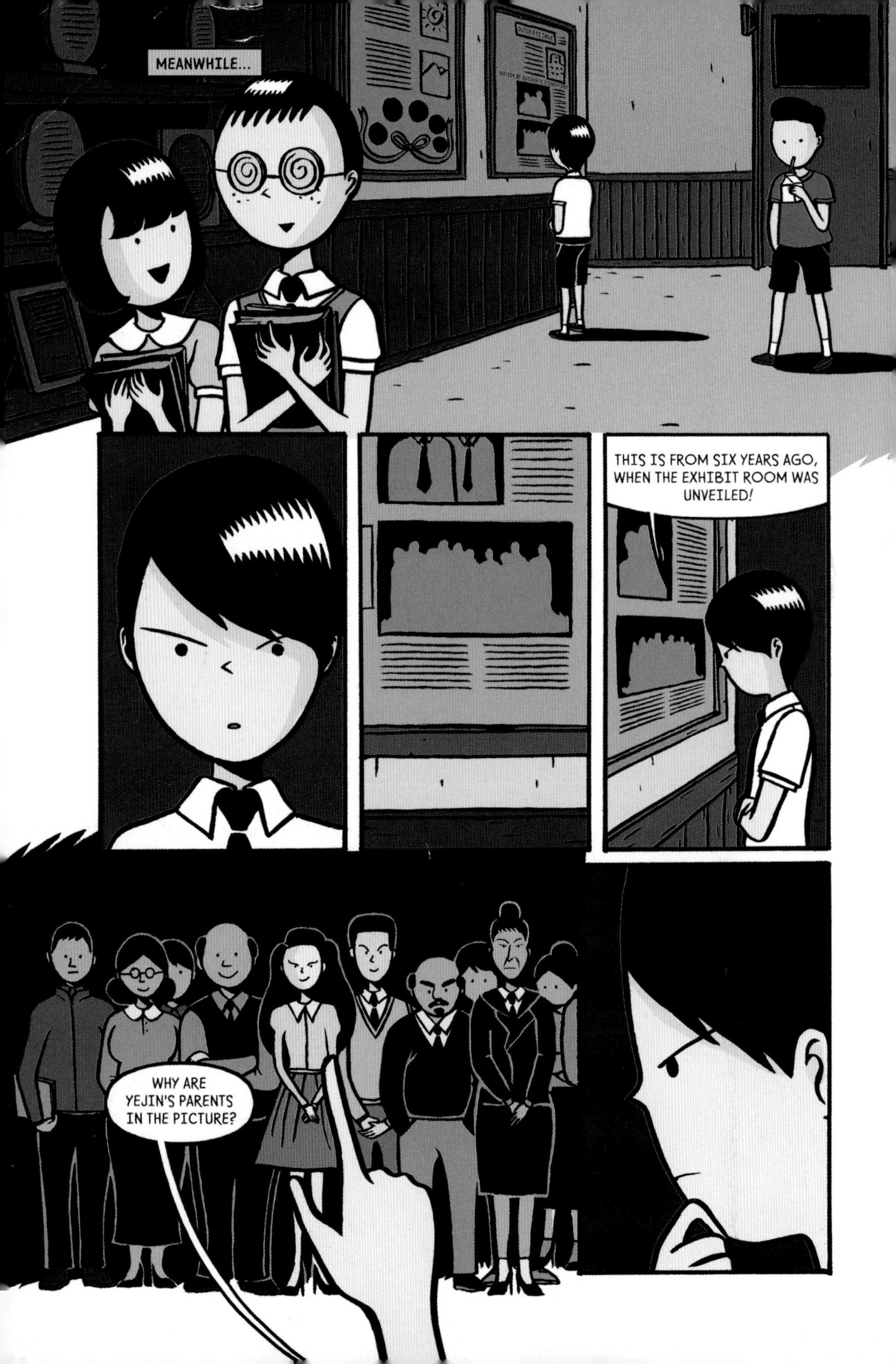
MEANWHILE...
THIS IS FROM SIX YEARS AGO, WHEN THE EXHIBIT ROOM WAS UNVEILED!
WHY ARE YEJIN'S PARENTS IN THE PICTURE?

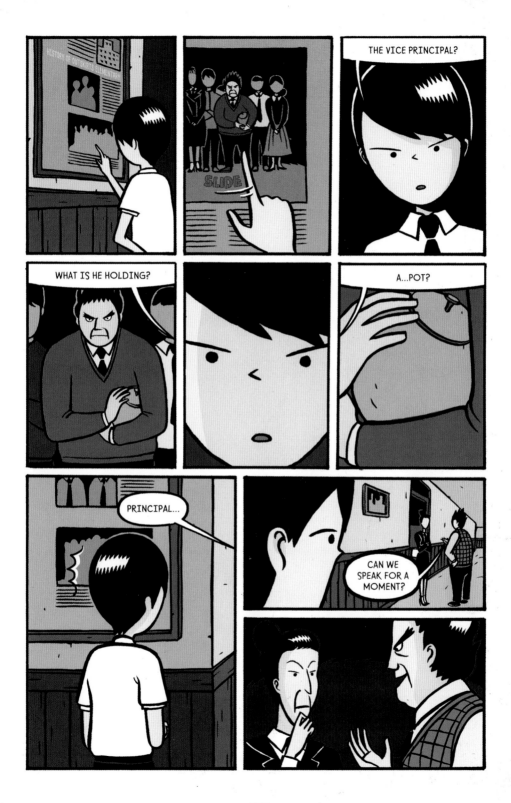

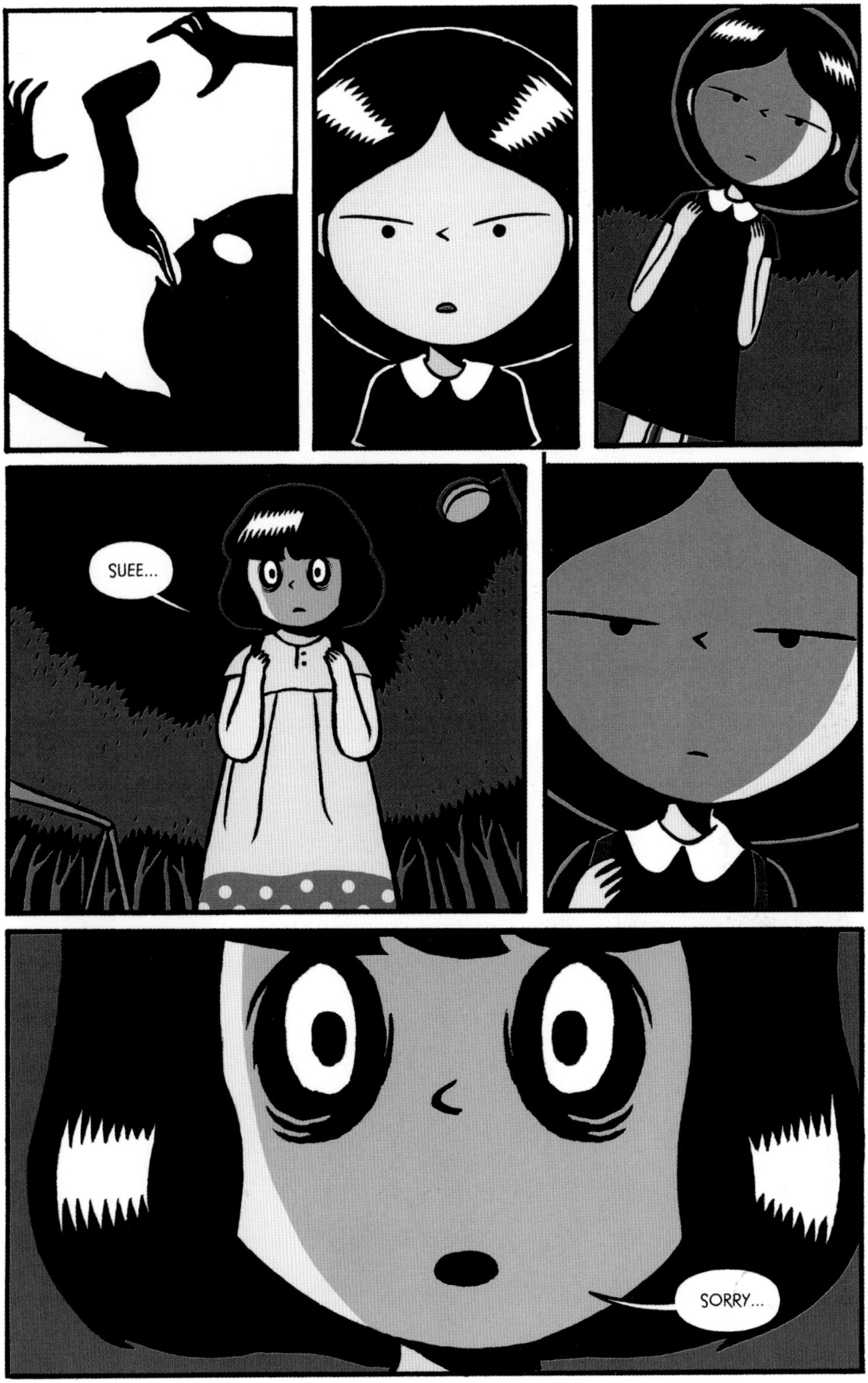
SUEE...
SORRY...

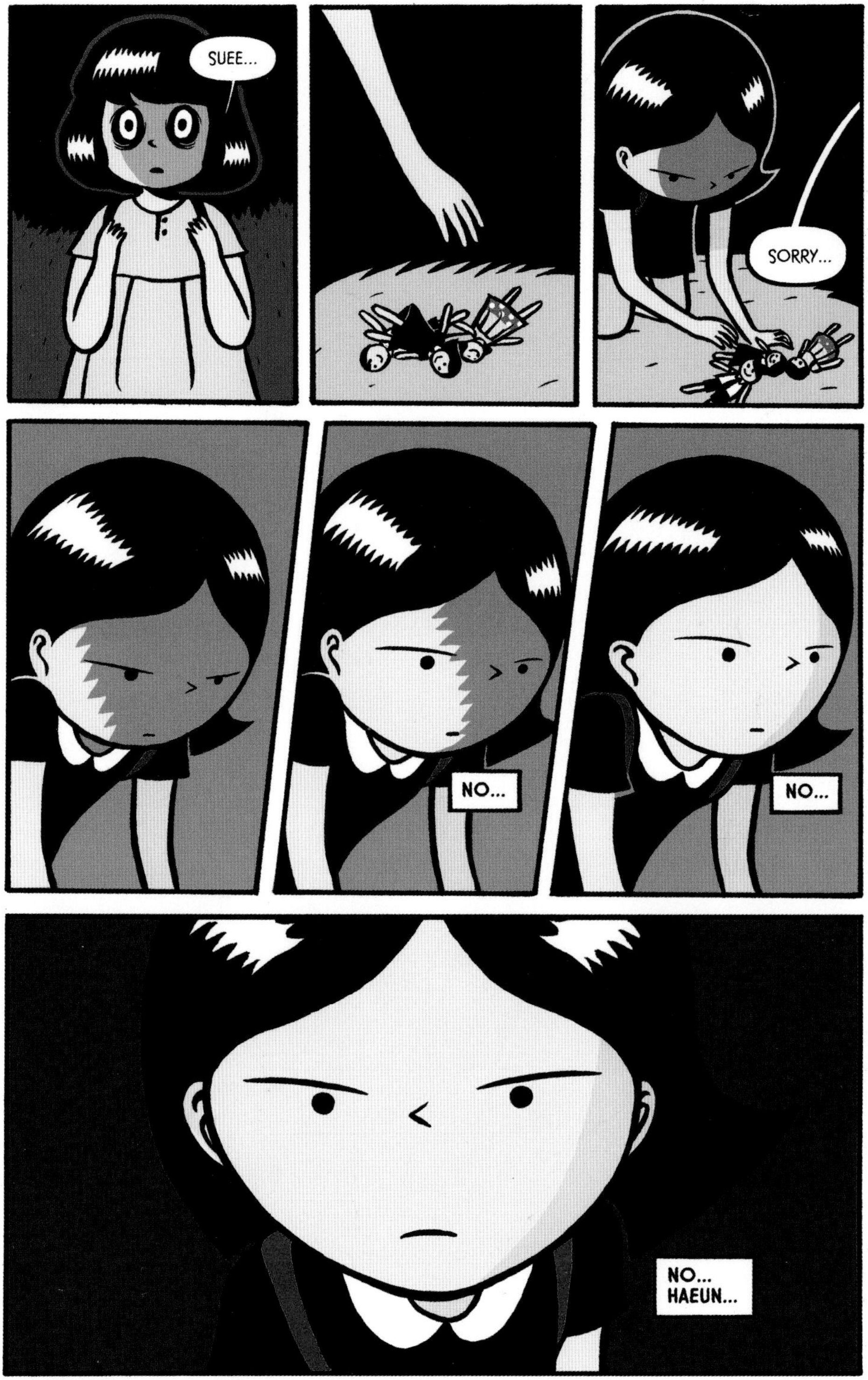
SUEE...
SORRY...
NO...
NO...
NO...
HAEUN...

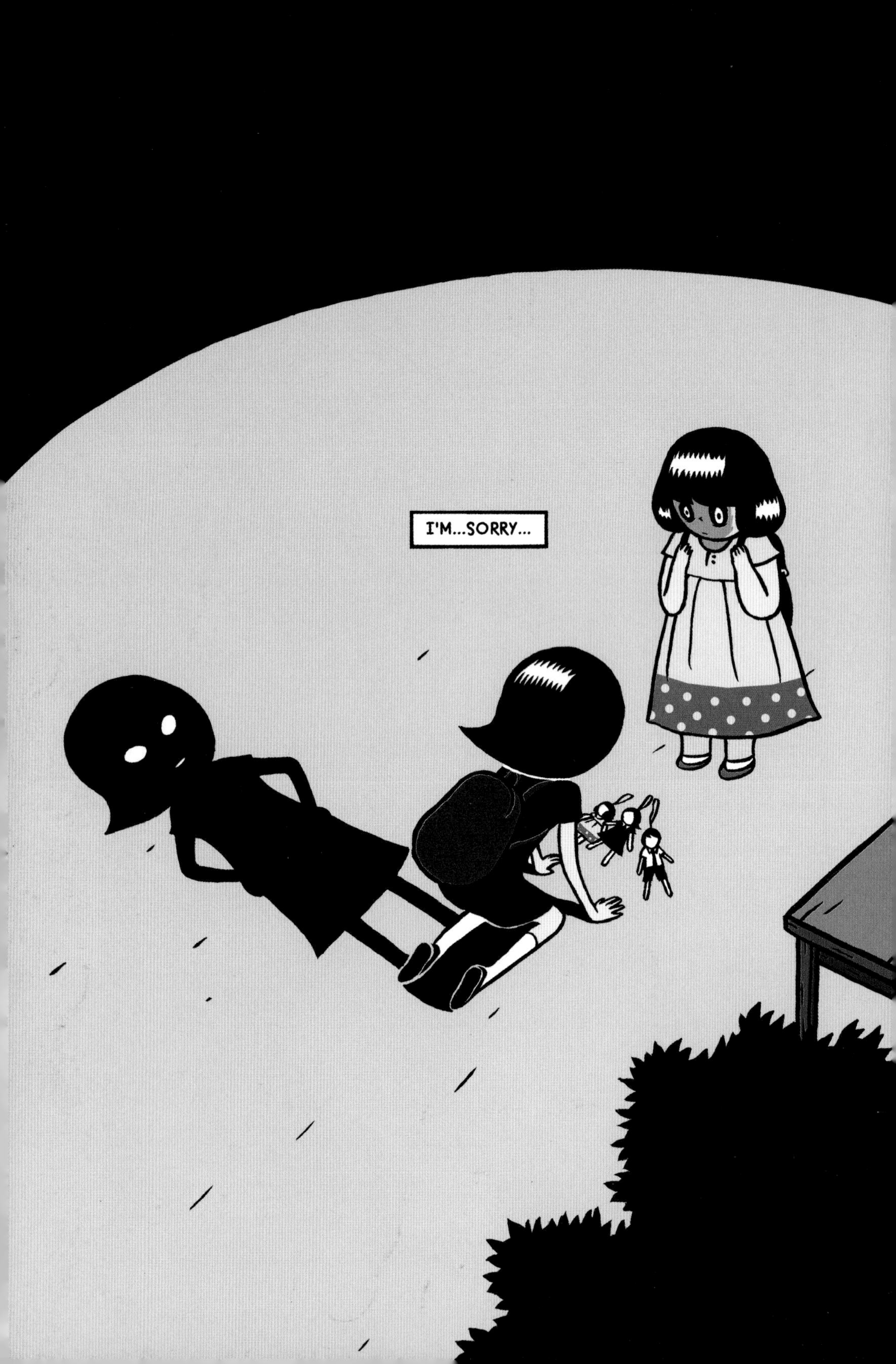
I'M...SORRY...

196

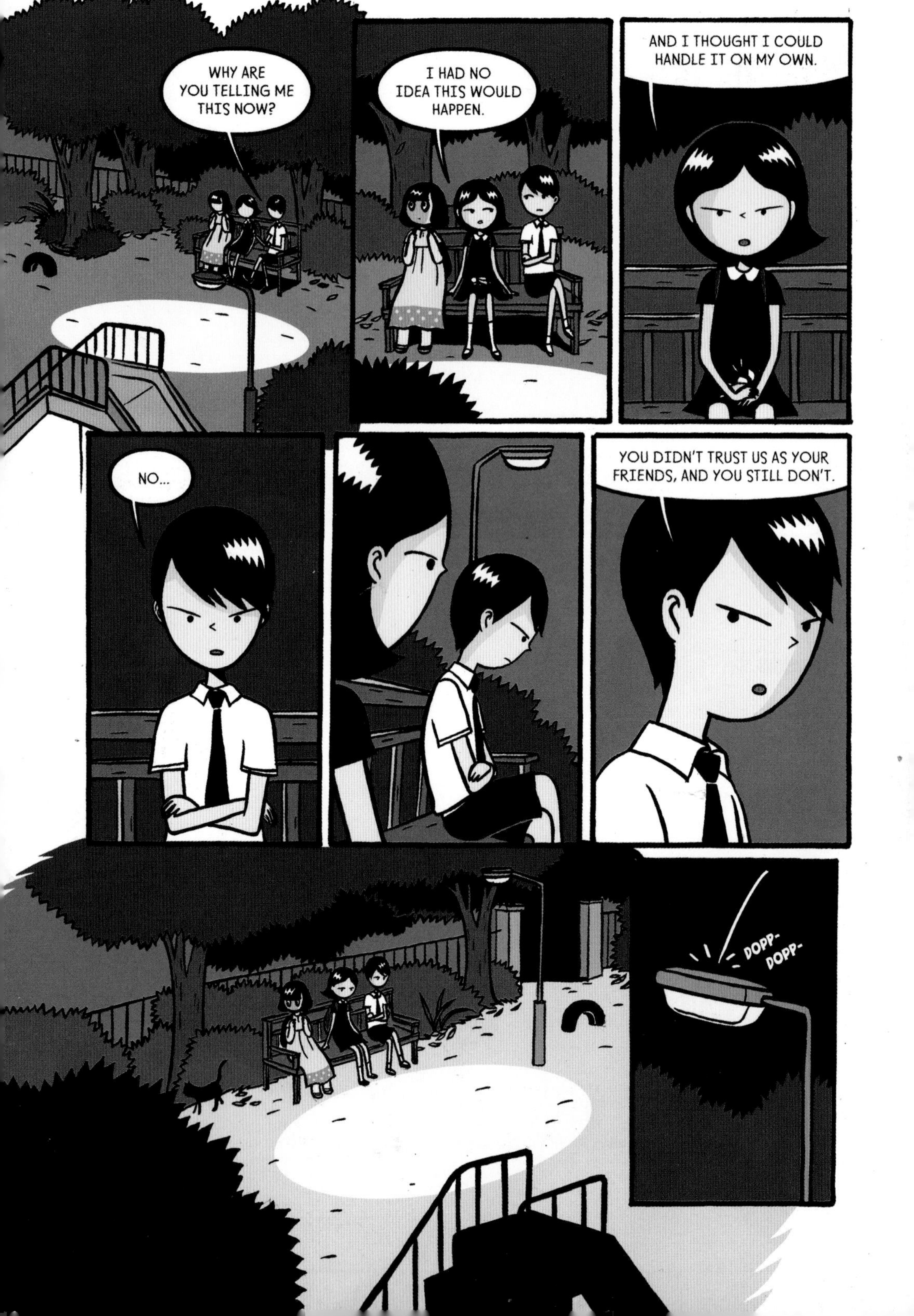
WHY ARE YOU TELLING ME THIS NOW?
I HAD NO IDEA THIS WOULD HAPPEN.
AND I THOUGHT I COULD HANDLE IT ON MY OWN.
NO...
YOU DIDN'T TRUST US AS YOUR FRIENDS, AND YOU STILL DON'T.
DOPP-
DOPP-

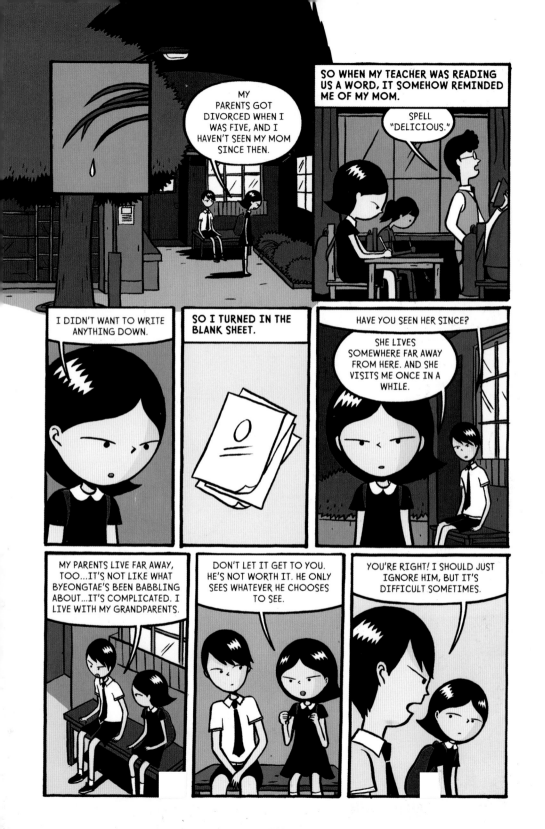

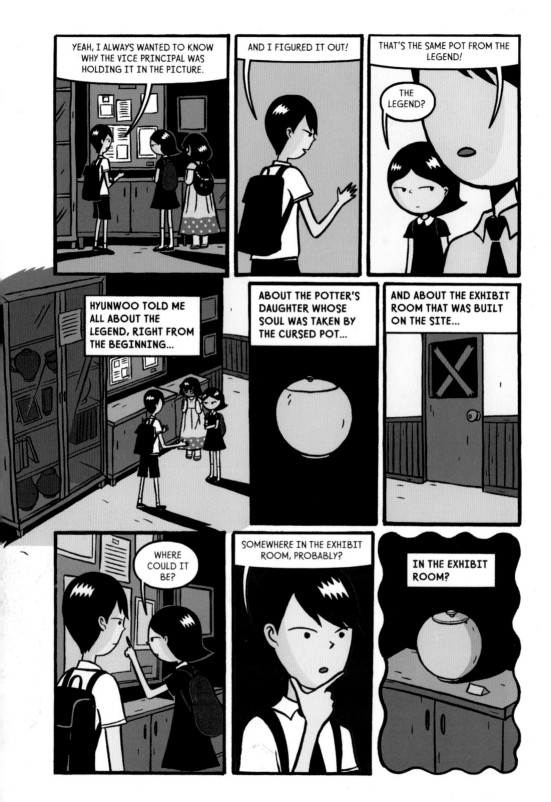

222

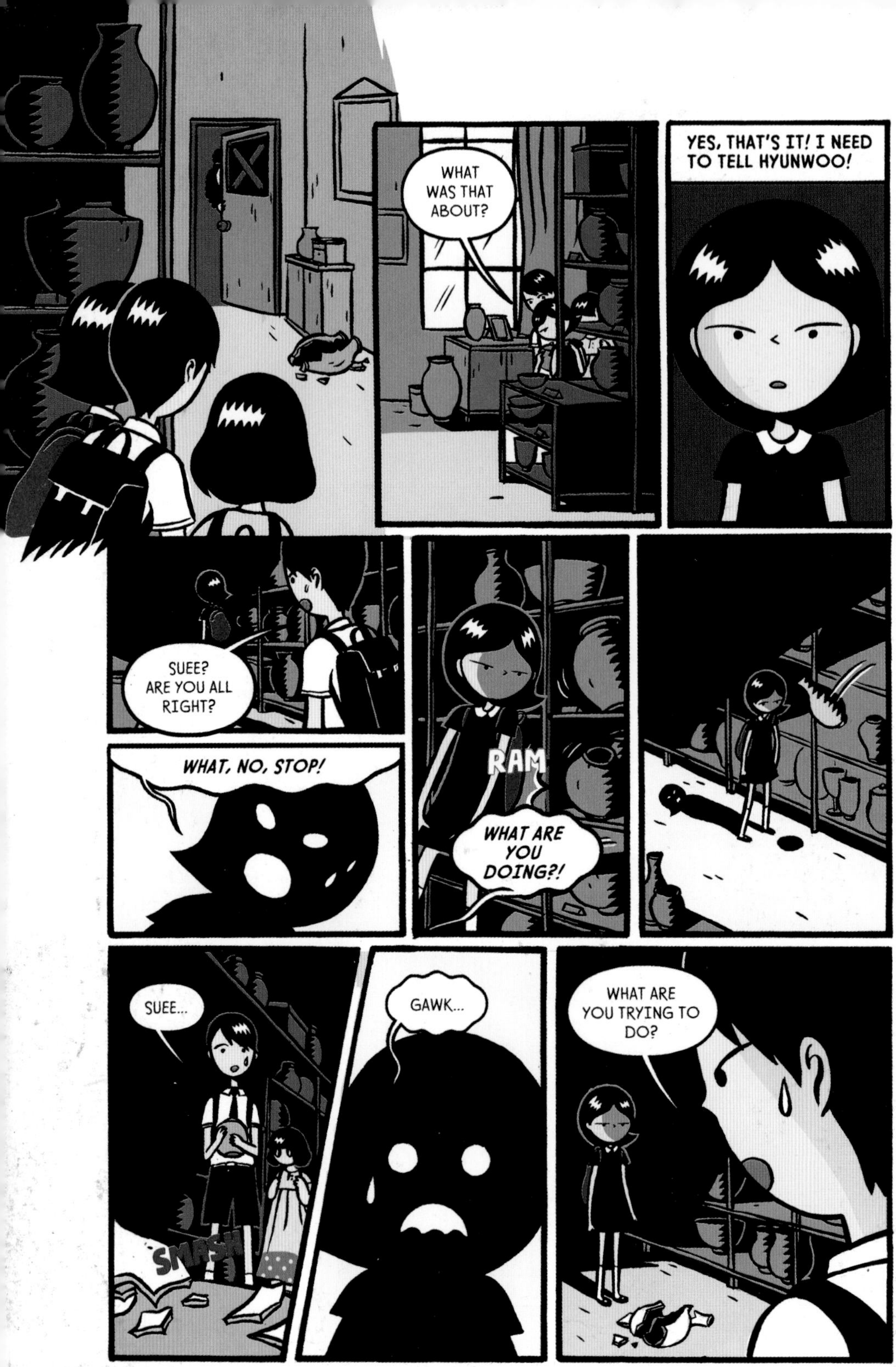
WHAT WAS THAT ABOUT?
YES, THAT'S IT! I NEED TO TELL HYUNWOO!
SUEE? ARE YOU ALL RIGHT?
RAM
WHAT ARE YOU DOING?!
WHAT, NO, STOP!
SUEE...
SMASH
GAWK...
WHAT ARE YOU TRYING TO DO?

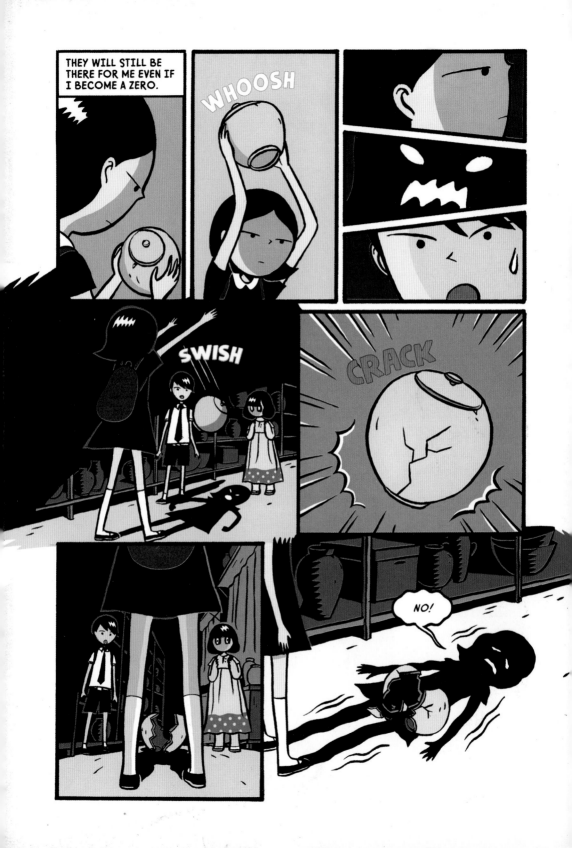

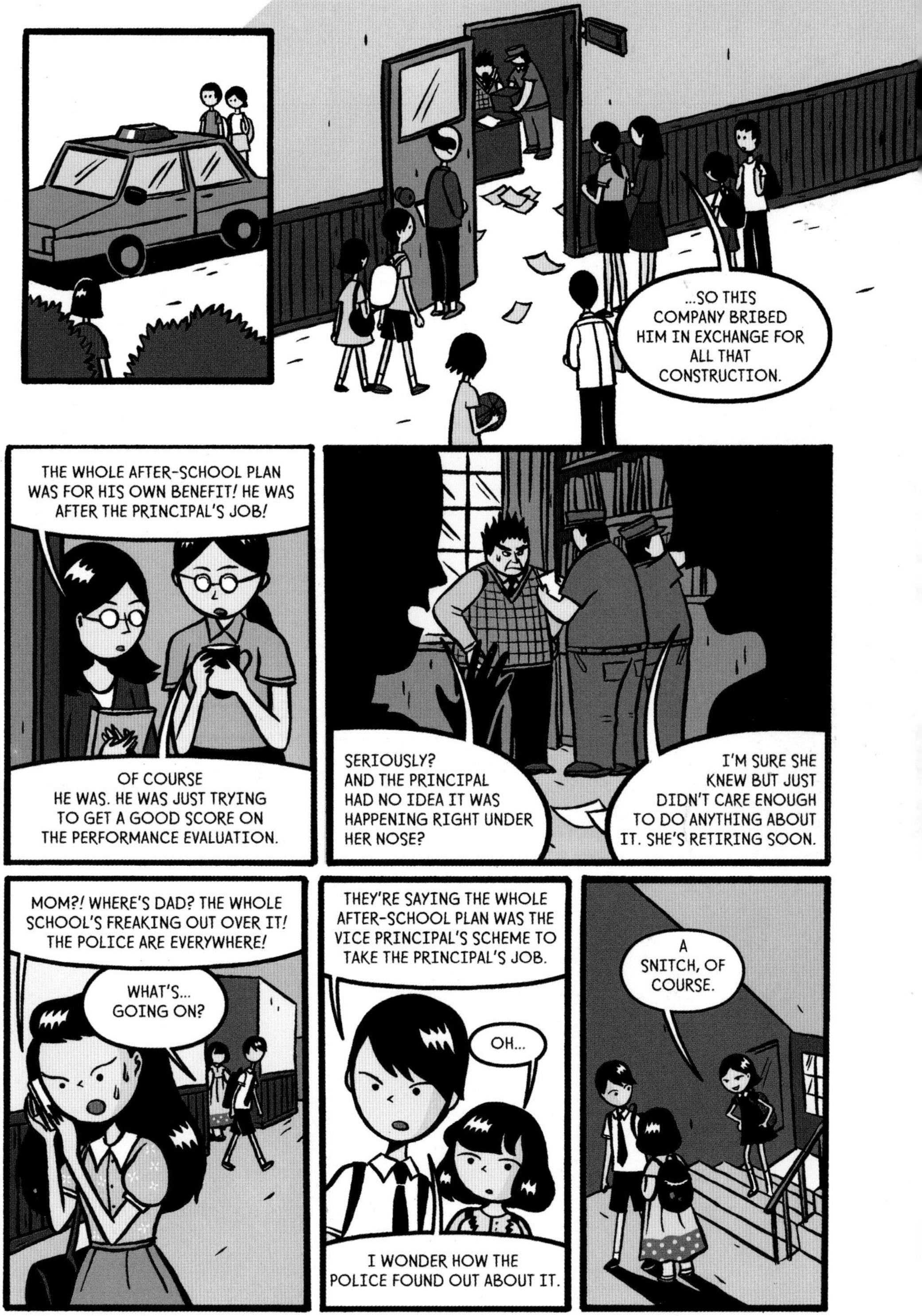
...SO THIS COMPANY BRIBED HIM IN EXCHANGE FOR ALL THAT CONSTRUCTION.
THE WHOLE AFTER-SCHOOL PLAN WAS FOR HIS OWN BENEFIT! HE WAS AFTER THE PRINCIPAL'S JOB!
OF COURSE HE WAS. HE WAS JUST TRYING TO GET A GOOD SCORE ON THE PERFORMANCE EVALUATION.
SERIOUSLY? AND THE PRINCIPAL HAD NO IDEA IT WAS HAPPENING RIGHT UNDER HER NOSE?
I'M SURE SHE KNEW BUT JUST DIDN'T CARE ENOUGH TO DO ANYTHING ABOUT IT. SHE'S RETIRING SOON.
MOM?! WHERE'S DAD? THE WHOLE SCHOOL'S FREAKING OUT OVER IT! THE POLICE ARE EVERYWHERE!
WHAT'S... GOING ON?
THEY'RE SAYING THE WHOLE AFTER-SCHOOL PLAN WAS THE VICE PRINCIPAL'S SCHEME TO TAKE THE PRINCIPAL'S JOB.
OH...
I WONDER HOW THE POLICE FOUND OUT ABOUT IT.
A SNITCH, OF COURSE.

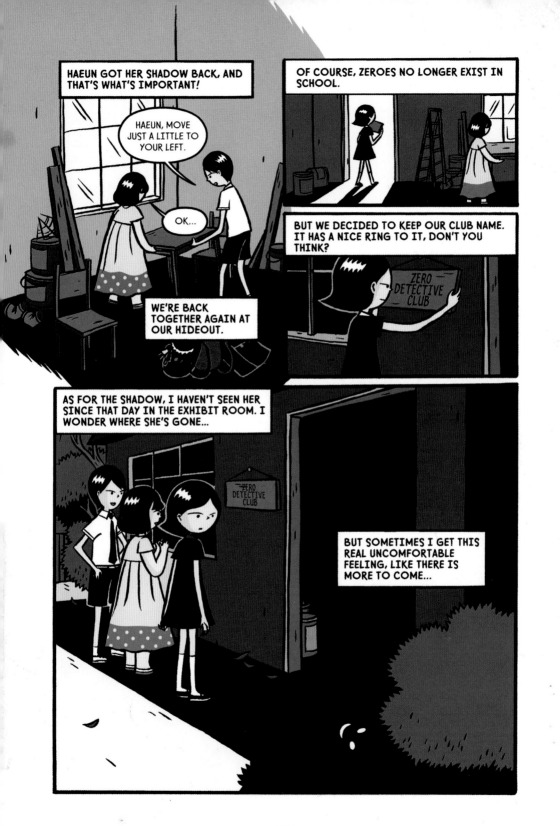

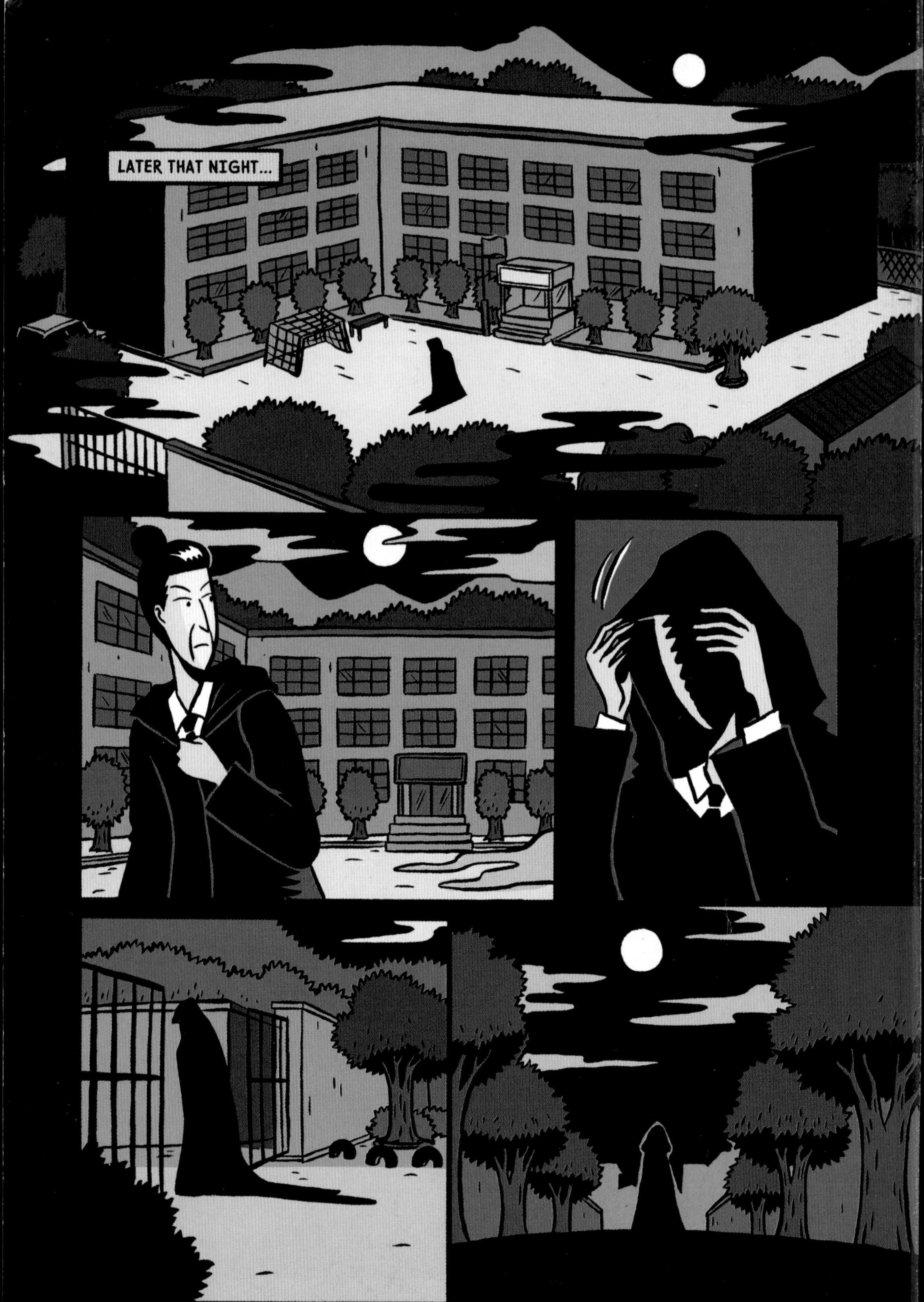
LATER THAT NIGHT...

To Mom and Dad
—Ginger Ly

GINGER LY worked as a designer before earning her master's degree in filmmaking from the School of the Art Institute of Chicago. She lives in the suburbs of Seoul, South Korea.

MOLLY PARK lives in Seoul, South Korea, with two black cats and a mouse, and they all get along very well.

Suee and the Shadow is their debut graphic novel.

PUBLISHER'S NOTE: This is a work of fiction. Names, characters, places, and incidents are either the product of the author's imagination or used fictitiously, and any resemblance to actual persons, living or dead, business establishments, events, or locales is entirely coincidental.

Library of Congress Control Number 2017937935

Hardcover ISBN 978-1-4197-2563-0
Paperback ISBN 978-1-4197-2564-7

Text and illustrations copyright © 2017 B Hive, Inc.
Illustrations by Molly Park
Cover and book design by B Hive, Inc. and Siobhán Gallagher
Translated by Keo Lee and Jane Lee

Printed and bound in China
10 9 8 7 6 5 4 3 2 1

Amulet Books are available at special discounts when purchased in quantity for premiums and promotions as well as fundraising or educational use. Special editions can also be created to specification. For details, contact specialsales@abramsbooks.com or the address below.

ABRAMS The Art of Books
115 West 18th Street, New York, NY 10011
abramsbooks.com